Duchess abruptly leaped to her feet and ran over to the door. She began to growl low in her throat.

Matt didn't waste a second. He grabbed his weapon. "Stay in the bedroom and don't open the door to anyone except for me or one of my brothers."

"Be careful," Lacy whispered.

Pressing himself against the wall, Matt opened the door.

Duchess was in full alert mode, her nose practically twitching with the need to track the intruder. Matt exhaled and then darted outside, Duchess hot on his heels. As they'd practiced earlier, he went left and Duchess went right. He heard Duchess moving through the brush.

The dog let out a sharp bark, and he instinctively lunged toward the sound, his heart pounding with adrenaline. He moved from tree to tree. Suddenly a sharp crack echoed through the night, followed by a burning sensation along the outer edge of his left biceps.

He'd been shot!

Ignoring the pain, he continued his zigzagging path toward the area where Duchess had barked, alerting him to the presence of the gunman, as he silently prayed that he and Duchess could hold the guy off long enough for his brother Mike to arrive.

And to keep Lacy and Rory safe.

USA TODAY Bestselling Author

Laura Scott
and
Debby Giusti

Seeking Refuge

Previously published as *Shattered Lullaby* and *Stranded*

HARLEQUIN® LOVE INSPIRED®CLASSICS

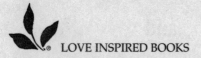

LOVE INSPIRED BOOKS

Recycling programs for this product may not exist in your area.

ISBN-13: 978-1-335-14306-8

Seeking Refuge

Copyright © 2019 by Harlequin Books S.A.

First published as Shattered Lullaby by Harlequin Books in 2018 and Stranded by Harlequin Books in 2015.

The publisher acknowledges the copyright holders of the individual works as follows:

Shattered Lullaby
Copyright © 2018 by Laura Iding

Stranded
Copyright © 2015 by Deborah W. Giusti

www.Harlequin.com

Printed in U.S.A.

CONTENTS

Laura Scott is a nurse by day and an author by night. She has always loved romance, and read faith-based books by Grace Livingston Hill in her teenage years. She's thrilled to have published over twenty-five books for Love Inspired Suspense. She has two adult children and lives in Milwaukee, Wisconsin, with her husband of thirty years. Please visit Laura at laurascottbooks.com, as she loves to hear from her readers.

SHATTERED LULLABY

Laura Scott

Blessed are they that mourn:
for they shall be comforted.
—*Matthew* 5:4

This book is dedicated to my cousin Joanne O'Connell. Thanks for all the awesome Tomahawk summer memories, especially teaching me how to water-ski!

ONE

Lacy Germaine woke to the sound of heated arguing. For a moment, she buried her head into the pillow in an effort to drown out her parents' fighting.

And then she remembered—her parents were long gone, both killed in a car crash several years ago. Abruptly, she sat bolt upright on the futon, her heart thundering in her chest.

One of the voices belonged to her sister, Jill, but who was she talking to?

Lacy leaped out of bed and went over to check on her three-month-old nephew, Rory, who was still sleeping, but not for long, considering the harsh tones coming from the next room.

At first the voices were low and angry but still incomprehensible. It didn't take long for the deeper male voice to rise. "Tell me the truth! Now! Or I'll kill you and the brat, too!"

Lacy sucked in a harsh breath, understanding with sick certainty that her sister's worst fears had become reality. Jill's husband, David Williams, had returned home.

And he was ambushing her sister after midnight.

Reacting instinctively, Lacy lifted her nephew from

the crib and grabbed the long shawl-type wrap, winding it around and around, swaddling the baby snugly against her body. Then she fumbled for her cell phone and dialed 911.

"What's your emergency?"

"Domestic violence at 1671 Elmwood Lane," she whispered into the phone. "Hurry!"

"Please stay on the line," the woman responded calmly.

Lacy wanted to yell that this was her sister's life at stake! But of course she didn't.

"I can't. He'll hear me." Lacy disconnected from the call. She needed both of her hands free in order to manage the baby.

Her brother-in-law obviously didn't know Lacy was there, staying with Jill to help out over spring break. If he found out Jill wasn't alone...

She couldn't finish the thought.

"No, please..."

Lacy hated the idea of Jill begging for mercy. Her sister had confided that she was filing for divorce from her husband because his anger and verbal attacks scared her.

Clearly, Jill had been right. Lacy was getting a first-hand idea of how frightening her brother-in-law could be.

"Please don't do this..." Her sister's voice was full of tears.

Bang! Bang!

No! Lacy gasped, her heart lodging in her throat. Dear God, what had David done?

There was nothing but silence after the gun went off, forcing Lacy to assume the worst.

Jill was dead. Shot by her own husband.

And if his threat was to be believed, Rory was next.

Lacy jammed her cell phone into her purse, slung the strap over her shoulder and shoved her feet into her running shoes. Where was the diaper bag?

In the kitchen.

Knowing she couldn't dare pass her sister's room to get the bag, she eased out from Rory's bedroom and darted around the corner in the opposite direction to go into the living room. She needed to get Rory out of the house, far away from his armed and dangerous father.

Thankfully, the patio doors slid open without a sound. She eased through into the mild April spring air. Relieved it wasn't too cold, she crossed the concrete patio until she reached the damp grass.

Grateful for the lack of snow, Lacy didn't hesitate, running around the house and toward the road. Her car was parked less than a block from her sister's home, on the opposite side of the street, and she hoped she'd make it to the vehicle before David realized the baby was gone.

Mud squished beneath her running shoes. The warm spring weather had melted what was left of the snow, leaving mush behind. She slipped, then steadied herself.

Twenty yards, fifteen, ten. A loud thud from inside the house caused her to misstep, and this time she fell, one knee hitting the ground. Clutching the baby to her chest, she braced herself with one hand on the ground, surprised to feel a hard ridge beneath her fingertips. Some sort of key. Instinctively she picked it up and shoved it into the pocket of her hoodie as she leaped up to her feet.

Still holding the baby close with one hand, she fished in her purse for her car keys.

Five yards. Three. She was going to make it! Using

her thumb, she pressed the key fob to unlock the driver's-side door. The car made an extraordinarily loud beeping noise, front and rear lights flashing. She winced, hoping David wouldn't hear. As if the car wasn't loud enough to broadcast her escape, Rory began to cry.

"Hey! Stop! Get back here!"

David's irate shout had her hunching her shoulders, half expecting to be hit with a bullet squarely in the back. Somehow, she managed to yank the driver's-side door open and to slide in behind the wheel. There was just enough room to maneuver with Rory bundled against her. She shut the door, jammed the key in the ignition and hit the accelerator, speeding away from her sister's house.

Lacy took a quick right and then a left, leaving the normally quiet neighborhood, expecting to hear the wail of sirens at any moment.

But there was nothing.

She'd called 911 for help, hadn't she? So where were the Milwaukee Police? How long would it take for them to show up?

What should she do? Even if the police would be there at any moment, Lacy didn't want to stop. What if David followed her? Every instinct she possessed told her to keep going, to put as much distance between herself and Rory's father as possible.

Think, Lacy, think! Where was the closest on-ramp? There! She found the sign and quickly took the ramp heading northwest, deeply afraid that David wasn't far behind.

No way would she allow him to lay one finger on Rory.

She would protect the baby with her own life if necessary. And she really, really hoped it wouldn't come to that.

Driving through the night, she kept her eyes peeled on the rearview mirror. She wished she could remember what kind of vehicle David drove, but she'd been focused only on escape, nothing more. She couldn't actually remember seeing any type of car, but David had to have driven to Jill's house in something. Her sister's house wasn't near a bus route.

Rory was still crying, signifying he was either hungry or needed his diaper changed, or both.

"Don't worry, I'll take care of you," she whispered in a soothing voice. Logically, she knew she should head to a police station, but nothing about this night made any rational sense.

And her sister's warnings echoed in her mind.

David's fellow police officers always cover for him; they believe whatever lies he's told them about me. Not one of them can be trusted.

At the time she'd thought Jill was being paranoid, but after this, she believed her sister had been right all along.

In fact, Jill had died because of it.

Tears welled in her eyes, blurring her vision. Lacy swiped them away, knowing she needed to be careful. In an effort to relax, she turned on the radio, searching for a soft jazz station, hoping the music would help calm Rory.

His crying had subsided to soft hiccupping sobs, the sound tearing at her heart. Keeping one hand on the wheel, she stroked his back as she drove, feeling guilty over not having him in a proper car seat. Driving with him in front of her was dangerous, but not as bad as staying behind where his father might try to kill him. Once again, her desperate need to flee wavered.

Should she turn around, go back to the police? But what if they were David's buddies? What if they didn't believe her?

If David succeeded in getting custody of Rory, what would prevent him from killing his son, the way he'd killed his wife?

No, she couldn't do it. She couldn't go back there. She had to wait until morning. There'd be plenty of time to find officers in another district far away from the one where David worked, who would listen to her side of the story. Surely they would believe her.

A weird beeping sound came from the radio, but before she could reach over to change the station, she heard the announcement of an Amber Alert.

"Missing three-month-old boy, Rory Williams, believed to be in a blue sedan belonging to his aunt, Lacy Germaine. The woman who took the child is in her late twenties and has long blond hair. Please call the Milwaukee Police Department if you see anyone matching this description."

Lacy tightened her grip on the steering wheel, feeling sick to her stomach. How was it possible that there was an Amber Alert so soon? Why would the police be looking for her and Rory? What had happened at her sister's house when the police had arrived? Had David played the role of grieving husband and father? Had he found a way to place the blame for what had happened to Jill on someone else?

On her?

She hadn't prayed in a long time, since before her parents had died. But desperate times called for extreme measures so she sent up a quick request, hoping God would care about an innocent baby.

Help me keep this child safe.

A sense of calm settled over her, slowing her breathing, but she still needed a plan. She took the next exit on the freeway and began searching for a convenience store. Rory began crying again and she knew she couldn't wait a moment longer. She needed diapers and formula, both essentials in caring for an infant. Good thing she still had one of Rory's bottles in her purse from their earlier outing to the park.

Once she found a safe place to stay and had the baby changed and fed, she would think about what she would do next. There must be a police department she could go to in order to turn herself in. A district that wouldn't believe David's lies.

Catching a glimpse of bright lights up ahead, she gratefully headed toward the store attached to a gas station. She pulled up to a pump and quickly filled her tank. She didn't have a lot of cash, however, forcing her to use a credit card, but having enough fuel was worth the risk. She knew the police would track her this far, but hopefully she'd be long gone before they could send a squad car to come pick her up.

She walked into the store and began searching the shelves for what she would need. There was a short, rotund man with a long scraggly beard behind the counter. He watched her like a hawk through thick, dark-rimmed glasses. Was he expecting her to steal something?

Or worse, had he heard the Amber Alert?

Praying it wasn't the latter, she tried to act natural, idly perusing the shelves, searching for the items she needed. She could feel the round bearded guy's gaze piercing her back, like tiny laser beams.

She tucked a package of diapers beneath her arm, then shifted a few steps to the right, looking over the various types of formula on display. Recognizing the yellow canister her sister used, she picked that one up.

Bright lights flashed through the window, startling her so much that she jumped a little. She cast a fugitive glance over her shoulder. Had the police found her already? She hesitated, wondering if she should just leave and go somewhere else.

The front door of the shop opened, and it took every ounce of strength she possessed not to turn and stare at whoever had come inside. She slid around the row of shelving, putting distance between herself and the newcomer.

A glimpse of black hair beneath a dark hat caught her eye and she ducked farther down, her pulse skipping several beats.

David had black hair. But he couldn't possibly have found her so quickly. Right?

She didn't want to believe it. Couldn't imagine how. Her sister's husband might have been a Special Ops soldier at one point, but he wasn't Superman.

Just her worst nightmare.

She tucked the canister of formula into the folds of the baby wrap and slipped a twenty-dollar bill from her purse, leaving it on the shelf to pay for the items she'd taken. Then she eased around another row of supplies, slowly making her way toward the main doorway.

After painstakingly slow maneuvering, she finally had a clear pathway to the door. Praying for safety, she took a deep breath, tucked her head and made a run for it.

Heading home after a long double shift, Officer Matthew Callahan and his K-9 partner, a tall German shepherd named Duchess, came upon a convenience store located six blocks from the church the Callahan family had attended ever since he could remember. His stomach rumbled with hunger, and since he knew there wasn't much food at home, he decided to stop for a bite to eat.

As he pulled into the parking lot, his headlights shined on a tall woman with long blond hair holding something bulky beneath her arm, running in a full-out sprint for the navy blue sedan sitting next to a gas pump.

What in the world?

Matt threw the gearshift into Park, hit the button to lift the tailgate so Duchess could jump down and then bolted from the vehicle.

Before he could yell at the woman to stop, he saw another tall man, a black cap covering his head, coming out of the convenience store, obviously following her. At first, Matt thought he was another cop, especially when he saw the gun in the guy's hand.

But then he lifted his weapon and aimed it directly toward the fleeing woman without warning.

"Stop! Police! Drop your weapon!" Matt shouted, turning his attention to the armed man. "Duchess, Attack!"

The man wearing the cap glanced over in alarm, lowered his gun and quickly took off behind the store with Duchess in hot pursuit. With the gunman covered, he went after the woman.

"Oh, no, you don't," he said, grabbing a hold of her before she could get into her navy blue four-door. "What's going on here? What happened inside the store?"

"Let me go! Didn't you see that man back there?" she demanded. "He's trying to kill me and the baby!"

Since he'd seen that much for himself, Matt couldn't

deny her statement held merit. Still, something about this entire scenario seemed off. "Who is he? What's his name?"

Before she could respond, his K-9 partner let out a yelp of pain.

Instantly he spun on his heel, alarm skittering through him. "Duchess!"

The dog came running toward him, her coat glistening with something wet and shiny. Then he noticed the blood trail behind her.

"Oh, no, he hurt your dog!" The woman said in alarm.

Duchess came up to rest against his leg. He reached down and saw there was a long laceration in her side, most likely from a knife. Thankfully, it didn't look too deep.

"Please don't arrest me," she said in a low voice. "My name is Lacy and I'm a schoolteacher on spring break. You need to understand that man is my brother-in-law, and he shot and killed my sister. Rory is my nephew and I heard him threaten to kill his son, the same way he murdered my sister. Please, you have to believe me!"

Oddly enough, Matt was leaning toward believing her. Not just because he'd watched that man point a gun at the woman, but also because he had lashed out at his partner. He glanced down at Duchess, who was still bleeding, and made a split-second decision. "Fine, but you're coming with me."

"No, wait…"

"Now!" Matt wasn't in the mood to quibble. He needed to get his partner's injury taken care of, and since this woman and the baby were also clearly in danger, he decided it was better to take them along.

He would figure out what to do with them later.

"Okay, but we need to hurry," she said.

Lacy surprised him by gathering up her items—baby things, he belatedly realized, such as diapers and formula—then heading over to his SUV without waiting for him.

Once she made up her mind about something, clearly, she acted on it. It was a trait he couldn't help but admire.

"Come on, Duchess." He led his partner back to the SUV and lifted her inside. Opening the first-aid kit he kept on hand for just these types of emergencies, Matt quickly pressed several gauze pads over the gash in her coat to stop the bleeding, then wrapped gauze around her abdomen as an added precaution. Duchess was trained well enough to leave the field dressing alone.

Satisfied he'd done what he could for the moment, he leaned over and rested his face against the animal's neck. "You're going to be okay, hear me? I'll get this taken care of right away."

Duchess licked his face, making him smile. He stepped back and closed the tailgate.

Gunfire erupted from the far east corner of the store, the same place where the gunman had disappeared. A bullet shattered the plastic sign hanging just over his head.

Matt didn't waste another moment. He jumped in behind the wheel and started the engine with a roar.

His tires screeched loudly as he drove away from the gas station. Once the lights from the store faded to nothing, he glanced in the rearview mirror at his passengers. He hated leaving the scene of the crime, but at the same time, Duchess's needs came first.

While he thought it was odd Lacy had chosen to sit in the back seat, he'd barely gotten onto the interstate when he saw the electric sign over the freeway blinking with the news of an Amber Alert.

The description on the sign matched the woman and baby sitting behind him.

He ground his teeth together, knowing this case was getting more complicated by the minute.

Somehow, some way, he needed to keep this woman and baby safe while he figured out what in the world was going on.

He couldn't bear the thought of losing another innocent child...

TWO

Lacy took a deep breath, desperately hoping she hadn't made a mistake going along with this cop. The fact that he was a K-9 officer irrationally soothed her fears.

Which was crazy and completely illogical. Anyone could have bad blood running through their veins. Her brother-in-law, Officer David Williams, was proof of that. He'd been so nice, so charming in the beginning.

But it soon became apparent that his niceness had been nothing but a facade hiding his cold black heart.

"Dispatch, this is Unit Twenty-one reporting gunfire at the Gas and Go store located on Bradley and Markwell. Send units out to that location. The perp who was last seen there injured my K-9 partner. He's roughly six feet tall wearing all black, including a dark cap over his head."

"Ten-four, Unit Twenty-one. Will send units to respond. What's your partner's status? Aren't you off duty?"

"I was off duty, but interrupted a crime in progress. I'm taking my partner in to be seen at the emergency vet. The perp tried to run, which is when my K-9 partner was injured." He glanced at her in the rearview mirror, then continued, "I'll write up my report as soon as my partner has been cared for."

"Ten-four."

Lacy let out her breath in a silent sigh. She'd wondered if the cop would mention her and Rory since David had clearly been after her, not the dog. And what about the Amber Alert? She knew this cop must have known about it. Or was it possible he'd missed the news since he was off duty?

The minute the thought entered her mind, she saw the Amber Alert flashing on the electric sign over the interstate.

Busted.

Rory was still crying, so she focused on caring for the baby. Since she was already breaking rules by not having him in a car seat, she decided to go ahead and get him changed. It was part of the reason she'd chosen the back seat. If she'd had water she would have made a bottle of formula for him, too. She should have thought of picking some up at the store.

So far, she was doing a lousy job of taking care of her young nephew. Not that she had much experience with babies. She taught fifth grade, not preschool.

"Shh, it's okay, Rory. Auntie Lacy is here. You're going to be fine. It's okay," she continued talking to the baby, who continued to wail. She glanced up at the officer, hoping he wasn't the type to lose his temper over a crying infant.

What did she really know about him? Other than he cared about his dog?

She deftly changed Rory, then bundled him back up in the sling, hoping he would calm down enough to fall back asleep.

Not hardly.

"Maybe the kid is hungry?" the officer suggested.

She stifled a sigh. "I'm well aware of that fact. I have

a can of powdered formula from the store, but it's useless without water."

"I have bottled water." He rummaged beneath the passenger seat and pulled out a fresh bottle of water, handing it to her over his shoulder. "I always keep a case in the SUV for my dog, Duchess."

"Thank you." The water wasn't warm, but it wasn't cold, either. Hopefully, he'd take it without a problem.

She made Rory's bottle, shaking the thing with enough force to make her teeth rattle in an effort to be sure the powder was completely dissolved. Then she shifted the baby in her arms so that she could feed him.

Rory latched onto the nipple with the strength of a linebacker. Apparently he was too hungry to care if the water bottle was warm or not.

With a sigh of relief, she gazed into Rory's wide eyes. This poor baby was in danger for no reason other than his father was an abusive, controlling lunatic.

She squeezed her eyes shut and lowered her mouth to press a kiss against the top of his downy head. He smelled like baby shampoo, and she had to fight against another wave of tears.

No child should have to grow up without his mother. Or with the knowledge that his father had killed his mother.

A sense of hopelessness hit hard, and she forced herself to shove it aside. Self-pity wasn't going to help.

She needed to remain strong, for Rory's sake.

Rory released his viselike grip on the bottle, so she lifted him up to her shoulder and lightly rubbed his back in slow circular motions. Duchess stuck her nose through the crate, pressing it along the back of Lacy's neck, making her smile.

Rory let out a wet belch and she instantly praised him. "Good boy! Yes, you're such a good boy!"

He lifted his head from her shoulder and smiled up at her with a toothless grin. She kissed him again, then turned him so that his head rested in the crook of her arm. As he finished the rest of the bottle, she glanced up and caught the officer staring at her through the rearview mirror.

"Where are we going?" she asked.

"To a twenty-four hour veterinary service," he answered. "Why don't you tell me exactly what took place tonight?"

"Look, Officer," she began, but he quickly interrupted.

"Matt. My name is Matthew Callahan."

Matt was a nice name, one that carried an inner strength. She shook her head quickly. She was acting irrational again. As if a name mattered. Wasn't David the one in the Bible who took down Goliath with a slingshot? It didn't mean her sister's husband was a good man.

Quite the opposite.

She gave herself a mental shake. "Okay, Matt. I'm sure you've figured out by now that I'm Lacy Germaine, and this baby is Rory Williams. There's an Amber Alert out on the baby and I understand we're in your custody."

"Is that why you chose to sit in the back seat?" he asked.

"No." Not only had she wanted to change Rory, but she secretly preferred being closer to the dog than to him. She forced herself to stay on track. "I've been staying at my sister's house for a few days to help her with Rory. I woke up to the sound of arguing and heard my sister begging not to be hurt. Before this happened, she had told me she was afraid of her husband, David

Williams, because of his temper. In fact, she recently filed for divorce. He was clearly angry about that—I overheard him threaten to kill her and Rory, too, right before I heard two gunshots. And the biggest problem of all is that David Williams is a police officer working in the third district."

"He's a cop?" Matt demanded, his expression turning grim.

"Yes." She could already tell that he didn't want to believe her. "When I heard them arguing, I called 911 and gave the dispatcher my sister's address. Then I took off with Rory."

"So why the Amber Alert?"

Rory had fallen asleep, the bottle just about empty, so she pulled it away and set it aside. "I don't know. I can only assume that David somehow convinced his cop buddies that I'm the one who killed Jill and took Rory. Which doesn't make any sense."

He snorted in derision. "I'll say. Even a rookie would have a hard time buying that story. There has to be something else going on."

She clenched her jaw. "I don't know what else is going on. You saw that David had a gun, didn't you? And he took a slice out of Duchess. What more do you want from me? I can't tell you what I don't know!"

Rory shifted restlessly in her arms, and she mentally berated herself for raising her voice. Rory shouldn't have to listen to her arguing with a cop. He'd had enough exposure to violence in his short life.

She let out a sigh and stroked the tip of her finger over his plump cheek. Now that Jill was gone, it would be up to her to take care of Rory. To raise him as her own.

To love him.

She swallowed a sense of panic. Okay, she didn't

know much about babies, but that didn't mean she couldn't take a crash course to learn.

Lacy silently promised to give Rory the stable life he deserved.

Matt didn't understand why he was so captivated by Lacy taking care of Rory. He came from a large family, sure, but he wasn't like his two eldest brothers, Marc and Miles, who'd both married women with children.

Truthfully, he'd gone down that path with devastating results. He'd begun dating a divorced woman named Debra who had a four-year-old daughter, Carly. He'd been about to propose when Carly had gotten sick and had been diagnosed with a rare form of lethal cancer. During the next few months, he'd been forced to watch the child he'd come to love die a horrible death. On top of that, the crisis had caused Debra and her ex-husband, Kyle, to grow close again. After Carly's death, Debra had broken up with Matt, claiming she and Kyle were going to reunite.

Logically, he knew he should have been happy for them, but he'd felt Carly's loss as keenly as they had. Losing a child, even one who wasn't his by blood, had been the most painful thing he'd ever experienced. Debra's rejection afterward hadn't helped.

When Debra walked away, he'd decided it was easier to avoid romantic entanglements and to focus on his career. Dogs were better than people any day of the week. He'd loved K-9 training, and Duchess made the best partner he could have imagined. He still had the closeness he shared with his twin, Maddy, and was truly happy she'd found love with his former partner, Noah Sinclair.

Using the rearview mirror, he kept a close eye on his

partner. If his gaze strayed on occasion to Lacy and the baby, he quickly caught himself and looked away. He didn't need to keep an eye on his passengers, as Duchess seemed to be enthralled by the woman and the baby in the back seat.

Or maybe his partner instinctively knew to offer her protection.

He grappled with Lacy's allegation that the dark-haired guy was a police officer. He could easily find out for sure, but he was loath to use his radio. He'd bought them a little time, but he couldn't postpone the inevitable forever. Now that he knew about the Amber Alert, he would have to take Lacy and Rory into custody so she could provide her side of the story.

In his gut, he believed she was telling the truth. But he also knew that David's being a cop would make things a lot more difficult.

Her word against that of a police officer.

He didn't like it.

Even worse, he wasn't sure he'd be able to continue investigating the case. In theory, once he handed her over, his role in this mess would be finished. The case would be given to one of the homicide detectives, not a K-9 officer.

The thought was depressing. Matt didn't want to become attached to the little guy, but at the same time, he worried about what would happen to him. The kid was the real innocent victim here. Would he end up in foster care?

Maybe, but it was likely a whole lot better than ending up with his father.

The lights from the emergency veterinary clinic loomed up ahead, so he turned in that direction.

He and Duchess had only been there once before,

and that was related to another on-the-job injury. Some perp had kicked Duchess in the head and he'd panicked, fearing she had suffered some sort of brain injury. She'd been fine, and he was determined she would get through this latest injury without complications as well.

After parking the SUV, he jumped out and went around to the back to get Duchess. She lifted her head, her tail thumping in greeting, but he could tell by the way she was acting that the wound along her side hurt.

"It's okay, girl. I have you." He scooped the animal into his arms—no small feat since she was a solid German shepherd weighing in at eighty pounds, hefty for a female.

She licked his face again and he used his elbow to close the back hatch. As he rounded the corner of the SUV, he realized that Lacy had gotten out of the vehicle with Rory swaddled against her. She held the door to the clinic open for him.

"Thanks," he said, carrying Duchess inside.

"You're welcome." She surprised him again by following him into the building.

He supposed it was better for her to be inside the building since her brother-in-law was looking for her. It bothered him to think about her need to escape with Rory in the middle of the night.

He focused on Duchess. Blood was seeping through the dressings he'd applied, so he looked around for someone to talk to. "I need some help here," he said in a loud tone.

The veterinary assistant came out of the back, then hurried over. "What happened?"

"This is my K-9 partner. She was cut by a sharp object," he said. "The laceration is roughly six inches long."

"This way." The assistant led the way through a door into a small exam room.

He eased the dog down on the stainless steel table, disconcerted to realize that Lacy had followed him again. Why her actions distracted him, he had no idea. Maybe on some level, he expected her to take off with the baby. In fact, he couldn't even say he would blame her if she did.

But she didn't.

The vet, a tall man who appeared to be in his early fifties, entered the room. After washing his hands in the corner sink, he approached Duchess. "I'm Dr. Hogan. Do you have any idea what was used to cause the laceration?"

"No, it was dark. I assume a knife, but couldn't say for sure." Matt stayed near Duchess, holding her in place, stroking the soft fur between her ears reassuringly. "Her name is Duchess and she's a K-9 officer."

"Hi, Duchess." The vet spoke in a soothing voice. He glanced at Matt. "I assume her shots are up to date?"

"Yes." Matt watched as the vet cut through the gauze he'd wrapped around the dog's torso.

"Well, I'm glad to see the cut isn't too deep," Dr. Hogan said. "I think we can close it up with glue. Hopefully, it won't bother her too much."

The huge wave of guilt rolled off his back. Duchess really would be okay.

"She'll need some antibiotics, since we don't know what cut her, along with some pain meds." Dr. Hogan lifted his gaze to Matt's. "First, we'll get this cleaned up, okay?"

He nodded again, grateful that his partner wouldn't need surgery. He sent up a silent prayer of thanks to God for watching over them.

Praying came natural to him. Growing up in the Callahan family meant they went to church every Sunday, followed by brunch at his mother's home. His father, Max Callahan, the former Chief of Police, had died in the line of duty over two years ago, but in some ways it felt as if the event that had so dramatically changed their lives had happened yesterday.

The perp who'd shot his father had never been caught, a fact that nagged at him incessantly. And he knew it bothered the rest of his brothers and his twin sister, too. He'd spent some time trying to investigate the case but had gotten sidetracked when he'd been selected for K-9 training.

His father had instilled a sense of serving the community in all six of his children. Most of them had gone into some type of law enforcement work; Marc was an FBI agent, Miles a homicide detective, Mitch an arson investigator, and Matt's twin, Maddy, a lawyer, working in the DA's office. Only his middle brother, Mike, had defied his father's wishes by becoming a private investigator.

"Matt?" Lacy's soft voice interrupted his thoughts. "I'm glad Duchess is going to be okay."

"Thanks." He forced a smile. "Me, too."

She took the baby bottle she'd used to feed Rory and washed it out in the sink. He couldn't help but admire how she managed to take care of an infant in less than optimal conditions.

The veterinary assistant came in with a razor and a bowl of soapy water. For the next five minutes, he held Duchess in place while the assistant first trimmed the dog's fur from the area around the laceration, then used the soapy water to clean it. By the time they were finished, Matt's uniform was almost as wet as Duchess's coat.

"Dr. Hogan will be back shortly," the assistant said,

emptying the bowl of soapy water into the sink, then rinsing it out.

An hour later, Duchess was ready to go. She took her antibiotics and pain pills in a ball of peanut butter like a pro. Since the leash was out in the car and he didn't want Duchess to pull on the glue the vet had used to close her incision, he once again scooped her into his arms.

Lacy went ahead to open the doors for him as they made their way back outside. The moon was high in the sky, and even though he was certain they hadn't been followed, the tiny hairs along the back of his neck lifted and pricked in warning.

"Take the baby and get inside," he said, once she'd opened the back hatch.

Lacy quickly scooted into the back seat. He closed the door behind Duchess, then hurried behind the wheel.

Twin headlights pierced the night, and he quickly started the engine and backed out of the parking spot. The headlights grew closer, and he couldn't ignore a sliver of apprehension.

Should he call for backup? Or was he being paranoid? Probably the latter, so he headed away from the lights, in the opposite direction. At two in the morning, he didn't expect there to be much traffic on the road.

The twin headlights followed.

He glanced in his rearview mirror at Lacy holding the baby and Duchess stretched out in the back. No way was he going to risk becoming involved in some sort of high-speed car chase.

Grabbing the radio, he quickly called it in. "Dispatch, this is Unit Twenty-one, requesting backup at my current location, about five miles away from the emergency veterinary clinic, heading westbound on interstate ninety-four."

"Ten-four, what's the problem?"

He wasn't exactly sure how to phrase his concerns. "I appear to have picked up a tail, and my partner is temporarily out of commission."

"Unit Five is only a few miles away. He should catch up with you shortly."

"Thanks." He disconnected from the radio, needing both hands on the wheel. The headlights grew brighter as the vehicle behind him began to close the gap.

Was it possible the guy dressed in black, David Williams, had come to finish what he'd started? Matt gave himself a mental kick. He shouldn't have announced over the radio that he was taking Duchess to the emergency vet. As a cop, Williams likely had a radio in his vehicle. Process of elimination would have made finding him and Lacy way too easy. There were only two emergency veterinary hospitals offering services around the clock in the area.

Swallowing hard, Matt pushed the speed as high as he dared, considering his precious cargo. Even though Lacy was wearing her seat belt, she didn't have the proper infant car seat for Rory, and he knew if they were hit hard enough, there was a chance she could lose her grip on the baby.

And Duchess wasn't up to par, either, considering she'd been given antibiotics and pain meds.

The headlights grew impossibly brighter. Was Williams gaining ground?

Where was his backup?

The headlights abruptly shifted, going into the left lane, coming up on his driver's side. Matt did his best not to panic. He decided to wait until the guy was almost upon him before he would abruptly slow down, hoping the guy would shoot past them.

"This is a good time to pray," he told Lacy. She looked surprised by his comment. "I'm serious. I know God will watch over us, and we need all the help we can get."

She gave a terse nod, then began reciting the "Our Father" prayer, which made him wonder if she wasn't used to praying on the fly.

"Dear Lord, give me the strength to keep us all safe," he murmured as the lights grew brighter and brighter.

Soon they were almost parallel to his rear bumper. Now!

He took his foot off the gas and pressed gently on the brake. The vehicle flew past him, and he didn't waste another moment. Wrenching the wheel to the left, he drove his SUV across the median, crossed the three lanes that were thankfully absent of traffic, and took the next exit he could find.

It was several miles before he could relax enough to breathe normally. But the close call bothered him.

At the moment, he didn't feel confident enough to take Lacy and Rory to the police station. They would be far too vulnerable there. He didn't want them anywhere near a place where the ex-husband who happened to be a cop could find them.

Nope. What he needed was a new plan.

There had to be some way to keep Lacy and Rory safe from harm while he tracked down the guy intent on killing them.

THREE

Lacy clutched Rory close, determined to hang on to him no matter what happened. She closed her eyes, the scenery flashing past the window making her dizzy. Duchess didn't much like the rocky ride, either, whining a bit and scrambling to regain her balance.

"Sorry, Duchess," Matt muttered.

Once again, she was oddly reassured by how much Matt cared about his dog. Not to mention that he'd told her now was a good time to pray. And most important, how he'd looked so concerned when he'd carried the animal in and out of the emergency vet clinic.

Surely, a guy who loved dogs couldn't be all bad.

After what seemed like forever but was probably less than twenty minutes, Matt spoke up from the front seat. "Sorry about the bumpy ride. Are you and the baby okay?"

"F-fine." Her breath hitched in her chest and she fought the urge to break down sobbing. When would this nightmare end? Why was David doing this?

Nothing made any sense.

"I've lost him for now," Matt continued. "You're safe."

She shook her head, knowing she and Rory wouldn't

be safe until somehow the authorities found David and arrested him. "He won't stop," she said in a low voice. "Jill told me that David is a terrible control freak. Who knows what horrible things he's capable of."

"I'm getting a pretty good idea," Matt said, his tone grim. "Apparently he doesn't mind taking out a fellow officer in his quest to get at his son."

"Not just his son, but me, too." She tried to think of a way to make him understand. "Not just because I'm Jill's sister, but he caught a glimpse of me taking off in my car. So he knows I'm a witness to her murder. My testimony could put him away for the rest of his life."

"I know and I believe you. I totally get that the guy is a serious head case. I need to call my lieutenant, but can't risk using the radio just yet."

The thought of Matt calling his boss made her stomach clench. "Please don't. Don't turn me into the authorities."

His gaze met hers in the rearview mirror. "I have to. When I explain what I know, my boss will call off the Amber Alert and put a BOLO—Be On the Lookout—on David Williams instead. Trust me, they'll find him and arrest him. You and the baby will be safe."

Having David locked up in jail was something she wanted more than anything, but she wouldn't be able to rest until she knew he'd been apprehended.

"It's so late. Can't you give me a little time?" She tried not to sound as if she were begging, even though she would if necessary. "Rory needs some rest. He's been through a lot over the past few hours."

"I know." Once again his gaze briefly met hers. "And so have you."

She didn't want to think about the fact that her sister was gone. Everything that had taken place seemed surreal. As if she might wake up in the morning to discover this was all nothing more than a bad dream.

"Yes," she agreed. "Both of us could use some time to rest and regroup."

There was a long silence before Matt spoke again. "Duchess could use a few hours off as well, so I'll find someplace to rest for what's left of the night. I'll report in to my boss first thing tomorrow morning."

Since it was already nearing 2:30 a.m., she didn't find that too reassuring. How many hours of rest would he give her? Five or six at the most?

Not nearly enough, but at this point she told herself to take what she could get. "Thank you."

"You're welcome."

The vehicle slowed and made a right-hand turn. She noticed that he'd pulled up to a motel with a bright *Vacancy* sign. She sat up straighter, keeping one hand against Rory, wondering if they had a crib available.

"This place will take cash from cops and they're pet-friendly," he said as he threw the gearshift into Park. "Two of my brothers are cops and have used this place to keep people safe before."

Brothers? Plural? A sense of unease niggled beneath her skin. What if one of them was friends with David Williams? What if they found a way to convince Matt that she was the guilty one, not David?

Why had she assumed she was safe with this particular cop? So what if he loved his dog? She still didn't know anything about him.

Except for the fact that he'd told her it was a good time to pray.

She didn't really know any men who actually prayed. Oh, sure, her father used to take them to church, but it was nothing more than an act. In private, he was anything but loving. Going to church had only been to make them look good in the community.

Sad to think that Jill had married a man who was exactly like their father.

Duchess pressed her nose against the back of Lacy's neck again, as if sensing her distress. She liked the dog better than she liked the master. The adrenaline rush had faded, leaving a nagging headache in its wake. Maybe that's why she was having trouble thinking clearly. Who could concentrate after witnessing a murder, being shot at and then followed?

"Stay inside for a moment," Matt said. "I'll see if I can get us adjoining rooms."

"Ask for a crib," she interjected before he could slam the door.

"Oh, yeah. Sure."

She rested back against the seat cushion, shivering in the night. A blanket of exhaustion dropped over her, and she had almost drifted off to sleep when Matt returned.

"We're all set." Matt slid in behind the wheel. "We have two adjoining rooms, one with a crib. The crib should be set up by the time we get inside."

"That's great, thanks." The fact that he'd gotten adjoining rooms was reassuring. Maybe his kindness wasn't just an act.

Matt drove around the motel and pulled up in front of two rooms on the ground floor, which would make caring for Duchess much easier.

After parking, Matt jumped out and opened the door for her. He offered his hand to help her out, and she took it, all too aware of the warmth of his fingers against hers. She dropped his hand, feeling self-conscious.

He used the key to open the door to room ten, then flipped on the light switch and handed her the key. She took Rory inside, grateful to see that there was in fact a crib in the room, set up near the bathroom.

The door closed behind her. She crossed over and gently began unwrapping the swaddling cloth that she'd used as an infant carrier. Rory squirmed, sighed and then quieted down again as she set him on his back in the crib.

For a long moment she stared down at his sleeping face, trying to find solace in the fact that he was too young to remember any of this.

A blessing, except for the fact that he would never know his mother. Fresh tears burned behind her eyelids, and she swiped them away and turned back into the room.

Rory wouldn't be alone. He'd always have her. She'd care for him the way she knew Jill would want her to. She wasn't sure how she would manage, but she would find a way.

There was a light tapping on the connecting door. Flipping back the dead bolt, she opened it up to see Matt standing there holding her purse, the diapers and the formula, with Duchess at his side. "I brought in your things."

"Thanks." She stepped back, giving him room to enter. He set everything down on the small desk, and she stole a glance at him. He was handsome, his mink brown hair longer than what most cops sported, with brilliant green eyes. He wasn't that much taller than her own five feet and eight inches, but he was broad across the shoulders in a way that made her feel smaller than she really was.

No question, Matt looked as if he could have his pick of women. If you liked a man in uniform.

Good thing she wasn't a fan. In her experience,

macho men like her father and brother-in-law were the ones to stay far away from.

Although if she were honest, she had to admit that Matt didn't act like her father or brother-in-law. Still, she wasn't going to take anything at face value. Not anymore.

She crossed her arms over her chest in a defensive gesture. "Will you talk to me before you call your boss?"

He lifted a brow. "Sure, if that's what you want."

"I'd appreciate it." Duchess moved over to sniff at the crib, then returned to stand beside Matt. The dog was more gold than black, the long laceration on her right side an aberration against her glossy coat.

"Let me know if you need anything," Matt said, moving back toward the connecting door. "And leave your side unlocked in case anything happens, okay?"

She gave him a terse nod. "Good night."

"Good night."

When he and Duchess left the room, she made sure the connecting door remained ajar as he'd asked before dousing the light and crawling beneath the covers fully dressed.

Sleep should have come easily, but for some reason her mind decided to replay the events of the past few hours. She pressed the pillow over her ears, as if that would help silence her sister's pleas. The subsequent gunshots.

Deafening silence.

She must have slept a little because Rory's crying woke up her up at quarter to six in the morning. Bleary-eyed, she dragged herself out of bed, stumbling a bit as she went over to make him a bottle.

She should have made it the night before. That's

probably what Jill would have done. Using warm water
from the tap, she made his bottle, then quickly changed
his diaper.

It was messy, and of course she'd completely forgotten about picking up wet wipes. The washcloth from
the bathroom seemed too rough against his skin, but it
did the trick. Finally, she had him changed and settled
in the crook of her arm with the bottle.

She eased down onto the bed and closed her eyes,
feeling like a failure. Being a mother wasn't as instinc-
tive as she'd hoped. What else had she forgotten? The
poor thing didn't even have a change of clothes.

She kissed the top of his head. "It's just you and me,
kiddo. Just you and me." Hopefully, she and Rory would
be able to figure things out, together.

Matt groaned when he heard the baby crying, tempted
to bury his head into the pillow to drown out the noise.

Although if Lacy was up, then he should be awake,
too. He squinted at the clock, realizing it was barely six.

He needed to talk to his boss, his lieutenant, not
his shift commander, but he wouldn't be in until eight
o'clock. A full two hours from now.

Beside him, Duchess thumped her tail and lifted her
head as if asking if it was time to get up.

"Easy girl," he soothed, lightly scratching her between the ears. "You need your rest."

Duchess licked his wrist, then set her head back down
on the mattress. Propping himself up on his elbow, he
gently palpated the long laceration. The wound looked
decent, considering what she'd been through. Still, she'd
carry the scar with her always.

A fresh burst of anger hit hard. Not just because of
Duchess's injury, but on behalf of the woman and baby

next door. That guy had killed his wife and had tried to kill a woman and her baby, not caring that he'd almost taken out two police officers.

Yeah, capturing David Williams and putting him behind bars was definitely at the top of his list of priorities. He'd have to find a way to convince his boss to let him assist in the investigation.

The crying next door subsided, but even in the silence, he couldn't fall back asleep. Dragging himself upright, he walked over to the window next to the door and pushed the curtain aside to sweep his gaze over the area. Convinced that nothing seemed out of place, he gestured for Duchess to come.

His partner ambled up and lightly jumped from the bed. He didn't carry her this time, needing to understand what she was able to do. Being the trooper she was, she moved as gracefully as ever, the pain from the incision apparently not bad enough to hold her back.

"Good girl," he praised, giving her a treat from his pocket. Deciding to leave her off leash, he pulled on his jacket and took her outside.

He was making his way back across the parking lot when the door to Lacy's room burst open. She had the baby wrapped against her with the cloth thingy, but the expression in her eyes was full of panic.

He immediately broke into a run, heading straight toward her, Duchess keeping pace at his side. "What is it? What's wrong?" He looked for signs of an intruder.

"I— Nothing, sorry. I thought you were leaving me behind." Her cheeks went pink and she averted her gaze.

"No, of course not." He was relieved there was nothing seriously wrong. He took her arm and drew her back inside the room, closing the door behind them. "I told you I wouldn't call my boss without talking to you first. He won't be in until closer to eight o'clock."

Her smile was weak as she dropped back down on the edge of the bed. "I'm sorry to overreact like that. It's just…." she shrugged. "Realizing that I'm all Rory has left in the world is a little overwhelming."

The baby was wide-awake, lifting his head and looking around with large curious blue eyes. Matt hadn't really understood until this moment just how big of a change this was for Lacy. The reality of her situation was clearly just sinking in.

"Looks like he's going to be up for a while. Should we find something to eat?"

Her tenuous smile widened, but then she grimaced. "That sounds great. Except for the fact that I don't have a car seat for Rory. I'm not sure I can manage a restaurant without one."

"Okay, how about I pick something up and bring it back? There's a family restaurant a few blocks from here. Tell me what you like."

"Scrambled eggs, wheat toast and bacon," she said. "Looks like the motel provides coffee in the room."

She had ordered exactly what he'd planned to get, which made him smile. "Yeah, but the pot only makes one cup. I'll get us both coffee to go, too." He turned toward his room, then looked back at Duchess. "Stay, Duchess. Guard."

Duchess instantly dropped to her haunches, sitting straight and tall. Lacy reached out to pet her, and he bit back a protest. It was clear Lacy was feeling emotionally fragile at the moment, and it wouldn't hurt for Duchess to get a little extra attention.

The trip to and from the restaurant didn't take long, but he didn't like leaving them alone. Duchess would protect Lacy and Rory with her life, but she wasn't bulletproof, either.

And he suspected that next time, David Williams wouldn't bother using a knife. In fact, he was surprised but glad he hadn't used his gun against Duchess.

Matt entered the motel through his room, then knocked on the connecting door that was still ajar. "Food's here," he called.

"Come on in."

Duchess greeted him with her usual tail wag, and he had to admit he loved that she was always happy to see him. Lacy had cleaned off the small desk so he could set the insulated containers down. He smiled when he realized she'd brewed herself a cup of coffee.

He pulled the two chairs over as Lacy set Rory back in the crib. Duchess went over and stretched out on the carpet in front of the crib, as if knowing it was her job to protect the baby.

"Duchess is amazing," Lacy said, dropping into the chair beside him. "Thanks for picking up breakfast."

"Yes, my partner is awesome, and you're welcome." He bowed his head and began to pray. "Dear Lord, we thank You for this food we are about to eat and for Your continued guidance and protection as we seek safety. Amen."

There was a brief pause before Lacy added, "Amen."

"Dig in," he teased, thinking about how they'd always said those words after their family prayer when growing up.

Lacy picked up her plastic fork and dug into her eggs. "Do you always pray like that?" she asked.

He bit into a crisp piece of bacon, glancing at her in surprise. "Yes, always. That's the way I was brought up."

"Hmm." Her noncommittal response made him frown.

"I take it you didn't grow up attending church?"

She let out a harsh laugh. "Oh, sure. We attended church every week, but it didn't mean much. My parents only went to put on a show for everyone else. At home they argued and…" She didn't finish, but he felt himself grow tense.

"Your father abused your mother?" He was horrified by the thought and hoped Lacy hadn't been subjected to abuse, too.

She shrugged and avoided his gaze. "It wasn't like she had to go to the emergency room or anything, but yeah, he liked to hit. I have no idea why she put up with him."

He couldn't stop himself from reaching out to put a hand on her arm. "I'm sorry, Lacy. That should never happen."

She abruptly dropped her fork and jumped to her feet. "It wasn't as bad as what you're thinking. He didn't point a gun and shoot my mother in cold blood the way David murdered Jill."

Before he could say anything she disappeared into the tiny bathroom, closing the door behind her.

He felt terrible for opening old wounds, and gave himself a mental kick in the pants. Losing Carly had gutted him. Debra had torn his heart out and stomped on it, but even those two things were a far cry from what Lacy had experienced. Just because he needed some emotional distance from her and Rory didn't mean he couldn't be more sympathetic and understanding.

After promising himself to do better, he finished his meal and then cleaned up his things, leaving Lacy's meal alone. After about ten minutes she emerged from the bathroom, her red, puffy eyes evidence of her tears.

She didn't say anything to him, but took her seat and continued eating her breakfast.

"I'm sorry," he said gruffly. "I didn't mean to upset you."

She nodded and finished her meal. "I know," she said after she'd tossed out her garbage. "I'm fine. Now, tell me how we're going to approach your boss. I'm not convinced going into the police station is the right move."

He stared at her in amazement, wondering if she'd read his mind. "How did you know that's exactly what my plan was?" he said. "Rather than call, I think we should show up and go straight in to talk to my lieutenant, Bill Gray."

Her eyes narrowed. "I don't know Lieutenant Gray, so who's to say he'll believe me?"

"I was there when David aimed a gun at you," he reminded her. "And he cut Duchess, remember?"

"We assume he cut Duchess. We didn't actually see it," she corrected him. "Duchess could have cut herself on a fence trying to chase him."

He didn't like admitting she had a point. "My boss has faith in me. There's no reason for him not to believe you."

"Except for another police officer telling a completely different story," she said. "And he's had three years of lies about my sister to back him up."

"Listen, the forensic evidence at the crime scene will speak for itself. The truth will prevail above the lies. You don't have anything to worry about." He hesitated, then added, "I need you to trust me on this, okay?"

Her expression was full of agony, and he felt so bad he almost gave in. But what other option was there? They couldn't hide out here in a motel room indefinitely.

"Fine," she reluctantly agreed. "I hope your boss is as good as you say."

"He is." Matt glanced at his watch. They still had almost twenty minutes before they needed to leave. He wanted to stop for warm clothes and maybe a car seat, but the stores wouldn't open for a couple hours yet.

Lacy went over to pick up Rory and brought him to the bed. For a moment, the memory of Carly lying sick in a hospital bed flashed in his mind, and he pushed it away with an effort.

Nothing was going to happen to Rory. He wasn't sick. And Matt would do everything in his power to keep the little guy safe from harm.

He left Lacy alone and checked his cell phone for messages. Then, since there was internet access in the motel, he decided to search for the closest big-box store, where they could get everything they needed for Rory.

The closest one opened at nine o'clock, so he figured they could stop there after talking to his lieutenant. It was tempting to call ahead to the department, to make sure Bill Gray would be there, but he restrained himself.

When it was time to go, he went back to Lacy's room to help carry the baby's things. He noticed she'd made a bottle for him, ready for whenever he became hungry. If she was intimidated by caring for her young nephew, she wasn't showing it. He had to give her credit for thinking ahead.

When he had the baby stuff loaded in the car, along with Duchess's food and water dishes, he went back inside. "Ready?"

Her expression was resigned, but she nodded. He opened the door and then escorted her to the SUV parked facing outward in the lot. Before she could get inside, the baby slipped down in the swaddling cloth.

She'd bent over in an effort to hoist him back up when a loud gunshot rang through the air. He pushed Lacy down, horrified to see a round hole in the passenger-side window where Lacy's head had been seconds earlier.

"Get in!" He shoved her inside and slammed the door. He jumped into the driver's seat, determined to escape from the gunman.

More gunfire echoed, and Matt drove like a demolition derby driver, clenching his jaw, praying that the bullets wouldn't find their mark. He headed toward the route that happened to be closer to the trees, hoping to use them as cover.

Thankfully, his ploy worked. They'd gotten away, for now. But he couldn't rest or relax.

How on earth had Williams known where to find them?

FOUR

Her heart in her throat, Lacy clutched Rory close to her chest and silently prayed for God to keep them all safe. The gut-level instinct surprised her—she hadn't really thought much about God in the years after her parents had died.

But right here, right now, with the wind whistling through the small round bullet hole in the passenger-side window, proof that David Williams hadn't stopped searching for them, she wanted to believe that God was up there, watching over them.

That she, Matt and Rory weren't completely alone in this.

"Are you all right?" Matt asked in a hoarse voice.

"Y-yes." She and Rory weren't hurt. Scared sense-less, but not physically injured.

"We need a new plan." Matt's tone was grim. "Williams is always one step ahead of us, and I don't like it. I can't figure out how he knew where to find us. Regardless, I'm not going to risk taking you anywhere near the police station."

The news should have been reassuring. She hadn't wanted to go to the authorities, afraid that even with Matt's support, his boss would lean toward believing

David's version of events over hers. At the same time, being here alone with Matt didn't make her feel that much better. Oh, she trusted Matt, at least as far as his ability to keep her and Rory safe. But for how long?

Duchess woofed softly behind her. Okay, they weren't completely alone, but still. Eventually, they'd need help of the two-legged variety. Someone to provide backup. It wasn't as if traveling with a three-month-old and a K-9 was inconspicuous.

They were bound to attract attention.

"Thank you," she said softly.

"For what? Almost getting you killed?" His harsh tone didn't make her flinch because she knew he was upset with himself rather than with her.

"You saved us," she corrected him. "And I can't deny I'm glad we're not going to the police station."

He was silent for several long moments. "We need a place to go where we can hide off-grid for a while. I want to dig into Williams's background a bit."

The idea of hiding somewhere off-grid was appealing, but the thought of his investigating David made her blood run cold. "He's a sociopath," she said in a flat tone. "His entire world revolves around him. I'm not sure you'll ever figure out the logic behind all this."

His gaze met hers in the rearview mirror. "Try not to worry about it, okay? Duchess and I will protect you and Rory."

She attempted to smile. "I know. But can we please stop at a store to pick up a few things? Rory needs clothes, baby wipes and extra bottles. Not to mention a proper car seat."

He sighed. "Yeah, okay. But I'm going to drive to a store located on the opposite side of town, just in case.

And once we have what you and Rory need, I'm going to call my brother Miles."

The news made her tense up all over again. "Are you sure it's safe? You said your brothers work in law enforcement. I highly doubt he'll be thrilled with the idea of us going into hiding rather than to the authorities."

Matt grinned. "You'd be surprised. Miles has done his share of breaking the rules. He'll be supportive of our plan, don't worry. Besides, I need a different vehicle and more cash."

Duchess pressed her nose against the back of Lacy's neck, making her smile. Between the K-9 officer and Matt's ever-present confidence, she was feeling better already. "All right. I'll trust your judgment."

Matt nodded and fell silent as they headed across town. The traffic wasn't too bad, and they reached a shopping area within thirty minutes. Lacy was relieved it was far away from the scene of her sister's murder.

She tightened her grip on Rory and blinked away the tears. Jill would want her to be strong for the baby, so she needed to stay focused on being a good mother. Once they were safe, there would be plenty of time to make sure Jill had a proper burial.

And hopefully by then David would be behind bars, paying for his crime.

"Ready?" Matt asked. He'd backed into a parking spot, and she belatedly realized he'd done that just in case they had to make a quick getaway.

"Yes." She unlatched the seat belt and curled her arm protectively around Rory as she pushed open the car door. Matt was there, offering his assistance. She put her hand in his, instantly aware of the warmth of his fingers curling over hers. As soon as she had her feet under her, she let go, uncomfortable about her odd awareness of him.

Matt was the complete opposite of the few men she'd tried dating in the past. One fellow teacher had expressed interest, but she hadn't experienced even the slightest flicker of attraction toward him. Then there was the accountant who did her taxes, but that hadn't been any better.

So why was she reacting to a man who was virtually a stranger?

No clue. And it needed to stop right now.

The stern lecture to herself helped. They entered the store and Matt grabbed a shopping cart. She wove through the aisles, quickly finding the baby items she needed. A glimpse of the prices on the car seats made her grimace.

"They're so expensive." She glanced at Matt. "I only have about fifty dollars on me."

"It's fine, I have enough to last until my brother brings more. Which one do you think is the best?"

She looked at the various styles, then pointed at the one Jill had purchased. "This one."

"Okay." He picked up the box and set it in the cart. "Pick out everything you need for the baby, then we'll get you a light jacket."

She wanted to protest, but spring in Wisconsin was unpredictable so she gave in. She picked out two outfits for Rory, a warm zip-up onesie with a hood to cover his head and then a packet of baby wipes. The smallest box of bottles contained six, so she tossed that in the cart, too. Silently counting up what they owed made her stomach clench with worry.

"Women's clothes are over there," Matt said, turning the cart in that direction.

"I'll just get a heavy sweatshirt. No need to pay for a coat."

"You should get both, just in case." He apparently wasn't about to take no for an answer. And he didn't stop there. After she picked out a navy blue jacket, he pushed the cart over to the sundries and waved a hand. "Get what you need—hairbrush, shampoo, etcetera. I'll pick up a few things, too."

She hesitated. "If we're going to another motel, they'll provide some of this stuff. No reason to waste your money."

"We're not going to a motel," he countered. "It's too hard to find the ones that are dog-friendly, and they're not all willing to take cash, either. Besides, I want you and Rory far away from the area."

"So where are we going?"

"I have a friend who owns a cabin located about thirty minutes outside the city limits. It's nothing fancy, but it's warm, has two bedrooms and a kitchen. It's the best place I know where we can hide out for a while."

A cabin sounded nice, if maybe a little too cozy. And since the accommodations sounded better for Duchess, how could she argue? She began filling the cart with the bare essentials. Matt tossed a few items in, too.

The grand total was just as bad as she'd feared, even though many of the items they'd purchased were on sale. She wondered how on earth she'd manage to repay Matt for his kindness.

Matt didn't seem concerned as he carried everything back out to the SUV. Right in the parking lot, he opened the box and quickly pulled out the infant car seat. Lacy bundled Rory into the new winter onesie and then fastened him into the car seat. Matt took over from there, securing the seat with ease.

"You look as if you've done that before," she said as she slid into the front passenger seat.

He froze for a moment, then shrugged. "A couple of my brothers have kids."

"A couple?" She fastened her seat belt then looked at him. "How many brothers do you have?"

"Four older brothers and a younger twin sister." He started the engine and let it run for a moment.

She tried not to gape at him. "Six? There are six of you?"

He pulled out his phone. "Yeah, crazy, huh? Marc is the oldest, and works for the FBI. He and his wife, Kari, are due to have another baby early next month. Miles is the second oldest and works as a homicide detective. He and his wife, Paige, are also expecting in early May. My twin, Maddy, just married my former partner, Noah Sinclair. Mitch, an arson investigator, and Mike, a private investigator, are still single, like me, which is good because we can balance things out."

All the information he was tossing out about his family made her head spin. And she hadn't missed the fact that he'd emphasized he was single and not interested in changing his status. Fine with her. "And you're sure they won't force you to take me in?"

"I'm sure." Matt reached over and lightly clasped her hand in his. "Trust me. In our family, Callahans always come first."

Strangely enough, she did trust him. As she listened to him leaving a message for Miles, she found herself relaxing for the first time since she'd woken up to the sounds of her sister arguing with her husband.

She reached back to place a soothing hand on Rory in his car seat. If Matt was right, and Callahans always came first, then maybe, just maybe, they'd find a way out of this mess.

* * *

Matt pulled out of the parking lot, hoping Miles would return his call soon. He didn't like thinking about the fact that as a cop, David Williams had access to information like Matt's cell number and his vehicle license plate number.

Five minutes later, his phone rang. He handed it to Lacy. "Place the call on speaker." When she'd done that, he quickly answered. "Miles, I need a hand."

"What's going on?"

"I need new disposable phones, a laptop computer, a new K-9 vehicle and cash."

"Anything else?" His brother's tone was all business. "What about a place to stay?"

"We need to remain off-grid, so I'm planning to head up to Valerie's father's cabin. Maybe you could give her a heads-up that I'll be staying there for a while, just in case she decides to take a trip."

"We?" Trust his brother to pick up on that slip.

He glanced at Lacy. "I'm keeping a woman and baby safe. There's already been three attempts to kill them. Honestly? The less you know, the better."

"Haven't I always supported you, Matt? I'm not about to turn you in, if that's what you're thinking."

Lacy relaxed in her seat, and he grinned. "I know that, and I trust you, bro. It's Lacy who's a bit skittish."

"Lacy obviously doesn't know us very well, does she?" Miles paused for a moment, then continued, "Okay, I'll meet you at Val's cabin in roughly forty-five minutes."

"Thanks, Miles. I owe you one."

"And don't think I won't collect. I think a night of babysitting should do the trick."

Babysitting? He grimaced but reluctantly agreed.

"Sure, Abby is a cutie. But let's do that before the baby is born, okay? I'm not sure I can handle two of them at the same time."

His brother let out a bark of laughter. "Done. Catch up with you later."

"I guess the Callahans really do stick together," Lacy said, a hint of wistfulness in her eyes. "I'm glad."

He thought about the way she'd lost her sister and knew he'd never rest if someone had murdered one of his siblings. In fact, he'd been secretly trying to investigate his father's unsolved murder. Max Callahan had been the Milwaukee Chief of Police for almost five years before his death. He'd been shot when he'd gone out to visit the scene of a crime. Matt continued to be angry and upset that the perp was still at large.

But right now, he had to remain focused on keeping Lacy and Rory safe. He headed toward his college friend's cabin, using side streets and lesser known highways to avoid the interstate.

Because he'd taken the longer route, he reached the cabin a few minutes before Miles. Matt took a moment to make sure they could get inside, using the key that was hidden in the bottom of a bird feeder. The door creaked open. While it was a little dusty, the interior looked just the way he remembered. He returned to the SUV and let Duchess out before carrying Rory's car seat inside, so the baby would have something to sit in. Lacy followed on his heels, bringing in the rest of their things. Duchess ran around for a bit, exploring the area before making her way back to the cabin. She barked, and he crossed over to let her in, taking a minute to check out her wound. Thankfully, it still looked good.

"Lacy, my brother Miles. Miles, this is Lacy and Rory."

"Nice to meet you," Miles said with a smile.

"You, too." Lacy shivered. "It's a bit chilly in here."

"I'll light the wood-burning stove. It will be warm in no time," Matt assured her.

Between the two men, they stacked armloads of cut wood near the vast iron stove. It didn't take long, and soon the logs were crackling and popping. He rose to his feet and turned toward his brother.

"Did you remember the computer?"

"Yep, it's in the SUV." Miles glanced at Lacy, who was busy unpacking their things. "Come outside for a moment."

Matt followed his brother outside. "What's up?"

"I'm sure you know about the Amber Alert. Lacy is wanted for kidnapping her nephew," Miles said. When Matt opened his mouth to protest, his brother waved a hand. "I told you I'd support you and I will. But I need to know what's going on."

Matt filled in the details, scant as they were. Miles scowled when he mentioned David Williams was a cop. "He's already tried to kill her three times. You'll find a bullet hole in my SUV to prove it."

They walked over to check out the damage, and Miles sighed heavily. "Okay, I trust you know what you're doing. The computer bag, cash and phones are in the front seat of the replacement SUV." His brother dangled the keys in front of him. Matt swapped with him. "Be careful, and let me know if you need backup."

"I will." Matt knew his brother probably didn't want to be too far from Paige, considering she was eight months pregnant, but he might need someone inside the police department to get him information. For any physical backup, he'd lean on either Mitch or Mike. "Thanks again."

"No problem." Miles slapped him on the back. "Lacy is pretty and the kid is cute, too."

Matt narrowed his gaze. "Just because you and Mark found the loves of your lives on a case doesn't mean I'm going to do the same. I'm finished with relationships, remember?"

"Yeah, we'll see." Miles grinned and slid in behind the wheel.

"Miles?" Matt put out a hand to stop him from closing the door. "Be careful, okay? Avoid taking the main highways. This vehicle has been targeted twice already. I need to know you'll be safe."

"I'll be fine."

Matt stepped back and watched for a moment as his brother drove away. He murmured a silent prayer for God to keep Miles safe before heading over to get the items Miles had brought for them. As soon as he had the computer up and running he wanted to start digging into David Williams's background.

When he entered the cabin, he heard high-pitched wails. Lacy was trying to get Rory to take his bottle, but the little guy wasn't having it.

A shiver of unease danced down his spine. "Is he okay?"

"I'm not sure." Lacy's expression reflected her concern. "I don't understand why he's suddenly so fussy."

He didn't know a lot about babies, but he'd heard that sometimes they cried because of gas pains. Maybe this was nothing more than that. "Here, let me try."

Lacy handed him the baby. He flipped the infant over his forearm so Rory was lying on his belly, and began rubbing his back in soothing circles.

The kid kept right on crying.

Matt tried walking around with him, putting an exaggerated bounce in his step. Duchess thought it was some sort of game and kept wrapping herself around his legs.

The kid continued to wail.

Was Rory missing his mother, instinctively knowing that he and Lacy were poor substitutes? Or was he just feeling colicky? He had no idea, but the incessant crying was making him feel a bit panicky.

"Here, I'll take him." Lacy extracted Rory from his arms, holding him protectively to her chest. There was a hint of fear in her eyes, and it took him a minute to figure out she was worried he was going to lose his temper over a crying baby.

"He'll likely cry himself out eventually. In the meantime, try changing him, then see if he'll eat," he advised calmly. "If not, we can take him for a car ride, see if that settles him down."

Lacy gave a tiny nod and hurried into the bedroom. The baby continued to cry, and when she returned five minutes later, she looked frazzled. "He still won't take the bottle. Let's try the car ride."

He closed the computer screen and nodded. He grabbed his jacket and gave his K-9 partner a hand signal that instantly brought the dog to his side. "Okay, let's go."

Lacy buckled Rory into his car seat, and he carried it outside and secured it in the back seat. He opened the back hatch for Duchess, then slid in behind the wheel.

"I hope nothing is seriously wrong. I don't even know the name of Rory's pediatrician," Lacy said in a low voice. "Maybe I should have purchased a thermometer. He feels a little warm, but maybe that's just because he's crying. I just don't know…"

"I'm sure he's fine." Matt did his best to infuse confidence in his tone.

Achoo! Achoo!

Rory's crying was interrupted by two consecutive sneezes. They would have been cute if they weren't so concerning. Matt didn't like thinking about how they'd been dragging this poor kid around the city, only just getting him something warm to wear a couple of hours ago.

He exchanged a worried glance with Lacy. What if the baby was indeed getting sick with some sort of flu virus?

No. Please, God, no. He couldn't bear the thought of something bad happening to Rory. He couldn't survive watching another innocent child struggle to breathe. To live.

Please, Lord, keep Rory safe in Your care!

FIVE

Lacy did her best to rein in her panic as she attempted to soothe Rory. So far, the car ride wasn't helping. She pulled out a tissue from the glove box and leaned back to wipe his face. The sound of his crying ripped at her heart.

The baby was so fussy, she knew something had to be wrong. This didn't seem like a simple case of colic, at least from what little she knew.

"Maybe we should take him to the emergency room." She looked at Matt. "I'd feel better if a doctor examined him."

Matt grimaced. "We can try, but without insurance information, they'll expect us to pay up front in cash."

Lacy had no idea how much an emergency department visit cost, but the fear of missing something serious with Rory outweighed her concern over money. "I still think it's worth it. What if he needs antibiotics? Babies are prone to inner ear infections, aren't they?"

"I think so," Matt agreed. "We'll take him in, but I'd rather go to a smaller hospital where we can be sure no one will recognize either of us, okay?" He hesitated, then added, "And we'll need to pretend to be married."

As much as she didn't like pretending to be something they weren't, she was relieved at the idea of Rory getting the help he needed. "Of course."

The baby's crying subsided to small hiccuping sobs that were no more reassuring than his loudest wails had been. His face was red and scrunched up, as if he were in so much distress that he couldn't stand it.

How did parents cope with the feeling of helplessness as they watched a sick child? A band of fear tightened around her chest. After everything Rory had been through, she couldn't bear the idea of his being ill. Although, maybe babies under stress were more likely to succumb to colds or ear infections.

She closed her eyes for a moment and sent up a silent prayer for God to watch over Rory.

"We're almost at the hospital," Matt said, drawing her attention from the baby. "We'll use my last name, if that's okay with you."

The thought of introducing herself as Lacy Callahan gave her a funny feeling in her stomach, but she nodded. Her name was linked to the Amber Alert, and the last thing she wanted was for the ER staff to call the police on them. In fact, she decided to use her middle name of Marie.

Yes, Matt was the police, but so was David Williams. Returning Rory to his father was not an option.

Matt pulled into the small parking lot in front of the ER and took the first available slot. By the time she slid out of her seat, Rory had stopped crying.

"He's finally fallen asleep," Matt said in a hushed tone as they stood beside the open door, looking down at the infant car seat. "What do you think? Should we still go in or head back to the cabin?"

"I don't know," she whispered, agonizing over the decision. If they left and he began crying again, they could turn around and come back, but what if the delay in obtaining care caused him more harm? The alternative was to go inside and have the doctor examine him, which would undoubtedly wake him up. If there was nothing wrong, they would have wasted a big chunk of their spare cash for no good reason.

Rory's face was still red, probably from his crying jag, but the thought of the baby suffering from a fever swayed her decision.

"We're going in to be seen." She looked up at Matt. "I won't be able to rest until I know for sure he's okay."

Matt nodded and, being careful not to jostle the sleeping baby, he unbuckled the car seat, lifting it out and then heading into the hospital's emergency entrance.

She closed the door quietly, then quickly followed them into the brightly lit building.

A nurse and registrar met them at the front desk. "Patient name and proof of insurance, please."

Fibbing didn't come natural to her, but for the sake of her nephew's health, she injected confidence into her tone as she used Rory's middle name. "Anthony Callahan, and unfortunately we don't have insurance. However, we do have money to pay our bill."

She held her breath as the registrar entered the information into her computer and then asked for a two hundred dollar deposit. Matt handed over the cash and they were led into the triage area, where a nurse began questioning them about Rory's symptoms.

"I believe he's running a fever, and I'm concerned he may have an ear infection," Lacy said. "I know we might be overreacting, but R—Anthony is such a good baby that this latest bout of crying and refusing to eat has me worried."

The nurse's smile was gentle. "I understand. I'm

going to get a quick set of vital signs, and then take a listen to his heart and lungs, okay?"

Lacy nodded and forced herself to step back as the nurse undressed Rory. He didn't like it and began to cry. She twisted her hands together, causing Matt to step up to put his arm reassuringly around her shoulders.

"He'll be fine," Matt said in a husky tone. She gave a terse nod but couldn't tear her gaze from Rory.

The nurse checked the baby from head to toe, listening with her stethoscope, although Lacy couldn't figure out what she would hear beyond his crying. She placed a device in Rory's ear that caused him to wail even louder.

"He is running a low-grade fever of 100.8," the nurse said. "He's acting like he may have an ear infection. The doctor will be able to tell for sure. Does your baby have any allergies?"

Allergies? She wracked her brain, trying to remember if Jill had ever mentioned anything like that. Lacy knew Rory had gone in for a two-month well-baby checkup, but had no idea if there had been other illnesses treated. "Not that I'm aware of."

The nurse nodded. "Okay, have a seat in the waiting room and we'll call you back when we have a doctor available to see your son."

She smiled, hoping the nurse couldn't tell it was forced. "Thank you."

Matt released her to step forward, lifting the car seat with ease.

They headed back to the waiting room, Rory's crying causing people to stare at them with obvious sympathy.

"I left his bottle in the car," she said as she unbuckled Rory from the carrier and lifted the baby in her arms. "Would you mind getting it for me? Maybe this time he really is hungry."

Matt nodded and headed outside. She stood and walked around with Rory propped against her shoulder, doing her best to soothe him. When Matt returned with the bottle, she took a seat and tried to coax Rory into taking it.

He latched onto the bottle, but after a few gulps began crying again. At least now it made sense—if Rory had an ear infection, his swallowing motion likely made the pain worse.

She set the bottle aside and lifted him back up against her shoulder. "It's okay, the doctor will give you some medication to make you all better."

"I hope so," Matt muttered. "I can't stand watching him suffer like this."

She wasn't so keen on it herself, but at least a simple ear infection wasn't anything to be alarmed about.

Twenty minutes later, they were taken back into a room where a physician soon joined them. He performed a full exam, including looking into Rory's ears and throat.

"Anthony has the beginning of an ear infection on the right side," he finally said. "Looks like you caught it early, so that's good. We'll start him on an oral antibiotic, amoxicillin, twice a day for the next ten days. After he finishes the medication, take him into your regular pediatrician to make sure he's fully healed." The doctor wrote out a prescription and handed it to her. "Any questions?"

"Not that I can think of." She glanced at Matt, who also shook his head. "Thanks, Doctor."

"You're welcome." He left the room, no doubt moving onto his next patient. Ignoring the incessant crying as much as possible, she bundled Rory back into his one-piece fleece jacket and then placed him back in the infant carrier.

"Let's find a pharmacy," Matt said as they went outside to the SUV. Duchess lifted her head and thumped her tail in greeting. "The sooner he gets those antibiotics, the better."

"Sounds good to me." Lacy was exhausted from the lack of sleep she'd gotten the night before and now it appeared she wouldn't be getting much tonight, either.

The pharmacy was strategically located not far from the hospital, and within the hour they were on their way back to the cabin. Getting Rory to take the antibiotic was another challenge, but they finally managed it. Then she sat down in the old wooden rocking chair and tried once again to feed him. He took another few sips of his bottle, then fell asleep.

She gazed down at Rory's sleeping face, almost too exhausted to get up to lie him down in the dresser drawer she'd lined with a blanket to use in lieu of a crib. She felt Matt come up beside her.

"Would you like me to put him down?" he asked in a low husky voice.

"Yes, thank you," she whispered.

Matt slipped his large hands beneath the sleeping baby and gently lifted him up into his arms. He carried Rory into the room she was using as a bedroom, over to the drawer/crib, and set him down.

She followed Matt into the room, and for a moment it felt as if they really were Rory's parents, taking turns caring for him. Of course, nothing was further from the truth. Normally, she didn't trust men in general, yet here she was trusting Matt.

Not just to keep her and Rory safe, but also to help her provide care for Rory. Matt was so kind and so considerate, not losing his temper even when the baby cried inconsolably. Ridiculous fantasy, since she knew that once the danger was over she would be raising Rory on her own.

Still, long after she'd shut off the lamp and crawled into bed, she couldn't shake the notion that with Matt at her side, she wouldn't be nearly as afraid of what her future as Rory's mother would hold.

Matt woke up to sunlight streaming in through the cabin's living room window. He sat up on the sofa where he'd slept, looking around for Lacy. It was still early, seven thirty in the morning, but the silence was a bit unnerving. He noticed an empty bottle on the counter, and assumed Lacy and Rory must have been up at some point.

Taking a few minutes to load more wood into the stove, he smiled when Duchess rose from the rug she'd been lying on and went over to stand by the door. Dusting off his hands, he latched the woodstove shut. He quickly let the dog out, then padded into the kitchen, relieved to find a coffeemaker. Since his brother had been smart enough to buy coffee along with eggs and other essentials, he quickly brewed a pot. Once he let Duchess back inside and gave her food and water, he set about making breakfast.

Lacy joined him a few minutes later, looking adorably rumpled and sleepy. "I smell coffee."

He grinned. "That's always the first thing on my morning agenda, too. Take a seat. I'll pour you a cup."

She seemed taken aback by his offer but dropped into the closest chair, her shoulders drooping with exhaustion. Duchess greeted Lacy with a sloppy kiss, tail wagging as Lacy scratched her behind the ears. He filled a large mug and brought over the milk, feeling guilty at having slept through Rory's crying.

"Did Rory keep you up a lot?" he asked.

She shrugged. "It's not his fault. Poor little guy finally fell soundly asleep around three in the morning. I'm sure he'll be up again any minute."

"Breakfast is just about ready. You eat, I'll take care of him when he wakes up." It was the least he could do, considering he'd been able to rest undisturbed.

She took a sip of her coffee and sighed with appreciation. "Boy, does that hit the spot."

"I remember you like scrambled eggs, so that's what I made. If you're tired of that, I can make them another way for you."

Her cheeks went pink. "Oh, please, don't bother. I'm not picky. I like eggs just about any way they can be made. No need to go out of your way on my account."

She acted as if no one had offered to do anything for her before, which was a concept he found disturbing. Granted, she'd witnessed her brother-in-law murder her sister, but surely there had been other men she'd had some exposure to? Men who didn't make a habit of hurting women?

He filled a plate full of scrambled eggs and set it on the table in front of her. "What's your favorite?"

"Favorite what?" Her blue eyes mirrored confusion.

"Breakfast food."

"Oh. I'm not picky, but if I had my top choice, I like French toast the best." She picked up the fork and dug into her meal. "Thanks, these are delicious."

"You're welcome." Her gratitude for basic things like a simple meal humbled him. But before he could ask anything further, he heard Rory begin to cry. "Finish your breakfast. I'll get him."

Hurrying into the bedroom, he found Rory squirming around in the blanket-lined drawer, arms and legs flailing. Duchess followed him and sat on her haunches, watching them. He lifted the little guy up in his arms, smelled the dirty diaper and sighed. Fine. He could handle this. Diapers and wipes were nearby so he changed the baby, the task taking twice as long as it should have. Rory stopped crying long enough to look up at him curiously with his wide blue eyes. Eyes that looked very much like Lacy's.

"Hey, big guy, I can tell you're much happier now, aren't you?" Matt used to smirk at how his brothers had talked to their kids, yet now he completely understood. The baby's wide eyes held a level of understanding that surprised him. "Let's go find you something to eat, okay?"

Rory grinned a toothless smile. He bent over to press a kiss on the top of the baby's head, trying not to remember how he used to do that with Carly.

Duchess once again followed him and Rory into the kitchen, where he found Lacy making a fresh bottle. Her plate was empty and he couldn't help but ask, "Did you breathe between bites?"

She raised a brow at him over her shoulder. "Maybe, but to be honest, I don't remember."

"I told you I'd take care of him. I'm perfectly capable of feeding a baby." Matt crossed over to take the bottle, but Lacy shook her head.

"You haven't had breakfast."

"I won't starve," he said drily.

"That's not the point. I may as well practice doing everything myself, since I'll be raising Rory alone." She set the bottle on the counter and took the child from his arms, then picked it back up and went over to sit in the rocking chair.

In his opinion, Lacy's logic was flawed. She didn't have to do everything herself right now. There was no reason she couldn't ease into the transition of being a single mom. Although, he didn't like the idea of her raising Rory alone.

Not his business. He forced himself to shake off the strange sense of regret. Losing Carly had only proven how tenuous life really was, so he hardened his heart and turned back to the counter. After cracking more eggs into the bowl and whipping them with some milk, he made another batch of scrambled eggs, thinking about the next steps he needed to take in the investigation.

Rory's ear infection had distracted him from digging into David Williams's background. He was a cop, so if he could get into the police department database, he should be able to find the details he was looking for.

He booted up the computer, searching through information as he ate. Once his eggs were finished, he filled his coffee mug and accessed the MPD database.

Rory let out a loud burp, making him smile. He glanced over to where Lacy was caring for Rory. With the sunshine streaming in through the window, her blond hair was a sheen of pale gold. His heart tightened in his chest as he acknowledged once again just how beautiful she was.

Even more so when she was cooing over Rory.

He must have been staring longer than he'd realized because she abruptly looked at him. "Is something wrong?"

"Huh? Oh, no. Um, I was just wondering when he was due for his next dose of medication."

A hint of uncertainty shadowed her gaze. "I was thinking it would be good to get him on a more normal schedule, like nine in the morning and nine at night. But he had his last dose at one in the morning. Do you think it's too soon to give it to him again at nine?"

He lifted a shoulder in a shrug, feeling helpless. In his opinion, babies should come with some sort of instruction manual, but no one had asked him. "Maybe we should do it more gradually, like eleven in the morning and at night for today, then nine tomorrow."

She nodded. "You're right. That seems reasonable."

He turned his attention back to the computer. Unfortunately, the cabin Wi-Fi was much slower than he would have liked, and when he tried to log in to the police database, his access was denied.

Scowling at the computer, he tried again. The same error message flashed on the screen.

What in the world was going on? For a moment, he wondered if his access had been disconnected on purpose because he'd been suspended, or worse, fired. But wouldn't Miles have said something if that was the case?

He pulled out his new disposable phone and dialed his brother's number.

Miles answered after four rings, his voice thick with sleep. "Yeah?"

"It's Matt, did I wake you up?"

"Abby was sick in the middle of the night, so yeah, I was trying to sleep in." As he spoke, Miles started to sound more awake. "What's up?"

"Sorry to hear about Abby. If I had known, I would have waited till later."

"Forget about it. I'm up now."

"Okay, here's the issue. I'm locked out of the MPD database." Matt fought to keep his voice level. "Do I still have a job?"

"What? Of course you have a job. Why wouldn't you?"

"Then why can't I log in?"

"We only allow officers to log in from secure networks. The cabin must not be secure enough. Here, give me a minute to log in and I'll find what you need."

"Thanks, bro."

He heard rustling sounds before Miles came back on the line. "Okay, I'm logged in to the database. What do you need?"

"Everything you have on David Williams." Matt felt a little guilty about Miles digging into this under his own name, but hopefully it wouldn't matter once they'd arrested the guy for murdering his wife.

And for attempting to kill Lacy, Rory and Duchess.

"I can send this to you electronically if you would like, but was there something in particular you were interested in?" Miles asked.

"Lacy mentioned David had some sort of Special Forces training. What branch of the military was he in?"

"There's nothing listed here about any military service. Are you sure you have your facts straight?"

Matt turned in his seat. "Lacy? Why did you think David worked in the Special Forces?"

"Because he told me and Jill all about his—" she made air quotes with her fingers "—high-level military training. Why?"

Interesting. Matt spoke into the phone. "Send me the file, Miles, thanks."

He disconnected from the line and waited for the email from his brother to pop up on the screen.

David Williams had lied to his wife about his military service. But why? For what purpose? To scare and intimidate her?

And what else had he lied about?

SIX

Lacy rose to her feet, propped Rory on her hip and crossed over to the kitchen table. "What did you find out on David?"

Matt seemed to hesitate, then shrugged. "He lied about being in the military. There's nothing listed on his police application. The department does extensive background checks on potential candidates. It's not something he would have been able to pretend never happened or fudge."

She sat beside him, setting Rory on her lap so he could look around. "That's so strange. Why did he tell us he was in the Special Forces?"

"I have no idea. Although, you were the one who described him as a sociopath. Maybe he's a chronic liar, too." Matt's gaze zeroed in on the most recent email. "Give me a few minutes to go through the information my brother sent me."

Rory was squirming around again, so she wandered around the inside of the cabin, checking things out. She found an old radio and plugged it in to see if it worked.

To her surprise it did, although the reception was a bit fuzzy. Curious about the Amber Alert—after all, they wouldn't be able to hide out forever—she tuned in to a news station.

The reporter spoke about the recent stats on the murder rate in the city of Milwaukee, which was nothing new. Normally, she avoided the news. How much bad stuff could a person hear in one day? But she forced herself to continue listening, certain the outstanding Amber Alert would be mentioned.

But it wasn't.

She frowned. Why on earth would the Amber Alert be dropped? Or had the radio announcer already discussed it before she'd found the radio? Anything was possible.

"In other breaking news this morning, Judge Dugan has received two separate death threats in the past week. When questioned, Judge Dugan believes these threats are related to a recent case he presided over several months ago, involving Alexander Pietro. Because of the extensive criminal network Pietro has been involved with, Judge Dugan is requesting around-the-clock police protection."

"What did they say about Alexander Pietro?" Matt asked, his head snapping around to face her.

"Something about how the judge who presided over the case is getting death threats."

Matt abandoned his computer to come over to stand beside her. "My twin was the assistant district attorney assigned to that case, but the trial ended abruptly after the first day in a plea bargain. She almost died because of her determination to prosecute Alexander Pietro. But at the end of the day, she and my former partner, Noah Sinclair, managed to find the dirty cop who attempted to sabotage Pietro's trial."

Lacy wasn't sure where he was going with this information. "So that means what? That Judge Dugan shouldn't be getting death threats?"

He grimaced and jammed his fingers through his hair. "I don't know. It just seems odd that these death threats would come three months after the aborted trial. You would think they would have taken place before the trial, right?"

"I guess." She hated to admit she didn't care, since it obviously had nothing to do with David Williams. Unless— A horrible thought hit her. "Do you think David might have been another dirty cop involved in the crime? One that somehow managed to escape unscathed?"

He slowly shook his head. "I can't say for sure one way or the other, although I can give Noah a call to see if Williams's name popped up anywhere during the investigation."

The thought of a potential link between David Williams and another crime caused a flicker of hope to burn in her chest. This could be the answer to her prayers! If David's name was linked to a known criminal like this Pietro guy, then the police would have to believe her side of the story. How she'd listened while David shot her sister.

She returned to the rocking chair while Matt made the call to his former partner. She lifted Rory up so that he could stand on her lap, then bounced him up and down a bit, enjoying his laughter. The antibiotics must be working because he was already so much better than he'd been the night before. The doctor must have been right about how they'd caught the infection early.

So she'd done one thing right. Despite being plagued by self-doubt.

"Noah? It's Matt. How's Maddy?" Matt paused and then continued, "Glad to hear it. Hey, I have a question about the Pietro investigation. Did a cop by the name of David Williams come up at all?"

There was a long silence as Matt listened to whatever Noah was saying. She tried to stay focused on Rory, but every muscle in her body felt stretched to a breaking point.

David had to be involved. Maybe that was part of the reason he'd killed Jill. Maybe her sister had suspected something was going on, so David silenced her once and for all?

Although, that certainly wouldn't explain why he had threatened to kill Rory, too.

"Okay, thanks for checking." The disappointment in Matt's tone was clear, and her shoulders slumped in defeat. "Keep your ears open for anything related to David Williams, okay? I have reason to believe he's involved in murder."

Lacy told herself not to lose hope. David could still be involved. Maybe he'd just been good at covering his tracks.

"No links to the Pietro case," Matt told her, confirming what she'd already suspected. "But Noah will remain on alert, and so will Miles. If Williams is involved in anything else, we'll find out about it."

"Thanks, but I think we have to consider the fact that David's crime is solely centered on murdering my sister—why, I'm not sure, especially since he threatened to kill Rory, too." She couldn't hide her stark disappointment. "Now that we escaped, I wouldn't put it past him to stage the scene of the crime so it looks like I had something to do with Jill's death."

"Try not to worry," Matt urged. "I know I told you this before, but I firmly believe the truth will prevail."

Maybe he was right, but she couldn't help thinking

that plenty of people got away with crimes every day. They weren't all brought to justice.

And the thought of David getting away with murdering her sister was too much to bear.

Needing distance, she abruptly shot to her feet, intending to head into the bedroom. But the front pocket of her hoodie got caught on the handle of the rocking chair, causing her to stumble.

Matt grabbed Rory as she struggled to stay upright. There was a tinkling sound as something metal hit the hardwood floor.

She stared in shocked surprise at the key that had fallen from her pocket. It took her a moment to remember how she'd accidentally stumbled upon the key in her haste to leave her sister's house the night of the murder.

"What is this for?" Matt asked, holding Rory close as he bent to retrieve the key.

"I have no idea." She reached over to take Rory, but the baby seemed to prefer being in Matt's arms. "I found it outside my sister's house the night I took off with Rory."

"You did? Is it possible Williams dropped it?"

"Maybe, but it's more likely to be Jill's, don't you think?"

Matt turned the key over with a frown. "It's too small to be a house key. In fact, it looks a little familiar."

"I don't know why I bothered to pick it up. Must have been pure instinct. All I could think about was getting Rory away from his father and keeping him safe." She shrugged, feeling guilty, as if she'd kept evidence from Matt on purpose. "I never gave the key another thought."

"That's okay. Better late than never." Matt slipped the key into the front pocket of his uniform pants. "I'll do some research on the computer, see if I can track down what kind of key it is."

Rory grabbed Matt's face and giggled. The baby clearly liked Matt, and for a moment her heart squeezed at the thought of Rory growing up without a father.

It wasn't as if she would be the only single mother in the world, though. Surely, those kids grew up to be well-adjusted adults. Having a two-parent household wasn't a requirement.

But watching Matt and Rory playing made her think about how much Rory would miss him once they went their separate ways.

The kid was too cute, and despite his need to protect his heart from caring too much, Matt found himself enchanted with Rory's antics. He sat on the edge of the sofa and gave Duchess the signal for Come.

The dog immediately came over, tail wagging. He instructed Duchess to sit. Rory reached out to pet Duchess's head, his movements clumsy. Duchess was infinitely patient, stoically tolerating Rory's tiny hands batting at her.

"Easy, Rory. Be gentle, like this." Matt took Rory's little hand and lightly stroked Duchess's fur. The baby followed his lead for all of a moment before waving his arms around again.

"Duchess is a trooper," Lacy said, dropping down to sit beside him.

"Yeah, she's well-trained." Matt lifted Rory up over his head, and the baby laughed and laughed. "I can't get over how happy he is today."

"I know. It's a total change from last night." Lacy stroked Duchess. "It's a little scary how quickly a baby can get sick. If we hadn't taken him in right away…"

His gut tightened, and he brought Rory back down to his lap. He knew all about how fast kids could get sick.

How they could even die.

"Here, I need to take Duchess outside for a bit." With an abrupt motion, he plopped Rory on Lacy's lap and jumped to his feet. Duchess followed as he grabbed his jacket and headed outside.

K-9 officers needed ongoing training and reinforcement, so he took Duchess through the paces, more to keep his mind occupied than out of necessity. It wasn't easy to erase the memory of Carly's pale wan face, the way she'd looked just before she'd taken her last breath and passed into God's arms.

Knowing Carly was at peace should have made him feel better. But it hadn't.

For months, he'd found it difficult to pray, to understand God's plan. Eventually, he found some measure of solace in church services, but there were still times, like this, where the unfairness of it all came rushing back, nearly choking him.

He continued working with Duchess until he managed to get some semblance of control over his rioting emotions. Feeling better after exerting some physical exercise, he headed back inside.

After filling Duchess's water bowl, he poured himself another cup of coffee and sat back down behind the computer. The shape of the key niggled at the edges of his memory, but he couldn't for the life of him figure out where he'd seen something similar like it before.

Hopefully it would come to him, but in the meantime, he resumed reviewing Williams's file. The guy had a couple of reprimands for excessive force, but there was really nothing else of interest. Truthfully, he figured there were several cops that had worse records than what he'd found in this one.

He'd hoped, for Lacy's sake, that Williams might have been linked to the Pietro crime boss. He typed Judge Dugan's name in the search engine and discovered the article that had been mentioned by the radio newscaster.

The details were just as sketchy, so the article wasn't much help. It was dated yesterday, so basically old news.

Pulling the key out of his pocket, he peered at it again. The letter *W* was etched on the side, but that could mean anything. They lived in Wisconsin.

Searching different kinds of keys online gave him a little more information. The key Lacy had found was a typical pin-tumbler lock key. It wasn't a car key, but it was also smaller than a typical house key.

He sighed and shoved the key back into his pocket. It was frustrating to have a clue that didn't lead anywhere, although Lacy could be right—for all they knew, the key belonged to her sister rather than to Williams.

Maybe once they had an inkling of where to find the guy, the key would prove more useful. He went back to the file, staring intently at David Williams's official photograph.

Angular features, narrow eyes and jet black hair. According to the report, he was six feet three inches tall and weighed two hundred pounds. Going by his photograph, the guy wasn't fat, but appeared to be muscular, especially around the shoulders.

He frowned for a moment, flashing back to the image of the guy wearing the black cap and taking aim at Lacy. His impression of the guy had been that he was lean rather than bulky with muscles. Also, the gunman hadn't appeared to be much taller than his own five feet eleven inches. Then again, Matt had only spared him a quick glance before rushing to protect Lacy, so he could have been wrong.

Or maybe, Williams had lost some weight since he'd initially joined the force.

Shaking off the sense of unease, he closed the file and sat back in his chair.

They weren't any further along on this case than they'd been on the night Lacy had escaped with Rory. He curled his fingers into fists, fighting back a wave of frustration.

There had to be something he was missing. Something he'd overlooked. He pulled out his phone and dialed Miles again.

"Now what?" Miles asked, a slight edge to his tone. "You do realize it's my day off."

No, he hadn't known that, but that would explain why Miles had been the one to get up with Abby. "I'm sorry, do you want to call me back at a better time?"

"No, it's fine. Ignore me. I'm just upset at Abby being sick and crabby from lack of sleep. What's up?"

"Do you have any idea which detective has been assigned to Jill Williams's murder?"

"Jill Williams?" Miles sounded confused. "I haven't heard much about it. When did it go down?"

Matt thought back. The night he'd rescued Lacy and Rory was late Monday night into early Tuesday morning. Today was Wednesday, but for some reason it seemed like they'd been hiding for weeks rather than a few days. "Monday night, same night the Amber Alert went out."

"It wasn't me, but I'll see what I can find out. Give me a couple of hours and I'll call you back."

"Thanks, Miles. I really appreciate it."

"No biggie. Later, bro." Miles disconnected from the call.

Matt didn't feel any better about his progress. Even knowing the name of the detective wouldn't help him much. It wasn't like he could call the guy up and ask for details related to the homicide investigation.

"Matt? Can you give me a hand with Rory?"

He swung around to face her, noticing she had the bottle of liquid antibiotic in her hand. Was it eleven o'clock already?

"Of course." He crossed over. "What do you need?"

"Hold him so I can get this syringe into his mouth. He's squirming around and I don't want to waste any of the medication."

He took the wiggling baby and cradled him so that his head was nestled in the crook of his arm. He trapped Rory's arm against his body and then lightly grasped his other arm. Rory didn't like it and let out a wail.

"Come on, sweetie, you need to take your medicine." Lacy tucked the blunt end of the syringe in the corner of his mouth and gave him a little bit of the thick white stuff.

"Looks disgusting," Matt muttered.

She glared at him. "You're not helping. You don't want to go back to the ER, do you?"

"Yum, yum," he encouraged. "Come on, Rory, take your medicine like a man."

Lacy snorted but managed to encourage Rory to swallow more of the antibiotic. It seemed to take forever, and by the time they were finished, they were both feeling flustered.

"That was fun," Matt said with a wry smile. "Good thing we only need to do it twice a day."

"You're telling me," Lacy said, taking the syringe

over to rinse it out in the sink. "When he started to spit some of it out, I panicked."

"I'm sure they factor some of that into their dosing," he assured her. Now that the medicine was in the baby's stomach where it belonged, Rory was back to his usual cheerful self. "I feel bad that we didn't buy any baby toys for him."

"I have a rattle in my purse, but he's pretty tired of it." She dried her hands on a dish towel. "Who would have thought it would be such hard work entertaining a three-month-old?"

Not him, that was for sure. "Do you need me to hold him?"

"No thanks, I'm going to set him down on the floor for a while." She disappeared inside the bedroom, returning a few minutes later with the blanket they'd used to cushion the drawer that was doubling as a crib. "I think babies start to roll over at three months, don't they?"

Again, he had no clue. As much as he'd enjoyed spending time with Carly, much of that togetherness had taken place in the hospital where he'd held her during needle sticks or other painful tests and treatments. Plus, she'd been four, so the milestones of rolling and walking had long passed. Shying away from those memories, he focused on the present, setting Rory down in the middle of the blanket and placing the rattle out of reach, yet directly in his line of vision. Lacy sat on the floor watching him.

Rory bobbed his head up and down as if trying to move in order to get what he wanted. His little feet kicked out behind him as if he could propel himself forward.

When that didn't work, he arched his back. The motion caused him to roll over, and he looked about as surprised as he and Lacy were.

"Did you see that?" Lacy cried with excitement. "He's so smart."

It felt crazy to be ecstatic about a baby learning to roll over, but he couldn't deny feeling proud of the little guy. "Yeah, he sure is."

Lacy looked up at him, her smile lighting up her face, and for a moment he wanted nothing more than to kiss her.

Whoa, where did that come from? He abruptly stood and moved away, putting distance between them.

Kissing Lacy was not going to happen. He needed to remember that he was here to protect her, not to start something he had no intention of following through on.

No matter how beautiful she was.

He wished he could put even more space between them. The cabin was too small for his liking. He considered taking Duchess out again, but what he really wanted was physical activity to let off steam.

His gaze landed on the small pile of split logs sitting beside the woodstove. "I'm going outside to chop wood," he said. "Duchess, Guard."

Duchess plopped down beside Lacy and Rory, sitting with her head high and her ears perked forward. Smiling grimly, he headed out to find the ax.

It was propped near the woodpile, so he shed his jacket and began to chop wood. Within five minutes, he'd built up a sweat.

He paused and swiped a hand over his brow. This type of workout was just as good as heading to the gym after a long shift.

In fact, splitting logs might even be better than pumping iron.

An image suddenly flashed in his mind. Instantly, he remembered where he'd seen that key before!

Matt dropped the ax and dug into his pocket to look at the key. The *W* etched on the face clinched it. The Milwaukee Police Department provided a discount to all police officers to the Wisconsin Fitness Center. He personally used the facility on a regular basis, and there were several branches scattered around the city. Members could use a locker for free, or they could rent one and keep their stuff inside rather than hauling workout gear back and forth.

This key opened a gym locker!

SEVEN

Lacy's gaze strayed to watch Matt chopping wood, regardless of how hard she tried to remain focused on Rory. The baby was obviously feeling better, managing to entertain himself without her assistance.

Matt didn't need her attention, either, but he looked so athletically amazing, swinging the ax in a choreographed rhythm, that she couldn't seem to tear her gaze away. Normally, she wasn't impressed by a muscular guy, but watching as the force of the ax cut through the wood with a single blow, she felt a bit mesmerized by Matt's physical strength and ability.

In the past, physical strength in a man caused a sense of fear of that power being turned against her. But she didn't feel that way about Matt.

Instead, she was attracted to him.

Rory rolled over again, this time bumping into her knee. She glanced down in alarm. He didn't cry, but looked a little bemused, as if he didn't understand what had stopped him. She lifted him up, smiling at his wide toothless grin, then set him down in the middle of the blanket.

Once again, her gaze found Matt. He'd stopped chopping and was staring down at something in the palm of his hand. She frowned, wondering if he'd hurt himself. A blister, maybe?

He turned and strode purposefully toward the cabin. She leapt to her feet. Was there a first-aid kit? She hadn't seen one, but she also hadn't opened every single cupboard and drawer.

Matt burst in through the door.

"Are you bleeding?" she asked, crossing over to meet him. "I'll look for bandages."

"What? I'm not bleeding." Belatedly, she realized he had the key in his hand. "This belongs to a locker at the WFC. Wisconsin Fitness Center."

"Really? Which facility?"

He grimaced. "I'm not sure. Did your sister have a membership?"

"Not that I'm aware of, but Jill used to complain about how many hours David spent working out." She swallowed hard, trying not to dwell on the fact that she'd never see her sister again. "The key must be his."

Matt nodded. "Makes sense, although we can't necessarily rule out other gym members. WFC offers a discounted rate to the MPD." He turned the key over in his hand. "The key is marked with a *W* on one side and the number eighteen on the other. Eighteen could refer to a locker number."

"We should check the gym closest to my sister's house."

"Or the facility closest to the district Williams works out of," Matt said. "I tend to use the one closest to where I work."

Lacy crossed over to the laptop and opened a search engine. Before she could type in the name of the gym, Rory began to cry.

"Oh, no." She quickly rushed over to find he'd rolled

off the blanket and was smooshed up against the leg of the end table, a red mark on his forehead. She scooped him into her arms, inwardly berating herself for being so inattentive. "I'm sorry, Rory," she murmured, pressing a kiss on the red mark. "It's okay, you're fine, I'm sorry…"

"What happened?" Matt came over, his green eyes shadowed with concern.

"I'm not a very good mother." She couldn't believe she'd even temporarily forgotten about Rory being on the floor. What if he'd hurt himself worse and needed stitches?

"Cut yourself a little slack, you've only been a mother for two days." Matt reached up and smoothed his hand over Rory's back. "Besides, I can't imagine he's the only baby who's ever rolled into something and bumped his head."

Logically, she knew he was right, but her pulse still raced with fear and worry. Obviously, she needed to make the cabin baby-proof. There were electrical outlets to worry about, and maybe other potential hazards she hadn't considered.

She battled back a wave of overwhelming helplessness. Lots of women raised a child on their own. She wasn't the type to shirk responsibility.

Yet any mistakes she made along the way could have serious consequences. It made her sick to think about inadvertently doing something to cause harm to an innocent baby. Rory had stopped crying for now, but what about next time?

"Lacy? Are you all right?" The tenderness in Matt's voice brought tears to her eyes.

She nodded, but kept her face hidden against Rory.

Her throat was thick with emotion, making it impossible to speak.

Suddenly, Matt's arms came up around her, holding her and Rory close. His masculine scent was amazingly reassuring. "Shh, it's okay. I know God is guiding us on His path and that He'll keep Rory safe from harm."

Oddly enough, the idea of not being in this alone caused her tension to slip away. "I hope you're right, Matt. I'll need all the help I can get."

"You're going to be fine, Lacy. Just remember you're not alone," he said, his voice muffled against her hair. "God will always be there for you, and so will I."

She knew Matt had included himself just to be nice, because as soon as David was arrested, she and Rory wouldn't see him again. But right now, being held in his arms, she couldn't deny feeling stronger and more confident in her abilities. She thought it was related to Matt's influence, but maybe he'd been right to remind her about God. It never occurred to her to lean on God in times of trouble or distress.

Please, Lord, help me be a good mother to Rory.

A sense of peace filled her heart. She began to ease away from Matt's embrace, but he didn't seem inclined to let her go.

As much as she didn't want to leave, she sensed Rory had fallen asleep, and she needed to put him down for a nap. She placed her hand on Matt's chest and gently pushed. He dropped his arms and stepped back.

"Will you put the blanket back inside the drawer?" she asked in a hushed tone. "He's fallen asleep."

Matt nodded, swept the shawl wrap from the living room floor and lined the drawer/crib. When he finished, she gently set Rory down, hoping he wouldn't wake up.

Rory made a mewling sound and waved his arms

for a moment before falling back to sleep. She watched him, noticing the redness across his forehead was already beginning to fade.

She turned away and bumped into Matt. He captured her shoulders with his hands to steady her. He wasn't much taller than she was, their eyes almost level. She noticed his gaze lingering on her mouth and felt herself flush with awareness.

"Lacy." Her name was barely a whisper as he slowly drew her into his arms. He lowered his head, giving her plenty of time to stop him.

Ignoring the tiny voice in her mind that urged her to break away, she waited breathlessly for his kiss. His mouth lightly caressed hers, as if he didn't want to scare her.

She'd only kissed two men, and neither one of them came close to what she was experiencing with Matt. When he deepened their kiss, her legs wobbled, forcing her to cling to his shoulders.

This was everything a kiss should be.

But then Matt abruptly broke away from her, breathing heavy. "I have to get that," he said.

"What?" She had no idea what he was talking about.

"The phone. It's probably my brother." Matt turned and headed into the kitchen.

She dropped onto the edge of the bed and tried to pull herself together. No doubt the kiss they'd just shared had meant far more to her than it had to him. She hadn't even heard his phone, she'd been so caught up in the kiss. She needed to remember that men kissed women all the time. It didn't necessarily mean anything.

Except to her.

She told herself that Matt had only kissed her because she'd been upset over Rory's bump on the head.

Being here in the cabin and hiding from David had created a false sense of intimacy. She was depending on him for safety, and he was depending on her to assist in testifying against her sister's murderer.

Losing her heart to Matthew Callahan wouldn't be smart. Rory was the priority here.

She'd gladly give up her personal life to provide a safe and stable upbringing for her nephew.

It was the least she could do.

Matt stumbled toward the kitchen, knocked seriously off balance by the sweetness of Lacy's kiss. He found the phone and quickly answered it. "Yeah?"

"What, did I interrupt your beauty sleep?" Miles asked in a dry tone.

Matt wasn't about to tell his brother that he'd interrupted an intense kiss. "No, I've been up for hours. Just finished chopping wood."

"That explains why you sound out of breath. Guess you're getting soft, huh?"

Matt wasn't in the mood for his older brother's teasing. Being the youngest of the four boys, not to mention the shortest, he was constantly trying to hold his own against their incessant banter.

"I'll take you on anytime, bro. Did you call for something important or just to hear yourself talk?"

Miles chuckled. "But you love hearing me talk. Actually, I just wanted to let you know that David Williams has gone AWOL and there's a warrant out for his arrest."

"He hasn't shown up for work? That's good news." Matt gathered his scattered thoughts. "When was the last time he was seen? Lacy thinks he's the one who issued the Amber Alert against her. I'm a little surprised he was able to deflect attention onto her."

"I haven't been able to get ahold of the police report from the night of Lacy's sister's murder," Miles said. "The homicide detective doesn't like me and is refusing to share any of the details, keeps insisting it's none of my business."

Technically, that was true, and Matt knew his brother well enough that if the situation were reversed, Miles wouldn't give out any information, either. "Thanks for the update. I found something else, too."

"What?" Miles sounded very interested.

"The night Lacy took off with her nephew, she found a key. I believe it belongs to a locker in one of the Wisconsin Fitness Centers."

Miles whistled. "Any idea which one?"

"Not yet, but I'm working on it." He trapped the phone between his shoulder and his ear, and typed the name of the gym in the search engine. "Which district does Williams work for?"

"The third district. I'm pretty sure there's a WFC nearby."

"Found it," Miles said, peering at the map that bloomed on the screen. "Five blocks south on Rochester Street. Although, there could be another one closer to where he lives."

"Hey, I have to go," Miles said abruptly. "A call just came in about a fresh homicide. So much for my day off. I'll check in with you later."

Matt absently disconnected from the line, zooming in on the fitness center closest to the third district police station. He didn't know Lacy's sister's address, so it was possible the key belonged to a locker at a different location, but he didn't think so. His gut told him that a guy like Williams would want to work out with his cop buddies, not a place closer to home.

Lacy came into the kitchen. "Are you hungry for lunch? I can throw together some soup and sandwiches."

"Sure, that would be great." He jotted down the address of the gym on Rochester, wondering when would be a good time to go. According to the website, the place was open 24/7, and he was certain it would be packed during the daytime.

But later, in the middle of the night? Might be easier to get inside to access the locker without a lot of curious eyes on him. Besides, he knew for a fact that a lot of cops used the gym either before or after their work shift.

Lacy brought over two bowls of soup and two turkey sandwiches. If she was angry at him for kissing her, she didn't show it. He reminded himself to stay on task. Lacy was a distraction he couldn't afford.

He closed the computer and smiled at her across the table before bowing his head to say grace. "Dear Lord, thank You for providing us with food and shelter, and please guide us as we continue to seek the truth. Amen."

"Amen," Lacy echoed.

He took a bite of his sandwich, wondering how she made a simple turkey and cheese sandwich taste so good. "Thanks, this is delicious."

"I'm glad."

He lightly tapped the computer. "I think my next step is to check out the gym locker. It's open all night, so I'll wait until you and Rory are asleep before heading out."

Her head snapped up. "What? You're leaving us here alone?" The sharp edge of her voice made him wince. "What if something happens? We won't have a vehicle to use if we need to escape. Are you taking Duchess, too?"

"Okay, you're right." He should have anticipated her reaction. "Leaving you alone isn't a good idea, with or without Duchess. I'll have one of my brothers come out for protection." If he could find one of them who wasn't too tied up in other cases. Miles was already a no-go, and he knew his oldest brother, Marc, was knee-deep in an FBI case. Mitch happened to be out of town for some arson training seminar, which only left Mike. He could potentially ask Noah for backup, but that would mean explaining Lacy to Maddy and he wasn't in the mood. As close as they were, she could be relentless when it came to questions about his personal life.

"I'd rather stick with you," Lacy said softly. "Rory may not be comfortable around a stranger."

She had a point, although in his opinion, the baby had adapted pretty well so far. Besides, if he left after they were asleep, Rory wouldn't even know a stranger was here. He pulled out his phone, determined to see if Mike was even available.

No answer. Possibly because Matt's call was coming in from an unknown phone number. He left a brief message, asking for a return call, then set the phone aside.

"What if he doesn't call back?" Lacy asked.

"I won't leave you here," he promised. "If Mike can't come, then we'll all go, okay?"

Lacy nodded, looking relieved.

He secretly hoped Mike wasn't also in the middle of a case. Working as a private investigator meant his brother set his own hours, yet it also meant that his paycheck was dependent on finishing his cases.

So what if Mike was busy? Matt didn't really believe that driving to a fitness center even late at night posed some sort of threat. Especially now that Miles had given him a different K-9 SUV. It wasn't likely that anyone would be able to find them.

Rory began to cry. Duchess lifted her head from the

sofa, as if instinctively knowing the baby needed attention. Lacy jumped up and disappeared into the bedroom. While she changed and fed Rory, he cleaned up
the lunch dishes, washing everything by hand.

He checked Duchess's incision, glad to see it still
looked good, before they both went outside to walk the
perimeter of the property. When he'd assured himself
everything was fine, he stacked the wood he'd cut earlier into a neat pile. When that was finished, he carried
several logs inside to stoke up the woodstove.

The rest of the afternoon dragged by slowly. He
wasn't used to being this inactive. It wasn't until well
after they'd finished eating dinner that Mike returned
his call.

"What's up?" his brother asked, getting straight to
the point. "I only have a few minutes."

His heart sank. "I could use some help later tonight,
if you aren't too busy."

"Unfortunately, I'm in the middle of something. Can
it wait until tomorrow?"

Matt hesitated. "No, it's fine. Not a big deal. But if
anything changes, give me a call back, okay?"

"Are you sure?" His brother's voice held indecision.
"If it's important, I can bag my case."

"I'm positive. No need to drop everything. But make
a note of my new number okay? I'll call you if things
heat up."

"Sounds good. Talk to you later."

Matt felt the pressure of Lacy's curious gaze so he
forced a smile. "Mike is busy, but I'm not worried.
This is a low-risk endeavor. I'd like to leave around
one o'clock in the morning. It will take roughly forty-
five minutes to get there."

"All right," Lacy agreed.

"I can sit up with Rory for a while if you want to take a nap," he offered.

"I'll lie down to get some rest after Rory takes his antibiotic at eleven o'clock." Lacy bounced Rory on her knee, but her blue eyes were serious. "Please don't leave without me, okay?"

"I won't," he assured her, remembering the panic on her face when he'd taken Duchess out for a walk at the motel.

An hour later, the cabin was quiet. Rory, Lacy and even Duchess had fallen asleep.

But Matt couldn't seem to relax. He dimmed the lights, stretched out on the sofa and closed his eyes, but his mind continued to race. He firmly believed David Williams would be arrested within the next day or so, and once the guy was behind bars, Lacy and Rory could return home.

Was that why he'd kissed her? Because he'd sensed their time together was coming to an end? And so what if it was? He wasn't interested in opening himself up to another relationship. And Lacy would have her hands full with caring for Rory, too.

This attraction they seemed to share couldn't go anywhere.

He must have dozed a bit because he woke abruptly at one in the morning, his internal alarm clock going off at just the right time. When he stood and headed into the bedroom to wake Lacy, Duchess followed, as if sensing the need to be back on guard duty.

It took almost twenty minutes for them to get on the road. Rory barely moved as Lacy tucked him in the car seat, and Matt hoped the little guy would sleep through the entire trip.

At exactly two o'clock, he pulled into the parking lot

of the Wisconsin Fitness Center on Rochester Street. He backed the SUV into a space closest to the exit, more out of habit than because he expected trouble.

"Keep the car running and your phone handy," he advised. "I won't be long."

She nodded. "Okay."

He flashed a reassuring smile before sliding out from behind the wheel. Through the windows, he could see the place wasn't very busy. There were long rows of exercise equipment and maybe one older man walking on a treadmill.

Matt entered the building with confidence. Even though he'd never personally been to this location, his membership allowed him to go to any of the WFC gyms. He flashed his card at the woman behind the counter, then ducked into the men's locker room.

The place was empty. He took out the key and walked directly over to locker number eighteen. The key slid in and turned easily.

The smell of stinky clothes made him grimace, but it didn't deter him from his mission. He pushed the clothing aside, hoping and praying this wasn't a wild goose chase.

At the bottom of the locker was a four by three inch spiral notebook. Curious, he pulled it out and flipped through it. There were letters and numbers listed, but at first glance it didn't make any sense.

He tucked the notebook beneath his arm and finished his search. The only item of interest was the notebook, so he quickly closed the locker and relocked it before heading out.

The woman behind the desk looked at him curiously, but he shrugged. "Gotta work," he said as an excuse, then ducked back out the front door.

He strode quickly to the SUV and climbed inside.

"What did you find?" she asked.

"This." He tossed the notebook in her lap, then clicked his seat belt into place. He put the car in gear just as a pair of headlights bloomed on the street, coming from the right-hand side.

Cars weren't completely unexpected at two o'clock in the morning, but still, he found himself going tense.

"Matt?" Lacy's voice was tentative. "What's going on?"

"Hang on," he said in a grim tone. He shot out of the parking space and instead of turning left, he turned right, directly facing the oncoming vehicle.

The headlights grew brighter, causing him to tighten his grip on the steering wheel. There was no doubt in his mind that the person driving the oncoming car was after the notebook. He'd walked into a trap.

"Matt?" Lacy's voice rose in panic. "Watch out!"

As the words left her mouth, the vehicle crossed the center line, heading straight toward them.

EIGHT

Lacy sucked in a harsh breath as the headlights grew large and bright and came straight for them. Bracing herself for the inevitable crash, she began to pray.

Dear Lord, protect us from harm!

Matt wrenched the steering wheel hard to the left in an attempt to avoid the oncoming car, narrowly missing a collision. Duchess scrambled for purchase in the back, as the SUV bumped wildly along the shoulder of the road. They were going the wrong way on the one-way street. At the next intersection, Matt turned left and then hit the gas hard to put distance between them and the vehicle that had tried to ram into them.

The headlights faded away behind them, but for how long? Had the driver gotten a good look at their license plate?

Lacy twisted in her seat, reaching out to make sure Rory was okay in his car seat. Amazingly, he was still sleeping. Duchess, too, appeared to be doing fine.

They were safe, at least for the moment.

Thank You, Lord!

"How did they know where to find us?" Lacy asked, breaking the strained silence.

Matt shook his head. "They must have had someone

staked out at the gym. Although, to be honest, I'm not sure why they didn't just go inside and break into the locker themselves."

She thought about that. "They probably didn't know which locker belonged to David. I doubt the gym administrator would give out that type of information." The notebook had fallen to the floor in the chaos, so she bent forward and picked it up.

"They would in an official investigation," Matt said. "We know Williams is a cop. I'm sure his buddies would have been able to get the information they needed."

"Maybe they're not involved." She opened the notebook and squinted in the darkness, trying to read what was written inside. There were initials and numbers—was it some sort of code? "What does all this mean?"

"I don't know," Matt said slowly. "But my gut tells me Williams is likely involved in something illegal."

"More illegal than murder?" Lacy closed the notebook, thinking back to the night she'd been woken by the sound of voices arguing. Granted, she hadn't heard much, but there was no question that her sister had begged for her life and that Rory had been threatened seconds before the gunshot had echoed through the house.

From that moment on, everything was a blur. She still couldn't believe she'd managed to get Rory away unharmed.

"Is it possible your sister found out he was doing something illegal?" Matt asked, breaking into her thoughts.

She lifted her shoulders in a helpless shrug. "If so, she didn't mention it to me."

"But she did file for divorce."

Lacy shifted in her seat so she was partially facing

him. "Yes. She was afraid of David, the way he seemed to get out of control when he was angry. Not only did he lash out at her, sometimes physically, but he was super controlling. He expected her to stay home every day, ready to answer his call no matter what she was doing. And if she did decide to go out, even to shop, he'd demand to know exactly what stores she'd gone to and who she'd talked to along the way. He'd often accused her of being a bad mother to Rory." She remembered Jill's tearfulness as her sister had finally told her everything that had been going on. "I hate that he started to hit her, the way our father lashed out at our mother. Jill didn't understand why David had turned so hateful. As if the man she'd married had ceased to exist."

Matt nodded thoughtfully. "Tell me again exactly what you overheard the night you escaped with Rory."

Lacy closed her eyes for a moment, trying to push past the painful memories. "They were arguing in low voices. I couldn't make out the words until David's voice got louder. He said, *Tell me the truth! Now! Or I'll kill you and the brat, too.*"

"The truth about what?" Matt asked.

"I assumed it was about her reason for the divorce. He never thought any of their problems were his fault. Or maybe he thought Jill was cheating on him." Although, now that she thought about it, the phrasing was a bit…off. "Since I couldn't hear the beginning of their argument, I can't say for sure what he wanted to know. But shortly afterward, Jill was begging for him to stop, pleading with him not to hurt her. I picked up Rory and called 911 to report the abuse, but right after I disconnected from the line, I heard two gunshots. I knew Rory would be his next target, so I ran."

Matt glanced at her, his expression serious. "I'm sorry. That must have been very difficult for you."

She swallowed hard, tearing up as the memories rushed back. It was all still so hard to believe. David had killed her sister without a moment's hesitation.

What kind of man could do something like that?

Immediately her father's harsh features flashed into her mind. Okay, maybe some men were just made that way. Yet, how was it that Jill had allowed herself to marry a guy who was so much like their father?

The night her parents had died in a car crash, the police had told them they believed their father had crashed into the side of the building on purpose, in a dual homicide/suicide attempt. Their rationale was that there had been no evidence of drugs or alcohol in their father's bloodstream and no sign that he'd even attempted to slam on the brakes.

The crash had killed both of them instantly. Leaving Lacy and Jill alone in the world at twenty-one and eighteen, respectively. Lacy had been able to finish her teaching degree, but Jill hadn't wanted to attend college. She'd met David at a mutual friend's party and married him a few years later.

Lacy had always suspected that Jill had been trying to replace the family they'd lost. A fact that had bothered her, because it wasn't as if they'd had a wonderful and happy childhood. What Lacy remembered most was tiptoeing around the house when their father was home, everyone avoiding the possibility of making him mad.

"Lacy?" Matt sounded worried. "Are you okay?"

It wasn't easy to push her tumultuous past aside. Her parents were gone, and so was her sister. She needed to remain strong for Rory's sake.

She looked at Matt. "I just wish I would have convinced Jill to open up to me about her problems sooner. Maybe if I had, we could have gotten away from David before that night. Maybe Jill would be alive right now, caring for her son…"

"Lacy, this isn't your fault. Or your sister's fault." Matt reached over and took her hand, giving it a gentle squeeze. "Williams is the one responsible. And this notebook is actually proof that there is more to the story."

"David being involved in something illegal won't bring my sister back."

Matt continued to hold her hand. "I know. But we'll find him and arrest him. He'll pay for his crimes."

She wanted to believe Matt was right. But somehow, even the idea of having David locked up in jail where he belonged didn't make her feel better.

As if sensing her despair, Matt swept his thumb over the back of her hand, in a sweet reassuring caress. She stared at their joined hands, grappling with how much her life had changed in the past two days.

She was a mother now. Logically, she knew the full impact of that hadn't quite sunk into her brain. Having Rory fully dependent on her was scary. She was so afraid of failing.

Strange to think that a future with Rory could be any harder than being on the run from a crazy man determined to kill her and an innocent baby. The difference was, she had Matt to lean on, his strength and support to share the burden.

Of course, this dependency on Matt couldn't continue. Eventually, she would have to stand alone on her own two feet.

Her chest tightened with panic, but then she remembered last time, how Matt had taught her to lean on God in times of stress.

She wasn't completely alone. God would be there, guiding her.

The tightness eased in her chest as the realization sank deep. She'd be all right, as long as she had her faith.

Yet, she would miss Matt. He'd been a rock during this entire nightmare. And while he'd claimed that she could call him anytime, she knew she wouldn't.

Rory was her responsibility. It was up to her to provide Rory with a stable upbringing.

She would just have to find a way to survive without Matthew Callahan.

Matt drove in a circuitous route back to the cabin, unwilling to risk the possibility of being followed. Thankfully, at three in the morning, it was easy to make sure no one was on his tail.

It bothered him to think about how someone was watching the gym. He replayed in his mind the brief conversation Lacy had overheard the night of her sister's murder. He had the niggling suspicion that he was missing a key piece of the puzzle. It made more sense that Williams would want to silence his wife if she'd found out about his illegal activities. So what truth had he wanted to hear? And why would he stay at the scene of the murder to accuse Lacy and put out the Amber Alert?

Rory woke up crying as he pulled into the driveway at the cabin. He let Duchess out the back, then carried Rory's car seat inside.

Lacy unbuckled the baby and took the bottle she'd premade for him from her purse.

"Why don't you let me feed him?" Matt asked, noticing her weary expression. "I'm wide-awake anyway, but you look as if you could use some rest."

"Rory is my responsibility," she protested.

"And I'm here to help." Matt kept his tone firm. "I won't be able to sleep, anyway. No reason for both of us to be up."

She wavered, then nodded. "All right. Thank you."

Matt cradled the baby in his arm and made himself comfortable in the rocking chair. Rory must have been hungry because he drank from the bottle with a single-minded intensity, his wide eyes glued to Matt's.

He tried not to compare Rory's glowing health to the emaciated way Carly had looked by the time she'd died. He'd loved that little girl, and his heart had broken in two when she had slipped away into God's arms. When Debra had announced she was reconciling with Kevin, the second blow had sent him to his knees.

He'd sought solace at church, trying to make sense out of God's plan. It took a while for him to accept that he might not ever understand what that plan may be. His job was to simply accept it.

God must have brought Lacy and Rory into his life for a reason. He'd been so determined not to let anyone get close to his heart again, but gazing down at Rory's innocent face, he realized he'd failed.

He cared about this little guy, far more than he should. Was this how his brothers had felt when they'd met their wives? Marc had met Kari when she had been pregnant, and even though their son, Max, wasn't a Callahan by blood, he was an integral part of the family. And the same could be said for Abby. Miles's wife, Paige, had been a single mother to the six-year-old when he'd met her.

Both of their families were tied together by love

rather than blood. And it occurred to him that love was the most powerful bond of all.

When Rory released his grip on the bottle, Matt carefully propped the baby up against his shoulder, rubbing his back the way he'd watched Lacy do. Rory's muffled burp made him smile.

The baby's eyelids began to droop. Rory took the last bit of his bottle and almost instantly fell asleep. Matt rose to his feet and silently padded into Lacy's room to set Rory into his makeshift crib.

He returned to the kitchen and began to examine the notebook. The initials likely represented people's names, and he soon realized there were dollar amounts attached to each one.

A blackmail scheme? Highly likely. But what was the source of the blackmail? Drugs? Gambling? Prostitutes?

There was no hint as to the source of the payments, either. The initials could have belonged to anyone—other cops, maybe, or politicians.

Matt set the notebook aside, turned off the lights and lay down on the sofa. Duchess came over to stretch out on the floor beside him.

He awoke to Rory's crying. With a groan, he forced himself upright, wishing for a solid four hours of sleep. He was about to get the baby, but when Rory quieted down, he knew Lacy had beaten him to it.

Duchess thumped her tail, got up and went over to the door, waiting patiently for him to join her. He took the dog outside, shivering in the cool brisk wind.

Another sweep of the perimeter reassured him their location hadn't been found. Satisfied for the moment, he waited for Duchess to finish her business, then headed back inside.

Lacy had Rory propped in his car seat as she made a fresh bottle. "Coffee is brewing. Should be ready soon."

"Okay." He glanced at his phone, wondering when Miles would call him back. Matt figured the police would apprehend David Williams sooner rather than later.

The police administrators wouldn't like the idea of a rogue cop running loose. They would want him behind bars as soon as possible. Matt figured every squad car on the streets was keeping a watchful eye out for him.

"Are you listening to me?"

He jerked around in guilty surprise. "No, sorry. I'm a bit distracted."

Her gaze was sympathetic. "I guess you didn't get much sleep. I was just saying how great it is that Rory and I might be able to go home."

"I don't think it will be safe enough for you to head home," he said cautiously. He didn't like the thought of leaving Lacy and Rory vulnerable. "This notebook complicates things."

She frowned, shaking the bottle to disperse the formula. "You don't think the notebook is proof that David is involved in something illegal? With something solid to go on, wouldn't the police take the investigation from here?"

He could, but that would take the case out of his hands. He trusted his brothers and his brother-in-law, Noah, but everyone else? Not so much. "I'd like to understand what crimes the notebook is linked to before I do that."

Lacy picked up Rory from the car seat and sat down at the kitchen table to feed him. "I'm sure David will explain everything once he's arrested. Isn't that the way these things work? He gives the police information in exchange for a lighter sentence?"

"Sometimes," he agreed. "But he'd have to give up a lot of people in order to knock a few years off a murder charge."

Lacy grimaced and nodded. "You're probably right." She lightly stroked Rory's plump cheek. "I just hope David stays in jail long enough for me to raise Rory. The idea that he could get out early and insist on visitation rights…" She shivered.

"He won't get visitation rights," he assured her. "Especially when you testify to the fact that he threatened to kill him. No matter what happens, when this is over, you'll be able to raise Rory without Williams interfering."

He went over to get some coffee, then set about making breakfast. French toast was Lacy's favorite, so he went through all the cupboards until he found a bottle of maple syrup.

"French toast coming up," he announced.

She smiled with gratitude, and he found himself momentarily captivated by her beauty. Not just on the surface, although the wavy golden blond hair framing her oval face was certainly attractive. But there was a light radiating from her blue eyes that came from within, giving her a loveliness that was more than skin-deep.

He was so distracted, he nearly dropped the egg in his hand, managing to catch it before it hit the floor.

Focus, he reminded himself. He was here to keep her safe while figuring out why her brother-in-law wanted her dead.

When she'd finished feeding Rory, she once again spread the blanket out on the floor and set the baby down in the middle of it. Rory was a quick study and quickly began rolling over to get toward the rattle.

"You're so smart, aren't you?" Lacy picked him up again, moving him back to the center. He instantly rolled over, giggling at his new trick. "I wish your mommy was here to see this."

Matt tried to think of something to say that would make her feel better, but in the end he simply announced, "Breakfast is ready."

Lacy picked up Rory and set him back in his car seat. Duchess sat beside the baby, as if to watch over him.

He was surprised when Lacy led the mealtime prayer. "Dear Lord, we thank You for this food we are about to eat. We also thank You for watching over us last night and keeping us safe from danger. Please continue to guide us on Your chosen path. Amen."

"Amen," he echoed. "It's nice to hear you praying."

Her smile was shy. "It's nice to know God is always there for me."

He wanted nothing more than to lean over and kiss her. His phone rang, saving him from himself. He recognized his brother's number. "Hey, Miles, what's up?"

"I have some interesting news," Miles said. "Your case has officially intersected with mine."

Matt frowned. "What do you mean? How are you linked to Lacy's sister's murder?"

"Remember the call I took last night?" Miles asked. "I reported in at a murder scene. Adult male body had been dumped out in the middle of a stone quarry and was difficult to identify since the animals had gotten to him before we arrived."

An adult male? Matt's stomach clenched. "Did you get an ID on the victim?"

"Just now. Victim is none other than your missing

cop, David Williams. The ME estimates he's been dead for at least twenty-four hours, maybe longer. We won't know more about the estimated time of death until the autopsy is completed."

"Williams is dead?" Matt echoed, his gaze locked on Lacy. She froze, her fork halfway to her mouth. "I get you don't know how long he's been out there, but what about cause of death?"

"Oh, yeah, forgot to mention that. Cause of death was a gunshot wound to the chest from close range. No gun found at the scene, either. No question it's a homicide."

Someone had killed David Williams. Who? And why? Either way, Matt was convinced the guy's death was linked to Jill's murder, or to the notebook he'd found in the gym locker.

Likely both.

He set the phone aside, his mind whirling. The driver of the car that had tried to ram into them hadn't been Lacy's brother-in-law.

Which meant Lacy and Rory were still in danger, but from an unknown assailant.

NINE

The loud clank Lacy's fork made when she dropped it from nerves made Rory startle and cry. The little guy's distress was enough to pull her back together, and she quickly pushed away from the table to pick up the baby, cradling him close.

David Williams was dead. He'd never have a chance to hurt anyone else, especially Rory.

She closed her eyes for a moment, struggling between being grateful that the man she'd feared was gone for good, and despairing over the horrible way Rory had lost both of his parents.

Each one, a victim of murder.

"Lacy? Are you all right?"

She opened her eyes to find Matt standing beside her, concern darkening his green eyes. "I...guess. I can't deny I'm relieved to know the danger is over."

Matt's jaw clenched, and he momentarily glanced away before letting out a heavy sigh. "I'm sorry, but the danger isn't over. Don't you remember how we barely escaped from the vehicle that had staked out the fitness center? Who was driving? Obviously not Williams."

A trickle of unease made her shiver. "But maybe the

driver was only interested in the notebook you found, not in harming me or Rory."

Matt was shaking his head. "Listen, my brother seems to think that Williams has been dead for at least twenty-four hours, maybe longer. We won't know the exact timing of his murder until after the ME finishes the autopsy, but we have to consider the fact that someone else has been tracking us. Someone who thinks you know something important."

Rory had stopped crying and was wiggling around in her arms, so she placed him back down in the center of the blanket on the floor. Duchess came over as if offering her protection. "But I don't know anything."

"Are you sure? Maybe you need to think back to the day before Jill's murder. Could she have mentioned something that didn't seem important at the time?"

Rory rolled onto his back, kicking his feet and waving his arms. She watched him for a moment, trying to remember the conversations she'd shared with Jill.

Her sister had confided being afraid of David's temper and filing for divorce. Jill had mentioned that David had punched holes in the wall of their bedroom and that he'd slapped her across the face in a moment of anger. Lacy remembered thinking it was a good thing Jill had taken that first step of filing for divorce, and she had encouraged her to obtain a restraining order against him, too.

Other than that, they'd mostly talked about Rory. Lacy had agreed to help with childcare duties whenever possible, and they'd worked out some scheduling issues.

Nothing that would cause somebody to come after her like this.

"Lacy? Let's finish our breakfast before it gets cold."

She wrinkled her nose, her appetite having disappeared, but followed him into the kitchen, anyway. She knew she needed to remain strong enough to care for Rory, so she ate a few more bites of her French toast.

Duchess let out a short bark, causing her to turn around in her seat.

"Hey, where are you going?" Matt jumped up from the table and rushed over to pick up Rory, who was trying to roll into the small stack of logs he'd brought in for the woodstove. Duchess had put her nose down in an attempt to stop him. "Good girl, Duchess. Rory, you're getting a little too good at rolling around. We need to find a way to keep you in one place."

Lacy swallowed the last bite of her breakfast and rose to her feet. "I can take him for a bit. Unless you'd rather I do the dishes?"

"No need, I can wash them." Matt handed her the baby, then returned to his meal. His appetite didn't seem to have suffered, she noted as he finished off the rest of his breakfast.

Bouncing Rory on her knee, she couldn't help but smile at how he laughed with glee. He was such a happy baby, at least now that he was taking antibiotics for his ear infection. Which reminded her, it was almost time for his morning dose.

"Matt, will you help me for a moment?"

"Sure." He didn't hesitate to come over. When he saw the bottle of liquid antibiotic in her hand, he grimaced. "Our favorite part of the day, huh, sport?"

Rory bobbed his head as if in agreement.

Lacy filled the oral syringe and waited for Matt to get a good grip on the baby. Rory still didn't seem to like the medicine, but most of it went into his tummy.

Mission accomplished.

She took the sofa cushions and used them to protect

the perimeter of the blanket so Rory could roll around without her worrying about him getting hurt. Knowing the cabin wasn't exactly baby-proof made her wish she'd picked up a swing or some other baby items to help keep Rory occupied.

When Matt finished cleaning up in the kitchen, he refilled his coffee mug and returned to the kitchen table. Since Rory was content and well-protected, she walked over to add more coffee to her own mug, then joined him at the table.

"What's our next step?" she asked.

He shrugged. "I wish I knew."

She leaned in to take a closer look at the notebook. "Are those people's initials followed by dollar amounts?"

"That's my theory," Matt said.

"Blackmail," she whispered. "I wish I could say I'm surprised that David would become involved in something like this, but I'm not."

"Do you think your sister knew?"

She glanced at him in surprise. "Absolutely not. I'm sure if Jill had known, she would have told me and would have used it as leverage in the divorce."

"I suppose you're right," he agreed. "No reason not to use it against him."

"And no reason not to confide in me," she insisted. "I was already staying over on my school break to help out."

Matt's expression turned thoughtful. "When you found the locker key, did you have the impression it was dropped recently? Or is it possible it had been there for a while?"

"I have no clue. I guess if you're asking for a gut reaction, I believe it had been dropped recently." She thought back to the moment she'd slipped and had stopped herself from falling. Her hand had instantly felt the raised edges of the key. "It wasn't imbedded in the dirt the way it might have been if it had been lying around for a while."

"So David must have dropped it."

She lifted her shoulders. "Who else?"

He nodded and went back to paging through the notebook. She crossed over to the radio, tuning in to the same news station she'd listened to before.

"What are you doing?" Matt asked, his gaze curious.

"I'm wondering if the Amber Alert has been discontinued. It should be now that David has been found dead, right?"

"I would assume so," he agreed. He returned to the notebook as she listened to the news. The announcer seemed obsessed about Judge Dugan's death threats, since that was all he talked about.

Apparently judges ranked up there along with celebrities. Or maybe in a city as small as Milwaukee, political figures counted as celebrities.

After fifteen minutes, she shut the radio off and turned back to Matt.

Sensing her gaze, he pushed the notebook aside and gestured for her to take a seat beside him. He turned in his chair to face her. "Let's go at this from another angle. You mentioned that Jill didn't think anyone would believe her because Williams had friends on the force. Do you know who they were?"

"I can only remember Jill talking about two guys, Randal Whalen and Jeff Jones. But to be honest, there could be others. I had the sense he hung out with a group of guys."

"Those two are a good starting point." Matt pulled the computer closer and began a simple search. She was amazed at how quickly he found pictures of both cops. "Do either of these men look familiar?"

"Not really. I hate that I'm not being very helpful. I can't remember anything significant Jill might have told me, and I don't recognize these guys."

"Hey, it's all right." Matt must have heard the frustration in her voice because he reached out and took her hand. "You're a huge help—don't forget, if you hadn't picked up that key we wouldn't be on the right track."

Matt's hand was nice and warm around hers, and she wanted so badly to lean against him in an effort to absorb some of his strength. His fingers tightened around hers, causing her to blush. She hoped her thoughts weren't transparent.

He must have sensed her longing, because he slowly stood, pulling her up to her feet. Then he carefully cupped her face in his hand and leaned forward to capture her mouth in a gentle yet warm kiss.

In some tiny corner of her mind, she knew she shouldn't be kissing him like this. That her priority shouldn't be giving in to her deepest yearning to be held by a man who'd proven to be strong, yet gentle, caring and compassionate and, most of all, not the kind of man who would ever yell and hit.

"Waaah!"

Rory's shrill cry brought her crashing back to reality. She pulled out of Matt's embrace and hurried over to where Duchess was standing over the baby, as if determined to protect him.

"I'm here. Mommy's here." The word slipped from her mouth without conscious thought as she lifted the baby in her arms. He continued crying, and she propped him against her hip as she headed into the kitchen to make him a bottle.

"Let me help," Matt said in a low, gravelly voice.

She knew she needed to figure out how to do everything for Rory alone, but his crying grew louder, so she quickly nodded and handed him over to Matt.

She made Rory's bottle, mentally berating herself for not being better prepared. If she'd made several bottles ahead of time, she wouldn't have needed any help.

Then again, Rory could cry in his car seat as easily as he was crying in Matt's arms.

Shaking the formula in the bottle, she did her best to ignore the niggling panic. No more being distracted by Matt's kisses and warm embrace.

Rory needed her. Taking over as his mother was the least she could do for her sister.

She needed to remember that Rory was her single most important priority.

Matt reluctantly handed the baby over to Lacy, watching with admiration as she made herself comfortable in the rocking chair and began feeding him.

He forced himself to turn away, although it wasn't nearly as easy to push the memory of their kiss aside. Lacy was a bit like a skittish colt, coming close enough to hug and kiss him, but only briefly before running away.

Turning his attention to the two cops who were Williams's friends, Randal Whalen and Jeff Jones, he tried to find out more about their respective pasts. He found via social media they were both listed as single. Although searching deeper into the Milwaukee County case review, he discovered Whalen had divorced two years ago. There was no divorce on record for Jones.

That knowledge wasn't very helpful. He picked up his phone to call Miles.

"Yeah?" his brother answered. "Something wrong?"

"No, but I wanted you to know that Williams was close to a couple of guys on the job, Randal Whalen and Jeff Jones. Figured you might want to talk to them about when they last saw Williams."

"Thanks for the help, but I already got their names, in addition to a guy called Hugh Nichols."

Matt punched Nichols's name into the computer, bringing his picture up beside the other two officers. He looked vaguely familiar. "What else have you found out?"

His brother hesitated. "Matt, you know I'd help if I could, but I can't afford to compromise my case."

"You're the one who told me our cases are linked. Why wouldn't we share information?" Matt hesitated, then added, "I have some info that might be pertinent to Williams's murder."

"What?"

Matt pulled the notebook close. "The night Lacy's sister was murdered, she found a key outside. We figured out the key belonged to a locker at the Wisconsin Fitness Center, so we went over there last night."

"You found something in the locker? And you're just telling me now?" Miles's voice rose with indignation.

"I'm sorry, I should have mentioned it sooner, but hearing that Williams had been shot distracted me. Yes, we found a notebook. Looks as if your victim was involved in a blackmail scheme."

"What kind of blackmail?" Miles demanded.

"No idea. There's a list of initials followed by what appear to be dollar amounts. No other indication of what might be involved."

Miles was silent for a moment. "Okay, I'll head out to meet up with you shortly. I need that notebook."

"No way, Miles. I need it just as much as you do." Matt didn't like the idea of giving his brother the only clue they had. "Lacy and Rory are still in danger, and whoever is after them knows we have it."

"I'll figure out something. Maybe I can bring a portable scanner so that we can each have a copy. Give me a couple of hours. I'm still wading through evidence surrounding the crime scene."

"What kind of evidence?"

"Tire tracks near the edge of the quarry. Our theory is that the killer had Williams's body in the trunk and drove there to dispose of it. There isn't much blood at the scene, so the murder must have happened somewhere else. Also we found a small thread of fabric stuck to a prickly bush not far from the tire tracks, also possibly left behind by the killer."

"That isn't much," Matt said on a weary sigh.

"I know, but we're still going over things. There may be other clues, too. Oh, and I almost forgot to mention, Williams had last been seen three days ago."

Matt leapt to his feet. "Three days?" He counted backward from the night he'd witnessed the guy wearing the black cap pointing a gun at Lacy. Exactly three days ago. "You sure?"

"That's what we're hearing. Of course, these buddies of his could be lying, but he hadn't been at work for three days, either. The first two were normal days off, and the last day was when he was reported as AWOL."

"Okay, thanks, Miles. I appreciate you filling me in."

"You were right. We need to share information since our cases are linked. See you later."

"Bye." Matt disconnected and glanced over to where Lacy had Rory up against her shoulder, waiting for the infamous burp. The kid didn't disappoint.

"Sounds like you learned something new," Lacy said as she continued feeding Rory.

He nodded. "I'll give you the details when you're done."

While he waited, he took Duchess outside to let her run for a bit. His K-9 partner wasn't used to being cooped up inside for so long, and he felt guilty that he hadn't spent as much time training and working with her as he should have been. She ran as if she'd never been cut by the knife, and he was glad her wound was healing well.

He put her through a few commands, and she responded like a pro. Satisfied the incision hadn't interfered with her performance, he carried another armload of logs back inside.

Lacy was in the bedroom, no doubt putting Rory down for his nap. He stoked the woodstove, then went over to sit in front of the computer.

He didn't like the idea of Miles taking the notebook, but there was no denying it was linked to the guy's murder. He opened the notebook again, going down the list of initials. For the first time, he noticed that some were just two letters, such as R.B., and others were three letters, like J.L.J.

Middle names? Maybe. But why did some have middle initials and others didn't?

He caught the hint of lavender and looked up to see Lacy standing beside him. She had her arms crossed protectively across her chest, as if warning him not to try kissing her again.

"Have a seat and I'll tell you what I know."

She sat, making sure that there was a good foot of space between them. The way she held herself away from him stung, but he told himself to get over it. He filled her in on the tire tracks and thread that Miles had found at the quarry, along with the fact that Williams's coworkers claimed no one had seen him for three days.

"That doesn't make sense," she said with a frown. "David murdered Jill and then called his buddies to put out an Amber Alert. They must have seen him."

"Agreed, although it's odd they would lie about that since whoever had gone to the house that night would have called in Jill's murder, along with putting out the Amber Alert."

She lightly tapped the third face on the computer screen. "Who is this?"

"A guy by the name of Hugh Nichols, another of Williams's coworkers."

"Hugh Nichols, Jeff Jones and Randal Whalen," Lacy repeated softly. "I wish I'd paid more attention to what Jill told me about David's friends."

A series of initials caught his eye, three in a row. H.N., J.L.J. and R.W.

His pulse jumped, and he stared in shock. The three cops he was close friends with? All in a row?

This couldn't possibly be a coincidence. For one thing, he didn't believe in coincidences. Not when it came to linking clues to a murder.

A puzzle piece clicked into place. These guys weren't loyal to Williams because of friendship.

It made far more sense that they had been forced to support Williams because he had something to hold over their heads. Information to blackmail them with.

Certainly money, either from drugs, guns, prostitutes or gambling.

But which one? What was the blackmail scheme that Williams had been involved with that had ultimately resulted in his own demise?

TEN

Lacy leaned over to see what had captured Matt's attention in the notebook. It didn't take long for her to see the three initials listed one after the other and to understand the implication.

"He was blackmailing cops from his precinct?" she whispered in horror. "That's crazy."

Matt's expression was grim. "With what he was holding over their heads, it's likely they would have testified that you must have been the one to kill Jill in order to have Rory for yourself."

Her stomach twisted. "I'd never do something like that. Why would I? It's not as if being a single mother is glamorous. In fact, it's been downright scary having sole responsibility of a three-month-old baby."

"I'm not saying I believe it, just what they would have claimed. Although…" His voice trailed off. "It doesn't quite fit now that we know Williams was murdered."

She remembered listening to his part of the conversation with Miles. "But they're still looking for clues, right? I'm sure they'll find something that will help."

"Yeah, maybe." Matt's voice lacked conviction. "Now that we know Williams's buddies are involved,

I think I need to talk to my lieutenant, bring him up to speed on the latest developments in this case. Especially since we never showed up to report in."

Lacy understood Matt's concern about his job being on the line, but she really, *really* didn't want him to call his boss. Then again, she didn't want Miles to come and take possession of the notebook, either.

Since it wasn't possible to stay here in this cozy cabin forever, she forced herself to nod. "Okay, if you think that's what we need to do, then you should call your boss. Just…don't tell him where we are, okay?"

"I won't." Matt reached for his phone and began dialing.

She tried to ignore the sliver of apprehension by reaching over to scratch Duchess behind the ears. The K-9 officer made her long for a pet of her own. Maybe once Rory grew older, and she felt more competent caring for him.

Who was she kidding? It was doubtful she'd ever feel comfortable taking care of Rory by herself. Especially since she was bound to make mistakes along the way.

"Lieutenant Gray? This is Matthew Callahan. I have an update."

Matt's boss spoke so loudly she could hear everything without a problem. "Where have you been, Callahan? You were ordered to report in two days ago!"

"Yes, sir, but if you'd let me explain—"

"Explain what?" his boss interrupted harshly. "That you Callahans think the rules don't apply to you? That just because your old man was once the Chief of Police that you can do whatever you want? What part of 'an order is an order' do you not understand?"

"Sir, I picked up a tail that morning and the driver pulled a gun and tried to shoot us. I managed to lose him, but I wasn't about to risk bringing trouble to your office, so I found a place to hide out for a few days." Matt's voice was amazingly calm, as if he was used to getting yelled at.

She was tempted to pull the phone away so she could tell the lieutenant that Matt would never break the rules without a good reason. Somehow she knew this, even though she'd only known him a few days.

"Why didn't you call in before now?" Lieutenant Gray thundered. "Where are you?"

"I can't tell you that, sir. Not without putting an innocent woman and baby in danger." Matt glanced at her and flashed a reassuring smile. "However, I can tell you that David Williams has been murdered. And I think I know why."

"Murdered? Let me guess, your brother was the one to give you that information?"

"Yes. Because David Williams's murder is linked to the murder of his wife, Jill Williams. I have proof that these cases intersect."

That made his lieutenant pause, and she couldn't hear him yelling anymore.

"The night of Jill's murder, Lacy found a key to a gym locker. We found a spiral notebook inside with initials followed by what appear to be dollar amounts. We believe that Williams was murdered because of his blackmail scheme."

Matt listened in silence for a few minutes, and she thought back to the night she'd overheard Jill's murder.

Tell me the truth! Now! Or I'll kill you and the brat, too.

A chill snaked down her spine. What if David wanted to know what Jill had learned about his blackmail scheme? Wasn't it possible that Jill had suspected something was going on? Say, for example, if someone had come to the house looking for David and alluded to the fact that he owed David money? Maybe while Lacy had been out at the park with Rory?

"Yes, sir. I'll report in tomorrow morning." Matt's voice brought her back to the present. "And I'll bring the notebook. My brother will likely join us."

Lacy wanted to cry out in protest. It was one thing to call his boss, but she didn't want to leave the cabin. It was the only place since this nightmare began that made her feel safe.

Of course, it wasn't the cabin itself, but staying in an isolated location with Matt and Duchess watching over them.

She glanced at the clock, noticing it was close to one o'clock in the afternoon. Seventeen hours at the most before they would be forced to leave.

Matt disconnected from the call and reached over to pat her arm. "We'll be okay, Lacy. You need to trust me on this."

She lifted her gaze to meet his. "I do trust you, Matt. But you're asking me to trust your boss, too. We already know that David's buddies were being blackmailed, and you have to admit there are likely others, too. Cops who would do anything to prevent the truth of whatever is indicated by that notebook from ever seeing the light of day."

"My boss isn't listed in the notebook," he assured her. "There are no B.G's or W.G's listed. And his middle name is Wayne, and there are no B.W.G's or W.W.G's, either. He's not involved in this."

"Still…" She was glad the lieutenant's initials weren't in the notebook, but that didn't mean they were in the clear.

"Besides," Matt continued, "we need to have faith in God's plan. He'll watch over us, Lacy."

She swallowed hard and tried to nod. Sure, she'd felt strong and calm when she'd prayed, but to blindly believe that God's plan included keeping her and Rory safe? They'd already been in danger several times since the night she'd listened to her sister beg for her life. God may have sent Matt and Duchess to the rescue, and she was grateful for that, but she was forced to admit that the danger wasn't over yet.

"Lacy?" Matt's husky voice saying her name caused a ripple of awareness to dance up her arm.

Battling a strong urge to throw herself into his arms, she abruptly stood, pulling away. "I need to check on Rory." Skirting around Duchess, she left the room, seeking the solace of the bedroom.

The baby was sleeping, his expression so peaceful and serene she felt tears well up, clouding her vision. She closed her eyes and dropped to her knees beside the drawer. She bowed her head and opened her heart.

Please, Lord. Please help me find a way to keep this innocent baby safe. I need You. Rory needs You, too. Please?

A sense of calm settled over her, and she slowly rose to her feet. They only had what was left of today and tonight before they had to leave. Since it was past lunchtime, she decided to go and see what she could make that would tide them over until dinner.

When she returned to the kitchen, Matt was on the phone again. She made grilled cheese sandwiches, listening as he told his brother about Lieutenant Gray's insistence on reporting in and bringing the notebook.

There was a long silence as Matt listened to whatever

his brother was saying. She could only imagine Miles wasn't happy with this latest news.

"Tell you what, Miles, bring a portable scanner," Matt suggested. "That way you can have the information, even if you don't have the actual notebook."

Another pause. "You found the gun?" Matt asked. "Where?"

She glanced over her shoulder, intrigued by the news. If they'd found the murder weapon, it was possible they were one step closer to making an arrest.

"Okay, we won't expect you until later, then. If you decide to meet up with us at Lieutenant Gray's office, that's fine, too. Whatever works." There was a brief silence, then Matt nodded. "Just call if you decide to come out to scan the notebook, okay? Bye, Miles."

Lacy finished making the grilled cheese just as Rory woke up from his nap. That kid sure did have a knack for knowing when she was about to eat.

"Sit down, I'll get him…" Matt started, but she quickly shook her head.

"No, thanks." She set a plate of food in front of Matt, then disappeared into the bedroom.

As she changed the baby, she thought about how soon she would be on her own caring for Rory.

"We're going to be all right," she whispered against his downy head. "I promise I'll do my best for you."

Rory smiled up at her with his wide toothless grin, and her heart filled with love.

Maybe Matt was right, and God would protect them. She needed to believe that in order to have the strength to move forward with whatever waited for them back in the city.

And if she missed Matt once this mess was over,

she had no one to blame but herself. She'd become too dependent on him, and that had to stop—right now.

Before she lost her heart.

Matt wrestled with guilt as he stared at his sandwich. Why did he feel as if he'd betrayed Lacy by agreeing to meet with his boss?

He took a bite of his grilled cheese, glancing around the interior of the cabin. This place had been their temporary home for two days, nice and cozy in spite of the stressful circumstances.

But it was already clear that Rory needed his own room, a place to play. A house that had been baby-proofed with an actual crib and play area, something other than sofa cushions and Duchess watching over him.

Her sandwich was no doubt growing cold, and he wished there was a microwave to heat it up for her when she'd finished with Rory.

He assumed the reason she hadn't taken him up on his offer was because she was upset he'd called his boss. Still, it didn't make sense that she insisted on doing everything herself, because soon enough she really would be on her own.

The thought bothered him. A lot.

Lacy returned to the main area of the cabin with Rory propped on her hip. He scarfed down the rest of his sandwich and held out his arms. "My turn."

She hesitated, then shook her head. "No need. I'll set him down on the blanket for a bit."

He frowned but didn't argue. As much as he liked the little guy, he knew his focus needed to be on uncovering the details of the blackmail scheme.

The computer wasn't much help, so he turned back

to the notebook. Now that Miles had found the murder weapon, Matt knew his brother would likely be tied up for the next several hours, watching over the crime scene as a team of officers searched the rock quarry for shell casings.

Duchess rose to her feet and stretched. She headed over to where Rory was rolling around on the blanket, as if sensing it was part of her duty to watch over him.

Matt knew Duchess would do exactly that. Without hesitation. The same way he himself would.

Lacy joined him at the table and pried her cold sandwich apart.

"How about I make you a new one?" he offered.

She frowned. "No reason to waste food. Find anything interesting?"

"Not yet." He ran his finger down the list of numbers. "I can't even say for sure whether these figures represent tens or hundreds."

"Hundreds?" She looked horrified at the thought. "Surely not that much."

At this point, he wouldn't put anything past Williams, not even bilking hundreds of dollars from his fellow officers. But who else was on the list? Highly unlikely that it was all cops. Most of the officers he knew were good, law-abiding citizens. Business owners? Relatives of cops? Who else had Williams come into contact with?

Wait a minute—maybe he was looking at this all wrong. If this was blackmail for, say, either gambling or prostitution, then Williams must have known details. Which meant the guy somehow stumbled upon the illegal activity, and instead of arresting those involved, he had begun his blackmail operation.

A thrill of anticipation hummed in his blood. If he

could figure out what cases Williams had been working on, he might find a hint of what the basis for the blackmail was about.

Matt made a mental note to ask his lieutenant for permission to review Williams's case files. When Lacy finished eating, he quickly went over to help clean up the dishes.

Lacy looked as if she was about to argue, but he shook his head. "Don't bother. We'll get this finished faster if we work together."

"Okay," she reluctantly agreed.

"I'm going to train Duchess for a while this afternoon," he said as he dried dishes. "Ongoing drills are important."

"Sounds good." Lacy's tone was polite, and he didn't quite understand why she was acting like they were nothing more than strangers, when in fact they'd kissed—not once, but twice.

Then it hit him. This was likely her way of keeping distance between them, preventing him from holding her and kissing her again.

His heart squeezed painfully in his chest, but he ignored it. Wasn't that best for both of them? He wasn't interested in getting involved—with anyone, but especially someone who had a kid. A kid he could get too attached to.

They finished the chore in silence. When the last dish was put away, he hung up the towel and turned toward the living room.

"Duchess, Come."

His partner instantly rose and trotted over to sit right beside him, her spine straight, her tall brown ears perked forward as she waited for the next command. He pulled on his leather jacket and then opened the cabin door. Making a motion with his hand, he indicated that Duchess should accompany him outside.

The air was warming up, laden with the scent of spring. He put Duchess through the paces, rewarding her with toys and the occasional treat. Thankfully, his partner enjoyed training. Matt was exhausted and sweaty by the time they'd finished, but he also felt good about the way he and Duchess were able to connect and communicate with verbal commands or hand signals.

After four hours, he called it a day. Back inside the cabin, he found Lacy playing with Rory. She'd made a cloth doll out of rags and was using it to keep the baby occupied. He hung his coat on the hook by the door and checked his phone again.

Nothing yet from Miles, and he wondered if it wouldn't be better for his brother to just meet up with him in the morning.

The rest of the evening passed with excruciating slowness. Partially because he couldn't think of another angle to investigate, but mostly because of Lacy's aloofness.

The camaraderie they'd once shared had vanished as if it had never existed. Several times he found himself about to broach the subject but held back.

He didn't know what tomorrow would bring. It was entirely possible that the job of protecting Lacy and Rory would be handed off to someone else. He didn't like it, but that was the reality of working in law enforcement.

After a dinner of canned beef stew, Lacy fed Rory his bottle. When she finished, she turned toward him.

"I need your help to give Rory his antibiotic," she said in a low voice. "I just can't figure out how to do it by myself."

"I don't mind helping, Lacy." He gently took Rory from her arms, holding him so she could get him to take his medicine.

"Thanks." Lacy's smile was strained. "You seem to have a way with kids."

His gut clenched as he remembered caring for Carly. All the love in the world hadn't been enough to prevent the little girl from dying.

"I have some limited experience," he said. Confiding about his feelings wasn't easy, but he wanted to tell Lacy the truth. "I dated a woman who had a four-year-old, but things didn't work out."

"I'm sorry." Her expression was full of compassion. "That must have been rough."

"Yeah." He hesitated, then pushed on. "Carly had an aggressive form of leukemia and died. Afterward, Carly's mother dumped me to reunite with her ex-husband. I ended up losing them both in a matter of days and it was the hardest thing I've ever gone through."

Lacy's eyes widened. "Really?"

"Yes." He flashed a lopsided smile. "I don't talk about it much, but I wanted you to know we all have hidden issues in our past, they're nothing to be ashamed of. And I'm here if you ever want to talk."

She opened her mouth as if to say something, but then clamped her jaw shut and rose to her feet. The closed expression on her face wasn't reassuring.

"Hey." He put his hand on her arm to stop her. "I don't like it when you're upset with me."

"I'm not," she denied, avoiding his direct gaze.

"You are," he countered. "I'm sorry, I didn't intend to say things that would upset you."

Finally she looked at him. "You didn't, I appreciate your honesty. But you're right about the emotional turmoil related to the past. As you've figured out, I'm not good with trusting men. And I'm really not accustomed to being around someone like you."

"Like me?" he echoed in confusion.

"Nice and considerate and…" Her voice trailed off and she shook her head. "Never mind, I'm exhausted and not making much sense. If you don't mind, I'm going to head to bed early."

"Of course." He wanted to say more, to continue their conversation, but he let her go, sensing she'd already said more than she'd intended. Holding Rory in one arm, she picked up the blanket from the floor and disappeared into the bedroom.

Stretching out on the sofa, he bent his elbow behind his head and tried to relax. He felt better after telling her the truth about Debra and Carly, but wished she'd been as comfortable opening up to him. Maybe it would come over time. The idea that Lacy didn't know about nice men didn't sit well. She deserved so much better.

Duchess came over and curled up on the floor beside him. He hadn't expected to sleep, but must have because a soft noise woke him up.

He blinked in the darkness, trying to figure out what he'd heard. Lifting his head, he noticed Lacy was in the kitchen, pouring water into a kettle.

"Can't sleep?" he asked softly.

She spun around to face him, her hand hovering over her heart. "I'm sorry if I woke you."

"No biggie." He was about to sit up when Duchess abruptly leapt to her feet and ran over to the door. At first he assumed the dog had to go outside, but then she began to growl low in her throat.

Matt didn't waste a second. He shoved his feet into his shoes, then grabbed his weapon and his jacket. He picked up the phone, dialing Miles. "Go into the bed-room and watch over Rory," he commanded. "I'm call-ing my brother for backup."

"But that will take too long, won't it?" she protested as she turned off the burner beneath the tea kettle.

He didn't want to admit she was right. "Duchess and I are a team. We'll be fine. Stay in the bedroom and don't open the door to anyone except for me or one of my brothers."

"Be careful," Lacy whispered.

He nodded and called Miles. When he didn't answer, Matt tried Mike. Thankfully Mike picked up almost immediately. "What's wrong?"

Duchess's growling was getting louder, and Matt could only hope that whoever was outside would think twice about coming after them. "I need backup, ASAP."

"I'm already on my way, because Miles asked me to pick up some book," Mike said. "I'm armed. Hang on till I get there."

"I'll try." He slid the phone into his pocket. Pressing himself against the wall, he carefully opened the door.

Duchess was in full-alert mode, her nose practically twitching with the need to track the intruder. He ex-haled and then darted outside, Duchess hot on his heels.

As they'd practiced earlier, he went left and Duch-ess went right. It took a few minutes for his eyes to ad-just to the darkness. The new moon was barely a sliver in the sky, and there wasn't any snow on the ground to assist in picking out an intruder.

He made his way to the corner of the cabin, making sure no one was using the SUV for cover. Once he'd cleared that area, he paused to consider his next move. He heard Duchess moving through the brush and hoped she'd picked up the scent.

His partner let out a sharp bark, and he instinctively lunged toward the sound, his heart pounding with adrenaline. He moved from tree to tree. Suddenly a sharp crack echoed through the night, followed by a burning sensation along the outer edge of his left bicep.

He'd been shot!

Ignoring the pain, he continued his zigzagging path toward the area where Duchess had barked, alerting him to the presence of the gunman, silently praying that he and Duchess could hold the guy off long enough for Mike to arrive.

And to keep Lacy and Rory safe.

ELEVEN

Watching Matt and Duchess disappearing into the darkness outside gave Lacy an overwhelming sense of dread. Nausea swirled in her belly. She felt acutely vulnerable and alone, but forced herself to push aside her emotions in order to check on Rory.

The baby was sleeping. She watched him for a moment. Her instincts were to lift him up and wrap him against her body with the shawl, the way she had the night she'd escaped from Jill's. But doing that would risk waking him up, so she hesitated and considered her options.

What she needed was some sort of weapon.

She quickly returned to the main living space, sweeping her gaze over the area. A kitchen knife? She wrinkled her nose. The attacker would have to get close for it to be of use.

One of the split logs? Too bulky.

Fireplace poker? She picked it up, testing the weight in her hand. Long enough to keep the intruder at arm's length, but not very heavy.

Since there wasn't anything better, she took the poker into the bedroom and stood protectively over Rory. Then she decided it would be best for Rory to be positioned well out of sight, so she slid the dresser drawer beneath the edge of the bed frame so he was completely protected, just in case whoever was lurking around outside managed to get past her.

Satisfied the baby was as safe as possible, she crossed over and stood near the doorway, her left side pressed against the wall, the fireplace poker resting on her right shoulder like a baseball bat.

Oppressive silence pressed against her chest, and every muscle in her body was tense. She silently prayed for strength and courage, hoping Matt was right and that God would watch over them. Especially an innocent baby like Rory.

A sense of calm nudged her fear aside. She would defend Rory, no matter what it took. No one would harm him, not while she was alive and kicking. If anyone but Matt or his brother came through the doorway, she would be ready.

The faint sound of Duchess barking reached her ears, causing her to hold her breath and listen carefully. Was that a good sign or a bad one? She didn't know, but hoped it meant Duchess had found the intruder's scent and was right now tracking him down.

A loud bang echoed through the night and she startled badly, gasping in horror. A gunshot? Was Matt the one shooting, or was it possible either he or Duchess had been the target?

And how had their location here at this remote cabin been found? The only call they'd made besides to Matt's brothers was to his boss.

Silence filled the cabin again, and she tried not to imagine Matt or Duchess lying on the ground bleeding. She swallowed hard, trying to decide what she should do. Matt had told her to stay here, but if he or Duchess were in trouble, shouldn't she take Rory and make a run for the SUV?

Or better yet, she needed to call 911 using the disposable phone. Matt said he'd called for backup, but she wasn't sure who would arrive first, the police or his brother. Being out in an isolated cabin didn't guarantee a quick emergency response. The shooter could easily break into the cabin before the police arrived.

That settled it. She had to do something.

Loosening her grip on the poker, she pulled the cell phone from her pocket and punched in the emergency number. Before she could push the send button, she heard the cabin door opening.

"Lacy, it's me, Matt. Are you and Rory all right?" Matt's voice caused a wave of relief to hit hard. She peeked around the corner, reassuring herself that he was really okay. He stood in the kitchen with Duchess at his side.

"I'm so glad to see you." She ran toward him, barely pausing long enough to toss the poker onto the sofa before throwing herself into his embrace. Matt wrapped his strong arms around her, holding her close. She closed her eyes for a moment, breathing in the aroma of pine trees mixed with his own unique scent and thanking God for keeping him safe.

"Hey, it's okay," he murmured, his face buried against her hair. "I'm fine and so is Duchess."

It took her a few minutes to find her voice. She didn't want to let him go but leaned back enough to look up into his eyes. "I heard the gunshot. Did you find him?"

"No, unfortunately he got away." The way Matt avoided her direct gaze made her frown.

"Did you get a good look at him?" she pressed. "Were you able to recognize him at all?"

"Not exactly." He dropped his arms and stepped away, and that's when she saw the dark wetness staining the side along his upper arm.

"You're hit!" Her voice came out in a squeak.

"It's nothing, just a scratch."

"Matt? Are you okay?" a voice called from outside.

"That's Mike." Matt opened the front door and gestured for his brother to come in. "Thanks for getting here so quickly. I think the perp saw your headlights and knew I had help coming, so he took off."

The man who entered the cabin resembled Matt in some ways, but was a little taller with long dark hair that he wore loose around his face. Lacy crossed her arms over her chest, feeling ill at ease, even though she knew Matt's brother wasn't anyone to be afraid of.

Pathetic that she was only comfortable around Matt. Clearly, she needed to curb her dependence on the man.

But not tonight.

"Sit down so I can take a look at your injury," she said, addressing Matt.

"I'm fine. Now that Mike's here, we need to head back outside to check the area for clues. We can only hope the shooter left something behind."

Lacy wanted to protest, but Rory began to cry. Remembering she'd tucked his drawer beneath the bed, she dashed into the bedroom and gently pulled him out.

"It's okay, sweetie, I'm here. You're fine. We're all fine." It occurred to her that she was telling all this to Rory in an effort to soothe herself. She nuzzled his neck, changed his diaper and then brought him into the kitchen.

Matt, Mike and Duchess had all gone back outside, but this time, she wasn't afraid to be alone. Granted, the danger wasn't over, but she felt more secure knowing that Matt and Duchess had assistance. They would be okay.

She fed Rory his bottle, gazing down at his sweet face, her heart full of love.

This was what was important. Not her tangled feelings toward Matt, but caring for this little boy who'd already been through so much. She took a deep breath and let it out slowly.

She could do this. With God's help, anything was possible.

When Rory finished his bottle, she set him in the infant car seat and began washing bottles. She kept glancing at the clock, wondering what was taking the guys so long.

Had they found something?

It suddenly occurred to her that whether they had found a clue or not, this idyllic time at the cabin was over.

The wave of despair returned full force. Now that they'd been found, she was certain they would have to go back on the run once again.

"Over here," Matt called, when Duchess alerted near the base of a tree. The way she sniffed the ground, then sat down made him realize she'd discovered something. He crouched near the ground and carefully flashed a light over it.

Mike came over to join him. "What is it?"

Matt used his gloved hand to pick up the shell casing. "Belongs to a thirty-eight, standard issue weapon for cops. Proof the shooter was in this area when he took his shot at me."

"Okay, but where did he go from here?"

Matt glanced around and shrugged. "I'm not sure. But Duchess can help."

Mike nodded and stepped back, giving him room.

"Find, Duchess. Find!" He pointed to the ground where his partner had picked up the shooter's scent, and Duchess immediately went to work.

The dog sniffed around on the ground, then began following the scent, heading due south.

Matt trailed behind his partner, giving Duchess plenty of space to do what she was best at. Duchess was smart, but her path was anything but straight. In fact she wove in and around trees, often backtracking to alert on an area where the gunman's scent was particularly strong.

"Good girl," Matt praised. "Find, Duchess. Find!"

That was all the encouragement she needed to get back on track. On the third spot where Duchess alerted, Matt caught a glimpse of white. He went down on one knee and found what looked like a partial gum wrapper that still carried a hint of cinnamon.

It had definitely been left recently, but not necessarily by the gunman. Still, he picked it up with gloved fingers and placed it in an evidence bag with the same care he'd taken with the shell casing.

"What's that up ahead?" Mike asked.

Matt frowned and straightened. "I'm not sure. A road?"

"Duchess is heading straight for it," Mike pointed out.

Matt nodded and hurried to catch up with his partner. Duchess had indeed found what appeared to be a dirt road, with a fresh set of tire tracks.

Duchess alerted on the spot then picked something off the ground, bringing it over to Matt. He knelt down to take the item from his partner.

A black knit cap, just like the one he'd seen on the guy who'd shot at Lacy outside the gas station.

"Good girl," he praised.

"Nice," Mike agreed. "There may be a stray hair in there that we can use to match DNA."

Matt nodded, placing the hat in the evidence bag. Then he gestured to the ruts in the ground. "What kind of vehicle do you think was here? These look too small to belong to a truck."

Mike nodded. "I have to agree. They're barely fourteen-inch tires. My best guess? They belong to a sedan of some sort."

"We can take pictures," Matt said thoughtfully. "It might be possible for someone in the forensic lab to find out more."

"You trust the forensic lab?" his brother asked drily. "I got the impression that you were pretty much working this case on your own, without support from the precinct."

That much was true, but then again, they would need this evidence to prosecute the case at some point. "Yeah, for now, but I'd still like you to take some photos."

"Fine with me." His brother went to work, taking photographs of the tire marks.

When Mike finished, Matt gestured toward the cabin. "Come on, let's head back. I don't feel comfortable leaving Lacy and Rory there alone any longer than necessary."

Mike quirked an eyebrow. "Really? Is that because of the potential danger, or because she's pretty and you're emotionally involved?"

He refused to take his brother's bait. "The danger is real. I have the wound, shell casing and hat to prove it. Come, Duchess," he commanded. His partner instantly came over, and he turned to head back toward the cabin. Thankfully, Mike left the subject of Lacy and Rory alone.

The interior warmth of the cabin greeted them. Or maybe it was Lacy's tentative smile he was reacting to. He hadn't realized just how nice it was to have someone waiting when he walked in the door.

Man, he needed to get a grip. His brother was right—he shouldn't allow himself to become emotionally involved with the woman and baby he was duty-bound to protect.

"Did you find anything?" Lacy asked.

Matt nodded. "Yeah, the perp went through the woods until he came upon the dirt road where he must have left his car."

"Or where someone with a car was waiting for him," Mike added. "You don't know he was working alone."

"True." Matt shrugged out of his jacket, wincing as the movement aggravated his injury. "I need to wash up, then we'll have to hit the road. The cabin's been compromised."

"Yeah, any idea how this guy tracked you here?" Mike asked.

"It had to be the phone call Matt made to his boss," Lacy said, opening the small first-aid kit. "Sit down. I need to look at your arm."

"I'm fine," he protested.

"I'd rather decide for myself. The last thing I need is for you to get sick from some sort of infection."

He dropped into the chair but didn't dare glance at Mike, afraid he would see the all-too-familiar knowing smile.

Lacy filled a bowl full of warm water and brought it over to the table. He shrugged out of his shirt, thankful he was wearing a T-shirt underneath. She leaned close, and he smelled a hint of baby shampoo mixed with lavender.

"This is more than a scratch," Lacy said sternly. "You should probably go to the ER. Antibiotic ointment may not be enough protection against a possible infection."

"I'm not going to the ER," he said, his tone sharper than he'd intended. "Just wrap it up for now. We can't afford to linger. The gunman could easily come back."

He could tell she wasn't happy, but she went about cleaning the wound, drying it and adding antibiotic ointment before wrapping gauze around his arm. He was acutely aware of the gentle touch of her fingertips against his skin and prayed she would hurry up already.

"Mike, don't you think he should go to the ER?" Lacy asked, stepping away, finally, to dispose of the bloodstained water in the sink.

"No, I don't." Matt shrugged back into his shirt, hiding a smile at his brother's blunt statement. "Gunshot wounds need to be reported to the police, and we don't have time for that nonsense."

Lacy scowled but didn't argue.

"Get your and Rory's things together, okay?" Matt caught Lacy's gaze and gave her a reassuring smile. "It will be fine."

Lacy nodded and disappeared into the bedroom. He opened cupboard doors, pulling out the food items they'd purchased along with the containers of formula. Mike helped, and it didn't take long to fill a couple of grocery bags.

"Guess there's no such thing as traveling light when it comes to a baby," his brother muttered.

"No, there isn't." He glanced down at Rory, who'd

fallen back asleep after being fed. "For such a little guy, he needs a lot of stuff."

"I'll say." Mike hoisted the bags off the counter. "I think we should take my SUV into town. I'll get a ride back here to pick up this one. I don't like the idea that the gunman may have the license plate number."

Yeah, Matt didn't much like it, either. He took the last of the kitchen grocery bags, then slung the computer case over his shoulder, making sure the notebook was safely secured inside before following his brother out the door. Mike was in the process of securing Duchess's crate in the back of his SUV.

"Thanks for backing me up," Matt said, storing bags in the back seat.

Mike shrugged. "You'd do the same for me."

True. They walked silently back into the house, and Matt noticed that Duchess was standing protectively over Rory's car seat. Lacy came out of the bedroom carrying three more grocery bags, her expression softening when she saw Duchess and Rory.

"She's so amazing," Lacy said in a low husky voice. "I had no idea what I was missing growing up. We never had pets. Jill and I always asked for one but our dad refused."

The thought of Lacy never owning a pet made him sad and angry at the same time. He truly didn't get people who didn't value pets. "You should get a dog, once this is over."

Her faint smile vanished. "Maybe. But I'm sure I'll be busy enough between working and taking care of Rory."

Matt almost offered his help, but Mike chose that moment to step between them, reaching for the bags Lacy held that contained diapers, clothing and a blanket.

"I'll take these to the car," his brother offered. "Bring Rory and whatever else Duchess needs. And don't forget to put out the fire in the woodstove."

Matt moved away to take care of the woodstove first, then tucked Duchess's food and water dishes beneath his arm. Lacy was holding on to Rory's car seat, the shawl wrapped around him to keep him warm.

"Ready?" he asked, taking the car seat from her fingers.

"I guess. Where are we going?"

"There's a hotel outside town that's run by a former firefighter and his brother. They're cop-friendly—in fact, the owner used to work with my brother Mitch."

"Okay." She preceded him outside.

He shut off the lights. "Come, Duchess," he said. He tucked Rory's car seat in the back, leaving Lacy to secure it with the seat belt so that he could get Duchess into the back. He slid in the front beside his brother, not liking the thought of leaving the police-issued SUV behind, but knowing it wasn't worth the risk.

Ten minutes later they were on the highway. Matt couldn't help stewing about how the phone call to his boss had been intercepted.

"We're not going in to meet your lieutenant, are we?" Lacy asked.

He and Mike exchanged a glance, and he knew they were both thinking about that thirty-eight shell casing they'd found.

"No," Matt assured her. "Not until I can figure out what's going on."

"Good." Lacy's relief was palpable as she relaxed into her seat and closed her eyes.

Matt filled his brother in on the events that had transpired over the past few days, including the contents of the notebook they'd found in Williams's gym locker.

"So it's highly likely the gunman really is a cop," Mike said in a hushed tone. They were being careful not to wake up Lacy and Rory.

"That's the way I'm leaning," Matt agreed.

"You trust your boss?" Mike asked.

He hesitated, then shrugged. "Right now, I don't trust anyone outside the family."

His brother nodded, and Matt knew he understood. The Callahan clan was known to stick together, through thick and thin. Yeah, they sometimes fought or argued, but at the end of the day, Matt would drop what he was doing to help any one of his siblings.

And they would do the same for him. But he couldn't stay off-grid indefinitely. He needed to figure out the blackmail scheme and who else was involved.

The gunman was either the person who had the most to lose if the truth came to light, or was hired by someone whose name was in that notebook.

He needed to uncover the truth, before it was too late.

TWELVE

Lacy awoke to the sound of muffled male voices. It took a moment for her to realize the car had stopped moving. She lifted her head, wincing at the crimp in her muscles from the odd angle at which she'd fallen asleep.

Gently massaging the back of her neck, she first checked to make sure Rory was okay, then squinted through the passenger-side window to where three men were standing outside, talking. Duchess was out there, too.

Matt and Mike were easy to recognize, but the third man took a moment to place. Oh, yes, Miles, the homicide detective.

The three Callahans were similar in size and build, but her gaze lingered on Matt, the most handsome, at least in her opinion. He wasn't as tall as the others, but there was something so compelling about him. More than just the fact that he'd kept her and Rory safe.

Enough mooning over the man. She gave herself a mental shake and averted her gaze to assess the motel. The American Lodge appeared to have two levels. Mike broke away from the group to walk inside the building, returning a few minutes later with what looked like small plastic key cards.

She pushed open her door and jumped out, shivering in the cool night air despite wearing the jacket Matt had purchased.

"Hi, Lacy. Here." Matt handed over one of the room keys. "We have connecting rooms just like last time, and they're both on the bottom floor, rooms two and three."

"Okay." She tucked the key in her coat pocket and turned to grab Rory's car seat. Before she could even open the door, Matt stopped her with a hand on her arm.

"Let me take care of hauling everything inside."

She hesitated, knowing that she needed to learn to do this stuff on her own, but was too exhausted to put up a fight.

Matt opened the door and carefully unbuckled the car seat without jostling the sleeping baby. She leaned in behind him to grab two of the plastic grocery bags, carrying them over to room three. The interior of the place was clean and tidy, a pleasant surprise. As an added bonus, there was both a crib and a small fridge tucked into the corner, perfect for storing Rory's bottles.

"Hope you'll be comfortable here," Matt said, brushing past her to set Rory's car seat in the center of the bed.

"It's great, thanks." She quickly began to unpack their belongings so that she would have everything ready before Rory woke up. It was late, just past midnight, and she had no idea how much longer he'd sleep.

Logically, it made sense to try to rest while he did, but she heard the brothers talking through the connecting door that Matt had left ajar, and she wanted to hear the plan.

After all, she was in danger, too.

"My hunch is gambling," Miles was saying as she entered. "These dollar amounts are likely related to high-stakes poker."

"Couldn't they be just as easily related to drugs or prostitution?" Matt asked. He took the notebook from his brother's fingers, glancing at her as she took a seat beside him. "We can't guess. We need to find out for sure."

For some odd reason, she didn't want Matt to give his brother the notebook. Not because she didn't trust Matt's family, but it was one of the only tangible pieces of evidence they'd found.

"May I?" she asked, tapping the notebook in Matt's hand.

He hesitated, then shrugged. "Why not? Miles will be taking it to the precinct soon."

She slowly turned the pages, searching for—what exactly? She'd already looked over the contents, going through the initials and numbers written alongside in small cramped script.

While flipping through the pages, she came across the halfway point, where the notations abruptly ended. The last initials were J.B.D.

She frowned, thinking they sounded familiar. But either she was imagining it, or was simply too exhausted to think clearly because she couldn't figure out why they would be.

There were, however, slight indentations on the opposite page, as if someone had written a note, pressing hard enough on the pad beneath to leave a mark.

She jumped to her feet. "I'll be right back."

"Lacy?" Matt called after her, but she ignored him. Moving silently in her room to avoid waking up Rory, she pulled out the small drawer beneath the desk. She immediately found what she was looking for—a dull, stubby pencil.

Matt came up to stand behind her, but she did her

best to ignore him as she lightly brushed the lead tip over the page, revealing the markings that were left behind.

"Amazing," Matt whispered, his mouth close enough to her ear that she could feel his warm breath caressing her skin.

"I think it's an address." She picked up the notebook and gestured for him to follow her back into the other room, where they wouldn't disturb Rory. "See? 2220 S. Handover Lane."

"You found an address?" Miles leapt up to meet them.

"I don't recognize it, do you?" Matt asked, showing him the address. He unpacked the laptop.

"Nope." Miles joined Matt as they peered at the computer screen, waiting for the internet to connect.

Lacy walked over to stand on Matt's other side, curious as to what sort of building the address belonged to. A private residence? Or some sort of business? She was glad to note that the address didn't match her sister's home.

It seemed to take forever for the computer to boot up and connect to the motel Wi-Fi. It wasn't secure, but since they were only looking at Google Maps, she hoped it didn't matter.

"Are you sure that's it?" Miles asked with a frown.

"This is what comes up when I type in the address," Matt confirmed. "It looks like some sort of nightclub called Secrets."

Miles grimaced. "Never heard of it."

"I have," Mike said. When his two brothers looked shocked, he held up his hands. "Hey, I only staked the place out. I never went inside."

Lacy leaned forward, trying to get a better view on

the three-dimensional map. "It looks like a two-story building. Do you think they're both part of the night-club?"

"Good question." Matt drummed his fingers on the table, glanced at the time and sighed. It was heading into one o'clock in the morning. "We need a copy of the blueprints."

"I bet Mitch could get them," Miles said. "But not until daylight hours. He came back to town yesterday from his conference."

"I'll give him a call first thing in the morning." Matt closed the laptop. "It's late. Why don't you guys head out to pick up my SUV at the cabin, and we'll touch base tomorrow."

"Okay," Miles agreed. "Although, I'm going to need to take the notebook in as evidence soon."

Lacy was tempted to pluck the notebook off the table and hold it protectively against her chest, but she needn't have worried. Matt didn't seem willing to let it go, either.

"Give me another twenty-four hours," he said. "Let's just see if we can figure out the source of the black-mail scam."

"Fine. But I'm going to take a few pictures of the pages with my phone." He took out his cell and snapped several photographs.

"Mike, don't forget to email me the pictures of the tire tracks we found," Matt said as his brothers pre-pared to leave.

"Include me, too," Miles added.

Mike nodded, going outside with Miles, leaving a sudden quietness in their wake.

"That was good work, Lacy," Matt said, finally breaking the silence. "The nightclub is a great lead."

She flushed, touched by his praise. "I'm glad."

Matt took a step closer, then stopped. "You've been awesome through all of this. I'm sorry it's taking so long to get to the bottom of it."

"You've been trying, that's what counts." She told herself to turn around and get some rest before Rory woke up for his next feeding, but she wasn't ready to leave him.

She might not ever be ready to leave him.

The knowledge hit her with the force of a brick falling squarely on her head. Oh, no. No. She couldn't do this. She couldn't allow herself to start caring about Matthew Callahan.

"Excuse me, I need to get some sleep." She spun on her heel so fast she nearly fell over her own two feet. With as much grace as she could muster, she ducked into her room.

It was tempting to close and lock the connecting door, but what would that accomplish? Other than to let Matt know how rattled she was.

And prevent him from reaching them in an emergency.

Lacy pulled herself together and closed the connecting door so there was barely a sliver of light shining through. Then she turned and used the bathroom to brush her teeth before sliding into bed.

But as exhausted as she was, sleep didn't come easily. She kept thinking of Matt. Of what her life would be like without him.

About how much she would miss him.

After an hour of struggling with her emotions, she turned to God.

Please, Lord, give me the strength to walk away and to raise Rory on my own.

* * *

Matt forced himself to let Lacy go. Kissing her wasn't smart. She'd been traumatized by her past and so had he. This wasn't the time to dwell on their personal issues. He needed to stay focused on the case so that Lacy and Rory could get back to their normal everyday life.

He took Duchess outside for one last bathroom break, then stretched out on the bed. Duchess lay on the floor beside him. He slept in snatches, attuned to the slightest sound, anxious to get started investigating the nightclub. He felt certain that the place was the key to the information they needed.

The baby's crying brought him upright, and he wiped the sleep from his eyes and rose to his feet. Duchess thumped her tail, but didn't move. He padded through the connecting door. Lacy was still asleep, so he quickly picked Rory up from the crib and looked in the fridge for a bottle.

"Shh, it's okay. I've got you." He tucked the bottle beneath his arm and picked up the diaper and wipes before sneaking back into his room.

Lacy deserved a chance to sleep in. Changing dirty diapers wasn't at the top of his list of fun things to do, but he managed. After washing up, he began warming Rory's bottle under the hot water. Duchess languidly rose to her feet and stretched. She came over, sniffed the baby and licked Rory's cheek.

Rory didn't seem to mind. The baby smiled and played with his feet, then waved his arms around as if he might fly. Matt couldn't help but grin. He didn't have a lot of firsthand experience with babies. Sure, he'd given his brother Marc a hand on occasion, but he'd never taken care of Marc and Kari's son, Max, for more than a couple of hours.

Both Kari and Paige were due to deliver in the next few weeks, so the size of the Callahan family would be increasing very soon. Looking down at Rory, he could easily picture Lacy and Rory fitting right in.

Except he didn't do relationships. He wasn't interested in a ready-made family.

Was he?

Rory and Lacy were tempting, in more ways than one.

When Rory finished his bottle, Matt burped the baby and then held him up so the little guy could stand on his feet. Well, not stand exactly, but exercise his chubby legs.

Duchess went over to position herself by the door, signaling the need to go outside. He debated bundling up Rory and taking him out when he heard Lacy's voice.

"Matt?" She hovered uncertainly in the doorway between their rooms. "I'm sorry if he woke you."

"I don't mind," he responded. "Figured you could use the extra hour of sleep. And you have good timing. I need to take Duchess out."

Her expression turned troubled. "Okay. When you get back we need to give Rory another dose of antibiotic, too. But—did Rory cry? I mean, I can't believe I would sleep through that."

He didn't want her to feel guilty. Everything she'd been through the past few days was stressful enough. "He's a good baby. After I take Duchess out and give her some food and water, we can have breakfast. Are you hungry for anything in particular?"

She came in and lifted Rory from his arms. "I'll have whatever you're having."

"Sounds good." He resisted the urge to plant a kiss on both the baby's head and Lacy's cheek, instead he took Duchess outside while she did her business.

When he returned to the motel room, Lacy was playing with Rory. He dug in his pocket for the car keys Mike had left behind. "Give me a few minutes, okay? I'll leave Duchess here to keep an eye on things."

"All right." If Lacy was afraid to be alone, with only Duchess watching over her, she didn't show it.

It was well over an hour later by the time they'd finished eating and giving Rory his medicine. He called his brother Mitch, relieved when he picked up on the first ring.

"Hello?" his brother answered cautiously.

He realized Mitch hadn't recognized the number. "It's Matt. I need some help if you can spare it."

"Sure, what's up?"

"Are you familiar with a nightclub called Secrets?"

"Is this a test? Did Mom put you up to this?"

"No, it's related to a case I'm involved with." The reference to their mother, Margaret Callahan, made him smile. Their mom lived with their grandmother, Nan, and the two of them would be upset if their sons decided to start frequenting the local nightclubs. "It's located at 2220 South Handover Lane."

"What kind of case?" Mitch asked. "Does it involve arson?"

"No, but I need a copy of the blueprints for the building. As an arson investigator, you have access to them, right?"

"Yeah, I can get them from the city," Mitch agreed. "When do you need them?"

"As soon as possible. We're staying at the American Lodge. If you could bring them over I'd appreciate it."

"We?" his brother echoed. "Who's we?"

"I'm protecting a woman named Lacy Germaine and her three-month-old nephew, Rory."

There was a pause as that information sank in. "Sure, why not? Good thing it's Friday. Otherwise, we would have to wait until after the weekend. Give me a couple of hours in case I have to cut through some red tape."

"You got it. Thanks, Mitch. I really appreciate it."

"I'll call you at this number when I'm on my way."

"Okay. Later." Matt disconnected, glancing over to where Lacy stood with Rory perched on her hip. "It's all set. We'll have the blueprints in a couple of hours."

"Good." She tipped her head to the side. "I'm supposed to report in to work on Monday. Do you think we'll have this wrapped up by then?"

He hesitated, unwilling to gloss over the truth. "I don't know, Lacy. I can promise to do my best, but it all depends on what we find out about the blackmail scheme."

"I know. But since today is Friday, I'll need to let my principal know if I won't be there on Monday."

He walked toward her, wishing he could do something to make this situation better. "You would have to arrange day care for Rory before returning to work anyway, right?"

Her eyes widened and she went pale. "You're right. How could I be so stupid? Of course, I need to arrange child care."

"Hey, give yourself a break. Four days ago, you weren't solely responsible for Rory. Of course, there are a few things that you need to arrange. Will your principal give you time off?"

"I...guess he'll have to." She still looked a bit shell-shocked.

His heart ached for her. "Listen, I'm sure you deserve some bereavement time after your sister's death. And if he won't help you out, I'm sure my mother and grandmother wouldn't mind watching Rory for a couple of days."

Her face drained of color. "No! I mean, I couldn't possibly impose on them like that. They don't even know me."

"Hey, they've watched my brother's kids on occasion. I can guarantee they won't mind."

She swallowed hard, nodded and turned to go back to her room. He listened at the doorway as she called her principal to fill him in on her sister's murder and her need to take custody of her nephew. By the time she finished the conversation, she looked calmer. It seemed her boss had been understanding and had provided her the time off she needed.

Matt couldn't help feeling a little put off by the fact that she hadn't wanted his mother's and grandmother's help. Yeah, she'd mentioned several times that she needed to be independent, but there was no reason for her to turn her back on his offer.

His phone rang, and he absently answered it. "Hello?"

"Matt? I'm on my way, but there's a small problem," Mitch said.

"What kind of problem?"

"I've picked up a tail. Don't worry, I'll lose him, but it's going to take me longer than planned to meet up with you. Gotta go." Mitch abruptly disconnected.

Matt stood there for a moment, his mind reeling. How in the world had Mitch picked up a tail? His brother hadn't even gotten his phone number until an hour ago.

Was the shooter having every member of his family

watched? It didn't seem possible. Then he thought back to the three officers whose names were in the notebook.

Three cops to keep an eye on his brothers, the ones most likely to give him a hand.

If that was the case, he shouldn't keep asking his brothers for help.

Once he had the blueprints, he would think of a way to work the case with Duchess as his only partner.

THIRTEEN

Principal Joel Harty had been understanding about her request for time off, even though it put him in a bind to find coverage for her at the last minute. Her teaching contract provided for bereavement leave, which took care of the first three days, and there was also a provision for adoption. If Jill didn't have a will it would take time for her to go through the formal adoption process.

Securing a couple of weeks off work should have made her feel better, but the reality of her situation was sobering. She needed to arrange day care, clean and put her sister's house up for sale, then find a new place to live. She didn't want to raise Rory in an apartment—besides, she only had one bedroom. And she also didn't want to live in Jill and David's house, not when her sister had been murdered there.

A wave of panic seized her by the throat, the enormity of the task ahead stealing her breath away. How on earth would she manage all of that in a couple weeks?

By taking it one step at a time and leaning on God's strength. Peace washed over her, wiping the panic away. She wasn't in this alone any longer. She had faith. And for now, she had Matthew Callahan. None of the arrangements she needed to make would matter until she and Rory were safe.

"Lacy? Are you all right?" Matt's voice mirrored his concern.

She smiled and nodded, shifting Rory to her other hip. "Sure. My boss granted me the time off. I don't need to report back to the classroom for three weeks. I can ask for another three weeks off, but it would be unpaid time. I figured I would hold off on that for now."

"Great. I'm happy to hear it."

She glanced around the motel room, realizing she'd been in her own little world for the past half hour. She hadn't paid the least bit of attention to Matt's side of the conversation. "So Mitch is bringing the nightclub blueprints?"

Matt's expression sobered. "Yeah, but there's a slight complication. He's picked up a tail. He needs to get rid of whoever is following him before heading over."

She dropped into the closest chair, her knees feeling weak. What next? First, being found at the cabin, and now this. It seemed like the gunman was always one step ahead of them. "How? What does that mean?"

"I'm afraid that Williams's cop friends must have figured I'd turn to my brothers for help, and they're attempting to keep an eye on them."

Lacy strove to remain calm, but it wasn't easy. She should be used to this type of thing by now. She thought about the fact that both Mike and Miles had come to their rescue. "Is it possible this motel is compromised? Do we need to move to a different location?"

"I don't think so. I know for a fact we weren't followed last night." Matt's gaze turned thoughtful. "But having a leak within the department isn't reassuring, either. They have access to a lot of resources. For all we know, there are other cops involved in the black-mail scheme. I can't stand the idea of placing my family in danger."

She shivered and cuddled Rory closer. "Okay then. We'll stay put for now. But we really need to understand what's going on. Why are they after us? Because of the notebook?"

Matt shrugged. "Probably. It shows a motive related to Williams's murder."

"Jill's murder, too," Lacy murmured. "I'm a witness, at least to what I overheard. But now that David is dead, it doesn't make sense that some guy is still coming after me."

"Keep in mind, you found the key to the locker," Matt pointed out. "It's possible he assumes you know more than you do. That you overheard information that might be used against them. Think about it—David kills your sister, then his buddies come out to help him. Only at some point, they kill him. Maybe Williams gave them some reason to believe you know all about the blackmail scheme."

Matt's theory was horrifying, yet logical. She swallowed hard. "All right, so they think I know details about the blackmail, and obviously, since you're helping me, they're assuming I've told you everything." Saying the words out loud didn't make them less terrifying. "What's to prevent them from assuming your brothers know everything as well?"

It was Matt's turn to drop into a chair. Duchess must have sensed his distress, because she came over and nudged him. He absently petted the dog. "You're right," he agreed, his voice low and gravelly. "It's too late. I've already put Mitch, Miles and Mike in danger."

"Hey, this isn't your fault." She edged her chair closer

so she could rest her hand on his arm. "That's what you told me, remember? This is the gunman's fault, along with those cops who are trying to keep their little blackmail scheme a secret. They are the ones breaking the law. The ones who placed your brothers in danger. Not you."

"I know." His tone lacked conviction. "I just— If something happens to them…" His voice trailed off and he shook his head helplessly.

"We need to keep our faith in God," she reminded him. "I hadn't really believed until you taught me about faith. Helped me to understand and to trust in God's plan."

After a long moment, he sighed, covered her hand with his and nodded. "You're right, Lacy. We needed someone to trust, and I would be there for any one of them."

"Of course you would." She was awestruck at how it must feel to have so many siblings, along with a mother and a grandmother, and hoped Matt knew how blessed he was.

Rory batted at her, and she looked at the baby, who happened to be the only family member she had left in the world.

Enough with the pity party. She disentangled her fingers from Matt's and rose to her feet. Rory was getting antsy, so she placed the blanket on the motel room floor and set him down. He immediately rolled over, giggling with joy. Then he planted his arms and lifted his head high, looking around at his surroundings.

"He's getting so strong," she said, amazed at how quickly Rory was changing right before her eyes.

"Yeah, he sure is." Matt's phone rang and he quickly answered it. "Mitch? Everything okay?"

This time, she paid attention, keeping an eye on Rory so he wouldn't roll into the furniture. There wasn't nearly as much space here for him to move around as there had been at the cabin. She had to pick him up several times, placing him back in the center of the blanket.

"I'm glad to hear you lost him," Matt was saying. There was another long pause as he listened. "Okay, see you in fifteen."

Rory giggled again, obviously enjoying the game of rolling away from her. They played until there was a sharp knock at the door.

She picked Rory up off the floor and turned to meet yet another member of the Callahan clan. Like the other two brothers, Mitch was taller than Matt, but he had dark blond hair cut short. His eyes were bright blue compared to Matt's green ones. He had a long roll of papers tucked beneath his arm. He took a moment to bend over to rub Duchess before facing her and Matt.

"Thanks for coming. This is Lacy and her nephew, Rory."

Lacy stepped forward, offering her hand. "Nice to meet you."

"Likewise," Mitch said with a smile. "I'm sorry to hear you're in danger."

She nodded, glancing at Matt. "We're all in danger."

"We'll keep you and Rory safe," Matt assured her.

"I know." She held Matt's gaze for a long minute. He'd opened up to her about his past, but she hadn't been as good about telling him about herself. "I trust you more than I've ever trusted anyone in my entire life."

He took a step toward her, then abruptly stopped, as if remembering they weren't alone.

The air between them shimmered with awareness.

For several long moments it was as if she and Matt were completely isolated in the room. She couldn't help thinking about their last kiss and wishing he would kiss her again.

Then Mitch seemed to notice the tension, too. "I'll—um—wait outside for a bit, give you guys some privacy."

"No need," Matt said, tearing his gaze away. "We have to focus on work."

That quickly, the moment was broken, leaving Lacy to wonder if Matt was fighting his feelings for her, or if it was nothing more than wishful thinking on her part. For all she knew, he wasn't ready for a relationship after the way he'd lost his former girlfriend and her daughter.

Which meant she was in big trouble.

Because she was certain her feelings for him were moving beyond the friendship category, morphing into something deeper.

"Thanks for getting the blueprints," Matt said, taking them from his brother and spreading them out on the bed. He needed to pull himself together. Thinking about how sweet it was to kiss Lacy wasn't smart.

In fact, one slip could get them all killed.

"What exactly are you looking for?" Mitch asked, staring down at the drawings.

He was keenly aware of Lacy leaving them alone, presumably to put Rory down in his crib. He reminded himself to focus on the case, not Lacy. "I'd like you to walk me through them first," Matt said. "I need to understand the layout of the place. This is the main floor, right?"

"Yes." Mitch pointed to the south side of the building. "This is the front door. The dance floor is here, and the bar area is along the east wall. There are a few offices here." He traced a finger over several small boxed-in shapes. "And an exit along the back of the building."

"Okay, what's on the second floor?"

"More club space, another dance floor and another bar."

Matt's shoulders slumped. He'd been so sure this place was the key to figuring out what was going on. "I was hoping there would be private rooms of some kind."

"There's a large private room and a few smaller ones on the lower level." Mitch shuffled the blueprints around, pulling one from the bottom and laying it across the top. "Right here, see?"

"That's it," Matt said, satisfaction surging through his bloodstream. "I bet that's the location. Whatever they're doing down there would be drowned out by the loud music and dancing on the upper levels of the nightclub."

"Gambling?" Mitch suggested.

Matt nodded slowly. "Yeah, that's what Miles and I think. The notebook has initials with what look to be dollar amounts. There are other possibilities, but looking at the layout of the nightclub, I'm convinced they're running an illegal gambling ring."

"Why gambling?" Lacy asked from the connecting doorway, her pretty brow puckered in a frown.

"I think there are extra zeros that belong on the end of these dollar amounts. In other words, these are thousands, not hundreds. I can't imagine prostitution costing that much, or drugs for that matter." He dropped his gaze to the blueprint of the lower level of Secrets. "High-stakes gambling seems to fit the best."

Lacy approached the drawings. "And you think

David found out about the gambling and was black-mailing the players?"

Matt hesitated, then shrugged. "This is all specu-lation at this point, but yes, let's say that he found out about the illegal gambling, maybe even played along for a while. But then he realized he could make more money by getting a cut of what the players won. So he began to blackmail them, threatening to go to the po-lice commissioner with what he knew."

"But he was a cop, just as several of his buddies were cops," Lacy countered. "He couldn't possibly think he could blackmail them all."

"From what you described, Williams thought he was tough stuff. He claimed to be in the Special Forces, which wasn't true." Matt shrugged. "Maybe his bud-dies didn't figure out he was the one doing the black-mailing until recently."

"And that's when they killed him," Lacy agreed. "Ex-cept they didn't realize that David had hidden away his notes related to the people involved."

"Until we found it in his gym locker," Matt finished. "And only because you managed to find the key."

A faint smile tugged at the corner of Lacy's mouth. "Yeah, I guess I did."

Matt couldn't tear his gaze away from Lacy's. How was it that he hadn't fully appreciated everything she'd contributed to the case so far? Without the notebook, they wouldn't even know about the blackmail.

"So what's the next move?" Mitch asked.

He turned toward his brother. "I think Duchess and I need to scope this place out, see if she can pick up the scent of the gunman."

Mitch looked perplexed. "How would she be able to do that?"

"One of the perps dropped his knit cap while escaping from the cabin." He pulled the evidence bag out of his pocket to show his brother. "We know the nightclub is tied to the blackmail. If we can connect the gunman to the nightclub, then we'll know for sure we're on the right track."

"Isn't it likely that the gunman is one of David's cop friends?" Lacy asked.

"Yes, but which one?"

"Maybe they're in it together," Mitch pointed out.

Matt hesitated, then shrugged. "I don't know, maybe. I saw one gunman attempt to kill Lacy outside the convenience store. And I think there was only one gunman outside the cabin. If he was working with someone, they would have attempted to flank the place in order to trap us. The more I think about it, the more I'm convinced we are hiding from one guy. A well-connected, talented cop who knows how to use his resources in tracking us down."

Mitch's cell phone shrilled loudly, drawing his attention to it. His brother turned away to answer it, and it didn't take long for Matt to realize that his brother was being called to the scene of a fire. "I'll be there in thirty minutes," Mitch promised, then faced him. "I'm sorry, but I have to go."

"I understand. Thanks for the blueprints." He walked Mitch to the door.

"Listen, be careful, okay?" Mitch said as he opened the motel room door. "Don't go into the club without backup."

"I won't," Matt assured him. "But I still need to do a little reconnaissance."

"Yeah, well, stay safe. I'll check in with you later." Mitch waved at Lacy before heading to his car.

"I hope you're not planning to leave me and Rory here alone," Lacy said, leveling him with a narrow glare.

"No, of course not." It would be one thing to leave Duchess behind to act as a guard, but he needed his partner's assistance in tracking the gunman's scent. "I guess we should wait for Rory to wake up."

"That would be nice," Lacy agreed. "And it won't take long for me to feed him first, either."

Matt used the time to work with Duchess for a bit outside, then to study the blueprints Mitch had left behind. There was only one door leading down to the lower level from outside the building. There was another stairwell leading down from the offices located on the main level.

After Lacy had taken care of changing and feeding Rory, they headed out to the SUV. He put Duchess in the back, while Lacy buckled Rory into his car seat. Finally, they were on their way back into the city.

The nightclub wasn't difficult to find, although the building sure looked empty and vacant during the daytime. He was glad the place was closed down. It made it easier for Duchess to pick up the scent.

He drove past the building, then circled around to a spot located a couple of blocks away. "We're getting out here," he explained to Lacy. "I want you to drive around for a while, staying far away from here."

She gnawed at her lower lip. "For how long?"

"Twenty minutes. If Duchess can't pick up the gunman's scent by then, it's not likely she'll find it at all."

Lacy gave a tight nod. "Okay, so I'll meet you right here in twenty minutes."

"Yes. Keep your phone handy, just in case." He shut the engine down and handed her the keys. Then he released the back hatch, letting Duchess out. "If something happens, call one of my brothers," he added, as he slid out from behind the wheel. "Start with Miles, then Mike, then Mitch."

Lacy switched places, climbing over the console to the driver's seat. "Matt?"

He glanced over his shoulder. "Yes?"

She pressed her lips together, then tried to smile. "Be careful, okay? I expect to see you here in twenty minutes."

"Will do." He shut the car door and waited for her to pull away before turning his attention to his partner. "Come, Duchess."

The dog came to stand beside him and he walked toward the nightclub, scanning the area for anything suspicious.

A block from the building, he stopped and offered the scent in the evidence bag to Duchess. "Find, Duchess. Find!"

Duchess buried her nose in the knit cap, then went to work. She sniffed the ground, weaving back and forth as she attempted to pick up the scent. The conditions weren't ideal—finding a scent in nature was easier than in the city—but he hoped, prayed, Duchess would come through for him.

She alerted on a spot where a grassy area met up against the sidewalk. "Good girl," he praised, rubbing her glossy coat. "Find, Duchess."

Duchess continued tracking the scent, leading him to the back door of the building, the one that would take people down to the lower level and the private rooms there.

"Good girl, Duchess." Now he knew for certain the gunman had been here.

Glancing at his watch, he realized that he only had six

minutes to get back to the meeting spot. He put Duchess on the leash and left the nightclub the way he'd come.

Matt stopped short when he caught a glimpse of another man coming toward the building from the opposite direction. Reacting quickly, he ducked into a doorway, bringing Duchess with him.

He waited for what seemed like eons, but was barely a full minute, for the man to go past him on the opposite side of the street. Staying deep in the shadows, Matt was able to get a good look at the man's face.

The familiar features made him freeze.

No, it couldn't be. Matt held his breath, watching as the man's determined stride took him directly toward the nightclub.

When the guy was out of his field of vision, Matt edged closer, peeking around the corner just in time to see him walk up to the door leading downstairs to the lower level. He knocked twice, the door opened and he disappeared inside.

Matt stood there, trying to wrap his mind around it. The man who'd just walked into the nightclub was none other than Judge Byron Dugan. The judge who'd presided, albeit for only one day, over his twin sister, Maddy's case against Alexander Pietro.

The judge whose name had been all over the news because he'd been receiving death threats.

Related to the blackmail scheme? Oh, yeah.

There was no denying it. Judge Dugan was involved in the gambling ring.

The fact that the judge was heading inside made him think there was a game starting any moment. Matt knew he needed to move fast if he wanted to catch them in the act.

FOURTEEN

Lacy felt vulnerable as she drove away, watching Matt and Duchess in the rearview mirror. There was no reason to be concerned. She knew Matt was armed and that he and Duchess were only attempting to track the gunman's scent, nothing more.

Still, it wasn't easy to shake off the niggling worry.

She turned the radio up and began to sing along with the happy rhythmic song. Thankfully, Rory was content enough to ride in the car, waving his arms and kicking his legs in the seat as if following along with the beat.

After several turns, she feared she might get lost, so she stopped singing and paid closer attention to the street signs. She didn't know this area very well. Her life had revolved around teaching, getting together for monthly book clubs with her teacher friends and checking in on her sister.

All of which seemed like a lifetime ago. Today, in this moment, it was difficult to remember what her life had been like before Jill's murder.

Before Rory. And Matt.

Pushing thoughts of her tangled feelings for Matt aside, she focused on her surroundings. After another right turn, she found a familiar street and let out a relieved sigh. Even though she was a good five minutes early, she decided to head over to their designated meeting spot. Better to be early than lost and late.

The bright sunlight warmed the interior of the vehicle, so she shut off the engine and turned in her seat to check on Rory. The baby was gnawing on his fist, and she wondered if he was starting to cut teeth.

There was so much she didn't know about babies. When to start solid foods, when they began to teethe. She had a lot to learn, but didn't every new mother? It wasn't as if women were born with this type of knowledge imprinted in their brains.

Sitting and waiting for Matt and Duchess, time crawled by with incredible slowness. Five minutes passed and Matt still hadn't returned.

Tearing her gaze from the clock, she peered out at her surroundings, hoping to catch a glimpse of him and Duchess. But there was no sign of them. In fact, there was hardly any pedestrian traffic at all.

Another minute went by. She shifted in her seat, debating her options. Matt had instructed her to call his brothers for help, but surely nothing terrible had happened in broad daylight? She imagined she would be able to hear a gunshot from this close range.

She released her death-like grip on the steering wheel, straightening her fingers and forcing herself to take several deep breaths. Maybe Duchess had caught the gunman's scent and they'd followed it farther than Matt had anticipated.

Seven minutes past their meeting time, she finally saw Matt and Duchess approaching the vehicle. Her breath whooshed out in relief, and she forced a smile.

But her grin quickly faded as she caught the grim expression on Matt's face. She pushed the button to open the back hatch for Duchess, then scooted over the console so Matt could climb in behind the wheel.

"What happened?" she asked the minute he was seated.

"We need to get back to the motel, ASAP," he said. He didn't waste any time in pulling away from the curb and heading back toward the interstate. "I think there's a game in progress, and I want to catch them in the act."

Her mind spun at what he was saying. "Why do you think there's a game going on now?" Then it dawned on her, and she answered her own question. "You saw someone go inside."

"Not just someone," Matt corrected, glancing over at her. "Judge Byron Dugan."

"A judge?" She frowned. "Dugan? Isn't that the same guy who was getting death threats?"

"Yes. I was in the courtroom for the first day of the Pietro trial and remembered seeing him." Matt shook his head. "I still can't believe it. Judge Dugan is one of the best judges on the bench. He's fair and doesn't tolerate any nonsense. It's inconceivable to me that he's involved in this."

She hated seeing him so upset and reached out to rest her hand on his forearm. "No one is perfect, Matt. A good man can easily get swept up in an addiction."

"Yeah." He let out a harsh laugh. "I know you're right, but it's the illegal part that's sticking in my throat. A judge is sworn to uphold the law. What if he's used his judicial power to skew a case?"

"I'm not sure what to say." Lacy tightened her grip on his arm, wishing there was more she could do to make him feel better. "We have to believe that he maintained his integrity on the bench. It's possible this part of his life hasn't touched his professional side."

Matt clenched his jaw so tightly, she could see a small muscle pulsing at the corner of his mouth. "Yeah, maybe. But something like this is bound to hang over his head like a dark cloud, tainting every decision he's made. The only consolation is that the DA's office made the deal with Pietro, not Dugan."

She couldn't argue—after all, the same thing would happen to a teacher. The barest hint of a scandal had far-reaching consequences.

They made it back to the motel in record time. She carried Rory's car seat inside, leaving Matt to take care of Duchess.

"So now what?" she asked, as she unbuckled Rory from the infant carrier.

Matt already had his phone to his ear. "Mike? I need backup. How soon can you get here?" There was a slight pause, then he added, "Okay, thirty minutes is reasonable. I'm going to need Mitch and Miles, too. Oh, and make sure you're armed. I'll explain everything once you get here."

Lacy picked up Rory, to comfort herself more than the baby. "What's the plan?"

"Arrest everyone involved in the gambling ring." Matt's voice was flat and clipped. She could tell he was still angry about the ramifications of arresting a judge.

And really, who's to say there weren't other high-profile people involved? Her stomach knotted with tension, and she remembered the initials in David's notebook.

Shifting Rory in her arms, she picked up the notebook. It was easy enough to find the initials J.B.D. She showed the notation to Matt. "This looks like it matches up with Judge Byron Dugan."

He scowled and punched in another phone number.

"Do me a favor and see if you can find the initials for Assistant District Attorney Blake Ratcliff."

"Who is he?" she asked in confusion.

"A guy who tried to hurt my sister. It wouldn't surprise me to find out he's involved in this, too."

She sat on the edge of the bed and looked through the pages. Finding A.B.R. wasn't difficult, but there was no way to know for sure if they corresponded to Ratcliff.

"Mitch, it's Matt. Call me. I need backup." Matt punched more numbers into his phone, and this time, it sounded as if his brother answered. "Miles? I have new information and reason to believe that there's a game going on in the lower level of Secrets right now. Mike is meeting me here in thirty, can you make it, too?… Great, see you soon."

Matt set his phone aside and she frowned. "Shouldn't you call all of your brothers? There's no telling how many people are involved, but we do know several are cops."

He scrubbed his hands over his face, looking suddenly exhausted. "Yeah, you might be right. But Mitch is obviously tied up, and Marc is also up to his eyeballs in a hot case." He looked thoughtful for a moment, then reached for his phone. "I'll give Noah a call."

"Noah?" That name didn't sound familiar, and her stomach knotted at the thought of bringing in somebody who wasn't part of the family.

"My new brother-in-law. He's a cop, too."

"Oh, yes you mentioned you were partners before you went into K-9 training." Her relief didn't last long, though, as it sounded from Matt's side of the conversation like he wasn't close enough to help.

"It's okay, Noah, just meet us at the nightclub when you can, or maybe head out to the American Lodge instead. Thanks." Matt sighed. "So far I can only count on Mike and Miles for backup. Noah might get there, but he's almost an hour away. I was hoping to get one more. I don't like the thought of leaving you here alone."

Alone? She swallowed against a hard lump of fear that threatened to choke her. "I'm sure Rory and I will be all right."

Matt leaned over to pet Duchess. "I can leave Duchess here with you. She's a good protector."

"Are you sure?" She loved Duchess, but it seemed as if Matt might need her more than she would. "I would rather you have more backup. Two guys, only one of them a cop, isn't going to be enough."

"We'll be okay," Matt assured her. "Mike actually went through the police academy, but decided at the last minute to drop out to start his own private investigator business. I've always thought there was some external reason that factored into his quitting, but he claims it was his choice. He told our father that he didn't like the idea of taking orders from others." Matt shrugged. "Regardless, he's trained as a cop, so there's truly nothing to worry about."

"Okay." Rory chose that moment to start fussing, and she realized it was well past time for his bottle.

She had just finished feeding Rory when Matt's brothers joined them. Both Mike and Miles looked serious as he filled them in on what had transpired in the short time he and Duchess had been outside the nightclub. He showed them the blueprints, indicating the entryway that led to the lower level.

"I can't believe they're meeting during the daytime," Miles said, rubbing the back of his neck. "It's Friday—shouldn't the judge be in court?"

"I have no idea how flexible their schedules are," Matt said. "But I know it was him."

"I'm going to need the notebook, Matt," Miles said. "I know you don't want to give it up, but…"

"It's fine." Matt handed the book to Miles. "Take it in as evidence."

"Will do," Miles agreed.

Lacy turned and went back through the connecting door to place Rory in the crib. He fussed for a moment, but once he settled down, she went back to join the Callahan brothers.

Mike glanced at her as she walked in through the connecting door. "Shouldn't someone stay here with Lacy and the baby?"

"I thought I'd leave Duchess behind. We weren't followed, so I think they'll be safe enough," Matt said. "And I asked Noah to head out this way when he has a chance. Give me a minute to strap on the dog's bulletproof vest."

At the sound of her name, Duchess wagged her tail and stood patiently while Matt buckled a vest over her chest and abdomen. When he finished, Lacy reached out to scratch the animal behind the ears. She attempted a smile. "I've seen Duchess in action. I'm sure we'll be fine."

Matt nodded. "I wouldn't leave you here if I didn't trust my partner. Guard, Duchess," he commanded. "Guard Lacy and Rory."

Duchess instantly sat at Lacy's side, her ears perked forward on alert.

"Ready to go?" Miles asked, his hand already on the doorknob. "We don't know how long the game will last."

"I'm ready," Matt said, but he was looking at her intently, as if he didn't want to leave.

Acting purely on instinct, she crossed over to wrap

her arms around his neck. "Please be careful, Matt," she whispered.

He clutched her close. "I will."

She leaned back to look at him. "I'll pray for God to watch over you."

His green eyes bored into hers for a hard moment, then he swept her close and kissed her. She kissed him back, wishing he didn't have to go.

Miles coughed as if hiding a laugh, and Mike sighed. "We'll meet you outside," Mike said in a loud voice. "Just remember, you were the one in a hurry."

She was vaguely aware of the motel room door slamming shut behind them. Matt's kiss was wonderful, and when he finally raised his head, breathing hard, she rested her forehead on his chest.

"I'll be back as soon as possible," he promised in a low husky voice. "Call me if you need something."

I need you, she thought, but managed to stop herself from blurting out her feelings. This wasn't the time. Matt needed to concentrate on the danger he was about to face.

"I will." She forced herself to release her grip on his shoulders long enough to take a step back. "Be safe, Matt. Call me when you have everything under control."

He nodded, looking as if he was about to say something more, but then silently turned away. He left the motel room to join his brothers outside.

Duchess paced the length of the room for a moment before coming back to sit beside Lacy. She rested her hand on the dog's glossy coat.

"He'll be back for us soon," she assured the dog. "You'll see."

Then she added a silent prayer. *Please, Lord, keep the Callahans safe from harm.*

* * *

Matt hated leaving Lacy and Rory behind, but taking them along to an illegal gambling bust wasn't an option.

"Give up the moony face already, would you?" Mike groused. "You're acting as if you'll never see her again."

Matt lightly punched his brother in the shoulder. "I don't have a moony face. Is it wrong to wish there was someone standing by to watch over her?"

"Hey, I know it's not easy," Miles said from the back seat. "But Duchess can hold her own."

Mike shook his head. "Man, you have it bad. Does Lacy have any idea how you feel about her?"

His chest tightened, but he strove to keep his tone light. "I care about her as a friend, okay? Enough about my personal life, let's focus on breaking up this gambling ring. We still need to figure out who's responsible for murdering Williams and attempting to shoot Lacy."

"By the way, I participated in the Williams autopsy early this morning," Miles said. "The ME is convinced Williams died the night before Lacy took off with Rory."

"Wait, what?" Matt locked gazes with his brothers in the mirror. "Is he sure?"

"*She's* positive," Miles corrected. "There's a new female pathologist working in the ME's office, Dr. Grace Goldberg, and she seems to know what she's doing. She puts the time of death almost twenty-four hours before Jill's murder."

Matt turned his attention toward the road, his mind whirling with possibilities. "I don't understand," he said. "Lacy heard the argument that preceded the murder. She repeated it to me twice."

There was a long silence before Miles spoke up. "Don't you think it's possible that Jill was murdered by the same gunman who tried to finish Lacy off at the convenience store? The same guy who followed her trail to the cabin? Maybe he thinks she can identify him?"

He felt as if someone had body slammed him against the wall. Of course, his brother's theory made sense. Why hadn't he thought of that possibility before?

"The guy said something to Jill about telling him the truth." Matt glanced at Miles again. "At the time, Lacy had thought it was related to David's assumption that she was being unfaithful, but if Williams was already dead, then the gunman was likely looking for the notebook. The truth about the blackmail scheme."

"Exactly," Miles agreed.

The pieces of the puzzle fit, except for... "What about the Amber Alert?" he asked. "Lacy assumed that David was the one to put out the alert in an attempt to get custody and to pin the murder on her, but why would one of his cop buddies do that?"

"Same reason," Mike pointed out. "The dude wanted a good reason to arrest her. If the same guy killed David, he could easily claim that Williams was afraid Lacy would try to get Rory away from Jill. That Lacy influenced her sister and convinced her to file for divorce. I imagine he would want to cover his tracks by pretending David was still alive and well."

"Makes sense," Matt agreed. "I wish I knew which cop was the shooter."

"You have it narrowed down to three possibilities, don't you?" Miles asked.

"Hugh Nichols, Jeff Jones and Randal Whalen." Matt exited the interstate and headed for the same place he'd used as a meeting spot with Lacy ninety minutes ago. "We found all three of their initials in the notebook."

"Okay, then," Miles said, crossing his arms over his

chest. "We'll focus on the three of them. Would make our job easier if they all happened to be at the club today."

"Yeah." But Matt wasn't holding out much hope that it would be that easy. His motto was to hope for the best while preparing for the worst. He threw the SUV into Park and shut down the engine. "We'll walk in from here."

"How do you want to do this?" Mike asked once they were all standing outside beside the vehicle.

"Two of us go in from the back doorway, the one Judge Dugan used to access the building. The third guy goes in from the front, in case they scatter."

"I'll go in with you," Miles offered, slapping Matt on the back. "Since we're both working the case, it only makes sense for us to stick together. Mike, take the front."

Mike shrugged. "Fine with me."

Matt hesitated, unable to shake the sense that he was missing something. He shrugged off the sensation, assuming that the reason he was feeling off was because Duchess wasn't there. He'd grown used to working with his K-9 partner, and it felt odd to be without her.

"This way." He took off down the street to the corner. "The back door is straight ahead," he said to Miles. "Mike, you'll want to go down another block to the front of the building. We'll breach the doors in exactly ten minutes. Ready?"

"Ready," Miles and Mike agreed simultaneously.

Mike set off at a jog while he and Miles approached the back entranceway. There weren't many people around, thankfully, since the nightclub didn't open for a few hours yet.

He took the lead position on the right side of the door, leaving Miles on the left. They flattened themselves against the building and waited.

Exactly ten minutes later, Miles gave him a nod. Matt kicked in the door and went in first, holding his weapon ready. There was an identical sound of a door bursting open from the front simultaneously.

He could hear voices questioning what was going on in response to his and Mike's noisy entrance into the building. Matt clamored down the stairs. "Police!" he shouted. "We have the place surrounded. You're all under arrest. Hands in the air! Now!"

There were three gaming tables, but only one was in use. Five men, including the judge, were rising from their seats around it, a large pile of cash heaped in the center, mostly one hundred dollar bills. Cards flew as the men attempted to flee, one heading for the staircase along the wall that would take him right toward Mike.

A shot rang out, and Matt dropped to one knee. He took aim at the shooter, recognizing him as police officer Jeff Jones. "Drop it!" he shouted, then when the guy didn't listen, pulled the trigger. Jones fell to the floor with a cry.

One down, four to go. But he didn't see the other two cops, Hugh Nichols or Randal Whalen.

Chaos erupted, but it didn't take long for the three Callahans to apprehend the poker players. But even after they had read them their rights and cuffed them, he knew this mess wasn't over.

In fact, it might only be the beginning.

Two officers were still at large. He needed to apprehend them before deeming Lacy and Rory safe.

FIFTEEN

As Lacy walked the length of the motel room holding Rory, back and forth, over and over, Duchess kept pace, close at her side. So close that she almost tripped over the animal. Twice.

She found herself talking to the dog like she spoke to Rory. "Sorry, girl, but give me a little room, okay?"

Duchess didn't seem to get it, nudging her thigh with her nose as if to tell her to keep walking.

So she did. Rory was being unusually fussy. She jiggled him in her arms as she paced in an attempt to calm him down. When that didn't work, she tried giving him a bottle. Unfortunately, that didn't help, either.

Being left alone to care for Rory caused her insecurities to return. She had thought she'd been doing a fairly decent job of taking care of him, but of course five minutes after Matt and his brothers had left, Rory had begun to cry.

"Shh, it's okay, I'm here. You're fine, everything's going to be all right."

He only cried louder, pitiful wails that she had no idea how to fix. What was wrong with him? Why was he crying? Was he missing Matt? Or worse, had he finally realized that she was all he had left in the world?

She battled back a wave of helplessness. She'd been overwhelmed before, and there was no reason to fall back on the old feelings of inadequacy.

She could handle this. Lots of women did this every day. She might make mistakes, but she and Rory would figure things out, together.

Feeling more self-confident, she continued pacing for another ten minutes before setting him down to change his diaper. Once that was finished, she walked the room some more, then decided to lay him down in the center of the bed on his stomach. Babies sometimes had gas pains, so maybe lying down would help.

Rory stretched and rolled from side to side, then finally, thankfully, stopped crying.

She'd done just fine. She didn't need Matt or anyone else to help her out. She could do it on her own.

On the heels of that thought came another. She might not need Matt's help with Rory, but the thought of not seeing him again once this was over left her feeling sad and alone. The sadness she could understand; after all, they'd been through a lot together. But the loneliness? That was just crazy. She hadn't been seeing anyone before meeting Matt and, frankly, hadn't wanted to. Normally she didn't trust men, didn't believe that the kindness they showed to the world didn't also hide a dark temper. Yet nothing about the time that she'd spent with Matt was normal.

How could she miss a man she barely knew? A man she'd come to care about far more than she should have?

Duchess sat straight and tall at the foot of the bed, as if instinctively knowing the infant was an important part of her protection detail. She looked like a furry sentinel, especially with the way her ears perked forward.

Lacy smiled and rubbed the silky spot at the nape of Duchess's neck.

"Good girl," she whispered. "I'm glad you're here."

Duchess licked her arm, but didn't move from her spot. Lacy watched as Rory wiggled around a bit, then rolled over onto his back. The crying must have tuckered him out, because he finally closed his wide blue eyes and drifted off to sleep.

Lacy's shoulders slumped in relief. Giving herself a pep talk was one thing, but fully believing in herself was another. She couldn't help wondering how many more instances like this she would face over the next, say, eighteen years.

Don't go there. One day at a time.

As a teacher, she knew how to deal with fifth graders, so really, all she needed was a few more years with Rory and the rest would come naturally. Isn't that how all parents coped?

Of course, it was.

Wearily, she rose to her feet, glancing around the cluttered motel room. Probably best to clean this mess up now, but then again, wasn't the advice given to new mothers to rest while the baby slept?

Maybe she should give it a try.

She glanced down at Rory again, realizing she couldn't leave him in the bed. If he woke up and began to roll again, he might fall off.

Gingerly, very gingerly, she eased her hands beneath his sleeping body, hoping and praying he wouldn't wake up. Lifting him up, she carried him the few steps over to the crib, letting her breath out in a silent whoosh when he continued sleeping.

One task accomplished. Ignoring the mess, she stretched out on the bed and closed her eyes. She wasn't good at taking naps, but obviously this was one skill she would need to work on.

It seemed like only a few seconds that she'd had her eyes closed when Duchess began to growl. She blinked and sat up, feeling groggy. The light shining between the drapes over the window was different, so some time had passed, although she didn't think it was much more than thirty or forty minutes.

A spike of fear stabbed deep when she saw Duchess standing at the door of the motel room, low, continuous growls coming from her throat.

Any other dog and she might assume the person outside was a maid, or maybe some guy delivering pizza to the room next door, but not Duchess. She never growled.

Except when there was potential danger.

Lacy's thoughts turned razor sharp and she leaped into action, grabbing the shawl and picking up Rory from the crib. She wrapped him tightly against her body, the same way she'd done the night of Jill's murder. The parallel between that night and today felt frighteningly real.

Only this time, she couldn't risk running outside. The only way out would take her directly past the gunman.

Which meant she and Rory were trapped inside, with little to no place to hide.

She swept the mobile phone off the bedside table and held her breath as she squeezed past Duchess and ducked through the connecting door into Matt's motel room. Feeling guilty at leaving Duchess behind, she closed the connecting door and slid the dead bolt in place. Then she sought refuge in the bathroom, closing and locking that door behind her, too.

She stepped into the tub and sank down until she was

reclined against the cold ceramic, keeping low. Despite the two closed doors, she could hear Duchess's growls getting louder and more insistent.

Frantic, she dialed Matt's number and listened to the endless ringing on the other end of the line. When he didn't pick up she disconnected and tried Miles. Then Mike—both with the same results. Finally, she called 911.

The muffled sounds of loud banging on the motel room door reached her ears, and she winced when they were followed by Duchess's sharp staccato barks.

"911, what's your emergency?"

"Someone is breaking into my motel room." She kept her voice low, even though she knew it wouldn't take long for the intruder to find her in the bathroom. Sure, she'd given herself an extra couple of minutes, but once he'd cleared her room, he'd make short work of the connecting door.

But where else could she go?

The dispatcher repeated her request. "I'm at the American Lodge motel, room three. Please hurry!"

"Is the intruder armed?" the operator asked. Lacy could hear clicking keys in the background and hoped that meant the woman wasn't just chatting, but had already sent a message to alert the closest police officer to the danger.

There was another loud bang against the door, and she imagined the gunman kicking it in. How long would it hold?

Not long enough.

"I don't know! Hurry! I'm alone with a baby and a K-9 officer. I'm afraid he's going to kill us!" She wanted to scream, but forced her voice to remain soft and quiet.

"Please stay on the line," the dispatcher said in her cool, controlled tone.

Another loud bang and the sound of splintering wood. A yelp of pain made her think Duchess may have gotten a piece of the guy. She sucked in a harsh breath, her heart jackhammering in her chest.

She held Rory protectively, turning so that her back was facing the door, shielding him as much as she was able to with her own body.

"Hurry," she begged the dispatcher. "I think he's inside the motel now. Please hurry."

For some odd reason, Rory didn't cry, maybe because he was all cried out from his earlier fussiness. Or maybe he instinctively knew that they needed to be quiet. She pressed her mouth against the downy softness of his hair, closed her eyes and began to pray, repeating the words frantically over and over in her mind.

Lord, spare this child's life. Please keep him safe in Your care!

At Secrets, the five men, including the one who'd tried to escape out the front door, were easily subdued. Judge Dugan hung his head in shame, especially once he'd recognized Matt as Maddy's twin.

Matt kept his distance from the judge, hoping this arrest wouldn't cast doubts on all the cases Judge Dugan had presided over. He pulled out his phone, intending to alert his sister so she would be prepared before any of this hit the news, when he saw the missed call from the disposable phone he'd given Lacy.

He quickly pressed his thumb on the number in an attempt to return the call, but she didn't pick up.

Not good.

"I missed Lacy's call," Matt told Miles. "We need to get back to the motel right away."

"You go with Mike. I'll stay here to wrap this up," Miles said.

Matt wasn't about to waste another second. "Mike! Now!" He took off running up the stairs to the street level, barely hearing Mike's footsteps behind him. Outside, he sprinted toward the SUV. When he reached the driver's seat, he wrenched open the door and jumped in behind the wheel. His brother managed to stagger into the passenger side before he hit the gas and shot out onto the road.

"Thanks for waiting," Mike said in a dry tone. "I wouldn't want to hold you up or anything."

"The other two cops are unaccounted for and I missed a call from Lacy," Matt said. "What if they figured out where she was? What if their plan was to set up this game to distract us? Then head out to the motel with the intent of silencing her once and for all?"

"Duchess will protect her," Mike said in a soft, reassuring tone. The hint of joking had vanished. "And we'll be there soon."

"I know. I'm trying to have faith in God's plan." Matt hated the thought of Duchess facing potentially two gunmen on her own. He'd thought for sure that at least two of the cops would have been at the poker game. Three hadn't been likely, but two had seemed plausible. One thing he hadn't seriously considered was the idea that two of the cops had bonded enough to work together.

He mentally berated himself for not doing as he'd promised himself, preparing for the worst.

He pressed down hard on the accelerator, the sense of worry blooming larger in his chest. He'd felt as if something was off earlier, and maybe this was it. A poker game during the day, especially during the week, had been nothing more than a clever ruse. A trap to get Lacy and Rory alone.

Hang on, Lacy. I'm coming!

The houses passed by in a blur. The exit came up quickly, and he slowed enough to get safely off the interstate. The motel wasn't far now, and he tightened his grip on the steering wheel, praying he wasn't too late.

The long, white two-story motel loomed ahead, and he watched in horror as a man with dirty blond hair lifted his leg and kicked at Lacy's motel room door. In the nanosecond during which he'd gotten a glimpse of the man's profile, Matt knew he wasn't the same perp who'd gone after Lacy with a gun. He was wearing off-duty black jeans and a black leather jacket.

"No!" Matt shouted, when the motel room door shuddered beneath the force of the guy's heel. Where was the motel manager? Why wasn't anyone else out there helping?

His brother rolled down the window and aimed his Glock toward the intruder. Mike fired a round, but they were moving too fast for accuracy.

The intruder ducked and kicked again. This time the frame broke and the door snapped open. He could hear Duchess barking, then heard a shout of pain from the intruder.

Bitter fear for Duchess coated his tongue, and he steered erratically into the parking lot and abruptly stopped the car.

Mike was out in a flash, with Matt hard on his heels. They heard a gunshot, and his heart squeezed painfully.

"Duchess!" Matt screamed. He knew his partner would protect Lacy and Rory with her life if necessary. The night that the gunman had sliced her with a knife burned in his mind.

Mike reached the door first and the gunman staggered around to face him. Duchess had her jaw latched around his ankle, hard enough to draw blood. He couldn't see any blood marring the animal's coat, but that didn't mean she hadn't taken a bullet. Had the vest protected her?

Before Matt could say anything, Mike lashed out with his foot in some sort of weird martial arts move that Matt had never seen before, kicking the gun right out of the guy's hand. Then Mike lifted his Glock, pointing it squarely at the cop's chest. "Don't move."

"Hands up!" Matt said, finding his voice. "Which one are you, Randal Whalen or Hugh Nichols?"

The guy's eyes widened in shocked surprise. "Whalen," he grudgingly admitted.

If this was Randal Whalen, that left Hugh Nichols as the original gunman—the one who'd tried to kill Lacy outside the convenience store. Had these two idiots decided to work together after all? If so, where was Nichols?

Matt stepped close enough to grab the man's wallet out of his back pocket to verify he was Whalen. "Duchess, Release."

Duchess let go and backed away, growling fiercely. "Guard, Duchess," he commanded, before turning his attention to the cop. "Randal Whalen, you're under arrest for attempted murder of a police officer and participating in an underground gambling ring. Oh, and I reserve the right to bring other charges forward at a future date."

The man who'd kicked in the door lifted his arms up over his head. "I'm gonna sue. That dog bit me. You gotta take me to the hospital, man, I can hardly walk. I might get rabies."

"Duchess is the one who should be taken in to be examined," Mike shot back. "We don't know what kind of diseases you've got running through your bloodstream."

Mike's remark made Matt smile grimly. "Duchess, Come."

His partner loped toward him, and Matt nearly wept with relief when she appeared unharmed. He sent up a silent prayer of thanks to God for keeping his partner, Lacy and Rory all safe.

"Cuff him and take him outside," Matt said, tossing his handcuffs to his brother. "I need to check on Lacy and Rory."

"My pleasure." Mike caught the cuffs one-handed. Apparently, his reflexes had been honed by whatever martial arts he was practicing these days. Matt waited until he knew that the cop was securely restrained.

"Duchess, Come." He crossed the threshold into the motel room, sweeping his gaze over the area. There was a lot of stuff around, but no sign of either Lacy or Rory. A sliver of unease worked its way under his skin.

"Lacy? It's Matt. Are you okay?"

The room was empty; the bathroom door was open and the interior was dark. He glanced over, noticing how the connecting door between their rooms was closed from the opposite side. When he pushed against it, he found it was locked. Good thinking on her part, he thought with a grim smile.

"Lacy? It's safe! You can come out now!" he called loudly. Pressing his ear to the door, he listened, but didn't hear anything. If she was hiding in the bathroom, which is exactly where he would have gone if he were in her shoes, then she might not have been able to hear him. Duchess stood patiently while he dug in his pocket for his own room key. No reason he couldn't go in through the main door.

He moved past the broken door to head outside. He stopped abruptly when he saw a police squad parked beside his SUV, blocking the view from the lobby area of the motel. The red and blue lights weren't flashing the way they should have been during an emergency response.

Then he swallowed hard when he noticed the tall man with familiar features standing in full uniform, holding a gun pointed directly at Mike. He took a step back, but it was a fraction of a second too late.

"Don't move, Callahan," the guy called. "Put your hands up where I can see them."

He did as instructed, realizing this was the same man who'd leveled a gun at Lacy outside the convenience store. Who'd sliced Duchess with his knife and had shot at Matt outside the cabin. And the way things stood right now, anyone looking over here would assume that he and Mike were the criminals, not the other way around.

Had the 911 operator called him to the scene? Or had this been part of his and Whalen's plan?

Either way, it was clear Officer Hugh Nichols had found them.

SIXTEEN

When Lacy heard the reassuring sound of Matt's voice, she let out a long sigh of relief.

It was over. Matt was here, and she was sure he'd brought along at least one of his brothers. Whatever had transpired at the nightclub hadn't taken long.

She rolled on her back in the bathtub, holding Rory against her, then awkwardly rose up to a partial sitting position. With Rory bound against her, she couldn't bend at the waist, so she threw one leg over the edge of the tub and then grabbed on to the sink in an attempt to haul herself upright.

It wasn't pretty, but she managed to leverage herself out of the ceramic tub. *This must be similar to how it would feel to be pregnant*, she thought with a wry smile. She hadn't really entertained the idea of having a child of her own, since she'd never trusted a man long enough to get to the point of considering even a long-term relationship. But spending the past few days with Matt had given her all kinds of ideas related to the future.

Ideas of seeing him again, once the danger was over.

If he was even interested, which she wasn't sure he was. Oh, he'd kissed her, not once but three times! But that might not mean much. After losing his girlfriend and her child, he wasn't likely to be in the market for a relationship. He was probably just being nice to her.

Enough. This wasn't the time or place to think about what might happen tomorrow. In fact, she had other, more pressing, priorities. Such as working with Social Services to begin the adoption process so she could keep Rory. Somehow, she didn't think her sister had gotten around to making a will. If Jill had, she'd never mentioned it.

Shaking off the distressing thoughts, she opened the bathroom door and poked her head out to survey the room. She expected to see Matt there, but the room was empty. The connecting door was still closed and appeared to be locked, the way she'd left it.

A trickle of unease raised the hair on the back of her neck. Where was Matt? She'd heard his voice.

Surely, he hadn't left her and Rory behind?

She took several tentative steps forward. The silence was eerie and strangely threatening. Approaching the window, she could hear the low rumble of deep voices, and through a gap in the curtains she saw a police car outside.

For some odd reason, the lights on the rack along the top of the car weren't flashing, which wasn't reassuring. She slipped closer to the opening between the curtains to get a better look at what was going on.

She froze when she realized Matt was standing there with his hands up in the air. A cop dressed in full uniform, no doubt the one who'd arrived in the patrol car, was standing several feet away, pointing a gun toward Matt. Mike was there, too, also holding his hands up in a gesture of surrender.

What was going on? And where were the motel staff?

Although, it occurred to her that the cop dressed in uniform would hardly be viewed as the bad guy.

In fact, quite the opposite.

Easing back from the curtains, Lacy swallowed hard and tried to figure out what she should do. She could call 911 again, but what if the next cop to arrive was an enemy as well? There could easily be others.

She hadn't seen Duchess, either, which was weird. Surely, Duchess would stay near Matt?

Unless— Her gaze landed on the connecting door. She silently unlocked the dead bolt and inched the door open.

Duchess hovered near the broken door of the motel room, hugging the wall and apparently out of sight from the men standing outside. Duchess must have caught Lacy's scent through the crack in the doorway, because the animal turned and came over to sniff at the opening.

Lacy eased the door open enough for her to get her fingers through. She lightly stroked Duchess's fur, grateful to see that she appeared unharmed. But the dog didn't stay near the connecting doorway. She turned and softly padded over to stand near the broken door, as if awaiting a signal.

Was Matt able to see Duchess? If so, he might be able to use her help. Having Duchess, a trained K-9 officer, available meant they weren't completely sunk, not yet. But it wouldn't take long. She scooted closer to the window, hoping to overhear what they were saying.

"I'm telling you, he has a dog! It attacked me," a whiney male voice said.

"You hurt my partner," Matt said in a sharp tone. "Don't you think she would be out here if she wasn't hurt?"

Lacy could tell Matt was trying to buy them time, but for what?

"Where is it? I want that notebook now!" The deep male voice of the cop holding the gun sent goosebumps along her arms. It was him! His voice was the one she'd overheard the night of Jill's murder.

All this time, she'd assumed the intruder was David, but she'd been wrong. David hadn't killed Jill.

It was the man standing outside, wearing a full cop uniform, who'd committed the murder.

All because of David's notebook.

She felt sick to her stomach, knowing that Jill had died for nothing more than greed.

So now what? She needed desperately to find some sort of diversion. As much as she didn't want to close the connecting door, she knew it was probably for the best. The last thing she wanted was to get between Duchess and Matt.

She was glad Matt had given the notebook to Miles, although handing it over wasn't likely to get them out of this.

The cop had been searching for her, no doubt because he knew she would be able to recognize his voice as the man who'd murdered Jill. Matt would stall as long as he could, attempting to convince the cop that she and Rory weren't here.

But eventually the situation would unravel, and she and Rory might be exposed.

She glanced toward the bathroom, wondering if she should hide in there with Rory. The baby deserved to be safe from harm, didn't he?

A movement from outside caught her attention. She eased closer to the window, being careful not to be seen.

There it was again. A figure was crouched behind the squad car. The brown hair looked familiar.

Miles! Matt's brother had come to rescue them.

But how could she get the news to Matt? A text message? No, he couldn't look at his phone.

She needed a diversion. What could she toss outside to cause a distraction?

There were two small, fist-sized glasses in the bathroom. She picked one up, leaving the other behind. Returning to the center of the room, she assessed her options.

Tossing it out through the open doorway of the adjacent room was her best bet. That way, she could use this room as a refuge, at least for a few minutes.

Should she leave Rory in the bathtub? The idea of being separated from him didn't sit well, but better that than risk having him hit by a stray bullet. She set the glass down and began to unwrap the shawl. When she finished, she tucked it around Rory in the tub as a cushion. He cried a little but then thankfully settled down.

Lacy unlocked the connecting door and opened it. Then she picked up the glass and slipped through into the motel room where Duchess still waited patiently for Matt's signal. Being this close to the broken doorway was scary, but she pushed past her fear long enough to find a spot where she could see through the narrow opening.

Once she identified her target, an open spot of the parking lot, she brought her arm back and threw the glass with all her might. Before she heard the glass shatter against the concrete pavement, she was already making her way back through the connecting doorway.

The rest was up to Matt, Duchess, Miles—and God.

"I don't have the notebook," Matt insisted for what felt like the tenth time in less than five minutes. Although, truthfully, every minute was a gift. He hoped and prayed either Miles or Noah would show up soon. "I've given the notebook over to the authorities, so there's no point in holding us at gunpoint, Nichols. The gig is up. Game over. We've already arrested Judge Dugan and the others involved in the poker game less than an hour ago."

"I know you have the notebook, Callahan," Nichols sneered. "Stalling is a waste of time. Maybe I'll shoot your brother in the kneecap, a painful but not lethal wound. Just something to show I mean business."

The barrel of Nichols's gun shifted toward Mike. Matt knew he couldn't wait a moment longer. It was now or never.

He gave Duchess the hand signal for Attack at the exact same time he heard the distinct sound of glass shattering somewhere off to his left.

From there, several things transpired at once. Miles jumped out from behind the squad car at the same second Duchess sprinted toward Nichols. The first cop that they'd cuffed, Randal Whalen, took off running away from the scene. The sound of gunfire echoed around him. There was a burning sensation in his left leg, but he ignored the pain. He hit the pavement and rolled toward Mike, wishing desperately that he had a backup weapon.

"Matt!" Mike's shout caused him to lift his head. A small pistol came flying through the air toward him, and he caught it with his right hand. In a smooth motion, he turned and aimed at Nichols.

But he didn't shoot. Couldn't, not without risking his partner. Duchess and Nichols were rolling around on the ground, Duchess's jaw latched onto the cop's shoulder in a firm hold. Unfortunately, Nichols was still holding on to his gun, attempting to angle it around so that he could shoot the animal.

"No!" Matt shouted hoarsely. He staggered to his

feet, wincing as pain shot through him. Blood ran down his leg, but he managed to get closer to where Duchess and Nichols fought for their lives.

"Stay back," Miles ordered.

Matt came to an abrupt stop but couldn't tear his gaze away from Duchess. If anything happened to his partner, he knew it would be his fault. It was bad enough that Nichols had hurt Duchess before.

Out of nowhere, Mike's foot lashed through his field of vision, kicking the gun right out from Nichols's hand and sending it spinning across the asphalt parking lot.

"Don't move," Miles said, placing the barrel of his gun against Nichols's right temple.

"Release! Heel," Matt ordered. Duchess responded instantly, releasing her grip on Nichols's shoulder and spinning away from the assailant, returning to Matt's side. "Good girl," he praised, leaning down to give her coat a nice rub.

"She okay?" Mike asked.

He nodded. "Yes, thanks to you. I want to know where you learned martial arts. Those moves are nice and handy."

"Where did Whalen go?" Mike demanded.

"Good question." Matt took one step, then another. "Unfortunately, I'm in no condition to track him down."

"I'll get him," Mike said. "He's handcuffed, so he won't get far."

"Hugh Nichols, you're under arrest for the murder of David Williams and Jill Williams," Miles said, as he tossed a pair of handcuffs to Mike. "You have the right to remain silent. Anything you say can and will be used against you in a court of law. You have the right to an attorney…"

Matt's vision blurred and he suddenly felt light-headed. He blinked, trying to focus.

"Looks like you guys have everything under control," Noah said, stepping out from behind the SUV. Matt stared at his brother-in-law for a moment, wondering where in the world he'd come from.

"Yeah, you're late as usual," Mike said in a dry tone. "How does Maddy put up with you?"

"She loves me," Noah said, putting his hand over his heart. Then his tone changed to one of concern. "Hey, Matt, are you okay? You're losing a fair amount of blood over there."

"I am?" He glanced down, realizing there was a dark reddish-brown puddle forming on the ground around his left foot. Noah was right—the pool of blood was getting larger and larger.

The earth tilted again and Matt felt himself slipping downward. Strong arms supported him, easing him slowly onto the pavement.

"Call an ambulance!" Noah shouted.

Matt reached up to grab Noah's shirt. "Grab the key out of my pocket," he said in an urgent tone.

"Huh?" Noah looked confused. "Hey, just relax, okay, Matt? I'll take good care of you. Maddy would never forgive me if I let something happen to you."

Matt closed his eyes for a moment, fighting the dizziness. He needed to stay conscious. "Listen! Lacy and Rory are inside the motel room. Someone needs to go inside to make sure they're okay. Use my key."

"I'll do it." Miles slid the room key out of Matt's back pocket and held it up. "I'll take good care of Lacy and Rory. Just stay put for a minute. The ambulance is on its way."

Matt struggled to remain conscious, determined to

see for himself that Lacy and Rory were unharmed. Against his will, his eyelids slipped closed.

"Matt!" Lacy's voice roused him, and he forced his eyes open with superhuman effort. He saw Lacy standing there, clutching Rory to her chest. "It worked. My diversion worked!"

Diversion? At first he didn't understand, but then he remembered the sound of breaking glass. He hadn't realized Lacy had been the source.

"You were great." Matt squinted up at her. "Are you and Rory okay?" he asked, blinking in an effort to keep her in focus. "You're not hurt?"

"We're fine," she assured him. She knelt beside him, her lips soft against his forehead. "God was watching over all of us today."

"Yeah," he agreed in a faint tone. He'd saved Lacy and Rory, despite being unable to save Carly.

Was this part of God's plan? Debra breaking up with him so he would be there to help keep Rory and Lacy safe from the gunman? From Hugh Nichols?

"He's losing a lot of blood," Miles said, coming over to kneel beside him.

"I'm right here," Matt managed to say. "I can still hear you. Why are you guys talking about me as if I'm already dead?"

"Of course you're not dead. But you are seriously injured. The bullet must have nicked your artery," Lacy said in a worried tone. "We need to place a tourniquet above the wound in an attempt to slow down the blood loss."

Matt was vaguely aware of his belt being slipped out of the loops and wrapped around the top of his thigh. He groaned in pain, clenching his jaw as Noah cinched it tight.

Boy did that hurt. Worse than getting shot.

"Keep it in place for five minutes, then loosen for a minute," Lacy instructed. "Keep repeating the pattern until the ambulance arrives."

He didn't like feeling helpless. There was still work to be done. Had Mike caught up to Whalen? He certainly hoped so.

Duchess licked his cheek, making him smile, despite the way his leg felt as if it were being seared by a bonfire.

Focus, he reminded himself. "Someone hasta take care of Duchess…" His voice trailed off as weakness overpowered his determination.

"Shh, it's okay. I'll take care of Duchess," Lacy said, putting her hand on his cheek. "Rest now, the ambulance is almost here. It just got off the interstate."

"Lacy," he whispered. There was something important he needed to tell her. What was it? He couldn't corral his scattered thoughts.

"I'm here, Matt." Her voice was beautifully melodic, and it pained him to realize he might not get a chance to hear it again. "You're going to be fine, you hear me? The ambulance crew is here and they're going to take you to the best hospital in the city."

"Lacy, I lo…" His voice trailed off and he knew staying awake was a lost cause. He simply couldn't hold back the darkness for a moment longer.

Time to stop fighting against the inevitable. He relaxed and let go, giving himself up into God's care.

SEVENTEEN

"Matt? Can you hear me?" Lacy watched in horror as Matt's eyes closed and his face went slack. "Matt?"

"Hey, it's okay, he still has a pulse," Noah said in a tone that she assumed was meant to be reassuring. She didn't like the pallor in Matt's face, though. "We need to give the paramedics room to work."

Hugging Rory to her chest with one arm, she clung to Matt's hand with the other, reluctant to let him go. He'd lost so much blood... She shuddered at the possibility of losing him.

"Come on, Lacy." Noah gently placed his hand under her elbow, helping her upright. "The danger is over. We have both Hugh Nichols and Randal Whalen in custody."

"You do?" Dazed, she looked around the parking lot of the American Lodge, surprised to realize Mike had returned with Whalen in tow.

It really was over, although not without casualties. Matt's gunshot wound was the most serious, since Nichols's shoulder injuries proved to be superficial and Whalen's ankle hadn't been bad enough to stop him from running away.

More police officers had arrived on the scene, and

she could see that Mike and Miles were in deep conversation with them, no doubt providing a detailed timeline of the events that had taken place over the past thirty minutes or so.

Thirty minutes that had seemed like a lifetime.

As she watched the paramedics work over Matt, providing badly needed fluids, Rory began to fuss, waving his arms and legs as if tired of being held. She shifted him in her arms, grateful for the fact that he'd waited until now to show his displeasure. He'd been amazingly quiet while they'd hid in the bathroom, keeping them safe.

"Do you need something?" Noah asked. "You want me to hold him for a bit?"

She hesitated, then nodded. Matt was right about learning to accept help when it was available. Her desperate need to remain independent seemed foolish now. "I'd appreciate it if you could take him long enough for me to make a bottle."

"No problem." Noah took the baby, then lifted Rory high in the air, distracting him from his hunger and making him giggle. She ducked through the broken doorway to find the formula and the bottles. When she returned outside, she caught a glimpse of Matt stretched out on a gurney, sliding into the back of the ambulance.

"Wait!" she called out, rushing toward the paramedics. "You're taking him to Trinity Medical Center, right?"

"Yes, ma'am," the paramedic said with a nod.

The tightness across her chest eased. She was glad they were taking him to the level-one trauma center. "Okay, thanks."

She stepped back, watching as they shut the ambulance doors and pulled away, red lights flashing and sirens screaming. She didn't move until they approached the highway.

When she felt Noah's presence beside her, she turned toward him. "Here, I'll take him."

"Sure." Noah handed Rory over, then jammed his hands into his pockets. "Listen, a Detective Styles just showed up, along with Matt's boss, Lieutenant Gray. Miles is soothing the lieutenant's ruffled feathers, but Styles needs your statement."

"Okay. I can talk while giving Rory his bottle, but I need to sit down." Exhaustion had hit hard, so she headed back inside the motel room to find a place to sit. Less than a minute later, Detective Styles came in and introduced himself.

After asking some basic questions, such as her name, age and occupation, he requested she start at the beginning—the night she'd overheard her sister's murder and had taken off running. It seemed as if that night had been months ago instead of days, but she reiterated the events that were seared into her memory.

The interview took much longer than she'd anticipated. In fact, he might have continued firing questions at her if not for Rory needing to have his diaper changed.

"Excuse me," she said, rising to her feet. "I have to take care of my nephew. Can we continue this at a later time? It's getting dark, and I need to get over to the hospital to check on Matt, er, Officer Callahan."

"Uh, yeah, okay." The detective seemed a bit annoyed but didn't argue. "Here's my card. I need to know how to reach you."

That comment brought her up short. Where was she going to stay now that the danger was over? Her single bedroom apartment?

And what about Duchess? She'd promised Matt she'd take care of her while he was in the hospital.

Her mind whirled as she changed Rory, considering her options. For now, her best bet was probably to go back to Jill's place if the police had finished processing it as a crime scene. That's where all Rory's things were, and she could sleep on the futon again.

"Lacy?" Mike poked his head through the doorway. "Are you ready to go? I thought you'd like to stop at the hospital for a bit before you head home."

"Yes, but give me five minutes to get everything together." Lacy placed Rory in his car seat and then packed what was left of the diapers, formula and bottles into a plastic bag.

Outside, she found Mike, Miles and Noah deep in conversation. Whatever they were discussing ended abruptly when she approached.

"Lacy, we think it's best if you stay at Matt's house for the next few days," Miles said. "Gives us time to take turns checking in on you, Rory and Duchess. I've turned over all the evidence to Styles, who's taking over the case. Matt's boss isn't happy with us—not that I care."

She was taken aback by their offer but quickly nodded in agreement. Truthfully, she liked their idea better, since she wasn't sure she had the option of staying at Jill's. "Thank you, I'd appreciate that."

"Good. Let's stop there on the way to the hospital."

The next few hours passed in a blur. She left Rory's things at Matt's house, fed Duchess and then caught a ride to the hospital with Mike. But Matt was still in surgery and Rory grew even more fussy, so in the end she accepted Mike's offer to return to Matt's place, providing Rory the opportunity for a good night's sleep.

She stayed in the guest bedroom, and Duchess remained close at hand, but she still felt as if she were intruding in Matt's personal space. Rory fell asleep quickly, but she was wide-awake, worrying about Matt. When the phone rang at ten o'clock at night, she quickly answered it.

"Lacy? It's Mike. Just wanted to let you know Matt is out of surgery and doing fine. The artery was repaired and he was given a few units of blood. He looks great."

She closed her eyes on a wave of relief. "That's wonderful. Thanks for letting me know."

"One of us will stop by tomorrow to pick you up if you want to see him," Mike continued.

"I'd like that, thanks." She disconnected from the call and closed her eyes, thanking God for giving Matt the strength to pull through surgery.

The welcome news about Matt helped her to relax enough to fall asleep. Rory woke up at 5:30 a.m. for a bottle. It was the longest he'd slept through the night since this nightmare had started. She fed him and let Duchess out. Since Rory showed no interest in going back to sleep, she stayed up, making a pot of coffee and helping herself to a slice of toast for breakfast.

Dawn crept over the horizon. She sipped her coffee, wondering how long they would keep Matt in the hospital. Probably a few days at the most, which meant she would need to find an alternative place to stay.

Not to mention she had things to do. Starting with filing the paperwork to adopt Rory and enrolling him in a day-care center. And looking for a new place to live.

She had to accept the fact that her time with Matt had come to an end. Matt needed to focus on recovering from his bullet wound and subsequent surgery. The last thing he needed was to deal with her and Rory. Especially after what he'd been through in his past.

And she needed to remember that her priority was Rory. Not Matt.

Lacy packed all her belongings into a small pile. Most of it belonged to Rory. Once she made sure Matt was truly all right, she would ask his brothers to take her home. Her apartment was small, but it would have to do for now.

The hours dragged by slowly, to the point where she was beginning to wonder if Mike and Miles had forgotten about her.

Had Matt's condition taken a turn for the worse?

No, someone would have called her. It was more likely they were continuing to discuss the case with the detective.

By ten o'clock in the morning, her worry had grown to astronomical proportions. She let Duchess out into the fenced-in backyard, then called both Mike and Miles, but neither one of them picked up.

Ten minutes later, she heard a car pull into the driveway. With a sense of relief, she set the disposable phone down and went over to greet one of Matt's brothers.

She opened the front door, expecting to see Mike or Miles. The moment she opened the door, Duchess let out a series of staccato barks from the backyard.

By the time she realized it wasn't one of Matt's brothers but a dark-haired stranger at the door, he'd pushed his way inside, holding a gun pointed at her chest.

And she knew, with a sick sense of certainty, that the danger was far from over.

"Let me up," Matt said, pushing Miles out of the way. "I'm getting out of here."

His brother let out a heavy sigh. "The doctor recommended you stay another day."

Matt reached for the crutches that were propped at the end of his bed. The wound in his thigh ached, especially when he'd pulled on the sweats his brother had brought in for him to wear, but he ignored it. "Yeah, but that was before you told me Styles thinks someone else is the brains behind the murder of David and Jill Williams. That both Nichols and Whalen are refusing to give up the guy's identity. You shouldn't have left Lacy and Rory alone."

"Duchess will watch over them," Miles assured him. "But if you insist on leaving, I'm going to get the doctor. And you're going to explain this to Mom and Nan."

"Yeah, yeah." Matt vaguely remembered seeing his mother and grandmother standing at his bedside last night when he'd returned from surgery. Maddy and his other brothers had been there, too.

But he hadn't seen Lacy. Which had bothered him, far more than it should have.

Logically, he understood she had Rory to care for, but he didn't feel comfortable having her out of his sight. He knew the police were likely still grilling Nichols and Whalen to give up their source, but he didn't like thinking about someone still out there as a potential threat.

It was twenty minutes before ten in the morning. The surgeon had come by several hours earlier. Physical therapy had arrived by eight with the crutches, and once he was mobile, there was no reason to hang around.

And two very good reasons to leave: Lacy and Rory.

Despite his grumbling, Miles escorted him out to the car and helped him inside. Once they were on the road, Miles's phone rang. Since he was driving, Miles didn't bother to answer it.

"Give it to me," Matt said. "I'd like to call Lacy."

"Hang on a minute," Miles said. "I need to get on the interstate first."

Matt waited impatiently, then took the phone Miles finally handed over. "Hey, we just missed a call from Lacy."

"We did?" Miles looked surprised. "I wonder why she was reaching out to us?" Matt quickly called Lacy back. She didn't pick up. He tried not to panic, and just when he was going to try calling again, the phone rang in his hand. Unfortunately, the caller was Mike, not Lacy.

"This is Matt, what's going on?"

"I just missed a call from Lacy, so I'm heading over to your place," Mike said. "Have you heard from her?"

"No, my phone battery is dead. She tried to call Miles, too. We're on our way."

"Meet you there," Mike said and disconnected.

Matt gripped the phone tightly in his hand, nausea swirling in his gut. "Hurry, Miles."

Miles gave a terse nod and pushed his foot firmly on the accelerator.

Both of his brothers made good time. When Miles arrived, Mike was already pulling into the driveway of his small ranch house. There was a strange car parked on the street, and Duchess was barking like mad from the backyard. Matt reached over to grip Miles's arm.

"Someone's inside. I need a weapon. I'll go around back to get Duchess—you and Mike cover the front."

"Let me call for backup first." Miles wrestled the phone to make the call, then dug a second gun from the glove box.

Matt tucked the weapon into his waistband and then pushed open the passenger-side door. With the help of his crutches, he hobbled over to the backyard and used his key to open the lock on the fence.

Duchess came right over to greet him but didn't stay. She raced over to the back door leading into his house.

Matt hobbled—slowly on the crutches—over to the doorway, pausing long enough to take a deep breath. He listened intently and then used his key to unlock the door.

Duchess stayed close. He didn't hear anything from the front of the house, but he was sure his brothers were there, waiting. Matt propped his right crutch against the side of the house and pulled out his weapon. He'd have to make do with one crutch from here on. Moving silently, he eased inside, giving Duchess the Stay command to keep her close.

"I don't see how planting evidence here is going to work," Lacy said from the living room. "No one will believe Matt is responsible for blackmail and murder."

"I'm not going down for this," a male voice said. "Trust me, I have enough connections who will believe Callahan is responsible. Once he's dead and I get rid of you and the kid, I'll come out looking like a hero."

Matt peered around the corner in time to see Assistant District Attorney Blake Ratcliff standing there with a gun pointed at Lacy and Rory.

"Drop it, Blake!" he shouted. "Attack!"

Duchess shot out of the kitchen directly toward Blake. The ADA turned and took aim at the dog, so Matt pulled the trigger on his weapon, hitting Blake in the stomach and sending him stumbling backward. He hit the ground and Duchess planted her paws on Ratcliff's chest, as if determined to make sure he couldn't get back up again. His brothers burst in through the front door, and just that quickly, it was over.

For good this time.

"Matt? What are you doing out of the hospital?" Lacy ran toward him, her expression etched with concern. "Mike, Miles? Why did you bring him here? He needs to go back right away."

"I'm fine," he assured her, reaching out with his free hand to give her a hug. He vaguely remembered telling her that he loved her last night before he had fallen unconscious, but he couldn't remember if she'd responded.

"Who is he?" Lacy asked, glancing over her shoulder at the man stretched out on the floor.

"Assistant District Attorney Blake Ratcliff." Matt reluctantly let her go. "I knew he was trouble when Noah confided how he assaulted my sister, but I never expected this. He was crazy if he thought he could pin this all on me."

"When did he assault Maddy?" Miles asked with a frown.

Matt winced. "I'm not sure. She didn't tell me, Noah did. So don't say anything."

"Backup will be here shortly," Mike said. "I guess he was the brains behind the murders. Do you want to go back to the hospital?"

"No." He may as well stay. He would have to deal with Ratcliff, anyway. Then he caught sight of Lacy's things gathered together in a neat pile. "Why is all your stuff sitting there?"

Lacy shrugged, avoiding his gaze. "It's time for me to go home. I have a lot of things to do over the next few weeks."

"But I thought…" He wasn't sure what he'd thought. "Couldn't you wait until we have a chance to talk?"

"Matt, you've been wonderful. I can't thank you enough for helping me find strength in faith and in

God. I know now, with God's help, Rory and I will be just fine."

He stared at her for several long seconds, trying to think of an argument that might change her mind. But what else was there to say? He'd already declared his love.

Clearly, she didn't feel the same way.

Mike's phone rang, and his brother quickly answered it. "Marc? What's wrong? Hey, stay calm, bro, Kari will be fine. We'll meet you at the hospital, okay?"

"Kari?" Matt asked, when Mike disconnected from the phone. "Is she all right?"

"She went into premature labor. The baby is three weeks early. Hopefully, Kari will be fine. Marc's a wreck, though."

"I don't blame him, but we can't just leave," Miles pointed out. "We have to explain what happened here."

"Call Detective Styles," Lacy suggested. "He'll understand."

The backup police officers arrived shortly thereafter, but Detective Styles didn't arrive for another twenty minutes. He wasn't surprised to see Ratcliff—apparently Whalen had finally broken down, confessing everything and implicating the ADA, who'd paid them to get the notebook at any cost.

Combined with the rest of the evidence that Matt, Miles and Mike had gathered, the two officers involved would go to jail for a long time.

Finally, a good hour later, the Callahans were free to go.

"Lacy, will you please come with us to the hospital?" Matt asked. "For one thing, I can't drive, and we need to check on my brother and his wife before we take you home."

She hesitated, then nodded. "What about Duchess?"

"She's coming, too."

"Sounds good, but I'd like to take my things now, so we can head straight to my place when we're finished."

He wanted to argue, but his brothers helped gather her stuff together, putting it all into the back seat. Soon they were back at the hospital where the rest of the Callahan clan had already gathered in the waiting room.

"Kari and Marc are in the labor room," his mother announced. "This baby is determined to be born early, that's for sure."

Miles crossed over to his hugely pregnant wife, Paige. "Guess our baby isn't going to be born on the same day as Marc and Kari's," he said in a soft voice, placing his palm protectively over her abdomen.

"I guess not," Paige responded with a wry grimace. "Although, I can't deny feeling a tiny bit jealous."

Matt shook his head. There were so many babies that he could barely keep up. Then again, the idea of having a ready-made family was growing on him.

Despite his intention to avoid complications, he'd fallen in love with Lacy. Somehow, he needed to find a way to convince her to give him a chance.

"I'd like to introduce you to my mother and grandmother," he told Lacy.

"Oh, well, okay…" Lacy looked uncertain as he gestured for his mother to join them.

"Mom, this is Lacy Germaine. Lacy, this is Margaret Callahan, my mother, and Nan, my grandmother."

"Nice to meet you," Lacy said with a small smile.

"You, too, dear. Oh, and who's this little cutie?" his mother asked, beaming at Rory.

"My orphaned nephew, Rory," Lacy answered. "I'm planning to adopt him."

"Oh, I'm so sorry for your loss." His mother gave Lacy a quick hug. "But I'm sure you'll be a great mother to Rory."

Lacy nodded with confidence. "Yes, I will."

Maddy crowded in, not one to be left out. "Hi, Lacy, it's great to meet you. I've heard so much about you."

"You have?" Lacy appeared taken aback.

"Noah was there last night, remember?" Matt leaned heavily on his crutches, unwilling to admit how much he wanted to sit down.

"Oh, yes. Of course." Lacy's puzzled expression cleared. "It's nice to meet you, too, Maddy."

"It's a girl!" Marc's excited announcement echoed loudly throughout the waiting room. "Kari and I have a beautiful baby girl!"

"Oh, Marc, that's wonderful." Matt's mother rushed over to give her eldest son a hug. "What are you going to name her?"

Marc grinned. "Since our firstborn is Max after our dad, we decided to name our daughter Maggie after you."

"Oh, that's so sweet." Matt's mother's blue eyes filled with tears.

Matt groaned. "Don't tell me you're continuing on the *M* name madness," he protested. "It's crazy enough around here as it is!"

"Yep." Marc beamed. "But no worries, there will be plenty of *M* names to go around. I'm not sure Kari is up to having six kids."

"Yeah, and this probably isn't the right time to broach that subject with her, either," Mike added in a wry tone.

Matt coughed to cover up a laugh when his mother swatted Mike on the arm. "Enough, young man."

It took him a minute to realize that Lacy was edging toward the door. Was she planning to leave without him?

He quickly followed her out of the waiting room. "Lacy, what's wrong?"

"Nothing." She subtly wiped at her eyes. Was she crying? "Your family is great, Matt. But I'm tired and need to get home."

"Lacy, wait." He walked over to her with his crutches and then leaned on his good leg so he could take her hand in his. "I know it's too soon for you, but I can't stand the thought of living my life without you. I love you. Will you please consider giving me—us—a chance?"

Her mouth dropped open in shock. "You...love me?"

"Didn't I tell you that last night?" When she shook her head, he inwardly groaned at his stupidity. "Yes, Lacy, I love you. And Rory, too. I know that there's a long adoption road ahead, but I want to be there with you, helping you, supporting you along the way. But most of all, I can't imagine not having you in my life."

"Oh, Matt." Lacy's eyes filled with tears. "As much as I would love to have your support, this isn't a good time to start a relationship. Being responsible for a baby will be stressful enough."

He swallowed hard and nodded. "Adapting to a baby won't be easy, but we managed pretty well so far, don't you think? And we can take things as slow as you'd like, but please, please don't leave without giving me a chance."

Lacy swiped at her eyes, then unexpectedly threw herself into his arms. He dropped his crutches to hold her close. Well, as close as possible considering she still held Rory.

"I love you, too, Matt," she murmured against his chest. "I've always felt safe with you, and not just from the men chasing us, but on a personal level. If you're really sure about this, I'd love to give our relationship a chance to flourish."

Matt's heart swelled with gratitude and love. "I knew God brought us together for a reason," he said, pressing a kiss to her temple.

She lifted her head and kissed him until they were both breathless. "Me, too," she whispered.

He continued to hold her, thrilled with the knowledge that the Callahan clan would soon expand by two more.

"Another Callahan bites the dust," a wry female voice said from the doorway.

He ignored the fact that his twin had thrown his own words back at him. She was right.

And he would show Lacy and Rory how much he loved them, every day for the rest of their lives.

EPILOGUE

Three months later

Church services followed by Sunday brunch with Matt's family had become Lacy's favorite way to end the week. Especially now that school was over for the summer.

The past few months had been amazing. Matt's support during the adoption process had been invaluable, and she knew deep in her heart that she would soon legally be Rory's mother.

She'd managed to get a service to clean up Jill's house so she could put it on the market. As much as she missed her sister, she knew Jill wouldn't mind. It was better for her and Rory to have a new place to start over in.

Exactly one week after Maggie was born, Miles and Paige welcomed a son, whom they named Adam. Abby was thrilled to be a big sister. Apparently, they were going to stick with *A* names, which she privately thought was a smart idea.

"That was delicious, Mom," Matt said, rising to his feet. His thigh incision had healed nicely, and he'd been cleared to return to full duty within the week.

"Yes, it was," Lacy agreed, jumping up to assist in

clearing the table. "Thank you for including me and Rory."

"You're always welcome, dear," Margaret Callahan assured her with a knowing smile that never failed to make her blush. She was thankful the Callahans had been warm and welcoming, including both her and Rory in family gatherings.

"Noah and I will take cleanup duty," Maddy offered, taking the dirty plate from Lacy's hand. "I think you guys should take advantage of this beautiful day."

"Oh, it's fine, really..." Lacy was about to protest, but Matt came over to put his arm around her waist.

"Thanks, sis. Come on, Lacy, let's take Rory to the park. You know how much he loves the baby swings."

Leaving the mess for everyone else to deal with didn't sit well with her, but Matt was insistent. He pushed her gently toward the door, stopping long enough to raise Rory up into his arms.

Outside, the sunshine was bright and she grabbed Matt's arm to stop him. "Wait, we need Rory's hat."

"Got it right here." He pulled a blue baseball cap out of his back pocket and tugged it on over Rory's fine blond hair.

She smiled, knowing that she shouldn't be surprised by Matt's conscientiousness. He'd proven to be a great father figure for Rory.

And he'd been wonderful toward her as well. He'd never raised his voice in anger. If he grew frustrated, he insisted they sit down to talk things out. He'd shown her what being in a normal relationship was really like.

She loved that about him. In fact, she loved everything about him.

They walked to the park where Matt placed Rory in

the baby swing, making sure he was securely buckled in before giving him a push.

Rory laughed in glee, enjoying every minute of swinging back and forth beneath the blue sky. At six months old, he was crawling, and she felt sure walking wasn't far off, either. Then things would really get interesting.

"Are you ready to head back to work?" Lacy asked, as Matt turned toward her.

He nodded, somewhat absently. "Sure, why not?"

"No nightmares about being shot?" she asked.

"Not at all." He gave Rory another big push, then abruptly turned toward her. "Lacy Germaine, I love you. Will you please do me the honor of becoming my wife?"

She gaped at him in surprise, and he winced.

"I did it wrong," he muttered, dropping down onto one knee. He pulled out a small velvet ring box. "I'm sorry, let me try this again. Lacy Germaine, I love you with all my heart. Will you please marry me?"

"Yes." She laughed and tugged him up to his feet. "Yes, Matt, of course, I'll marry you. I love you, too. I'd be honored to become a part of the infamous Callahan family."

Matt pulled her close, sealing the deal with a deep kiss.

Lacy kissed him back, knowing there was no better man on the face of the earth for her and for Rory.

She cherished becoming a Callahan for real.

* * * * *

Debby Giusti is an award-winning Christian author who met and married her military husband at Fort Knox, Kentucky. Together they traveled the world, raised three wonderful children and have now settled in Atlanta, Georgia, where Debby spins tales of mystery and suspense that touch the heart and soul. Visit Debby online at debbygiusti.com, blog with her at seekerville.Blogspot.com and craftieladiesofromance.Blogspot.com, and email her at Debby@DebbyGiusti.com.

Books by Debby Giusti

Love Inspired Suspense

Amish Protectors

Amish Refuge
Undercover Amish
Amish Rescue
Amish Christmas Secrets

Military Investigations

The Officer's Secret
The Captain's Mission
The Colonel's Daughter
The General's Secretary
The Soldier's Sister
The Agent's Secret Past
Stranded
Person of Interest
Plain Danger
Plain Truth

Visit the Author Profile page
at Harlequin.com for more titles.

STRANDED

Debby Giusti

Greater love hath no man than this,
that a man lay down his life for his friends.
—*John* 15:13

This book is dedicated to
Frank Forth,
a member of the
Greatest Generation
who fought in the
Battle of the Bulge.
Thank you, Frank, for your
service, your love and your support.

ONE

Gripping the steering wheel with one hand, Colleen Brennan shoved a wayward lock of red hair behind her ear with the other and glanced, yet again, at the rearview mirror to ensure she hadn't been followed. She had left Atlanta two hours ago and had been looking over her shoulder ever since.

Her stomach knotted as she turned her focus to the storm clouds overhead. The rapidly deteriorating weather was a threat she hadn't expected.

"Doppler radar...storms that caused damage in Montgomery earlier today...moving into Georgia."

Adjusting the volume on her car radio, she leaned closer to the dashboard, hoping to hear the weather report over the squawk of static.

"Hail...gusting winds. Conditions ideal for tornadoes. Everyone in the listening area is cautioned to be watchful."

The darkening sky and gusting winds added concern to her heavily burdened heart. She didn't like driving on remote Georgia roads with an encroaching storm, but she had an appointment to keep with Vivian Davis. The army wife had promised to provide evidence that would convince the authorities Trey Howard was involved in an illegal drug operation.

Hot tears burned Colleen's eyes. She was still raw from her sister's overdose and death on drugs Trey had trafficked. If only Colleen had been less focused on her flight-attendant career and more tuned in to her sister's needs, she might have responded to Briana's call for help.

Colleen had vowed to stop Trey lest he entice other young women to follow in her sister's footsteps. If the Atlanta police continued to turn a blind eye to his South American operation, Colleen would find someone at the federal level who would respond to what she knew to be true.

Needing evidence to substantiate her claims, she had photographed documents in Trey's office and had taken a memory card that had come from one of the digital cameras he used in his photography business, a business that provided a legitimate cover for his illegal operation.

She sighed with frustration. How could the Atlanta PD ignore evidence that proved Trey's involvement? Yet, they had done just that, and when she'd phoned to follow up on the information she'd submitted, they'd made it sound as if she was the drug smuggler instead of Trey.

Despite her protests, the cop with whom she'd dealt had mentioned a photograph mailed to the narcotics unit anonymously. The picture indicated Colleen's participation in the trafficking operation she was trying to pin on Trey.

Foolishly, she had allowed him to photograph her with a couple of his friends. A seemingly innocent pose, except those so-called friends must have been part of the drug racket. From what she'd learned about

Trey over the past few months, he'd probably altered the photo of her to include evidence of possession and then mailed it to the police.

Too often he'd boasted of being well connected with law enforcement. Evidently, he'd been telling the truth. In hindsight, she realized the cop had probably been on the take.

She wouldn't make the same mistake twice. No matter how much she wanted Trey behind bars, she couldn't trust anyone involved in law enforcement at the local level. For all she knew, they were all receiving kickbacks.

Later tonight, after returning to the motel in Atlanta where Colleen had been holed up and hiding out, she would overnight copies of everything she had secreted from Trey's office, along with whatever evidence Vivian could provide, to the Drug Enforcement Administration's Atlanta office. Surely Trey didn't have influence with the federal DEA agents, although after the pointed questions she'd fielded following her sister's death, Colleen didn't have a warm spot in her heart for cops at any level.

Glancing at her GPS, she anticipated the upcoming turn into a roadside picnic park. Vivian had insisted they meet in the country, far from where the army wife lived at Fort Rickman and the neighboring town of Freemont, Georgia.

Colleen glanced again at her rearview mirror, relieved that hers was the only vehicle on the road. Vivian was right. Meeting away from Freemont and Fort Rickman had been a good decision. Except for the storm that threatened to add an unexpected complication to an already dangerous situation.

Turning into the picnic park, Colleen spotted a car.

A woman sat at the wheel. Braking to a stop next to the sedan, Colleen grabbed her purse off the seat and threw it in the rear. Then stretching across the console, she opened the passenger door, all the while keeping the motor running.

Clutching a leather shoulder bag in one hand and a cell phone in the other, Vivian stepped from her car and slipped into the front seat. She was as tall as Colleen's five feet seven inches, but with a pixie haircut that framed her alabaster skin and full mouth, which made her appear even more slender in person than in the photographs Colleen had seen on Facebook.

Fear flashed from eyes that flicked around the car and the surrounding roadside park.

"Were you followed?" Vivian nervously fingered her purse and then dropped it at her feet.

"I doubled back a few times and didn't see anyone." Colleen pointed to the thick woods surrounding the off-road setting. "No one will find us here, Vivian. You're safe."

Rain started to ping against the roof of the car. Colleen turned on the wipers.

"I don't feel safe." Vivian bit her chipped nails and slumped lower in the seat. "And I'm not even sure I should trust you."

"I told you we'll work together."

"What if my husband finds out?"

Colleen understood the woman's concern. "He was deployed. You were depressed, not yourself. If you're honest with him, he'll understand."

"He won't understand why his wife accepted an all-expense-paid trip to a Colombian resort while he was deployed to a war zone. He also won't understand how I got involved with Trey Howard."

Colleen's sister had been as naive as Vivian. Briana had been used and abused by the drug dealer, which made Colleen realize how easily Vivian could have been taken in by Trey.

"My sister made the same mistake. Two other women did, as well. That's why I contacted you. You still have a chance to escape."

Vivian glanced out the window. "My husband has orders for Fort Hood. We're moving in three weeks." She raked her hand through her short hair. "I'll be okay, unless the cops find out I smuggled drugs into the country."

"I'll mail whatever evidence you brought today to the DEA without mentioning your name or mine. They won't be able to trace anything back to either of us." Colleen rubbed her hand reassuringly over the young woman's shoulder. "Besides, you didn't know what was in the package Trey had you bring into the US for him."

"I knew enough not to ask questions, which means I could end up in jail." Vivian shrugged away from Colleen and reached for the door handle. "I made a mistake meeting you."

"Vivian, please." Colleen grabbed the young woman's arm before she stepped from the car.

A shot rang out.

Vivian clutched her side and fell onto the seat.

Colleen's heart stopped. She glanced into the woods, seeing movement. A man stood partially hidden in the underbrush, a raised rifle in his hands.

Trey.

A car was parked nearby. She couldn't make out the make or model.

"Stay down," Colleen warned. Leaning across the

console and around Vivian, she pulled the passenger door closed.

Another shot. A rear window shattered.

Vivian screamed.

Fear clawed at Colleen's throat. She threw the car into gear and floored the accelerator. The wheels squealed in protest as they left the roadside park.

A weight settled on Colleen's chest. Struggling to catch her breath, she gripped the steering wheel white-knuckled and focused on the two-lane country road that stretched before them.

"He tried to kill me," Vivian gasped. Tears filled her eyes.

Colleen glanced at the hole in the window and the spray of glass that covered the rear seat. "He tried to kill both of us."

She should have known Trey would follow her. He loved fast cars, and no matter what he was driving today, her Honda Civic couldn't outrun his vehicle of choice.

Hot tears burned her eyes. "Our only chance is to find a place to hide and hope Trey thinks we continued north toward the interstate."

He'd eventually realize his mistake and double back to search for them. By then, they would have left the area by another route.

"I'm scared," Vivian groaned.

Refusing to give voice to her own fear, Colleen focused on their most immediate problem. "What's near here that could offer shelter? We need to stow the car out of sight."

"An Amish community." Vivian pointed to the upcoming intersection. "Turn left. Then take the next right. There's a small shop. An old barn sits in the rear. It's usually empty when I drive by."

Colleen followed the younger woman's directions, all the while checking the rearview mirror.

Vivian glanced over her shoulder. "If he catches us, he'll kill us."

"Not if we hole up in the barn. He won't look for us there."

The army wife pointed to the upcoming intersection. "Turn right. Then crest the hill. The Amish store is on the other side of the rise."

Colleen's stomach tightened with determination. She turned at the intersection and kept the accelerator floored until the car bounded over the hill.

The rain intensified. Squinting through the downpour, she spied the Amish store. One-story, wooden frame, large wraparound porch. Just as Vivian had said, a barn stood at the side of the shop.

Colleen took the turn too sharply. The tires squealed in protest. A gravel path led to the barn. The car bounced over the rough terrain.

She glanced at the road they had just traveled. Trey's car hadn't crested the hill. Relieved, Colleen drove into the barn. Before the engine died, she leaped from the car and pulled the doors closed, casting them in semi-darkness.

Outside, wind howled. Rain pounded against the wooden structure.

"Help me." Vivian's voice.

Colleen raced around the car and opened the passenger door. The woman's face was pale as death. Blood soaked her clothing. For the first time, Colleen saw the gaping hole in Vivian's side.

Removing her own coat, Colleen rolled it into a ball

and pressed it onto the wound to stem the flow of blood. Holding it tight with her left hand, she reached for her cell and tapped in 9-1-1.

Before the call could go through, a ferocious roar, both powerful and insistent, gathered momentum, like a freight train on a collision course with the barn. Even without seeing the funnel cloud, Colleen knew a tornado was headed straight for them.

The barn shook. Hay fell from the overhead loft. The noise grew louder. Colleen's ears popped.

Swirling wind enveloped them. Clods of Georgia clay and shards of splintered wood sprayed through the air like shrapnel.

She threw herself over Vivian, protecting her. *God help us*, Colleen prayed as the tornado hit, and the barn crashed down around them.

"Frank," Evelyn screamed from the kitchen. "There's a tornado."

Startled by the tremor in his sister's voice, Frank Gallagher pulled back the living room curtain. His heart slammed against his chest at what he saw. A huge, swirling funnel cloud was headed straight for her house.

"Get to the basement, Evie."

Her sluggish footsteps sounded from the kitchen as she threw open the cellar door and cautiously descended into the darkness below. Injured in a car accident some years earlier, Evelyn's gait was slow and labored, like a person older than her 42 years.

"Duke?" Frank called. The German shepherd, a retired military working dog, appeared at his side.

"Heel." Together, they followed Evelyn down the steep steps.

An antique oak desk sat in the corner and offered additional protection. Frank hurried her forward.

"Get under the desk, Evie."

A deafening roar enveloped them. Frank glanced through the small basement window. His gut tightened.

Debris sailed through the air ahead of the mass of swirling wind bearing down on them.

His heart stalled, and for one long moment, he was back in Afghanistan. The explosion. The flying debris. The building shattering around him.

Trapped under the rubble, he had gasped for air. The smell of death returned to fill his nostrils. Only he had lived.

Duke whined.

"Frank," Evelyn screamed over the incessant roar. She grabbed his arm and jerked him down next to her.

Frank motioned for Duke to lie beside them. The thunderous wail drowned out his sister's frantic prayers. All he heard was the howling wind, like a madman gone berserk, as chilling as incoming mortar rounds.

He tensed, anticipating the hit, and choked on the acrid bile that clogged his throat. Tightening his grip on his sister's outstretched hand, Frank opened his heart, ever so slightly, to the Lord.

Save Evie. The prayer came from deep inside, from a place he'd sealed off since the IED explosion had changed his life forever. Just that quickly the raging wind died, and the roar subsided.

Frank expelled the breath he'd been holding.

Evelyn moaned with relief. "Thank you, God."

Crawling from under the desk, he helped his sister to her feet and then glanced through the window. Mounds of tree limbs, twisted like matchsticks, littered the yard. At least the house had been spared.

He pulled his mobile phone from his pocket. No bars. No coverage.

Evelyn reached for the older landline phone on the desk. "I've got a dial tone."

"Call 911. Let them know the area along Amish Road was hit and to send everything available. Then phone the Criminal Investigation Division on post. Talk to Colby Voss. Tell him the Amish need help."

"Colby would tell you to stay put, Frank. You're still on convalescent leave."

Ignoring her concern for his well-being, Frank patted his leg for Duke to follow him upstairs.

Another close call. Was God trying to get his attention? A verse from scripture floated through his mind, *Come back to me.*

In the kitchen, Frank yanked his CID jacket from the closet and grabbed leather work gloves he kept nearby. Pushing through the back door, he stopped short and pulled in a sharp breath at what he saw—a different kind of war zone from what he'd experienced in Afghanistan, but equally as devastating.

The tornado had left a trail of destruction that had narrowly missed his sister's house. He searched for the Amish farmhouses that stretched along the horizon. Few had been spared. Most were broken piles of rubble, as if a giant had crushed them underfoot.

A sickening dread spread over him. The noise earlier had been deafening. Now an eerie quiet filled the late Georgia afternoon. No time to lament. People could be trapped in the wreckage.

"Come on, boy." Frank quickly picked his way among the broken branches and headed for the path that led through the woods. He ignored the ache in his hip, a reminder of the IED explosion and the building that had collapsed on top of him. Thankfully, a team of orthopedic surgeons had gotten him back on his feet. A fractured pelvis, broken ribs and a cracked femur had been insignificant compared with those who hadn't made it out alive.

Still weak from the infection that had been a life-threatening complication following surgery, Frank pushed forward, knowing others needed help. Skirting areas where the tornado had twisted giant trees like pickup sticks, he checked his cell en route and shook his head with regret at the lack of coverage.

At the foot of the hill, he donned his leather work gloves and raced toward the Amish Craft Shoppe. A brother and sister in their teens usually manned the store.

"Call out if you can hear me," he shouted as he threw aside boards scattered across the walkway leading to the front porch. "Where are you?" he demanded. "Answer me."

Duke sniffed at his side.

"Can you hear me?" he called again and again. The lack of response made him fear the worst and drove him to dig through the fallen timbers even more frantically.

An Amish man and woman tumbled from a farmhouse across the street. Their home had lost its roof and a supporting side wall.

The bearded man wore a blue shirt and dark trousers, held up with suspenders. Dirt smudged his face and his cheek was scraped.

"The store was closed today," he shouted, waving his hands to get Frank's attention. "The youth are at a neighboring farm."

"You're sure?" Frank was unwilling to give up the search if anyone was still inside.

The man glanced at the woman wearing a typical Amish dress and apron.

"*Jah*, that is right," she said, nodding in agreement.

"What about your family?" Frank called. "Was anyone hurt?"

"Thanks to God, we are unharmed, but our neighbors are in need." The man pointed to the next farmhouse and the gaping hole where the wall and roof had been. He and his wife ran to offer aid.

Before Frank could follow, he glanced at the nearby barn. The corner of one wall remained standing, precariously poised over a pile of rubble. At that moment, the cloud cover broke, and the sun's reflection bounced off a piece of metal buried in the wreckage.

Something chrome, like the bumper of a car. The Amish didn't drive automobiles, but a traveler passing by could have been seeking shelter from the storm.

He raced to the barn and dug through the debris. "Shout if you can hear me."

A woman moaned.

"Where are you?" Frank strained to hear more.

All too well, he knew the terror of being buried. His heart lodged in his throat as the memories of Afghanistan played through his mind.

Duke pawed at a pile of timber, his nose sniffing the broken beams and fractured wood.

He barked.

"Help."

Working like a madman, Frank tossed aside boards piled one upon the other until he uncovered a portion of the car. The passenger door hung open. Shoving fallen beams aside, he leaned into the vehicle's interior.

A woman stared up at him.

"Are you hurt?"

She didn't respond.

Hematoma on her left temple. Cuts and abrasions. She was probably in shock.

"Can you move your hands and feet?"

She nodded.

"Stay put, ma'am, until the EMTs arrive. You could have internal injuries."

She reached for his hand and struggled to untangle herself from the wreckage.

"You shouldn't move, ma'am."

"I need help." She was determined to crawl from the car.

"Take it slow." Frank had no choice but to assist her to her feet. She was tall and slender with untamed hair the color of autumn leaves. She teetered for a moment and then stepped into his arms.

He clutched her close and warmed to her embrace. "You're okay," he whispered. "I've got you. You're safe."

"But—"

She glanced over her shoulder. He followed her gaze, his eyes focusing on a second woman.

Black hair. Ashen face. A bloodstained jacket lay wadded in a ball at her waist.

Pulling back the covering, Frank groaned. Her injury hadn't been caused by the storm.

She'd taken a bullet to the gut.

TWO

Where were the emergency response teams?

Police, fire, EMTs?

Frank removed his belt and wove it under the victim's slender waist. Determined to keep her alive, he cinched the makeshift tourniquet around the rolled-up jacket to maintain pressure and hopefully stop the flow of precious blood she was losing much too fast.

He glanced at the redhead hovering nearby. She looked as concerned as he felt. They both knew that without immediate medical help, the injured woman wouldn't survive.

"If you've got a cell, call 911."

She pulled a phone from her pocket and shook her head. "There...there's no coverage."

The gunshot victim needed an ambulance and needed it fast. Frustration bubbled up within him. After ten years with the US Army's Criminal Investigation Division, Frank didn't like the only conclusion he could make with the information at hand.

"Why'd you shoot her, ma'am?"

Red shook her head, her eyes wide. "I did no such thing."

He pointed to the demolished car. "This is your Honda?"

She nodded.

"How'd she end up in your car?"

"I... I stopped at the picnic park about a mile from here. She needed help. I opened the passenger door, and a shot rang out."

"Did you see the shooter?"

Red rubbed the swollen lump on her forehead. "I... I don't remember."

"Don't remember or don't want to remember?" Even he heard the annoyance in his voice.

The woman stared at him, her face blank. Maybe she was telling the truth.

"What's your name, ma'am?"

"Colleen... Colleen Brennan."

"You're from around here?"

"Atlanta."

Which didn't make sense. "But you just happened to pull into a nearby picnic park?"

Her green eyes flashed with fear.

Trauma played havoc with emotions and memory. Frank wanted to believe her, but he knew too well that the pretty woman with the tangled hair could be making up a story to throw him off track.

Duke sniffed at her leg. She reached down and patted his head.

A raspy pull of air forced Frank's attention back to the gunshot victim. She moaned.

Sirens sounded in the distance.

He leaned into the car. "Stay with us, ma'am. Help's on the way." Hopefully it would arrive in time.

Her glassy eyes focused on Colleen. Frank turned to stare at her.

The redhead blanched. The lump on her temple cried

for ice, and the scrapes to her cheek and hands needed debridement.

"After your friend's treated, we'll have the EMTs take a look at you."

"I'm fine." Colleen's voice was lifeless.

Slipping past her, he waved his arms in the air at the approaching first responders. Two ambulances and a fire truck from one of the rural fire stations.

The emergency crew pulled in front of the Craft Shoppe. Frank motioned them closer to the barn, where they parked and jumped from their vehicles.

"Two women are injured." Frank pointed to the collapsed structure. "One with a bullet wound to her gut. She's lost blood. The other woman has a knot the size of a lemon on her forehead and could be in shock."

Hauling medical bags and a backboard, a pair of EMTs waded through the collapsed wreckage around the car. A second set of paramedics set up an emergency triage area near the second ambulance.

"We'll need you to step away from the car, ma'am," one of the EMTs told Colleen.

Her brow furrowed. She peered around them at Frank.

Seeing the confusion in her gaze, his anger softened. "It's okay," he assured her. "They're here to help."

Despite the niggling worry that Colleen Brennan may have been involved in the shooting, he reached for her. "Come toward me, and we'll get out of their way."

She offered him her hand. Her skin was soft, but clammy, which wasn't good.

"Let's see if someone can check your forehead."

She shook her head. "Vivian's the one who needs help."

"You know her name?" Although surprised by the

revelation, Frank kept his voice low and calm. "What's her last name?"

"I… I don't remember." Colleen pulled her hand from his grasp. "We were trying to get away—"

She hesitated.

"Away from—" he prompted.

"A man. He was in the woods. Tall. Dark jacket. Hood over his head. He had a rifle."

"Did you see a car?"

She shook her head. "Not that I remember."

Selective memory or a partial amnesia brought on by trauma?

"Come with me." Frank ushered Colleen to the triage site. Duke followed close behind.

A pair of EMTs helped her onto a gurney pushed against the side of the ambulance. One man cleaned her hands and face and treated the scratches on her arms while the other took her vitals, checked her pupils and then applied an ice pack to the lump on her forehead.

"You've got a slight concussion, but you don't need hospitalization," he said. "Is there anyone who can check on you through the night?"

She shook her head. "I… I live alone."

"In Atlanta," Frank volunteered.

An Amish man stumbled toward the ambulance. Blood darkened his beard. The EMTs hurried to help him.

"You'll spend the night here in the Freemont area," Frank told Colleen. Before she could object, he pointed to the one-story brick ranch visible in the distance. "My sister, Evelyn, owns the house on top of the knoll. There's an extra room. You can stay with her."

"I… I need to get back to Atlanta."

"From the looks of your car, travel anytime soon

seems unlikely. Downed trees are blocking some of the roadways and won't be cleared until morning."

"Is there a bus station?"

"In town, but you need to talk to law enforcement first."

The downward slope of her mouth and the dark shadows under her eyes gave him concern. She looked fragile and ready to break.

"I... I don't know your name," she stammered.

"It's Frank Gallagher, and the dog's Duke."

Her face softened for a moment as Duke licked her hand, then she glanced back at Frank.

"You're a farmer?"

He shook his head. "I'm an army guy. CID."

Seeing her confusion, he explained, "Criminal Investigation Division. We handle felony crimes for the military."

Her eyes narrowed. "You're a cop?"

He shrugged. "More like a detective. What about you?"

"Flight attendant."

"Hartsfield?"

She nodded, indicating the Atlanta airport.

One of the EMTs returned and pulled a bottle of water from a cooler. "I want you to sit up, ma'am, and drink some water. I'll check on you again in a few minutes."

Frank pointed to the nearby fire truck. "You relax while Duke and I talk to the guys from the fire department."

Rounding the ambulance, Frank glanced at the road. A line of first responders and Good Samaritan townspeople had arrived to help in the rescue effort. The scene farther south was probably the same, with people flocking to the area in hopes of aiding those in need.

Glancing back at Colleen, he was relieved to see she had closed her eyes and was resting her head against the side of the ambulance.

Static played over the fire truck's emergency radio. A tall, slender guy in his midtwenties stood nearby. He wore a navy blue shirt with the Freemont Fire Department logo and a name tag that read Daugherty.

His face brightened when he saw Duke.

"Nice dog."

"Daugherty, can you can patch me through to the local police?"

"No problem, sir."

Once Frank got through to the dispatcher, he explained about the gunshot victim. "Colleen Brennan was the driver of the vehicle. She'll be staying overnight at Evelyn Gallagher's house." He provided the address.

"Everyone's tied up with the rescue operation," the dispatcher explained. "I'll pass on the information, but be patient."

After disconnecting, he requested a second call to Fort Rickman.

"Did you want to contact the military police?" Daugherty asked.

"That works."

He connected Frank to the provost marshal's office. After providing his name, Frank requested all available military help be sent to the Amish area.

"Roger that, sir. I believe we've already received a request for aid, but I'll notify the Emergency Operations Center, just in case. They'll pass the information on to General Cameron."

"Any damage on post?"

"A twister touched down. Some of the barracks in the training area were in the storm's path. No loss of life reported thus far. The chaplain said God was watching out for us."

Frank wasn't sure he'd give God the credit. If the Lord protected some, why were others in the storm's path? "What about Freemont?"

"We've got some spotty reports. A trailer park on the outskirts of town was hit with some injuries. A few shops downtown and a number of the old three-story brick buildings on the waterfront."

"The abandoned warehouses?"

"That's correct. We're awaiting more details from the local authorities. The information I received is that Allen Quincy is heading the civilian relief effort."

"The mayor?"

"Yes, sir. He's asked for our help. We've called in all personnel. I'll pass on the information about the Amish area."

"Let the Red Cross and medical personnel know, as well."

"I'm on it, sir."

"Do you have landline access?" Frank asked.

"To main post only."

"See if you can contact CID Headquarters. Ask for Special Agent Colby Voss. Tell him Special Agent Frank Gallagher is at the Craft Shoppe, located at the northern end of Amish Road. We're going to need him."

"Roger that, sir."

Colby's wife, Becca, had been raised Amish. She knew the area and the local Amish bishop, but Becca was on temporary duty out of the state so Colby was the next best choice.

He and Frank had joined the CID years earlier and had served together before. Frank could attest to Colby's ability both as an investigator and diplomat.

The Amish were a tight community and preferred to take care of their own. After the tornado, they needed help. Colby might be able to bridge the gap between the Amish and their *English* neighbors.

Frank thanked Daugherty for the use of his radio. He and Duke returned to the ambulance in time to hear the EMT reassure Colleen.

"Looks like dehydration was the problem, ma'am," he told her. "Your vitals are better so you're good to go."

"What about that lump on her forehead?" Frank asked.

"She should be okay, especially if someone checks on her through the night."

"It's nothing to worry about," Colleen insisted as she hopped down from the gurney.

Frank reached out a hand to steady her. She held on to him for a long moment and then nodded her thanks. "I'm okay."

"Ma'am, you need to take it easy for the next day or two," the EMT cautioned.

"And the gunshot victim?" Frank asked, his gaze flicking to the other ambulance.

"They're preparing to transport her to the hospital at Fort Rickman, sir."

"Not the civilian facility in Freemont?"

"She was conscious long enough to give her last name. Her husband is a sergeant on post. Sergeant Drew Davis."

Frank didn't recognize the name, but if Vivian was an army spouse, the CID would be involved in the investigation. With the Freemont police working hard on the storm-relief effort, the military might take the lead on the case.

Tonight, everyone would focus on search and rescue.

By morning both the Freemont cops and the military law enforcement would have more time to question Colleen. Until then, Frank would keep her under watch.

Too many things didn't add up. In spite of being on convalescent leave, Frank needed to learn the truth about how a military wife with a gunshot wound had ended up in Colleen's car.

Colleen tried to ignore the pointed stare of the CID agent who had dug her from the rubble. His deep-set eyes and gaunt face were troubling and cut her to the core. In fact, the only redeeming quality about the guy was his dog.

She rubbed her temple, hoping to drive away the pounding headache that had come with the storm. Her memory was fuzzy at best, and she had difficulty recalling some of the most basic information, especially pertaining to Vivian. Without thinking, she'd left her purse in her car along with the memory card.

A pickup truck pulled to a stop in the triage area. The driver, a middle-aged farmer wearing bib overalls and a baseball cap, rolled down his window and nodded to the EMT.

"We found a guy hunkered down in a ditch just over that ridge." The farmer pointed to the rise in the roadway. "His sports car was destroyed, but he survived, although he's scraped up a bit. Face could have been in worse shape if he hadn't been wearing a sweatshirt. Looks like the hood protected him. A guy with an SUV is bringing him your way."

Hooded sweatshirt. Colleen's heart jammed in her throat. Trey had a sporty BMW, although she hadn't seen which of his many cars he was driving today.

If he was the injured man, Colleen had to get out

of sight. She'd come back later for the things she'd left behind.

A gold SUV headed down the hill.

Her stomach fluttered. She turned and started to walk away.

"Where are you going?" Frank called after her.

To hide.

What could she tell him? *Think. Think.*

Her stalled brain refused to work. Searching for an answer, she glanced at the house on the knoll.

"I'm taking you up on that invitation to stay with your sister." Even she heard the tremble in her voice.

Frank raised his brow. Surely he wouldn't rescind the offer?

Her pulse throbbed and sweat dampened her back.

The SUV drew closer.

Colleen waved Frank off. "Stay here and help with the rescue operation. I can find my way up the hill."

She lowered her head, wrapped her arms around her waist and started along the path with determined steps. Keeping her back to the approaching car, she was grateful for the descending twilight and the shadows cast from the tall pines. The path wound along the roadway for a short distance and then burrowed deeper into the woods.

If only she could reach the denser underbrush before the SUV got too close. She couldn't let Trey see her.

Flicking a quick glance over her shoulder, she recognized the firm set of Trey's jaw and the bulk of his shoulders as the car pulled to a stop.

No mistaking the man riding shotgun.

At that moment, he glanced up.

Ice froze her veins. Her heart slammed against her chest. If Trey recognized her, he would track her down.

Not only did Colleen have incriminating photos, but she had also witnessed him shoot Vivian in cold blood.

She increased her pace and darted along the path.

"Wait, Colleen."

The military CID agent ran after her, along with his dog.

Stay away from me, she wanted to scream, but reason won out. She needed Frank. She was stranded without a car with a killer on the loose. She needed the security of his sister's house and his protection throughout the night.

Later, she'd return to the wreckage and retrieve her purse and the memory card. Tomorrow, she'd catch the bus to Atlanta. From there, she'd hop a flight for the West Coast and disappear from sight. She'd leave Trey behind along with the special agent who didn't understand what she was trying to hide.

Frank wondered at Colleen's rush to get away, but then, he wasn't the best at reading women. Case in point Audrey, who said she'd wait for him. The memory still burned like fire.

"Wait up, Colleen."

Frank ran after her. His hip ached, and his breathing was tighter than he'd like.

Before the IED, he'd never questioned his strength. Now he had to weigh everything in light of his physical stamina.

Drawing closer, he grabbed her arm.

She turned troubled eyes filled with accusation. "Let me go."

Releasing his hold, he held up both hands, palm out. "Sorry. I didn't mean to upset you."

She glanced through the bramble to the triage area,

where a cluster of rescue workers gathered. "I'm still shaky."

An understatement for sure. "You've been through a lot today. The temperature's dropped since the storm. You must be cold."

"A little."

He shrugged out of his windbreaker and wrapped it around her shoulders. "This should help."

"What about you?"

"Not a problem." He pointed to the path. "Let's keep going while there's still some light."

"Are you sure your sister won't mind taking in a stray?"

He almost smiled. "She welcomed me a few weeks back with open arms. If I had to guess, I'd say she'd enjoy having another woman in the house. She claims I get a bit snarky at times."

"I'm sure she loves your company."

"She loves Duke."

Colleen almost smiled. "Who wouldn't?" She patted his head, and he wagged his tail, enjoying the attention.

"You've got brothers?" Frank asked, hoping to learn more about the reclusive flight attendant.

She faltered. Her face darkened. "One sister. She passed away four months ago."

"I'm sorry."

"So am I."

"Watch your step." Frank pointed to an area littered with rocks. Taking her arm, he supported her up the steep incline.

"Thanks," she said when they reached the top.

Stopping to catch her breath, she glanced over her shoulder. Frank followed her gaze. Darkness had settled over the small valley, but headlights from the response vehicles and flashing lights from law enforcement cut through the night.

A number of Amish buggies were on the street. Lights from additional rescue vehicles appeared in the distance. Frank needed to get Colleen settled and then return to the triage area and wait for personnel from post to arrive.

If anything good came from the tornado, it was the wake-up call that Frank had been lingering too long, nursing his wounds. He didn't want to appear weak. Not to the military or the other CID agents. Most especially not to himself.

Colleen turned back to Evelyn's house and paused for a long moment. Perhaps she was as unsettled about moving forward as he was. Frank could relate.

But that wouldn't change the problem at hand. He needed to learn more about Colleen Brennan and the gunshot victim. Why were they on the run, and who was after them?

THREE

Some of Colleen's nervous anxiety eased when Frank opened the door to his sister's home, and she stepped inside. The dog followed.

A brick fireplace, painted white, drew her eye along with a beige couch and two side chairs, nestled around a low coffee table. An oil seascape hung over the mantel flanked by built-in shelves filled with books. She neared and glanced at the titles, seeing some of her favorites.

Frank came up behind her. "Did I tell you Evelyn is a librarian?"

"I'm in here." A voice called from the kitchen.

He motioned for Colleen to follow as he headed toward a small hallway that led to a keeping area and open kitchen.

A slender woman, early forties, with chestnut hair and big blue eyes, stood behind a granite-topped island and greeted Frank with a warm smile. She was fair and petite and contrasted with her brother's rugged frame and broad shoulders.

Colleen and her sister had shared similar facial structures, although Briana had been golden-haired like their mother, while Colleen inherited her flaming-red locks from her dad. Seeing the warmth of Evelyn's welcome made Colleen long for her own sister.

"I'm baking a ham and making potato salad for the rescue effort." She stirred mayonnaise into the bowl of boiled potatoes and sliced hard-boiled eggs.

As Colleen moved closer, Evelyn glanced up. The look on her face revealed her surprise at finding a visitor. She wiped her hand on a dish towel.

With a pronounced limp, she moved around the island and opened her arms to greet Colleen with a hug. "Welcome. Looks like you were caught in the storm."

The sincerity of Evelyn's voice touched a raw edge in the depths of Colleen's self-control. Her eyes burned and a lump formed in her throat in response to the genuine concern she heard in the older woman's voice.

Frank quickly made the introductions, his tone suddenly curt and businesslike and so opposite his sister's soothing welcome. As if unsure of where to stand or what to do next, he headed for the coffeepot.

"Care for a cup?" he asked Colleen before glancing at his sister. "Decaf, right?"

"Always at this time or I'd never sleep."

"A glass of water might be better," Colleen said. "But I don't want to trouble you."

Duke nuzzled her leg. He held a tennis ball in his mouth and wanted to play. Before she could take the ball, Frank motioned him to the corner, where he dropped the toy and obediently lay down.

"Good dog."

Frank turned to his sister. "Colleen's car was damaged by the tornado. She lives in Atlanta and hopes to return home in a few days."

"Preferably tomorrow," she quickly added.

"You need a place to spend the night." Evelyn's eyes

were filled with understanding. "We have a spare room. Of course you'll stay here."

Turning to Frank, she added, "Did you bring her luggage?"

"I've got a carry-on bag in the trunk of my car, but I didn't think about it until now," Colleen admitted.

"I'll get it when I head back to the triage area," Frank volunteered.

Colleen held up her hand. "No need. I'll get it in the morning."

"Is there anyone in Atlanta you want to call who might be worried about you?" Evelyn asked.

"That's kind of you, but I have a cell phone." Colleen patted her pocket, reassured by the weight of her mobile device.

"You might not have coverage," Evelyn said. "Some of the cell towers were hit by the storm. Thankfully our landline is still working."

"I take it you got through to the rural fire department," Frank said to his sister.

She nodded. "Which was a blessing. They passed on the information to emergency personnel in town. The local radio station quoted the mayor as saying search-and-rescue operations would continue into the night and throughout the next few days."

"At a minimum." Frank glanced at his watch. "I need to hurry back."

"You need to eat something," Evelyn insisted.

He shook his head.

"Then I'll make a sandwich to take with you."

"More of your attempts to fatten me up?" His tone held a hint of levity that surprised Colleen.

Evelyn opened the refrigerator and pulled out lunch meat, cheese and mustard. As she layered the meat and cheese on two slices of bread, Frank grabbed a glass from one of the overhead cabinets. He filled it with ice and added water from the dispenser on the door of the refrigerator.

"You'll need your coat," Evelyn said, cutting the sandwich in half and wrapping it in foil.

Colleen accepted the water from Frank. From all appearances, his sister was the nurturing type, and despite the macho persona he tried to impart, the CID special agent seemed to readily accept her advice.

"I'm changing into my uniform. Fort Rickman's getting involved, and I want to help them set up."

"You're still on convalescent leave, Frank."

"Only for another week."

He glanced at Colleen and then headed into the hallway that led to the front of the house. "Back in a minute."

While Frank changed, Evelyn showed her to a guest room located behind the kitchen. "This doubles as my office and sewing room. I hope you won't mind the clutter."

A computer sat on a small desk, and colorful baskets filled with fabric and threads were neatly tucked in the shelving that covered the far wall. A double bed, nightstand and small dresser took up the rest of the space.

"If the weather warms tomorrow, you can use the screened-in porch." Colleen pointed to the French doors leading to the private sitting area. "It's usually nice this time of year, although tonight the temperature's a bit chilly."

"It's a lovely room, Evelyn, but I fear I'm putting you out."

"Nonsense. I'm glad Frank found you."

Which he had. He and Duke had found her in the rubble. If they hadn't, no telling how long she and Vivian would have been trapped.

"You're fortunate the storm spared your house," Colleen said as she glanced outside at the downed branches littering the yard.

"God answered our prayers."

Colleen nodded. "I'm sure the Amish folks prayed, as well."

"Of course. Their faith is strong. In fact, they are a resilient community and a forgiving people. They'll rebuild."

"I hate to see dreams destroyed."

Evelyn nodded knowingly. "If only we knew what the future would hold."

The melancholy in her voice gave Colleen pause. Perhaps Evelyn had her own story to tell.

"Frank said there's a bus station in Freemont."

Evelyn raised her brow. "You're in a hurry to get back to Atlanta?"

The question caught Colleen off guard. "As…as soon as possible."

Mentally weighing her options, she realized none of them were good. She couldn't fly without her driver's license and airline identification. Both were in her purse, buried in her car.

She had planned on a fast trip to Freemont to gather the last bit of evidence she needed to send Trey to jail. Now Vivian was in the hospital, and Colleen was stranded in an area devastated by a tornado. To add to her situation, she was holed up with a law enforcement officer who made her uneasy.

A tap sounded at the entrance to her room. She turned to find Frank standing in the doorway. He was clean-shaven and dressed in his army combat uniform. Maybe it was the boots he wore or the digital print of the camouflage that made him seem bigger than life.

She needed to breathe, but the air got trapped in her lungs.

"I'll be back later. Don't wait up, sis."

"The sandwich is on the counter."

"You're spoiling me." Raising his hand, he waved to Colleen and then hurried toward the kitchen.

"The sandwich," Evelyn reminded him.

"Got it," he called before the front door slammed closed behind him.

"Why don't you wash up and come back to the kitchen for something to eat." Evelyn motioned toward the hallway.

"Thanks, but I'm not hungry."

"A bowl of soup might be good."

The woman didn't give up.

As if on cue, Colleen's stomach growled, causing her to smile. "A cup of soup sounds good."

Once Evelyn returned to the kitchen, Colleen pulled back the curtain in the bedroom and watched Frank lower the back hatch on his pickup truck. Duke hopped into the truck bed and barked as if eager to get under way.

Frank climbed behind the wheel. The sound of the engine filled the night. He turned on the headlights that flashed against the house and into the window, catching her in their glare.

She stepped away, hoping he hadn't seen her. Much as she appreciated Evelyn's hospitality and grateful though she was of having a place to stay, Colleen worried about Frank's questions and the way he stared at her when he thought she wasn't looking.

After her sister's death and her own struggle with the Atlanta police, Colleen wanted nothing more to do with law enforcement. Now she was seeking shelter in the very home of a man she should fear.

Only she didn't fear Frank. Something else stirred within her when he was near. Unease, yes, but also a feeling she couldn't identify that had her at odds with her present predicament. She needed to leave Freemont as soon as possible, but until she retrieved her purse and the photo card, she had no other choice but to stay with Frank and his sister.

Hopefully she wasn't making another mistake she would live to regret.

A desire to protect her stirred deep within Frank when he saw Colleen standing at the window as he pulled his truck out of the drive. She had a haunting beauty with her big eyes and high cheekbones and the shock of red curls that seemed unwilling to be controlled.

Did her rebellious hair provide a glimpse into who Colleen really was? She tried to maintain a quiet reserve, yet perhaps a part of her longed to be free like the strands of hair that fell in disarray around her oval face. That disparity between who Colleen tried to be and whom he had caught a glimpse of when she wasn't looking gave him pause.

Driving down the hill from his sister's house, Frank thought of his own past, and the picture he had painted for his life, all with broad brushstrokes. At one time, he'd had it all and thought the future would provide only more positive moments to share with Audrey. He found out too late that she lived life on the surface and wasn't willing to go beneath the false facade she had created.

Frank had thought she understood about sacrifice for a greater good. He'd realized his mistake when she left him, unwilling to be tied down to a wounded warrior who had to face a long, difficult recovery.

At this point, Frank didn't know who he was. Too

many things had changed that clouded the picture. He certainly wasn't the same man as the cocky, sure-of-himself CID agent patrolling an area of Afghanistan where terrorists had been seen. Perhaps he had been too confident, too caught up in his own ability to recognize the danger.

Not that he could go back or undo what had happened. He had to move forward. Donning his uniform tonight was a positive step. The stiff fabric felt good when he'd slipped into his army combat uniform.

At least he looked like a soldier, even if he wasn't sure about the future. Would he continue on with the military or put in his papers for discharge?

A decision he needed to make.

Headlights from a stream of military vehicles appeared in the distance when Frank parked at the barn. Two more ambulances from Freemont had arrived to transport the injured, and radio communication was up and running among the various search-and-rescue operations.

A fireman with wide shoulders and an equally wide neck approached Frank. "Thanks for helping with the relief effort."

"How's it look so far?"

"At least twelve Amish homes and barns have been destroyed. Close to twenty people have been identified as injured. No loss of life, but we're still looking."

"I heard Freemont had damage. A trailer park and some of the warehouses by the river."

"Might be time to clean out that entire waterfront," the fireman said, "but the mayor and town council will make that decision."

Noting the approach of the convoy, Frank pointed to a grassy area between the Amish Craft Shoppe and the collapsed barn. "Can you get someone to direct the military personnel to that level area where they can set up their operations center?"

"Will do." The fireman called two other men who used flares to direct the military vehicles into the clearing.

Frank saluted the captain who crawled from his Hummer.

"Thanks for getting here in a timely manner, sir." Frank introduced himself. "I'm CID, currently on convalescent leave, but I reside in the area and wanted to offer my assistance."

"Appreciate the help." The captain shook Frank's hand and then smiled at Duke. "Nice dog."

"He's a retired military working dog. Duke lost his sense of smell in an IED explosion, but that doesn't stop him from helping out when he can."

Frank passed on the information the fireman had shared about the damage and the injured.

"I've got engineers who will check the structural integrity of the homes still standing once we're assured all the victims have been accounted for." The captain pointed to a group of soldiers raising a tent. "We're setting up a field medical unit to help with the injured. That way the ambulances can transport those needing more extensive medical care to the hospital."

"The local fire and EMTs have a triage area you might want to check out, sir."

"Thanks for the info. I'll coordinate with them."

The captain headed for the civilian ambulances just as Special Agent Colby Voss pulled to a stop in his own private vehicle, a green Chevy.

He climbed from his car and offered Frank a warm smile along with a solid handshake. Instead of a uniform, Colby wore slacks and a CID windbreaker. "I thought you were still on convalescent leave."

"Another week, but I'm ready to get back to work."

"Wilson will like hearing that. We're short staffed as usual, and he'd welcome another special agent."

Frank appreciated Colby's optimism. "Did anyone notify you about Vivian Davis, a gunshot victim who got caught in the storm? She's a military spouse. EMTs took her to the hospital on post."

"The call could have come in while I was away from my desk. Do you have any details?"

"Only that she flagged down a driver at a picnic park farther south, saying she needed help. A shot rang out, the woman was hit. She and the driver escaped."

"Did you question the victim?" Colby asked.

"Negative. She was slipping in and out of consciousness. EMTs needed to keep her alive."

"I'll notify CID Headquarters. What about the driver?"

"Colleen Brennan. She's a flight attendant from Atlanta. Her vehicle is buried under rubble." Frank pointed to the spot where the barn had once stood. "She won't be driving home anytime soon. My sister has a spare bedroom. I invited her to stay the night. The local police don't have time for anything except search and rescue, and I know Fort Rickman is probably equally as busy. I thought keeping an eye on her here might be a good idea, at least until we get through the next twenty-four hours or so."

"Was she injured?"

"A slight concussion and some cuts and scrapes. Nothing too serious, although she was pretty shook up and not too sure about some details. I'm hoping she'll be less confused and more willing to talk in the morning." Frank pointed to the barn. "I'm planning to check out her car if you're looking for something to do."

"Sounds good, but I've got to call Becca. She left a message on my cell after seeing video footage about the storm on the nightly news. Give me a few minutes, and I'll catch up to you."

"The last remaining portion of the barn looks like it could easily collapse, so be careful. If you've got crime scene tape, I'll cordon off the area."

"Good idea. We don't need any more injuries." Colby opened his trunk and handed the yellow roll of tape to Frank.

He grabbed a Maglite from his truck and patted his leg for Duke. "Come on, boy."

The two of them made their way to what remained of the barn. Frank heaved aside a number of boards and cleared space around the rear of Colleen's vehicle before he opened the trunk.

Aiming the Maglite, Frank saw a carry-on bag with a plastic badge identifying Colleen's airline.

"Let's check up front," he told Duke, after he had retrieved the bag and placed it on the ground.

The dog whined.

"What is it, boy?"

Duke climbed over the fallen boards and stopped at the passenger seat, where Vivian had lain earlier. Blood stained the upholstery.

"You're upset the woman was injured." Frank patted the dog's flank. "I am, too. We need to find out who shot her and why."

Bending, he felt under the seat. His fingers touched something leather. He pulled it free.

A woman's purse.

He placed it on the seat and opened the clasp. Shining

the light into the side pocket, he spied Vivian's government ID card and driver's license. Tissues, face powder and high-end sunglasses lay at the bottom.

Leaning down, he again groped his hand along the floorboard. This time, his fingers curled around a smartphone. He stood and studied the mobile device.

An iPhone with all the bells and whistles.

He hit the home button. A circle with an arrow in the middle of the screen indicated a video was primed to play.

Colleen claimed to have happened upon the distressed woman, but if the two had arranged to meet, the video might have been meant for Colleen to view.

Frank hit the arrow, and the footage rolled. A man sat at a booth with Vivian sitting across from him. From the angle, the camera appeared to have been upright on the table, perhaps in a front pocket of her purse with the camera lens facing out.

The guy didn't seem to know he was being recorded.

The audio was sketchy. Frank turned up the volume.

"You brought the package?" The man's voice.

"Relax, Trey. I don't go back on my word."

Trey?

She slipped a rectangular object across the table. The man nervously glanced over his shoulder.

Frank stopped the video. His gut tightened. He'd been in law enforcement long enough to know what the small package, shrink-wrapped and vacuum sealed in plastic, probably contained.

Snow, Flake, Big C.

Also known as cocaine.

FOUR

While Evelyn busied herself in the kitchen, Colleen hurriedly ate a bowl of homemade soup and a slice of homemade bread slathered with butter.

"A friend is stopping by shortly." Evelyn wiped the counter and then rinsed the sponge in the sink. "He's a retired teacher and works with the hospitality committee at church. Ron's organizing a meal for the displaced folks and the rescue workers."

A timer dinged. She opened the oven and pulled out two green bean casseroles and a baked ham.

"The Amish want to take care of their own, but with so many homes destroyed they'll need help. Thankfully, I had a ham and fresh vegetables in the fridge, many grown by my Amish neighbors. They also baked the bread you're eating."

"It's delicious."

Finishing the last of the soup, Colleen scooted back from the table and headed to the sink. "I was hungrier than I thought. I'm sure the homeless will appreciate the food." She rinsed her dishes and silverware and loaded them in the dishwasher.

"I'd invite you to join us, but you look worn-out," Evelyn said. "Better to get a good night's sleep. There will be plenty of ways to get involved in the days ahead."

"I'm going back to Atlanta."

Evelyn nodded. "That's right. I didn't mean to change your plans, but if you decide to stay longer, you know you're welcome."

A knock sounded. She hurried to open the front door and invited a man inside. Returning to the kitchen, she introduced Ron Malone. He was of medium build and height but had expressive eyes and a warm smile, especially when he looked at Evelyn.

For an instant, Colleen had a sense of déjà vu.

Shaking it off, she tried to focus on what Evelyn was saying. Something about organizing the food.

"Colleen was driving through the area when the tornado hit," Evelyn explained. "Her car was damaged. She hopes to get back to Atlanta in a day or two."

Tomorrow.

"I'm amazed at the immediate response from so many who want to help." Colleen shook Ron's outstretched hand. "I doubt the same would happen in Atlanta."

"I think you'd be surprised about the number of caring people even in the city."

Colleen didn't share his opinion, but Evelyn's friend had an engaging manner, and from the way Evelyn was smiling, she must think so, as well.

"If you don't mind, I'll say good-night and head to my room."

Evelyn gave her a quick hug. "Hope you sleep well."

Colleen didn't plan to sleep. She planned to do something else, something she didn't want Evelyn to know about.

Timing would be important. She needed to be back at the house before Frank came home. He was the last person she wanted to see tonight.

Once the front door closed and Ron had backed out of the driveway, Colleen left the house through the French doors and scurried across the yard to the path in the woods. Gingerly, she picked her way down the hill.

A large military tent had been erected since she'd left the triage area. It was located close to the Amish Craft Shoppe and well away from the barn.

Staying in the shadows, she inched forward, grateful that her eyes had adjusted to the darkness. All along Amish Road, flashing lights illuminated the ongoing rescue effort.

Glancing back, she saw the glow in Evelyn's kitchen window like a beacon of hope in the midst of the destruction. The sincere welcome and concern she had read in her hostess's gaze had brought comfort.

If only she could sense a bit of welcome from Frank. He revealed little except a mix of fatigue and frustration. The only time she'd seen his expression brighten was when he'd talked to his sister. Other than that, he'd seemed closed, as if holding himself in check.

Judging by his appearance, he must have either been sick or sustained an injury. Her heart softened for an instant before she caught herself and reeled in her emotions. She didn't want to delve into his past or any pain he carried. She had enough of her own.

Her eyes burned as she thought of her sister. Too often, Briana had called begging for money to buy more drugs. Colleen had adopted a tough-love attitude that had backfired. She had hoped going after Trey would ease the burden of guilt that weighed her down. Now Vivian was injured, and the evidence she had planned to give Colleen was buried in the rubble.

Squinting into the night, Colleen saw the outline of her Honda, partially covered with debris. The passenger door was still open. Using her cell phone for light, she approached the car and leaned inside.

Working her hand across the floorboard, she searched for two purses, one of which contained the evidence Vivian had promised. The other—her own handbag—held the tiny memory card filled with digital photos.

Trying to recall the series of events when she pulled into the roadside park, Colleen bent lower. Vivian had dropped her purse at her feet as soon as she'd climbed into the car. Colleen extended her arm under the seat and then stretched down even farther.

A hand touched her shoulder.

She jerked. Her head knocked against the console, hitting near the spot injured earlier in the storm. The pain made her gasp for air. Rubbing the initial knot that was still noticeable, she turned to stare into Frank's dark eyes.

"Looking for something?" His voice was laced with accusation.

"My…my carry-on bag," she stammered.

He gripped her upper arm and pulled her from the car.

"What are you doing?" Her voice cracked, making her sound like a petulant child when she wanted to be forceful and self-assured.

"Let go of my arm," she demanded, more satisfied with the intensity of her command.

"Promise me you won't run."

She straightened her back. As if she could outrun Frank.

"I was searching for *my own* luggage in *my own* car. That doesn't warrant being manhandled."

His head tilted. He released his hold on her.

She rubbed her arm. He hadn't hurt her, but he had been aggressive.

Dark shadows played over his steely gaze. "What were you really looking for, Colleen?"

Refusing to be intimidated, she held her ground. "I just told you. My carry-on."

"Which I found in the trunk of your car." He held up the shoulder bag Vivian had carried. "Was this what you wanted?"

"That's Vivian's purse. She dropped it on the floor when she slipped into the car."

"Then maybe you were looking for her cell." He held up the iPhone.

"Should I have been?"

He leaned closer. "You tell me."

"Look, Frank, we're not getting anywhere fast. I'm sure Vivian would like her purse and phone back. As for me, I'm not interested in either item."

"Did Vivian tell you about the video? The near-field communication function was turned on. Had she planned to send a copy of the video to your phone?"

"I don't know anything about a video."

Vivian had evidence she'd wanted to share. A chill ran down Colleen's spine. Frank had found what Vivian had promised to provide.

He tapped Vivian's phone. A picture appeared on the screen of a rectangular object wrapped in plastic.

Colleen leaned in to view the screen. "What's in the shrink wrap?"

"Don't play dumb. You know exactly what the package contains."

She pulled back, frustrated by the hostility in his voice.

When she didn't respond, he took a step closer, too close.

"Coke. Crack. Crystal." He glared down at her. "You get the message?"

His eyes narrowed even more. "Were you and Vivian working for the guy in the video, only maybe Vivian was dealing on the side? Maybe she wanted to rip him off? He got angry and followed her."

Frank hesitated for half a heartbeat. "Or was he following you? Did you and Vivian plan to blackmail him? Maybe you wanted payment for the video. Did you ask for cash, or did you want the payoff in drugs?"

Anger swelled within her. Frank was just like the cops in Atlanta.

"Do you always jump to the wrong conclusion?" she threw back at him. "Must not bode well for your law enforcement career."

Fire flashed from his eyes. She had struck a sore spot. He took a step back and pursed his lips.

"We need to talk." He glanced up the hill. "At Evelyn's house."

"You mean you're not going to haul me off to jail?"

"Tell me the truth, Colleen. That's all I want. Why did you meet Vivian at the roadside park? Who's the guy in the video? Was he the shooter? If so, why'd he come after you? If you'll answer those questions, then I'll listen. If you're unwilling, I'll transport you to CID Headquarters tonight."

She raised her chin with determination and stood her ground. "I'm not military. You don't have jurisdiction over me."

A muscle in his neck twitched. "Then I'll contact the local authorities."

"They're busy, tied up with the aftermath of the storm. I doubt they'd be interested."

"You're wrong. A woman was shot. She was in a video and appears to have been dealing drugs. The local authorities may be busy, but they're not that busy."

Colleen breathed out a deep sigh of resignation. She didn't have a choice. "You're right, Frank. We need to talk."

"I've got my truck." He pointed to where it was parked on the far side of the Amish store.

If only she had noticed the vehicle earlier. She would have turned around and returned to Evelyn's house and not attempted to search her car while Frank was in the area.

Hindsight wouldn't help her now.

She walked purposefully toward the pickup with Frank following close behind.

Duke stared at her from inside the cab. Frank reached around her and opened the passenger door. "Down, boy."

The dog jumped onto the gravel driveway. Colleen slipped into the passenger seat.

Once Duke was secured in the back of the pickup, Frank returned to the barn and stretched crime scene tape around her car. Her heart skittered in her chest. The yellow tape made everything that had happened today even more real. She raked fingers through her thick curls. What had she been thinking, trying to cover up information from the authorities?

Her eyes burned. She clenched her fists, blinking back the tears. She needed to be strong. If she broke down, Frank would think she had something to hide.

Walking back to his truck, he raised his cell phone

to his ear. Was he answering a call or making one? To local law enforcement perhaps?

Would the police be waiting for her at Evelyn's house? She bit her lip and looked into the darkness. How had she gotten into this predicament when all she wanted was to talk sense into Vivian and gather more evidence against Trey?

Frank rounded the car and slid into the driver's seat. His long, lean body hardly fit in the confined space. She tried to imagine him bulked up. Perhaps he wouldn't seem as menacing then. Somehow his pensive expression and hollowed cheeks gave him a frosty appearance that was less than approachable.

He turned the key in the ignition. Colleen was glad for the rumble of the engine and the sound of the wheels on the gravel drive as he backed away from the Amish store.

She didn't want to talk to Frank, yet that's what would happen shortly. Colleen wouldn't lie, but she couldn't tell him everything. He'd be like the other law enforcement officers she had approached.

They hadn't believed her.

Frank wouldn't believe her either.

Instead of driving up the mountain, Frank headed to where the rescue crews were working farther south along Amish Road.

Colleen didn't question the change of direction. Instead she gazed out the passenger window as if distancing herself from Frank.

Through the rearview mirror, he saw Duke balanced in the truck bed, his nose sniffing the wind. The dog had an innate ability to read people. Duke had taken to Colleen from the onset, yet Frank wouldn't make a judgment about Colleen based on his canine's desire for attention.

Nearing the rescue activity, he pulled to the side of the road and cut the engine. "I'll just be a minute."

She nodded but didn't question the stop.

Duke whined to get down.

"Stay and guard the truck." *Guard Colleen, as well.*

Huge generators operated the emergency lights and rumbled in the night. Frank's eyes adjusted to the brightness, and he quickly searched for a familiar face in the wash of rescue personnel.

Spying Colby near one of the medical vehicles, Frank hurried forward. The other agent held up both hands and shrugged with regret.

"Frank, I'm sorry. I got caught up in a problem with the Amish and never made it to the barn. Did you find what you were looking for?"

"I found Colleen." Frank glanced back at the truck. She held her head high and stared straight ahead. If only he could tap into that defensive shell she wore as protection.

He turned back to Colby. "Any chance you can spare an hour or two?"

"We're in good shape here. What do you need?"

"Colleen was rummaging through her car. Supposedly she was searching for her carry-on bag. Earlier I had found Vivian's phone with a video showing what appeared to be a drug exchange."

"You know we're not allowed to search a suspect's cell phone without a warrant."

Frank nodded. "I was checking to see if it still had power. The video came up on the screen. I didn't have to search for anything, and I didn't access her call log, much as I would have liked that information, as well."

"You think both women were dealing?"

"I'm not sure what to think, but Colleen's ready to answer questions, and I want you there since I'm not officially on duty."

"You could take her into post."

Frank nodded. "That's an option, but Fort Rickman's digging out from the storm. I doubt anyone wants to stop that effort to question a witness when we can handle it here."

"Good point. I'd be glad to serve as another set of eyes and ears. Give me a minute to let the captain know that I'll be away from the area for a bit. I'll meet you at Evelyn's house."

Frank appreciated having another CID agent present when he questioned Colleen. She seemed legit, but even pretty young things with red hair popped pills and dealt drugs. Better to be cautious instead of making another mistake. Frank hadn't seen Audrey for who she really was. He needed to be right about Colleen.

Was she a deceptive drug dealer or an innocent woman caught in the wrong place at the wrong time?

FIVE

Knowing Frank would be thorough with his questioning, Colleen climbed from his truck as soon as they got back to Evelyn's house. While he tended to his dog, she headed for the kitchen. Working quickly, she filled the coffee basket with grounds and poured water into the canister. The rich brew would help her see things more clearly, and the caffeine would ease her fatigue.

The scent of coffee soon filled the kitchen. She pulled mugs from the cabinet and placed them on the counter. Frank entered the house and wiped his feet on the rug by the door before heading down the hallway.

Just as she expected, his gaze was filled with questions when he stepped into the kitchen.

"The coffee will be ready in a minute," she said, hoping to deflect his initial frustration.

"Are you and Vivian dealing drugs?" he asked without preamble.

"Of course not."

"A woman was shot and fell into your car. Your rear window took a hit, which means you could have been a target, yet you didn't know who the assailant was or why he was after Vivian. You didn't even claim to know her name until you inadvertently shared that information when she was fighting for her life."

Colleen bit her lip, not knowing what she should tell him and where she should start.

Frank continued to stare at her. "You know a lot more than you let on, Colleen. The video shows Vivian dealing drugs. She was injured in your car. Looks to me like you're involved. The CID will investigate, as will the local police. It's time to start talking."

Trembling internally, Colleen struggled to appear calm and in control. Thankfully, her hand didn't shake when she poured coffee and handed the filled mug to the man who had followed Frank into the kitchen.

He wore a CID windbreaker and had watched the exchange with a raised brow. The guy was shorter than Frank but carried an additional ten to twenty pounds—all muscle.

"I'm Colleen Brennan," she stated matter-of-factly. "And you are?"

"Colby Voss. Special agent, Criminal Investigation Division."

"From Fort Rickman?"

He nodded.

"Then you work with Frank," she added, following the logical progression.

"Not yet. He's on convalescent leave and will be assigned to the post CID when he goes back on active duty."

She turned to Frank. "So you're not officially on duty."

"My leave status doesn't change the fact that I'm a CID agent. We still need to talk." His gaze was chilling. He wanted answers, not random chatter.

"It's time for you to come clean, Colleen."

She nodded. After filling a cup for Frank and one for herself, she carried both of them to the kitchen table. "I'm sure you're as tired as I am. Let's sit while we talk."

He groaned with frustration, but pulled out a chair across from her and lowered himself into the seat. Grabbing the coffee mug, he took a sip.

Colby sat at the end of the table and retrieved a small tablet and pen from his pocket. "I'll make note of anything you want to share, ma'am."

"Thank you." She tried to smile. "You're investigating Vivian's shooting?"

The agent tapped his pen and then raised his gaze to meet Frank's. "Special Agent in Charge Wilson will make that call. Right now, I'm here with Frank to help with the local recovery effort."

She nodded and then hesitated, trying to determine where to begin. "At seventeen, my sister, Briana, ran away from home to marry a shiftless bum named Larry Kelsey. He promised her a lot of things, including an acting career in Hollywood. The marriage didn't last long. She got rid of Larry, but kept her dream of fame and fortune."

Colleen tried to smile. "In spite of Briana's skewed sense of what was important in life and her naïveté, she was beautiful and poised and articulate."

Everything Colleen wasn't.

"About a year after her divorce, she took up with an Atlanta photographer. Although somewhat successful, the photography business was a front for his drug-trafficking operation. He got Briana hooked and then used her as a mule to bring in drugs from Colombia. Four months ago, she overdosed from drugs he'd given her and died."

Colby shifted in his seat as he took down the information. Frank steeled his jaw and continued to stare at Colleen as she continued.

"One day, I… I ran into Trey in the grocery store." She played her finger around the rim of her mug. She wanted to laugh at the irony, but everything caught in her throat. "Our shopping carts collided, which he thought was accidental. He didn't realize I'd been watching him and had planned our meeting. Trey was apologetic and a perfect gentleman, or so he tried to seem. Because of Briana's married name, he never realized I was her sister."

"Trey's last name?" Colby asked.

"Trey Howard," she replied. "I let him take me out a few times. Nice places. Upscale eateries. Plays at the Fox, art shows at the High Museum. He said we liked the same things. At least that's what he thought." Again she hesitated.

"So you had a relationship," Frank pressed, his tone as hard as his gaze.

She held up her hand in protest. "If you're implying that we were involved or that anything happened between us, you've got it all wrong. As I kept telling Trey, we were friends, enjoying time together."

When she took a sip of coffee, Colby added, "But things changed."

"I'm a flight attendant with some seniority. I fly to Colombia two or three times a month. Trey mentioned having worked there on a resort property. He took photos for a brochure and pamphlets for vacationers looking for a new place to visit. The photos he showed me were lovely. He told me he'd arrange for me to enjoy an all-expenses-paid stay there on my next layover. The resort liked airline personnel and would be happy to have me as their guest at no expense to me."

"You took him up on the offer?" Frank asked.

"I made an excuse, but the next time I was scheduled to fly, he mentioned it again. He thought I didn't want to be beholden to anyone. He needed a package brought back into the US and suggested I do him the favor in return for the resort accommodations."

Frank leaned in closer. "Did you ask what was in the package?"

"No, but I didn't need a degree in law enforcement to know the package probably contained something the government might not want brought into this country."

"You notified the authorities?"

She pulled in a deep breath. "Trey was well connected. I needed evidence before I accused him of anything illegal."

"Go on," Frank encouraged.

"One night I surprised him at his condo. He was working in his office, but said he needed to take a break and was glad I had stopped by. We were in the living area when he got a phone call. He apologized for taking the call and said he'd be tied up for ten to fifteen minutes. I excused myself to use the restroom. His office was across the hall, but he didn't go there to talk. Instead, he went outside on the deck, which gave me the opportunity I'd been hoping for."

"You searched his office?" Frank seemed surprised.

"I had questions that needed answers and wanted to be sure I was right about who Trey really was."

"You put yourself in danger, Colleen."

"Maybe, but Trey trusted me at that point. Besides—" she raised her brow "—I'm sure you've been in harm's way a time or two."

"It's my job. You're a civilian and not law enforcement."

"That's correct, but if the authorities weren't interested in bringing down a known drug trafficker, I had to get involved."

At the time, she hadn't thought about the danger to herself. She'd thought only of gathering the evidence she needed.

"Give me all the information you have about Trey," Colby interjected.

She provided his address and phone number. "He's got a studio in College Park, not far from the airport, and another one in Midtown."

"What did you find that night?" Frank asked.

"A list of names that included two young women I'd read about in the *Atlanta Journal-Constitution* some weeks earlier. Jackie Leonard and Patty Owens."

Colby wrote the names in his notebook.

"Both women had disappeared months earlier. They worked in the King's Club downtown. Jackie's body was found stuffed in the locked trunk of an automobile in long-term parking at the airport. The car had been stolen. Patty's body was recovered in a shallow grave in Union City, south of the airport."

"Had you known the women?" Frank asked.

She shook her head. "I told you, I read about them in the *AJC*, but their stories aren't much different from Briana's. I'm sure Trey promised them payment in drugs if they brought a few packages into the country for him."

"Finding their names on a list doesn't establish the photographer's guilt."

"Maybe not, but it does increase the cloud of suspicion hanging over his head."

Frank pursed his lips. "Let's go back to when you were in Trey's office. You saw a list of names and recognized the two women in question."

"That's right." She nodded.

"Did you find anything else?"

"Trey said he'd been working, so I clicked on his computer. A photo appeared on the screen."

Colby glanced up.

"Go on," Frank prompted.

"The picture showed a table near a huge window that looked down on a swimming pool and lush gardens with the ocean in the distance. Bricks wrapped in plastic were on the table."

"Shrink-wrapped in plastic?"

She nodded.

Frank's tone hardened. "Just like the package Vivian handed off in the video."

Colleen raked her hand through her hair and sighed. "Yes."

Colby sniffed. "Seems I missed something."

Frank pulled the iPhone from his pocket and hit the home button, then the play arrow. He held it up for Colleen to see. "Who's the guy in the footage?"

She leaned across the table. "Trey Howard."

"That's what I thought." Frank handed the cell to Colby. "As I mentioned earlier, Vivian had the near-field communication function turned on."

"Because she planned to copy the video to someone else's phone." Colby made a notation in his tablet.

Frank turned back to Colleen. "How'd you hook up with Vivian?"

"Her name was on the list, along with a phone number. I recognized the Georgia area code, and did a search on the internet."

She glanced at Colby. "Vivian likes social media. I learned her husband was deployed to Afghanistan, and she was interested in modeling so she'd had photographs taken for her portfolio."

"Trey did the photography?" Frank asked.

"That's right. He can be charming when he wants something. I'm sure he told Vivian she'd be a successful cover model."

"But he wasn't interested in her career."

"Hardly." She pulled in a breath. "Trey needed another mule to transport drugs into the country."

"How can you be certain?"

"I called her. She was scared. Her husband had redeployed home, and she wanted to cut off all contact with Trey."

Frank shook his head and narrowed his gaze. His tone was laced with skepticism. "She admitted to bringing a package into the US from Colombia?"

"Not in so many words, but I understood what she was trying to tell me."

"Why would she reveal anything over the phone?"

"I knew enough about Trey and how he operated to convince her. Plus, she'd met Briana at Trey's photo studio the day she was having her portfolio done."

"Wasn't Trey afraid the girls he used would rat him out to the cops?"

"I don't know how Trey's mind functions, but he's despicable and conniving, and he kept close tabs on anyone who worked for him. If they talked about leaving his operation, he got rid of them."

"Do you know that for sure?"

She sighed. "I don't have proof. I do have what you'd call circumstantial evidence that points to him."

"You think Trey killed Jackie Leonard and Patty Owens?"

"Maybe not personally, but he could have ordered

one of the thugs who are part of his operation to do his dirty work."

"Could have?" Frank repeated the phrase she had used. "Did Trey kill your sister?"

"She overdosed on drugs he provided."

"You notified the authorities?"

"I did, but they had other, more pressing cases to investigate. Or so it seemed."

"Did Briana tell you about Trey?"

"She…she was slipping into a coma and died soon after I got to the ER. The only thing she said was to stop Trey Howard."

Which Colleen had vowed to do.

Had she made a mistake by taking on so much by herself? She rubbed her forehead and swallowed the lump that clogged her throat. She wanted to cry, but she couldn't appear weak. Not with Frank sitting across the table.

He scooted out of his chair and reached for the coffee carafe. He refilled her cup and his.

Colby held up his hand. "No more for me."

"Let's go back to Vivian," Frank said when he returned to the table. "You two decided to meet?"

"That's right. At the roadside park, but Trey was hiding in the woods."

"Why risk meeting her?"

"Vivian said she had something that would prove his guilt. I wanted that evidence."

"Evidence or drugs?"

Colleen didn't know whether to burst into tears or pound her fist on the table at his pigheadedness. She did neither. Instead she willed her expression to remain neutral and her voice controlled.

"I planned to mail whatever evidence Vivian provided, along with the list of names and the photo I found on Trey's computer, to the DEA."

"You have the photo?"

"I used the camera on my phone and took a snapshot of his computer screen. It's not the best quality, but I thought it was enough to get the police interested."

"If it's still on your phone, send the photo to my email," Frank requested.

"I'll need a copy," Colby added. Both men provided their online addresses. Colleen plugged the information into her phone and sent the photo as an attachment.

Frank left the kitchen and returned with his laptop in hand. He placed it on the table, hit the power button and quickly accessed his inbox. After opening the attachment Colleen had sent, he enhanced the screen.

"There's some type of case on the edge of the table with an identity tag, although it's too blurred to read."

She nodded. "The tag says Howard. It's Trey's camera case. That's why I thought the cop would be interested."

"But he wasn't?"

"He said I could have pulled the photo off the internet."

Colby glanced at the computer screen over Frank's shoulder. "Any idea where the picture was taken?"

"In La Porta Verde, the Colombian resort Trey wanted me to visit. As I mentioned, Trey had done the photo layout for their brochures and website when the resort was first built."

Frank tapped in the name of the resort. The home page appeared. He hit Additional Photos and clicked through a series of still shots. "Here it is. The same pool and gardens with the ocean as a backdrop."

Although still not satisfied with the direction of the

questioning, Colleen felt somewhat relieved that Frank and Colby recognized the connection between the photo from Trey's laptop and the resort website.

"I sent the website URL to the Atlanta police," she continued, "along with the photo. The officer who talked to me didn't see the tie-in and said neither seemed relevant to him."

"Who'd you deal with?"

"An officer named Anderson."

Colby returned to the table and made note of the name. "Did he want to talk to you in person?"

She shook her head.

"So your only dealing with the police was over the phone to a cop named Anderson?" Frank asked.

"I dealt with two different officers at two different times. After Briana died, I contacted a cop named Sutherland. He worked close to where she lived." Colleen glanced down at her partially filled mug, remembering the less than desirable area. "He was a tough guy who didn't seem interested in the fact that she'd OD'd. He kept asking pointed questions about my relationship with my sister and insinuated I had something to do with her death."

Frank shook his head. "That doesn't make sense."

Colleen bristled. "Maybe not, but I'm just telling you what happened."

Seeing the frustration plainly written on Frank's face, she glanced down and rubbed her hand over the table. "The cop talked about the free flow of drugs to the inner city often brought in by dealers who lived in the nicer neighborhoods."

"Did you mention the photographer's name?"

She shook her head. "Sutherland made it perfectly

clear that he wasn't interested in the accusations of a dying addict."

"What about Anderson? Did you have any more contact with him?"

"Not face-to-face, but someone came to my apartment."

Frank glanced at Colby then back at her. "Go on."

"I had a short overnight flight. The gal who lives in the apartment across the hall called to tell me someone had been looking for me."

"Anderson?"

"I'm not sure. He wasn't in uniform, but Trey had boasted of having connections with the Atlanta PD. I was afraid Anderson might be on the take."

"Why would you jump to that conclusion?"

She shrugged. "Call it woman's intuition, but a warning bell went off. I had my carry-on bag so I checked into a motel instead of going home."

"That's when you contacted Vivian."

"A few days later. I needed more evidence, which I planned to mail to the DEA."

"Calling them on the phone would be a whole lot easier."

"Vivian didn't want her name used, and I didn't want the call traced back to me."

"Because?" Frank asked.

"I didn't know if they'd believe me."

She stared across the table at Frank, who seemed like the other cops with whom she'd dealt. "You don't believe me either."

He hesitated for a long moment. "I'm not sure what I believe."

His words cut her to the quick.

She glanced at Colby. "What about you?"

"I'm just making note of your statement, ma'am. More information will be needed before I can satisfactorily evaluate your response."

"Lots of words to say you're not on my side." She shoved her chair away from the table. "Neither of you are."

Standing, she glared at Frank. "If you'll excuse me. I'll answer any additional questions you might have in the morning."

She turned on her heel and walked with determined steps to the guest room. Closing the door behind her, she dropped her head in her hands and cried.

Frank let her go. She was worn-out and on the brink of shattering. He felt as frustrated as she looked and needed time to process what she had already revealed. Parts of her story seemed valid, although her attempt to bring down a drug dealer single-handedly was hard to accept. Yet surely she could have made up a more plausible story—and one that was less convoluted—if she was trying to cover up her own involvement.

He turned back to his laptop. "Let's check out those newspaper articles about Jackie Leonard and Patty Owens."

Searching through the *AJC* archives, Frank located information on both women. Just as Colleen had said, the girls had worked at the King's Club in Atlanta. Frank checked the address and mentioned the location to Colby.

He nodded. "The heart of the inner city. Crime is rampant in that area. Those girls were flirting with trouble."

"Looks like they found it." Frank read the news stories about their bodies being found. "Know anyone in the Atlanta PD?"

"There used to be a guy. Former military. George Ulster. I could see if he's still there."

"Find out if he knows Sutherland or Anderson. Get his take on both guys. See if anyone suspects either of them is dirty. Then see what Ulster knows about the two women and whether the PD has any leads. Mention Colleen's sister, just in case there's a tie-in. Seems all three women were on a downward spiral." Frank shook his head with regret. "And hit bottom."

The front door opened, and Evelyn's laughter filtered down the hallway. Stepping into the kitchen, her face sobered. She glanced first at Frank, who quickly logged out of the archives, and then nodded to Colby.

Ron walked up behind her. "Evening, folks."

To her credit, Evelyn seemed to realize this wasn't the time for late-night chatter. She patted his arm. "It's late, Ron. We need to say good-night."

She hurried him toward the door. After a hasty few words, he left the house, and Evelyn headed to her room.

Frank closed his laptop and stood. The energy had drained from him. He grabbed the mugs off the table and placed them in the dishwasher.

Colby glanced at his watch. "It's late. I need to get back to post. I'll take the iPhone with me and stop by headquarters in the morning. Hopefully, I'll be able to talk to Wilson about getting a warrant to access her call list."

"The Freemont police need to be in the loop, but I want Wilson's approval before I do anything."

Colby headed for the hallway and then turned back. "Try to get some sleep, Frank. She's not going anywhere. At least not tonight. Besides, we all might think a bit more clearly in the morning."

Frank watched his friend leave the house. He planned to lock the doors and let Duke have the run of the house. If anyone tried to get in or out, the dog would sound a warning. Frank needed to be careful and cautious. He didn't want anything to happen to Colleen, whether she was telling the truth or not.

SIX

Colleen woke the next morning with a pounding headache. She touched the lump on her forehead and groaned, thinking back over everything that had happened.

Vivian! God, help her. Heal her.

If only she could get an update on the army wife's condition. As soon as Vivian was able to talk, the police and military authorities would question her. The video proved she had been working for Trey. Even if she claimed innocence, Vivian had brought drugs into the United States from Colombia and would, no doubt, be tried and prosecuted.

Would her guilt rub off on Colleen?

Throwing her legs over the side of the bed, she sat up and groaned again. How had her once orderly, controlled life gotten so out of hand? She longed to flee Freemont and Georgia and wipe everything she knew about Trey and his trafficking from her memory. As if she could.

Thinking back over Frank's barrage of questions last night, she sighed. She had kept some information from Frank, not wanting to fuel the flame of his disbelief. Still, she should have mentioned seeing Trey at the triage area right after the twister hit.

How could she have been so forgetful? Actually more like stupid. Probably because of her own nervousness and because Frank's penetrating gaze had left her frazzled and totally undone.

She specifically hadn't mentioned the memory card because of the digital photo she feared Frank might see. A photo taken of her with Trey's so-called friends, who were probably involved in his drug operation.

Frank didn't believe her now, and she refused to give him any more reason to doubt her. His cryptic and caustic tone had been hard enough to deal with last night. As much as she didn't want to face him in the light of day, he needed to know Trey could still be in the area.

Leaving the comfort of the bed, she walked to the window and opened the shades. Her mood plummeted as low as the gray cloud cover that blocked the sun and put a heavy pall on the day. At least it wasn't raining.

Needing something to hold on to, she once again reviewed the steps she needed to take to get out of Freemont. Once she retrieved her identification and the memory card, she would head back to Atlanta. Catching a flight to the West Coast seemed her best option. As Frank had suggested last night, she could notify the Atlanta DEA by phone—an untraceable cell—or even by email, all the while staying out of the agency's radar and away from Trey Howard and the men who worked for him.

A safer escape plan might be to drive to Birmingham, two hours west in Alabama, and fly out of that airport. If Trey's men or the Atlanta PD were checking Hartsfield, she didn't want to walk into a trap after all her hard work trying to prove Trey's guilt.

Had he already returned to Atlanta?

Or was he still in Freemont?

If so, it was because he was looking for her. Knowing how effective Trey was in getting what he wanted, she couldn't successfully hide out for long.

With a shudder, she yanked the curtain closed again and hastily slipped into jeans and a lightweight sweater from her carry-on bag.

Colleen looked at her reflection in the mirror after she'd brushed her teeth and scrubbed her face in the adjoining bathroom. Her cheeks were flushed from the abrasive washcloth she'd scrubbed with and the cold water she'd splashed on her face.

Running a comb through her hair, she hoped to untangle the mess of curls that swirled around her face. She usually relied on the products she'd forgotten to pack to tame her unruly mane.

All she could do was roll her eyes at the halo of locks that circled her face. She'd never liked her red hair, and this morning's frizz made her look like Little Orphan Annie, only older and in no way cute or endearing.

For a fleeting moment, Colleen wondered what type of woman Frank liked. Blondes, perhaps, with rosy cheeks and finely arched brows. Maybe jet-black hair and ivory skin turned his fancy. Or women with big eyes and tiny, bow-shaped mouths.

She scoffed at her foolishness. Why would she even consider such thoughts? As far as she'd seen, the CID agent was all business with no pleasure allowed.

Colleen made the bed and tidied the room. After ensuring the colorful quilt and lace pillow shams were in place, she let out a deep breath and opened the door to the hallway.

The smell of fried eggs and bacon, mixed with the rich aroma of fresh-brewed coffee, led her to the kitchen. Usually Colleen skipped breakfast, but this morning her stomach growled with hunger, and her mouth watered for whatever Evelyn was cooking.

Stepping into the airy room, she was greeted with a wide smile from her hostess. Standing at the counter, Evelyn was arranging biscuits, still warm from the oven, in a cloth-lined basket.

"Tell me all the food I smell isn't just for you and Frank," Colleen said with a laugh.

"Help yourself. I've got four egg-and-bacon casseroles in the oven for the rescue workers. Ron's coming over at nine-thirty to take them to the triage area. You're welcome to join us if you feel able, but first, you need breakfast."

"Coffee sounds good. Mind if I pour a cup?"

"Mugs are in the cabinet closest to the stove."

Colleen selected a sturdy mug with a blue design. "Polish pottery, isn't it?"

Evelyn nodded. "Frank gave me the set for my birthday two years ago. They're popular with the military."

Colleen enjoyed the weight of the pottery as she filled it with coffee.

"Cream's in the refrigerator. There's sugar on the counter."

"Black works for me."

"You're like Frank. He claims sugar spoils the taste."

Colleen tried to seem nonchalant as she took a sip of the hot brew and then asked, "Is Frank helping with the relief effort?"

"He's in his room getting ready. I tried to convince him to sleep in this morning. I heard him pacing until the wee hours. In case you haven't noticed, my brother has a mind of his own, which sometimes causes him problems. He thinks he can do the things he used to do before his surgery."

"I heard mention of convalescent leave last night. Was Frank wounded during a deployment?"

Evelyn nodded. "He entered a building while on patrol in Afghanistan. An IED exploded and trapped him in the rubble. Duke found him and alerted the rescuers who pulled him to safety the next day."

"No wonder dog and master are so close."

"Inseparable is more like it."

"They make a good team."

"Speaking of teams, Ron needs help with the breakfast line this morning. Are you interested?"

"Count me in."

A bedroom door closed, and footsteps sounded in the hallway. Colleen tightened her grip on the mug, unsure how to react when she saw Frank.

He nodded as he entered the kitchen, looking rested and self-assured. "Morning, ladies."

"Do you have time for breakfast?" Evelyn seemed unaware of the tension Colleen felt.

"Not today." He glanced at his watch, equally oblivious to her unease. "When do you expect Ron?"

"Soon."

"Tell him folks have been notified that food will be available in the triage area. The volunteers will arrive first, followed by Amish families."

"I'll let him know."

Frank glanced at Colleen. "Can you lend a hand?"

"Of course, if Ron needs help."

"I'm sure he will." Frank stared at her a moment longer than necessary, causing her heart to flutter, but not in a good way.

She kept remembering his pointed questions from the night before.

"Then I'll see you shortly." With another nod, he hurried outside along with Duke.

He had backed his truck out the driveway before Colleen could shake off the nervous edge that hit as soon as Frank had stepped into the kitchen. If only she could react to his nearness in a less unsettling way. He seemed like a good man, but Frank was a CID agent first, and he was convinced she had some part in the drug operation.

"What would you like for breakfast?" Evelyn asked, interrupting her thoughts.

Colleen smiled. "I'd love a slice of the homemade bread you served with the soup last night."

"That's easy enough. Toasted with butter and jelly?"

"You're spoiling me."

A knock at the door had Evelyn tugging her hair into place and glancing at her reflection as she passed the mirror in the hallway.

"You look lovely," Colleen assured her and was rewarded with a backward wave of hand as Evelyn hurried to open the door.

Ron stepped inside and followed her into the kitchen, where he greeted Colleen and then began carrying the casseroles out to his car.

Colleen downed her coffee, forsaking the toast she didn't have time to fix or eat, and then grabbed the bowl of fresh fruit from the counter and hastened outside.

She stopped short on the front porch. Her heart skipped a beat as she stared at the SUV parked in the driveway.

A gold SUV.

Ron started down the sidewalk toward her.

She'd had a sense of déjà vu when Evelyn introduced them last night. No wonder.

Ron was the driver who had transported Trey to the triage area.

* * *

The temperature had risen slightly, but the day was overcast and about as gloomy as Frank's mood. The military had erected a flagpole near the triage area, and the American flag flapped in the breeze that blew from the west.

Allen Quincy was spearheading the Freemont rescue effort. Midfifties with silver hair and bushy brows, the mayor quickly briefed Frank about the rescue operation.

The engineer from Fort Rickman had checked the houses that had remained standing. A handful of the structures needed to be shored up before they'd be safe enough for the families to occupy. The army was offering manpower and supplies to any of the Amish willing to accept the help.

Earlier this morning, Colby had met with Bishop Zimmerman and eased the Amish leader's concerns about accepting the outreach. Once he realized the aid was freely given and in no way meant that his community was beholden to the military, he willingly accepted the help.

With civilian and military personnel working together, the rescue and reconstruction was progressing, but people were still without homes and many had been hospitalized.

Colby pulled to a stop in front of the tent where medical triage and evaluations were being done and waited until Frank finished talking to the mayor.

"How 'bout some coffee?" Colby called from his car, holding up two paper cups.

Frank smiled and reached through the open window to accept Colby's offer. "You must have read my mind."

"My body needed caffeine. I thought you might feel the same, especially after the late night."

"Thanks for listening to Colleen and passing the information on to the chief."

Colby held up his hand. "I didn't get Wilson. He was tied up with the general, but he sent a message through Sergeant Raynard Otis. Wilson wants to see you. Ray will call and set up an appointment."

"When?"

"Probably when post gets back to normal."

"A couple days or so?"

"That sounds about right." Colby sipped the coffee.

"I'm sure Wilson wants to know when I plan to return to duty."

"Do you have an answer for him?"

Frank shrugged. "I'm ready now, if he can use me."

"My guess, he'd tell you to stay here in the area until the relief effort is behind us. You've done a lot already."

Frank shook his head. "This is basic military operations."

"I hear you, but even the bishop mentioned your name this morning."

"He's a good man."

"So are you, Frank."

As much as he appreciated Colby's comment, Frank wasn't sure where he stood with the chief. Wilson was a competent investigator, but tight-lipped, especially with subordinates, and always faint on praise.

"I called Atlanta PD and left a message for Ulster to call me when he reports to work."

"Has anyone talked to Vivian?"

"Negative. The docs have her in an induced coma. I alerted security at the hospital on post and asked the military police to station a man outside her room."

"In case Trey returns?"

"Exactly. If he tried to kill her once, he may try again."

Would he come after Colleen, as well?

Frank let out a stiff breath. "Did anyone look at the call log on Vivian's phone?"

"We're waiting for a warrant, but I ran the plates on the blue Honda this morning."

"Colleen's car?"

Colby shrugged. "A long shot but you never know."

"You think she's lying."

"Look, Frank, we both know things aren't always as they seem. Her story's confusing enough that it just might be true, but as I mentioned last night, facts need to be verified. I wanted to ensure the car was registered to Colleen Brennan. I should hear something shortly."

"Keep me posted."

"Will do."

The coffee tasted bitter. Frank poured the remainder on the ground as Colby drove away. He crushed the recycled cardboard in his hand and tossed it in a nearby trash receptacle.

Duke had lost the keen sense of smell that had made him a valuable military working dog in the IED explosion in Afghanistan. Evidently, Frank had lost his investigative edge and ability to see things clearly, as well.

He hadn't even thought to run the plates.

In spite of what he had told Colleen last night, he wanted to believe her. The tale she had told—as Colby mentioned—seemed a bit disjointed, yet if all the pieces had been sewed too neatly together, he might have been even more suspicious.

The old Frank went on gut feelings, and his gut was telling him that Colleen was not involved in any criminal activity. He shook his head, knowing all too well that a sound investigation was based on facts, not feelings.

He couldn't let any personal feelings for Colleen get

in the way of uncovering the truth. She was pretty and seemed legit, but as Colby said, looks could be deceiving. He thought of Audrey, which only drove home the fact that he wasn't a good judge of women.

Was Colleen to be trusted?

He hoped so, but he couldn't be sure.

Not with a supposed drug dealer turned killer like Trey Howard on the loose.

"What's wrong?" Evelyn asked, returning to the kitchen, where Colleen had fled, the fruit bowl still in hand, after seeing Ron's gold SUV. "I thought you were going with us. The food's in the car. Ron's ready to drive us down the hill."

"To the triage area?"

Evelyn nodded. "By the Amish Craft Shoppe."

As Frank had mentioned and where Colleen needed to go to find her purse.

Ron entered the kitchen and looked expectantly at Evelyn. "Are you ready?"

"I was just checking to ensure we got everything." After grabbing two additional serving utensils, she nodded. "I'm ready."

Evelyn pointed to the door and motioned Colleen forward. "Let's get the fruit in the car, and we'll be able to leave. People are hungry. We should hurry."

Ron and Evelyn were both staring at Colleen. She had to make a decision. Was Ron in any way involved with Trey? Or was it pure coincidence that the seemingly compassionate churchgoer had transported an injured man, who turned out to be a drug trafficker determined to cause her harm?

Colleen wasn't sure about Ron, but she trusted Evelyn, and she had to get back to her car. She'd go with them, but she'd keep her eyes open and watch for any signs that he wasn't who he seemed. For Evelyn's sake, she hoped Ron was a good man. For her own sake, as well.

SEVEN

Frank recognized Ron's gold SUV heading down the hill from Evelyn's house. The retired teacher was a nice guy who had been hanging around his sister recently.

Evelyn had been in love once, but she never talked about the guy or what had happened to break them up. Frank had been stationed at Fort Lewis, in Washington State.

About that same time, Evelyn had been involved in a car accident on a wet, slippery road that left her with a noticeable limp. Frank came home to help her recuperate. When he broached the subject about the former boyfriend, she had shrugged off his questions and indicated she didn't want to revisit the past. Frank had abided by her wishes. Now she seemed enamored with Ron, which made Frank happy for her sake.

Ron pulled onto the gravel path and braked to a stop. He waved as he stepped from his vehicle. "Hey there, Frank. We brought breakfast. Where do you want us?"

Frank looked past Evelyn and saw Colleen in the backseat. Her face appeared even more strained than when he'd seen her earlier in Evelyn's kitchen. They'd parted last night on an angry note, and he wanted to reassure her.

Colleen had nothing to worry about if she was telling the truth, but that was what hung heavy between them. The uncertainty of whether she was being truthful about her involvement in Trey Howard's drug operation.

Frustrated that everything seemed so complicated, even in the light of day, he turned back to Ron and pointed him toward the clearing. "You can set up your serving line in front of the tent."

The teacher helped Evelyn from the car. Frank hurried to assist Colleen, but she opened her door before he could reach for the handle.

She stepped from the backseat, looking almost hesitant, and glanced at the barn, where one wall still hung precariously over her car.

Ron pulled out the first of four folding tables from the back of the SUV. Frank helped with the setup. Once the tables were upright, Evelyn wiped them with a damp cloth, and Colleen dried them with paper towels.

"You were up early this morning," Frank told his sister.

"I was saying my morning prayers and giving thanks to the Lord for saving us in the storm. Knowing people needed food, I wanted to get a head start on the breakfast casseroles. As it was, Ron arrived soon after you left and just as I was ready to pull them from the oven."

"Perfect timing." Frank's gaze flicked to Colleen, who had yet to say anything. Her cheeks had more color, but lines of fatigue were noticeable around her eyes.

She wore an emerald-green sweater, and her hair was pulled into a bun at the base of her neck. He followed her to the SUV and took a large bowl of fresh fruit from her hands.

"How's that lump on your forehead?" he asked.

"It's fine, but I'm worried about Vivian. Do you have any news about her condition?"

"The hospital wouldn't tell me much when I called this morning. Only that she's still in ICU, and her condition's critical."

"Has anyone talked to her husband?"

Frank shook his head. "I'm not sure. CID may have."

"He didn't know about the trip to Colombia."

"That will have to be determined."

Colleen bristled.

"It's the way law enforcement operates, Colleen. Anecdotal information needs to be checked. We can't operate on hearsay."

Her eyes were guarded as she glanced up at him. "You think I'm covering up the truth?"

"I didn't say that."

"You didn't have to. You keep demanding answers to your questions, then when I provide information, you instantly discount it as not being factual."

She slipped on insulated mitts and grabbed one of the piping-hot casseroles. "I'd be better off not telling you anything, Frank. Then you could learn everything on your own, which you seem to need to do no matter what I say."

She huffed as she walked past him.

Anyone else and he wouldn't have been affected, but Colleen's sharp reproach made him flinch internally. She was right about his need to verify everything she said, but that was what investigators did, even when they believed a witness was being truthful.

He glanced at his sister, who didn't have a clue about what was going on. Ron was equally in the dark. Both of them smiled and chatted amicably as they transported the food from the SUV to the tables.

Two more carloads of volunteers parked near the Amish Craft Shoppe. They hustled forward carrying casseroles that, coupled with what Ron and Evelyn had brought, would provide an abundance of food for the workers and those displaced.

The military planned to set up a second tent this afternoon that would serve as a makeshift chow hall. Hot food in marmite containers was scheduled to arrive later in the day.

Ron would probably still be here helping out any way he could. Evelyn couldn't stand that long and would need a break. Colleen had to be tired, too.

Frank hadn't slept much last night, and he doubted she had either. He'd encourage her to rest, although he doubted she would want his advice.

A line of hungry rescue workers formed even before all the food had been placed on the tables. Ron raised his hands to get everyone's attention and offered a blessing over the food.

Colleen clasped her hands and lowered her eyes. A breeze played with a strand of hair that had come free from her neck. She pulled it behind her ear, her gaze still downward.

As Ron concluded the prayer, three flatbed trucks hauling bulldozers and backhoes came into view. American Construction was stenciled on the side of the earth-moving machinery.

Frank double-timed to the edge of the road and signaled where the vehicles should park. A man climbed down from the first truck. He wore a gray T-shirt with the construction company's logo of a bulldozer superimposed over a stenciled outline of the world.

Frank stretched out his hand and introduced himself. "You're the owner of American Construction?"

The big guy nodded. "Steve Nelson. I saw the report on the Atlanta news and called city hall in Freemont. They connected me to the mayor who's running the rescue effort. I told him we had some equipment and wanted to help."

The guy was built, at least six-two with huge biceps and a lot of definition under his shirt.

Steve wasn't a stranger to the gym. His strong grip and powerful forearm were evident when he shook Frank's hand.

"We appreciate the help."

The guy looked as Frank had at one time when weight lifting and training had been part of his daily routine.

"Frank Gallagher, Army CID. Nice to have you join us, Steve."

Two of his men approached, both big guys wearing the same company T-shirt and packing plenty of muscle. "Paul Yates and Kyle Ingram."

They shook hands. "Thanks so much," Frank said.

He filled them in on the stretch of homes that needed to be cleared along the road.

"There's food, if you want to grab some chow before you get started."

Steve held up his hand. "We ate before we left Atlanta."

Assessing the situation quickly, he sent one of the trucks farther south to connect with the effort closer to post.

"Paul and I'll get started here." Steve eyed the homes across the road still buried in debris. "You've completed the search for injured?"

"We have. Any structure that has a large X on its door has been cleared and is ready for your men."

He nodded. "We've done this a number of times over the twelve years our company's been in operation. Just tell me where you want me to start."

Frank pointed to the Craft Shoppe. Damage to the building was minimal, but fallen trees and debris littered the entranceway. "Having the Amish store open for business would lift everyone's spirits."

Steve nodded. "We'll start there. Then head across the street and work south."

"Sounds like a plan."

Frank hustled back to the breakfast line. Colleen stood next to Evelyn, and both of them offered smiles of encouragement along with the food they dished up to the hungry workers.

Colleen chatted amicably with one of the men in line. More of her hair had pulled from the bun and blew free. For an instant, Frank had a vision of who Colleen really was. She seemed relaxed and embraced life. An inner beauty that she tried to mask was evident in the attention she showered on each person in line.

In that same moment, Frank wished he could be one of the people with whom she was interacting. Each time he and Colleen were together, she closed down, as if burdened by the weight she carried. He wanted to see her smile and hear her laughter.

Duke nuzzled close to Frank's leg as if sensing his master's confusion about the woman from Atlanta. Colleen may have told him the truth last night, but she was still embroiled in a shooting. The video found in her car only compounded the situation.

Frank needed to tread carefully. She could be hiding something behind her guarded gaze and cautious nature. He couldn't make a mistake and allow an attractive woman to throw him off course. He may be physically compromised, but he needed to think clearly.

She was someone of interest. The problem was, a part of him was interested in a way that didn't mesh with his CID background. He needed to hold his feelings in check and use his brain instead of his heart when he was dealing with Colleen.

"Do you need anything?"

Colleen startled at the sound of Frank's voice. She turned to find him behind her, standing much too close. Needing space, she took a step back, but her leg hit the table.

Wanting to maintain her self-control, she raised her chin and stared up at his angular face. For one long moment, the hustle and bustle around her melted into the background. Her breath caught in her throat, and she forgot about his questions and the doubt she had heard in his voice the night before.

Just that quickly, reason returned. "I have everything I need, but thanks for checking."

Seemingly satisfied by her response, he moved on to Evelyn and asked her the same question.

Colleen turned back to the hungry people in line. Serving food to the workers lifted her spirits. She was grateful for the continuing assortment of breakfast casseroles, baked goods and fresh fruit that poured in from people in Freemont who wanted to help. The long line of hungry rescue personnel included firefighters and emergency personnel as well as military from Fort Rickman who appreciated the home-cooked meal.

The clip-clop of horses' hooves signaled the approach of Amish families in their buggies. Frank greeted the men with a handshake and offered words of welcome to the women and children. Duke frolicked with the youngsters, and they giggled as he licked their hands and wagged his tail.

As the families approached, the workers backed up to let those who had lost much move to the front of the line.

One of the men—evidently a spokesman for the Amish group—held up his hand. "We will wait our turn. We do not want to inconvenience you who are so willing to help us in our need."

"Please," a rescue worker insisted, speaking for the others in line. "You and your family need to eat. You've lost much."

"God provides," the man said with a nod. "We appreciate your generosity."

He motioned his family forward. Others followed. The eager faces of the children, when they held out their plates, hinted at their hunger.

Colleen was impressed by the children's politeness and the way they deferred to their parents. The mothers remained close and pointed to the various foods each child could take.

One little boy with blond hair and blue eyes took two bananas and then glanced at his mother, who shook her head ever so slightly.

The child quickly returned the extra piece of fruit and looked up at Colleen. "I must only take what I can eat and leave the rest for others."

He couldn't have been more than six or seven, but his demeanor and the apology he offered were that of a much older child.

During a lull in the line, she felt something rub against her leg and looked down to find Duke at her feet. She laughed at the sweet dog and watched him scamper off when Frank called his name.

He bent to pat the dog's neck, then glancing up, he stared at Colleen. Her heart skittered in her chest, and longing for some normalcy in her life swelled within her. If only she had met Frank under different circumstances.

A man in uniform tapped his shoulder, and Frank turned away. Suddenly, she felt alone in the midst of so many.

"I'm looking for a job to fill," a middle-aged woman said some minutes later as she approached Colleen. "Ron told me you need a break."

Although she was capable of working longer, Colleen knew the woman was eager to get involved.

"A break sounds good."

She looked for Frank and saw him in the distance. He was working with other military men setting up tables and chairs where people could sit while eating their meals. A large generator was humming, and fifty-cup coffeepots had been plugged into the electrical outlets. The smell of fresh-perked coffee wafted past her in the gentle breeze, and many people were enjoying the hot brew.

A ramp extended from the end of a flatbed truck. A man in a gray T-shirt drove a bulldozer down the incline and off the truck.

With a grateful nod, Colleen handed her serving utensil to the newcomer. The woman instantly began chatting with the people in line.

Retreating to the side of the military tent, Colleen grabbed a bottle of water from an ice chest. The cold liquid tasted good and refreshed her.

Everyone was busy, and no one seemed to miss her. After downing the last of the water, she dropped the bottle in one of the temporary trash receptacles and wiped her hands on her jeans. She glanced at the barn, where the back end of her car was visible under the wreckage.

Rubbing her forehead, Colleen mentally retraced her movements yesterday. Usually she kept her purse in the passenger seat, but as she pulled into the rest stop, she'd tossed it into the rear to make room for Vivian.

Again, she checked to ensure no one needed her. Evelyn was chatting with one of the Amish ladies. The other servers seemed content doing their jobs and were focused on feeding the workers and Amish who continued to arrive by buggy.

Seeing that Frank was still tied up with the military, she hurried to the barn area, gingerly picked her way through the downed timber and ducked under the crime scene tape. She peered through the back window into her car but saw nothing except broken glass.

Rounding to the passenger side, she leaned over the front seat, shoved her fingers between the rear seat cushions and sighed with frustration when she came up empty-handed.

In the distance, the bulldozer gathered downed tree branches. The driver piled them to the edge of the road, where they could easily be picked up and carted off later in the day.

Colleen rounded the Honda, only this time, she grabbed the beams that blocked the driver's door and shoved them aside. The wood was heavy, and her energy was quickly sapped, but she continued to work, intent on having access into the rear of her car, behind the driver's seat. Without doubt, she'd wake up sore tomorrow, but finding her purse would be worth the effort.

Her neck was damp, and her hands ached, but she smiled with success when she cleared away the last of the rubble. Opening the driver's door, she saw what she was looking for—a small leather handbag wedged under the driver's seat. The clasp had come open, and the purse was empty.

She stretched her hand under the seat and patted the floorboard, searching for the spilled contents. She found a lipstick and a comb and placed both items in her bag. Once again, she used her hand to search along the floorboard.

Please, Lord.

A sense of relief spread over her when her fingers curled around her wallet. Pulling it free, she ensured her credit cards, driver's license and airline identification were still inside.

The roar of the bulldozer grew louder.

She glanced at the food line, which had started to thin. Time was of the essence. Ron and Evelyn would begin cleaning the area once all the people had been fed.

But she still needed the memory card.

An Amish teen appeared from the rear of the barn. He stared at her for a long moment and then walked quickly to where the others were eating.

A nervous flutter rumbled through her stomach at the young man and the pensive look he had given her.

Someone screamed. Colleen turned at the sound and saw Evelyn staring at the barn with her hands over her mouth. Ron was standing next to the young Amish boy. In the distance, she saw Frank running toward her, as if in slow motion.

For the briefest second, Colleen wondered what had caused them concern. Then she heard the *whoosh* of air and the *creak* and *groan* of wood. Glancing up, she saw the lone portion of wall still standing. Only now it was crashing down around her.

She ducked and raised her hands to protect her head. The purse dropped to her feet, its contents spilling onto the ground.

The last thing she heard was Frank's voice. He was screaming her name.

EIGHT

Heart in his throat, Frank followed the ambulance to the Freemont hospital. He'd been the first to get to Colleen. Medical personnel were close by to respond to the emergency. They'd started an IV line, taken her vitals and then hastened to get her into the ambulance that was currently racing along River Road to Freemont.

Frank's phone rang. Relieved the cell tower was back in operation, he glanced at Colby's name on the monitor and pushed Talk. "What'd you find out?"

"The guy driving the bulldozer was Paul Yates. He claimed he'd checked the barn and hadn't seen anyone in the area before he picked up the first load of fallen timbers. According to him, he didn't get near the wall. Steve Nelson, the construction team boss, told me Paul was a conscientious worker and doubted that his man, even inadvertently, would have knocked the load he was carrying against the edge of the barn wall."

Frank sighed, frustrated at his own mistake. "If he did cause the wall to topple, I have to take some of the blame. I told Steve his men could clear the area around the Craft Shoppe. The store's structure was in good shape. I thought the sooner we start getting some of the businesses and homes restored, the better."

"Which was sound reasoning. You're not at fault, Frank. Yates probably thought he'd clean up around the barn, although—as I mentioned—he said he never saw anyone in the area."

"Colleen was standing in plain sight by the car."

"That's what Ron Malone told me. He verified she was clearly visible when the wall came down, but she could have been hunkered down and peering into her car when Paul checked. If he checked."

Frank glanced at the purse he'd pulled from under the fallen timber, which she must have found. Colleen had wanted to retrieve her identification and credit cards, yet nothing was worth putting her life in danger.

"Your sister said to let her know when you hear from the doctor," Colby added.

"Will do. Make sure Ron takes her home so she can rest. She not only looked upset but also exhausted. She worked late last night and was back at it this morning."

"They plan to leave soon."

"Have you heard anything from Atlanta PD?"

"Negative."

"What about the check on the Honda's plates?"

"I'm not sure what the holdup is. I'll give them another call."

"Let me know."

"Will do."

"Thanks, Colby." Frank hesitated for a long moment, choosing his words. "For being there, for helping."

"You mean calming you down? It wasn't your fault she was injured."

"She's staying at my sister's house. I feel responsible. I should have posted a guard at the barn."

"That's not CID's jurisdiction. The Freemont police needed to get involved, although everyone's overworked at this point. I don't know if you heard the news. The governor called in the National Guard, but he sent them farther east to Macon, where a second tornado touched down. According to the radio report I heard, he's satisfied Freemont is well taken care of with Fort Rickman's help."

"Only Rickman has their own damage to repair." The hospital appeared in the distance. "We're approaching the medical facility. I'll call you once the doctor makes his diagnosis."

Frank kept his focus on the ambulance ahead of him. The siren wailed as the EMT at the wheel entered the intersection leading to the medical complex. Frank followed close behind.

He kept seeing the wall crash down on Colleen. He hadn't been able to get there fast enough and had frantically clawed at the fallen timbers to save her. He'd found her dazed and bleeding from a head wound that was all too close to the blow she'd taken yesterday, which made him even more concerned.

The EMTs had been concerned, as well. They'd used a backboard and neck brace to stabilize her spine and had hurried her into an ambulance.

He hoped she wouldn't have any permanent injury or hadn't suffered internal wounds that would need further medical care.

The ambulance braked to a stop in front of the ER. The automatic doors opened, and medical personnel wearing pale green scrubs raced to meet their patient.

The EMTs lowered the gurney to the pavement and pushed her into the hospital. Nurses hovered close by, assessing her injuries as they rushed Colleen into a trauma room.

Frank found a nearby parking space and hurried inside. A nurse pointed him to a room where even more medical staff surrounded the gurney where she lay.

"Can you hear me?" a doctor questioned.

A nurse grabbed the telephone. "We've got an injury in trauma room two. I need a CBC and chemistry panel. Protime and PTT. Type and cross for two units." She nodded. "I'll place the order now."

After returning the phone to its cradle, she typed the lab orders on a nearby computer.

"BP's 130 over 70," a voice called out. "Pulse 65."

The doctor checked her pupils and had Colleen follow his finger with her eyes. All the while her head was immobilized on the backboard.

He glanced at Frank, hovering near the doorway. "Family?"

"Ah, no. I'm with the CID."

"Is she a victim of a crime?"

"Negative. Her injury was accidental."

"Then I need you to leave the room and give the patient privacy."

Frank understood the doctor's request, but he didn't want to leave Colleen. He knew how fast things could go south if an internal injury was involved.

When the medics had taken him to the field hospital in Afghanistan, he'd been in good shape. Or so everyone had thought. Too quickly his blood pressure had bottomed out. He'd gone into shock and had been rushed into surgery—the first of many.

As Colleen was being lifted into the ambulance, Evelyn had grabbed his hand. The concern in her eyes had made him aware of how much she understood the emotions that were playing havoc with his control.

"I'm praying for Colleen," she'd assured him.

Knowing his sister's deep faith and her belief in

prayer had brought a bit of calm in the midst of his turmoil. Evelyn would storm heaven, of that Frank could be sure.

He wanted to stand in the hallway outside the trauma room, but a nurse escorted him to a waiting area. She promised to notify him if there was any change in Colleen's condition. Not that he could sit idly by. He paced from the door to the bay of windows on the far wall and back again, feeling trapped and confined, like a caged animal.

He looked down, expecting to find Duke at his feet and needing his calm support, but Evelyn had kept the dog with her.

Every time the door opened, Frank hoped to see one of Colleen's nurses.

No one appeared whom he recognized. He glanced at his watch. The ambulance had arrived more than thirty minutes ago. How long would the medical team take before he would receive word of her injuries?

He pulled out his phone and checked his emails, searching especially for a message from Special Agent in Charge Wilson. Frank was ready to get back on active duty. Surely Wilson could use him.

Of course, the chief might not be willing to take a chance on him. Especially after the witness Frank needed to keep safe had been injured.

The door opened, and the nurse from Colleen's room motioned him forward.

"An aide is transporting Colleen Brennan to X-ray. They should return in a few minutes. The doctor will review the X-rays and test results once they're back from the lab. If you want to wait in her room, you can."

Relieved, Frank headed for the trauma room. His

stomach tightened when he saw droplets of blood on the floor.

His mind went wild with concern. "You mentioned X-rays. Does that mean internal injuries?"

"The X-rays will tell us a lot. The doctor may order a CT scan."

Bile rose in Frank's throat. He glanced at the vinyl chair shoved in the corner and knew he couldn't sit. Backtracking to the doorway, he peered into the hall, hoping to catch sight of Colleen.

Where was she? What was her condition? What was the doctor keeping from him?

The sound of a gurney rolling over the tile floor flooded him with relief. She was alert, and her color was good. The backboard had been removed, which was another positive sign.

"Did you find the Amish boy?"

Frank didn't understand what she was saying.

"You saw him, didn't you?" she insisted. "He came out from behind the barn just before the wall toppled."

"What'd he look like?"

"Straw hat, blue shirt, suspenders."

The same as every other Amish kid. "You think he caused the wall to fall?"

"I don't know. Ask Ron. He talked to him."

"Will do, but what about you?"

"I'm okay." She grimaced. "Except for my head."

"Another concussion?"

"They haven't told me yet. The patient's the last to know."

He followed the gurney into the room. The nurse's aide held up her hand. "Give us a minute, sir, until I get Ms. Brennan settled."

"Oh, sure. Sorry." He returned to the hallway. The door closed behind him.

Colleen needed her privacy. Shame on him for barging into her room.

He started to call Colby about the Amish boy, then disconnected when the door to Colleen's room opened. The aide scurried down the hall.

Frank waited a long moment, wondering if she would return.

He hesitated too long.

Another health-care worker, wearing a white lab coat, entered the trauma room and closed the door.

Frank shook his head with frustration. At this rate, he might never see Colleen. Patience had never been his strong suit, except when he pulled surveillance. Today's wait seemed especially trying.

The main thing was to ensure Colleen was okay.

His cell rang. Colby's number.

Frank raised the mobile device to his ear. "Did you find out anything?"

"Can you talk?"

Frank's gut tightened. Needing to speak freely, he headed for the empty waiting room. Colby had information to share, but from the negative overtones in his voice, the news wasn't good.

Did it involve Colleen?

Colleen hadn't expected Frank to follow her to the hospital and then wait while the various tests were being run. She thought he had stayed behind. Spotting him in the hallway when she came back from X-ray had been a surprise that added a hint of brightness to a very bleak day.

Although from what she knew about Frank, he probably wanted to question her about breaking through the crime scene tape. Was it against the law to search for her own missing purse?

She closed her eyes and tried to relax. Knowing Frank was in the hallway made her doubly anxious.

The door opened, and someone—no doubt, Frank—entered the room. Unwilling to face the confrontation she expected to see in his eyes, she pretended to be asleep.

His footsteps were heavy as he neared the gurney.

She sensed him staring down at her.

Unnerved, she opened her eyes.

She didn't see Frank.

She saw Trey.

NINE

Colleen screamed. Trey hovered over her. He raised his hand and pressed it across her nose and mouth, cutting off her air supply and blocking any additional sound she tried to make.

She writhed and scratched his face, then grabbed his nose and twisted.

He growled and clamped his hand down even harder.

Unable to breathe, she thrashed at him, kicked her feet and shifted her weight. The gurney was narrow, and the sheet covering the vinyl pad shifted with her.

With one massive thrust, she threw her legs up and over the narrow edge. Gravity helped.

She fell to the floor, along with the sheet.

Trey lost his hold.

Gasping for air, she crawled away from him like a crab.

He reached for her again.

She kicked and screamed.

Where was Frank?

Why wouldn't he come to her rescue?

"I got a call from Ulster," Colby said.

The cop in Atlanta. Frank shoved the cell closer to his ear.

"The two women Colleen mentioned who were murdered worked at the King's Club. Guess who else worked there up until four months ago?"

"You tell me."

"Briana Doyle."

"Colleen's sister."

"Roger that."

An interesting twist. "Anything else?"

"He also said Sutherland—that Atlanta cop who gave Colleen a hard time—suffered a nervous breakdown and had to retire."

"What about the plates on the Honda?"

"The car's registered to a Ms. C. A. Brennan."

Frank couldn't help but smile. "Do me a favor, Colby. See if anyone remembers an Amish teen hanging around the barn today."

"Do you have a name?"

"Negative, but Colleen saw him talking to Ron Malone."

"Evelyn's friend?"

A sound filtered into the waiting room, like a muffled cry.

Frank tensed. "Hold for a minute."

Lowering the phone, he retraced his steps into the hallway and listened.

A woman screamed.

Colleen!

Someone ran down the corridor.

Six foot. Stocky. White lab coat.

Frank's heart stopped. He crashed into her room. Colleen was on the floor, back to the wall.

She shook her head and pointed to the hall. "I'm not hurt. Go after him."

Frank raced into the corridor.

The man rounded the corner at the end of the hallway. Frank followed.

A nurse blocked his path.

He shoved past her.

A lab technician carrying a tray with tubes of blood appeared.

"Get back," Frank yelled. He sailed around her and turned left. The hall was empty.

Glancing back, he spotted a stairwell.

Frank shoved open the heavy fire door. A short stairway led to an emergency exit, leading out of the hospital.

He bounded down the steps.

Movement behind him.

Frank turned. A fire extinguisher sailed through the air, aimed straight for him. He lifted his hands to block the hit.

The canister crashed against his chest, knocked air from his lungs and forced him off balance. He fell down the steps. His head scraped against the wall.

The stairwell door opened, and the man in the lab coat walked back into the hospital.

Frank's ears rang. Pain screamed through his body. Fighting to remain conscious, he groped for his cell and heard Colby's voice.

"What's going on, Frank?"

He'd never disconnected.

"Someone attacked Colleen." Frank struggled to his feet. "A guy wearing a white lab coat. Six foot. Stocky. Call hospital security. Tell them to lock down the facility."

Frank grabbed the banister and pulled himself up the stairs. "Notify Freemont PD. The attack happened in trauma room two in the ER. He was last seen in the rear stairwell."

"Where'd he go from there?"

Back to Colleen!

Ice froze Frank's veins.

He jerked open the fire door and stumbled into the hallway.

"Colleen," he screamed, racing back to her.

Hurling himself into the trauma room, he expected the worst.

She sat crumpled on the floor, her face twisted with fear.

"Frank." She gasped with relief. Tears sprang from her eyes.

He was on his knees at her side, reaching for her. She collapsed into his arms. He pulled her trembling body close, feeling her warmth. Hot tears dampened his neck.

She was alive. Relief swept over him. A lump of gratitude filled his throat. He hadn't lost her. Not this time, but he hadn't reacted fast enough. She'd almost died because of his inability to protect her.

He rubbed his hand over her slender shoulders. "Shh. I've got you. You're safe."

For now. But someone wanted to kill her. Whether she had been working with Trey or against him, he was determined to end her life.

Trey would come back. No doubt about it. Would Frank be able to save her the next time?

TEN

"He must have headed down the east corridor and left from that side of the hospital," Frank had told the hospital security earlier and now repeated the details to the Freemont police officer who had answered the call.

The cop was pushing fifty with a full face and tired eyes. His name tag read Talbot. He had pulled a tablet and pen from his pocket and was making note of the information Frank provided.

As Talbot wrote, Frank rubbed his side that had taken the hit. The fire extinguisher had bruised a couple of ribs and the area around one of his incisions. The dull ache was aggravating but not serious.

Colleen was resting in the ER room across the hall, awaiting the doctor's decision about whether she would be released or admitted for observation. Frank had wanted to stay with her, but Talbot insisted on questioning Frank in private. The only way he would leave Colleen was if the door to her room and the door to the room across the hall where Frank now sat both remained opened.

The cop looked up from his notebook. "Did you see his face?"

"Only in profile, but Ms. Brennan gave you a description."

"That's correct. I just wanted verification."

Law enforcement's need to confirm anecdotal information was what Frank had tried to explain to Colleen. Now, as his own irritation began to mount, he understood her frustration.

"The man was approximately six feet tall, wearing a white lab coat. I can't be sure about his build. He appeared stocky. Muscular might be a better description."

"Ms. Brennan thought you were in the hallway. She screamed, but you failed to respond." The cop paused and pursed his lips. "Did she imagine raising her voice?"

"As I mentioned earlier, I went into the waiting room to take a call. Hearing a sound, I retraced my steps and realized Ms. Brennan was in distress."

"The person who phoned you was—"

Colby was busy dealing with the Amish. Frank didn't want him tied up, answering Talbot's questions, especially when Frank was at fault for letting Trey escape.

He scrubbed his hands over his face. What was wrong with him these days?

"The name?" the cop pressed.

"Special Agent Voss."

"First name?"

More irritation bubbled up within Frank. "Special Agent Colby Voss."

"Spelled?"

How else would Voss be spelled? "V.O.S.S." The cop was a jerk. Either that or he had a bone to pick with the military.

Needing to reassure himself that Colleen was all right, Frank glanced through the two open doorways to where she was resting in the room across the hall. Her eyes were closed and her hands folded at her waist.

He pulled his gaze back to Talbot. Dark circles rimmed his eyes.

Frank's temper subsided ever so slightly.

"Have you been involved with the search and rescue?"

The cop nodded. "When I'm not cleaning up my own property. My wife and I live on the west side of town. The twister tore the roof off our house. The wife was inside." He shook his head and looked as dejected as Frank had felt when he realized Trey had escaped. "We're living with our daughter and son-in-law. They don't have room for us."

"I'm sorry."

"It's not your fault. My wife blames God, but it's not His fault either."

Frank's opinion of the cop did a one-eighty. Although hard to admit, deep down Frank had blamed God after the IED explosion and Audrey's rejection. It was easier to claim the Lord was at fault instead of his own poor judgment.

The doctor entered Colleen's room.

"If there's anything else you need from me, call my cell." Frank gave the cop his number as well as the one for Evelyn's landline.

"I'll alert local law enforcement to be on the lookout for Trey Howard. As you're probably aware, the department's working long shifts trying to keep the peace in the areas hardest hit by the storm. Doubt we'll be back to normal operations for a few more days, so I wouldn't hold your breath about tracking him down anytime soon."

The doctor stepped into the hallway and motioned to the nurse. "Once pharmacy fills the pain prescription for Ms. Brennan, she's free to go."

The nurse nodded. "I'll get her meds and discharge papers."

Frank climbed from the table and shook hands with the cop. "I appreciate your help today. Let me know if you find out anything about Trey Howard."

"I've got your phone number, sir. I'll contact you first thing."

Frank left the room with a better attitude. He hated that he hadn't nabbed Trey, but he'd changed his opinion of the cop. The guy was carrying a lot on his shoulders.

He knocked on Colleen's open door. His heart softened when she looked up and smiled. She was carrying a lot, too. Her sister had died because of a drug dealer who seemed to escape apprehension. Frank had to find Trey before he hurt Colleen again.

Frank's head was scraped and he looked tired, but Colleen smiled when he stepped into her room. "Did you finish answering Talbot's questions?"

"The guy's thorough."

"Don't all of you law enforcement types follow the same playbook?"

He laughed. She liked the sound.

"How's the head?" he asked.

She shrugged. "Pain is relative. I'll survive."

"And the shoulder?"

"You mean where I hit the floor after I slipped off the gurney?"

Frank nodded.

"It's probably not as painful as that scrape on your forehead."

"You need to rest."

"That's what the doctor told me. Rest and protect my head. Two cranial blows in a short span of time aren't recommended for good health. The doc doesn't want me to end up like some old prizefighter. Research claims concussions don't lead to good quality of life."

"It's not something to joke about."

"I know, but if I don't laugh, I just might cry. That wouldn't be good."

"Sometimes shedding a few tears helps."

The nurse returned to the room and dropped a plastic medicine bottle in Colleen's hand. "Take every six hours as needed for pain. They'll make you sleepy. Don't operate motor vehicles when taking them."

"My car was totaled in the storm," Colleen said.

"Tough break, huh?" The nurse sorted through the papers she carried. "Have someone check on you in the night."

She handed Colleen the release instructions. "This covers most of the questions you might have. The doctor warned you to guard your head, and don't take any more hits."

Colleen smiled. "He mentioned that might be a problem."

"He's right. Be extra careful."

"I don't plan to get into any more dangerous situations."

"Could I get that in writing?" Frank asked.

The nurse pointed to the scrape on his forehead as she left the room. "As if you should talk."

Colleen turned to Frank when they were alone. "Thank you for going after Trey. I wouldn't be here if it weren't for you." She held out her hand and gripped his in a half shake, half high-five motion.

"I didn't react fast enough," he countered.

The nurse knocked and pushed the wheelchair through the door.

"I'll drive the car to the front of the hospital." Frank hurried to the parking lot.

"He seems like a nice guy." The nurse helped Colleen off the gurney and into the wheelchair.

"He's not sure what he wants in life."

"I can relate. I still don't know what I want to do when I grow up."

Colleen raised her brow. "But you've got a great profession."

"Sometimes I want more in life. Money, fame."

"Really? I just want to be safe."

The nurse patted her hand. "Looks like you've got a special guy who's all about protection."

Colleen was taken aback. Surely she wasn't talking about Frank?

"His face softens when he looks at you," the nurse added. "I'd say he's interested."

Colleen shrugged off the statements about Frank because they weren't true. The nurse was wrong, although Colleen would like having someone to protect her. Especially if that someone was Frank Gallagher.

ELEVEN

Frank called Evelyn and filled her in on what had happened after he and Colleen left the hospital. She was understandably upset about the attack and concerned about Colleen's well-being.

"Is Ron there?" he asked.

"He left a short while ago, why?"

"Just wondering." He didn't mention the Amish boy Colleen had seen earlier. Evelyn didn't need anything more to add to her concern.

"Be careful," she warned before they disconnected.

Lowering his cell, he glanced at Colleen. "Evelyn's worried about you."

"And I'm worried about putting both of you in danger."

"Hey, remember—" he pointed a finger back at himself "—I'm with law enforcement and used to dealing with criminals."

"Yes, but Evelyn doesn't need to get involved."

"She's not in danger, and with the BOLO out on Trey, he'll be in custody before long."

Colleen tugged at a strand of her hair. "I'm not as optimistic as you are. Trey's cunning. He tells a lonely woman lies she wants to hear and gets her to smuggle drugs into this country. If she balks, he overdoses her or shoots her at a roadside park. He doesn't think of anyone but himself."

She glanced out the window and sighed. "Maybe I should hole up in a motel someplace. You don't need trouble underfoot."

"And prevent Evelyn from extending her gracious Southern hospitality?"

"I don't want anyone else to get hurt."

He reached for her hand. "You're not going to a motel. Evelyn wouldn't think of it, and neither would I. Plus—" he smiled "—Duke's a good watchdog."

She smiled back, and relief swept over him. He squeezed her hand to reassure her and almost groaned when his cell rang. The last thing he wanted was to pull his hand away from hers.

He glanced at the screen and hit Talk. "Yeah, Colby."

"I tried to contact Ron Malone, but I couldn't reach him. Seems there were a number of teenage Amish boys getting a free breakfast this morning. I need a name or something to distinguish the kid in question from every other Amish youth."

"Ron was at my sister's house for most of the afternoon. Colleen and I are headed there now. I'll call him." Frank paused, wondering if Colby had anything additional to add.

"Stay safe," was all he said before disconnecting.

Seems everyone was worried about their well-being. Frank punched in Ron's home number.

"Good evening. Ron Malone speaking."

The guy was definitely old-school. "Ron, this is Frank Gallagher."

"How's Colleen? Evelyn phoned and filled me in."

"She's okay. I'm calling about the accident at the barn

today. Do you remember talking to an Amish boy just before it collapsed? He's probably sixteen or seventeen years old. Straw hat. Suspenders."

"That would be Isaac Fisher. He and his sister, Martha, work at the Amish Craft Shoppe."

Frank glanced at Colleen and gave her a reassuring nod as Ron continued.

"Isaac's math skills need help so I've been tutoring him. We were trying to schedule our next session around the relief effort. Why do you ask?"

"He was hanging around the barn today."

"And probably had his eye on the Craft Shoppe. He wants to go back to work. Money's tight for most of the Amish, especially for a young guy who's planning for his future."

"Any reason to think he might have done something to cause the wall to topple?"

"You're saying it wasn't an accident?"

"I'm just asking for your opinion, Ron."

"Isaac Fisher is a fine young man who would never bring dishonor to himself or his family."

"That's what I wanted to hear. Thanks."

Lowering his cell, he smiled at Colleen. "Ron vouched for the teen. Isaac Fisher. Ron called him a fine young man."

"But—"

"You don't believe Ron?"

"I'm not sure." She wrapped her arms around her waist and stared out the window.

Frank watched her out of the corner of his eye. "Take one of those pain pills when we get to Evelyn's."

"I'm fine."

But, of course, she wasn't. Frank still had a lot of questions about the photo she'd sent to the Atlanta police, about her sister knowing the two women who had been killed and about why she was suspicious of an Amish boy who sounded like a good kid.

As fragile as Colleen seemed, this wasn't the time to delve into anything that would increase her anxiety. The doctor had ordered her to rest, which was what she needed.

Frank's questions could wait until morning. Everything would seem more clear then. At least, that was his hope.

Colleen couldn't pull her thoughts together. She kept feeling Trey's hand covering her mouth and nose. Shaking her head ever so slightly, she tried to scatter the memory and focus instead on being with Frank.

"Are you sure you're okay?" he asked, concern so evident in his voice.

"I'm trying *not* to think about what happened."

He nodded as if he understood, but how could he know what she was thinking? So many questions swirled through her mind. About the man in Atlanta who had been snooping around her apartment, about whether Ron Malone could be trusted and whether a young Amish boy could somehow be involved in Trey's drug operation.

She fingered her handbag, grateful that Frank had pulled it from the debris today. At least she had her identification, but what about the memory card?

Would she ever feel confident enough to tell Frank?

He didn't need to see the photo of her with men who worked for Trey. She'd been foolish to allow Trey to take the picture. Too late, she'd realized that he wanted the picture to blackmail her, in case she decided to go to the police.

She'd outsmarted Trey, but not for long. Now he was after her. No matter what Frank thought, Trey was dangerous, and he wouldn't stop until he found her. Knowing he had been with Ron after the storm troubled her even more.

Pulling in a deep breath, she had to tell Frank.

"There's something I haven't mentioned."

He raised his brow but kept his gaze on the road.

"That first night, when the tornado touched down and then you found me—"

Frank nodded.

"I saw Trey with Ron Malone."

"Evelyn's Ron?"

"He drove Trey to the triage area."

"Ron transported a lot of folks that night." Frank glanced at her. "You took a bad hit to your head, Colleen. You couldn't remember a number of things. Are you sure you saw Trey?"

"I thought I did."

"You were frightened. Sometimes our minds play tricks on us."

"Maybe." Or maybe not. Colleen needed to find out the truth about Ron Malone and his relationship with Trey. Even if it put her in danger.

Colleen was quiet for the rest of the ride home. Frank helped her from the car, but she insisted on walking on her own.

Audrey had always sought his help and made him feel as if he was in charge. Looking back, she'd played him and fed his ego. Had he really been in love with her?

"Oh, Colleen, we were so worried." Evelyn gave her a warm hug when they got inside. She pointed to the scrape on Frank's forehead. "Looks like you and the doc came to fisticuffs."

Colleen tried to smile, then grimaced.

"You've got two choices." Frank ushered her into the kitchen and pulled out a chair at the table. "Sit down or head straight to bed."

"I'm fine."

Colleen had grit and determination, almost to a fault. She needed to let down that strong wall of independence at times. Like now, when she was shaky and her strength compromised.

The nurse had given them instructions. Colleen needed to be checked in the night. Nausea or a severe headache could signal life-threatening complications. She'd had one brush with death already. She didn't need any more problems tonight.

Frank pointed to the chair.

"If you insist." She sat, and he pushed her closer to the table.

"Can I fix you something to eat?" Evelyn asked.

"Is there any soup left?" Colleen asked.

"Of course." She glanced at Frank. "How about you? I doubt you've eaten today."

"Soup sounds good." Once his sister thought he needed nourishment, she wouldn't let up until he agreed to eat. He'd learned that early on after he moved in following his infection.

Of course, at that point, the MRSA had taken a toll on his body and nearly done him in. The highly contagious deadly organism he'd picked up in the hospital had been hard to overcome.

"Anything I can do to help?" he asked.

"Grab a couple placemats and some silverware. You know where the napkins are."

"You're not joining us?"

"I've already eaten." Evelyn glanced at the clock. "Ron's coming over. There's a new sitcom on television. We were planning to watch it together, although I can tell him tonight might not be a good idea."

Colleen held up her hand. "Don't change your plans on account of me. I don't need to eat."

"Nonsense. I'll heat the soup and let Frank take over while I freshen up."

"Ron's visiting quite often these days." Frank set the table and winked at Colleen.

Fatigue rimmed her eyes and her face was even more pale than usual.

The doorbell rang.

"He's early." Evelyn's voice held a note of flustered alarm.

"Go. Put on your lipstick." Frank pointed to her bedroom. "I'll take care of the door and the soup." He smiled as his sister scurried from the kitchen.

Frank lowered the heat under the pan and then hurried to open the door.

"Good to see you," Ron said as soon as he stepped inside. He glanced into the kitchen, where Colleen sat. "We were all concerned about you today."

"I'm fine. Just a bit worn-out."

"Evelyn and I prayed for you." He pointed his thumb at Frank. "We've been praying for this guy for a long time."

"No wonder I'm doing so well." Frank smiled. "Colleen's tired but pretending to be stronger than she looks."

"That last part sounds like Evelyn."

"She'll join you in a minute, Ron. Can I get you some coffee or a cola?"

"Thanks, but I'll make myself at home in the den."

"I need to ask you something, Ron." Colleen sat up straighter in the chair. She glanced at Frank and then back at the former teacher. "The night of the storm, do you remember transporting a man in a black hooded sweatshirt to the triage area?"

"Sure do. He was the first of many who needed help. I found him walking along Amish Road. He was shook up and didn't have much to say except that the twister had picked up his car. No telling where it landed. I left him with the EMTs, who said they'd take care of him. Do you know the guy?"

Frank nodded. "We think he's the man who came after Colleen today."

Ron gasped. "I had no idea. Is he from around here?"

"Atlanta."

"What brought him to Freemont?"

"It's a long story."

Evelyn's footsteps sounded in the hallway. Ron turned his full attention to her when she entered the kitchen. Her cheeks glowed pink, and her eyes were bright and focused on Ron.

"The show's almost ready to start," she said, motioning him into the den.

"Enjoy the program." Frank turned back to the stove. Steam was rising from the pan. He stirred the soup and dished up two bowls, placing them on the table.

Settling into the chair across from Colleen, he smiled. "Are you okay with Ron?"

"I'm sorry about all the questions I asked."

"Evelyn's a good judge of character."

"She met him at church?"

"That's right. He's started to come over more often

since I moved in." Frank hesitated. "I don't think he's involved with Trey."

"I'm sure you're right. It's nice that he's been praying for you."

Frank nodded. "I knew Evie prayed, but I didn't think other folks in her church were praying for me, as well."

"It may sound like a strange question, but how's that make you feel?" Colleen's gaze was intense.

"Humbled. At one point, the docs weren't sure I'd pull through. My sister must have spread the word that I needed prayer."

"Your injury was severe."

He nodded. "I walked into a building before Duke cleared it of explosives. Broke my pelvis and a few other bones."

Frank smiled down at the trusty dog at his feet. "Duke was scraped up pretty badly, but he stayed with me and alerted the guys who came looking for me the next day. I went to Lanstuhl in Germany for my first operation. Then Walter Reed. My final surgery was at Augusta, about five hours from here."

"Then you came here to recover?"

"Eventually. Somewhere along the line I was exposed to MRSA. My immune system was compromised, and I had a hard time fighting the infection."

He tried to smile. "You know how Evie likes to cook, which worked to my advantage since I'd lost so much weight and strength."

"Your sister's generous with her love." Colleen peered at Duke under the table. "How'd you end up with your sweet pup?"

As if knowing Colleen was talking about him, Duke pranced to her side of the table and sat at her feet.

"The explosion did something to his nose," Frank continued. "When a military working dog can't track a scent, he's forced to retire. I heard he was at Fort Rickman and asked if I could adopt him."

He smiled, watching as Colleen rubbed Duke's neck. "We've been through a lot together."

"Duke's probably enjoying retirement, but it sounds like you're ready to go back to work."

"That's my hope." Or was it?

Not wanting to open that door tonight, he pointed to the bowls of soup. "Dinner's getting cold."

"You're right." Colleen lowered her head.

"If you want to pray out loud, I'll join you."

She glanced up at him, seemingly startled.

"We both have a lot for which to be thankful."

Her face softened, and she smiled. Warmth spread through him.

Her hand was still on the table. He reached out and grasped it before his internal voice of reason could tell him to be cautious. After everything that had happened, he wanted to join Colleen in prayer, even if he didn't know what words to say. He'd let her lead this time. Maybe he'd be able to say his own prayers, in time.

After they finished the soup, Frank walked Colleen to the guest room and said good-night at the door.

"Is there anything you need?" he asked.

She shook her head, grateful for the concern she heard in his voice and the sincerity in his expression. Something had changed since the run-in with Trey at the hospital. Maybe Frank finally believed her.

"Thanks."

He raised his brow. "For saying good-night?"

She laughed. "For saving my life. If...if you hadn't been there—"

"I almost didn't make it in time."

"You scared Trey off."

"But he escaped."

"At that moment, all I cared about was staying alive."

The thought of what could have happened made her shiver.

Frank reached for her. She stepped closer, and his arms circled her shoulders. She laid her head on his shoulder.

Frank had to be as tired as she was, yet she could feel his strength and determination. He had saved her from Trey. She thought she could bring the drug dealer to justice on her own, but she needed help. She needed Frank.

At the moment, she didn't think of Frank as a cop. She thought of him as a man. He was tall and strong, even though he still wore some of the ravages of the infection he had battled.

Colleen had been so wrong about who he really was. Now she saw him in a better light, and she liked what she saw.

She allowed herself to rest in his embrace for a long moment before she pulled back. "Thanks again for today." She flipped on the overhead light in the bedroom. "If you'll excuse me, I'm tired and need to sleep."

Stepping into the room, she closed the door and sighed. Frank hadn't believed her last night. Did he now? She didn't know for sure.

Until she knew his true feelings, she had to be careful and guard her heart.

TWELVE

Colleen inhaled the clean smell of the outdoors as she snuggled between the crisp sheets—no doubt dried on the line—and pulled the quilt up to her shoulders. Feeling pampered by the fresh linens, she fell asleep quickly and woke with a start some hours later from a dream that seemed too real.

She saw Trey in the woods, rifle raised, and heard Vivian's cry for help, along with the deafening roar of the twister.

Throwing back the covers, Colleen grabbed the robe Evelyn had provided and shrugged into the soft cotton. Reaching to turn on the bedside lamp, she hesitated, her hand in midair.

A sound upset the stillness.

With every nerve on high alert, she turned her ear toward the double French doors leading to the porch and strained to decipher the sound that came again.

Metal on metal?

Ever so quietly, she slipped from the bed and tiptoed to the window. With her back to the wall, she lifted the edge of the curtain.

Darkness.

Staring into the black night, she willed her eyes to focus. Slowly, they adjusted.

Movement.

Snip. Then another.

Her pulse raced and fear clawed at her throat.

The sound repeated over and over again.

She strained to make out some faint outline that could identify who was trying to gain access.

There. A hand thrust through the porch screen.

A portion of the wire mesh pulled free.

She dropped the curtain and turned to flee.

Tired though he was, Frank couldn't sleep. He kept seeing Colleen buried in the rubble, first when the twister hit and then later when the barn wall had collapsed on top of her. He'd screamed and raced forward, but he couldn't get to Colleen in time.

Thankfully, the roof of the Honda had stopped the momentum of the wall's downward collapse. Colleen had been hit by broken boards, but not with the full force of the larger section.

He'd asked Evie to check on Colleen during the night. No doubt, his sister was also giving thanks to the Lord about the right resolution to a very dangerous situation today. Frank wasn't used to turning to God, yet a swell of gratitude rose within him.

Dropping his legs over the side of the bed, he sat up and stared into the darkness. "I don't know what to say except thank you, Lord."

Satisfied with his first significant attempt in years to communicate directly with the Almighty, Frank lay back down, hoping to grab some shut-eye.

Duke stirred at the foot of the bed.

"Easy, boy. What is it?"

The dog whined and trotted to the door.

"You hear something?"

He pranced and whined again.

Frank stood, slipped into a pair of jeans and grabbed his service weapon.

Opening the door ever so carefully, he glanced at the door to Evelyn's bedroom and stepped into the hallway. Duke trotted toward the kitchen and turned into the rear hallway leading to the sewing room, where Colleen now slept.

Frank followed and stopped outside Colleen's room. All he heard was the beat of his heart and the dog's even breaths at his feet.

Had he imagined something?

Duke had seemed a bit skittish since the tornado. Both of them were having problems settling back into a routine ever since Colleen had blown into their lives.

Convinced they'd overreacted, Frank started to turn away.

A sound made him pause.

A scurry of footsteps inside the room.

Before he could raise his hand to knock, Colleen's door opened.

Eyes wide. Hair in disarray. Lips still swollen with sleep.

"Someone's—" She gasped and pointed to the French doors. "Someone's on the back porch."

"Evie's bedroom is down the hall on the left. Stay with her. Lock the door. Don't let anyone in unless I tell you it's clear. Call 911 and notify the police."

She scurried past him.

"Come on, boy."

Duke followed him through the kitchen. Frank

grabbed his Maglite and slipped outside, the dog at his side.

A breeze blew through the trees, the sound of rustling leaves covering their footfalls. Frank's heart pounded. Trey wouldn't escape this time.

Gripping the Maglite in his left hand and his weapon in the right, Frank inched around the corner. A dark shadow, big and bulky, peered through the French doors into the room where Colleen had slept moments earlier.

At the same instant, sirens sounded in the distance.

The dark shadow turned and ran.

"Stop. Law enforcement."

The guy fled into the woods. Frank gave the command. Duke ran after him. Frank followed.

Shots fired.

Fearing Duke had been hit, Frank increased his pace and pushed harder.

The sound of a car engine filled the night. Tires screeched.

Frank whistled. The dog bounded from the wooded area.

Relieved to see his trusty friend unharmed, Frank slapped his leg. "Come on, boy."

They hurried back to the house. A police squad car pulled into the driveway.

"I didn't expect you to respond so quickly," Frank said to the cop who climbed from the car.

His name tag read Stoddard. He was tall and lean, midtwenties and blond. "I was in the area, sir."

Frank quickly filled him in on what he'd seen and heard.

Using the radio, Stoddard alerted other patrol cars. "The man is armed and dangerous."

While the officer examined the cut screen, Frank

stepped inside and headed to Evelyn's room. He tapped on the door.

"It's Frank. You can come out. The guy ran off."

Evelyn threw open the door and gasped with relief when she saw Frank. "Colleen and I thought something had happened to you. We heard the shots and—"

He patted her shoulder. "The shots were aimed at Duke."

Colleen looked alarmed. "Is he okay?"

"Seems to be fine."

"Did you see the guy?" she asked.

"Only from the rear. He was wearing dark slacks and a hooded sweatshirt."

"It was Trey."

"We don't know that for sure."

The cop called from the front of the house. Evelyn tied her robe more tightly around her. "I'll brew coffee."

She hurried to the kitchen.

Colleen stepped closer. "Something woke me. I couldn't recognize the sound at first. Looking out the window, I saw him cut through the screen."

"Frank." Evelyn's voice. "The officer needs to ask you some questions."

"He'll want to talk to me, too," Colleen said.

"I'll stay with you."

She nodded. "It's okay. I don't have anything to hide."

The officer accepted a cup of coffee from Evelyn and took down the information that Frank and Colleen provided.

"Ma'am, did you recognize the prowler?" he eventually asked.

"I… I couldn't tell who he was. It was dark. I don't know if it was Trey Howard or someone else."

"I'll check with Officer Talbot, whom you spoke with at the hospital, and see if he's uncovered anything new."

"The officer said he'd issue a Bee Low," she added.

Frank smiled. "That's BOLO. A Be On the Lookout order was sent to all law enforcement in the area."

The blond officer scratched his head. "Which I never received. I'll check that with Talbot, as well."

He glanced at Evelyn as he scooted back from the table and stood. "Thanks for the coffee, ma'am."

"I wish you'd take a slice of coffee cake for later."

He nodded his appreciation. "I'm training for a marathon next month and keeping my sugar to a minimum. But the coffee hit the spot."

Frank walked Stoddard to the front door and offered his hand. "Ms. Brennan's car is at the barn. See if your crime scene folks can get to it in the morning."

"I'll make that happen, sir."

The cop was young and seemed competent. Colleen had answered all the questions, but Frank wondered if she was holding something back.

Why did Trey keep coming after Colleen? Was it because of what she knew? Or did it involve more than a list of names and a photo?

There had to be something else that Trey wanted.

But what?

Just before Stoddard left the house, a car pulled into the driveway. While Colleen helped Evelyn tidy the kitchen, Frank opened the door, surprised to find Mayor Allen Quincy standing on the porch.

"Evening, Frank. Officer Stoddard." Tall, balding and wearing his fatigue, the mayor stepped into the foyer. He dropped his keys on a nearby table and shook both men's hands.

"Actually, sir," Stoddard said, "evening has long since passed. Everything okay?"

"Just doing a last-minute check in the Amish area." Pulling a handkerchief from his pocket, the mayor wiped his forehead and smiled. "Age seems to be catching up with me."

"I doubt that, sir," Stoddard was quick to reply.

The mayor smiled. "I saw your squad car when I drove by. The dispatcher said there was a break-in."

"An attempted break-in," Frank explained. "The guy got as far as the screened-in porch."

The mayor shook his head with regret, his shoulders sagging ever so slightly. "We've had vandalism in the trailer park that was hit by the tornado. I had hoped the Amish area wouldn't have that problem."

Evelyn wiped her hands on a towel and joined the men in the foyer. "Care for a cup of coffee, Allen?"

"Thanks, Evelyn, but I'll take a rain check."

Another knock. "Seems everyone's stopping by tonight." Frank opened the door.

A second police officer stood on the porch with his hand on the shoulder of a young Amish boy.

"Evening, Mayor. Ma'am. Sir." He peered through the crowd at Colleen and nodded to her, as well.

"I hate to bother you folks this late," the officer said, "but I found this young man walking through your property. I wanted to see if you could identify him as your prowler."

Colleen stared at the Amish lad. "You were behind the barn when the wall came down."

The boy tensed. "I did nothing wrong."

"What about tonight, son?" Frank asked. "What were you doing this far from home, especially so late?"

Evelyn reached for the boy's hand: "Isaac, it's good

to see you. Was Mr. Malone tutoring you? Did you have a night session?"

The boy shook his head. "I... I was talking to Lucy Wyatt."

"Marsha and Carter Wyatt's daughter?"

"*Jah*. They are her parents."

Evelyn looked at the two officers and the mayor. "I can vouch for Isaac. He works at the Craft Shoppe and selects the best produce and baked goods for me. He's a fine young man."

Recalling the bulk of the guy on the porch, Frank had to agree with his sister. "The intruder was taller and more filled out."

He turned to Isaac. "Did you see anyone in the woods when you were with Lucy?"

The Amish boy shook his head. "No one."

The mayor checked his watch. "I'm headed back your way, Isaac. I'll take you home."

He hung his head. "My *dat* does not know I left the house."

The mayor thought for a moment and then patted the boy's shoulder. "Then we won't tell him. I'll drop you at the end of your driveway. He won't hear my car."

Turning to the officer still standing on the porch, the mayor asked, "Does that meet with your approval?"

"Yes, sir. No need for me to file a report as long as you're taking the boy home."

"Thanks for your hospitality, Evelyn."

"Anytime, Mayor."

As he turned to leave, Colleen pointed to the keys on the foyer table. A plastic picture frame was attached to the chain.

Frank followed her gaze and stared at the photo of a young woman in a wedding dress.

The mayor patted his pocket and then laughed as he reached for the forgotten keys. "Isaac and I wouldn't have gotten far without these."

"The photo?" Colleen asked.

"That's my daughter." The mayor beamed with pride. "She got married in Atlanta last summer and gave the key chain with the attached picture to me for Christmas."

"She used an Atlanta photographer?"

"That's right. He seemed like a nice guy. My daughter was happy with the photos, so that's all that matters."

Once everyone left, Frank closed and locked the door. "A busy place tonight."

Evelyn shook her head with regret. "I fear Isaac's heart is going to be broken."

"Oh?"

"Lucy Wyatt is not Amish."

Evelyn returned to the kitchen.

Colleen's eyes were wide. She grabbed Frank's hand. "The bride's picture had the name of the photographer written in the corner."

Frank knew before she told him.

"The photographer was Trey Howard."

THIRTEEN

Colleen woke the next morning and stretched out her hand to pet Duke. Frank had insisted the dog stay in her room throughout the night. She had slept soundly knowing the German shepherd was standing guard.

"You're such a good dog." Duke lifted his ears and tilted his head, letting her rub behind his ears and pat his neck. "Thanks for taking care of me last night."

She glanced at the clock and groaned—9:00 a.m. She'd slept later than she wanted. At first, she'd tossed and turned while reviewing the questions the police officer had asked. True to his word, Frank had sat next to her and filled in any blanks when she got stuck on an answer. Evelyn had stayed up and encouraged them to eat the cake and cookies she served, never appearing fazed by Frank's explanation about Trey and his drug operation.

The arrival of the Amish boy and the mayor added to her concern, especially when she'd seen Trey's name on the key-chain photo. Surely the mayor wasn't involved in a drug operation, yet the coincidence added to her unease.

Crawling from bed, Colleen quickly showered and changed into jeans and a pullover top. The memory card was weighing heavily on her mind.

Hurrying into the kitchen, her enthusiasm plummeted when she found a note from Evelyn on the counter. "I have to work at the library for a few hours. I'll be home in time for lunch."

Knowing Frank was probably at the triage site, Colleen glanced out the kitchen window, searching for a glimpse of him in the valley below. Hopefully Evelyn wouldn't be gone too long. Feeling a bit skittish at being alone, she rubbed her hands over her arms and tried to still her growing anxiety.

Duke stood at the front door and barked. Of course, she wasn't alone. She had a wonderful guard dog.

"Sorry, boy, I wasn't thinking of you."

She let him out and returned to the kitchen to brew coffee. Evelyn had left coffee cake on the counter with a second note. "Help yourself. Eggs and bacon are in the fridge. Homemade bread is next to the stove."

She smiled, grateful for Evelyn's hospitality.

As the coffee dripped, Colleen hurried back to check on Duke.

Footsteps sounded on the front porch.

She stopped short. Her stomach tightened. She hadn't completely closed the door. Through the cracked opening, she saw a man, wearing jeans and a black sweater.

Heart in her throat, she backed into the kitchen and grabbed a knife from the wooden butcher block by the stove. Holding it close to her side, she mentally outlined her options.

How much protection would the knife provide?

Not enough.

She needed help.

She needed Frank.

* * *

"Colleen?"

Frank's voice. She gasped with relief and felt foolish for thinking Frank could possibly be Trey. She dropped the knife on the table and tried to blink back tears, but she couldn't stop the rush of emotion that swept over her.

Frank's face was twisted with concern. He opened his arms, and she fell into his embrace.

Her control broke. She sobbed, unable to stop the on-slaught. She had been so strong for so long. She'd stood by her dying sister and promised she'd bring Trey to justice, but she hadn't been able to gather enough evidence or convince law enforcement of his guilt.

No one believed her. Not even Frank.

Until now.

Much as she didn't want to admit the truth, Colleen felt responsible for her sister's death. She'd been so determined to show Briana tough love that she'd failed to respond to her plea for help.

Why hadn't she been more sensitive, more caring, more who Christ wanted her to be? Maybe because she'd been burned by Briana so many times in the past. Still, that wasn't reason to forsake her sister in a time of need.

Frank pulled her closer. His hand rubbed over her shoulders. Lips close to her ear, he whispered soothing words that were like a lifeline to a drowning woman.

"Shh, Colleen, I've got you. I won't let anyone hurt you."

"I… I thought you were—"

"I'm sorry for scaring you. I went out to get the morning paper. When I saw Duke, I wanted to make sure you were okay."

She nodded and wiped her cheeks, concentrating on Frank's strength and the understanding so evident in his voice.

"I… I closed my heart to Briana." The words came unbidden. She had to admit her mistake.

"It's okay, honey."

"She had nowhere else to turn except to Trey."

"Even with your help, she probably would have gone back to him. The statistics aren't good for anyone hooked on drugs. Without rehab, without the will to make a change—"

"Without God," Colleen added, her lips trembling.

"That's it exactly. As much as you wanted Briana to walk away from her addiction, she couldn't, and you couldn't do it for her. She went to Trey, not because of you, but because of her need for drugs."

"If only she hadn't gotten involved with him."

"Where'd they meet?"

"I'm not sure. She worked at the King's Club for almost two years. It's in the heart of the city and known to have the wrong type of clientele. Trey may have been a regular. I told her it was a bad place. I don't know if she quit the job because of me or if she got tired of what she saw."

"Did she know the two women who died?"

"She never mentioned them. The last time she phoned wanting money, I said no. She overdosed a few days later."

Colleen looked into Frank's dark eyes, which reflected the pain she was carrying.

"I have to stop Trey. That's the promise I made to Briana."

He nodded. "I'm in this with you. We'll get him. He won't hurt anyone again."

"There's...there's something else I have to tell you."

Frank tensed ever so slightly.

She felt the change, but she couldn't stop now. Everything needed to be revealed.

"When I entered Trey's office, I was searching for evidence that would convince the police. I told you about the picture on his screen."

Frank nodded. "Go on."

"That night, Trey was using an external card reader to view his digital photographs from a memory card. I needed more evidence, so I took the card, although I never had time to look at the pictures."

"He must have realized the memory card was gone. Didn't he come after you?"

"He sent one of his men to my apartment later that night. I was scheduled on a flight early the next morning. My carry-on was packed so I left through a back door, made my flight the next day and then checked into a motel when I got back to Atlanta. That's when the gal who lived across the hall called me. She said someone else had been snooping around."

"You thought that was Anderson, the cop from Atlanta."

"I'm not sure. Anderson or one of Trey's men. Soon after that, I called Vivian. She had evidence that would prove Trey's involvement. At least that's what she told me."

"The video."

"She didn't tell me what she had, but she did ask what type of phone I used."

"Why didn't you tell me before about the memory card?"

"Trey took my photograph with a couple of the men

who worked for him. I didn't want to be in the picture, but he insisted. If I made too much of it, I knew he'd get suspicious."

"What's that have to do with not telling me?"

"I... I wasn't sure how you'd react if you saw me with the men. You didn't believe me earlier. The photo wouldn't have improved my credibility, especially if they were known drug traffickers. Plus, I worried Trey might have doctored the photo to incriminate me even more. Guilt by association, they call it, but I'm innocent of any wrongdoing."

She glanced up, and her breath hitched. "Do you believe me, Frank?"

"Why wouldn't I?" His voice was flat and his eyes had lost their spark of interest. He was trying to cover up his true feelings.

"Where's the memory card now?" He took a step back, distancing himself from her.

She shook her head, struggling to control a second wave of tears that threatened. Frank didn't believe her.

"It was in my purse. The contents were strewn under the seat in the storm. I'm sure it's still in the car."

"I'll check it out."

He started to turn away from her. She grabbed his arm.

"I'm going with you."

She'd ride to the triage area with Frank. Hopefully they'd find the memory card, but then she'd leave Freemont and go someplace safe.

She never wanted Trey or his men to find her.

She didn't want Frank to find her either.

A stiff breeze blew as Frank pulled out of Evelyn's driveway. He'd left Duke behind, but Colleen sat next to him, her arms crossed and her shoulders straight.

Frank had been attracted to Colleen and ready to go the distance for her. Then she mentioned the memory card, which was another bit of evidence she had kept from him.

He didn't understand her or her actions.

She wanted Trey stopped, yet she refused to share crucial information with him. Didn't she trust him to be an effective investigator?

After his injury, he hadn't been enough of a man for Audrey. Evidently he wasn't enough of an investigator for Colleen.

He remembered the way she had felt in his arms. Truth be told, he hadn't wanted to let her go. Instead, he wanted to protect her and do whatever he could to stop her tears and bring joy to her life.

He hadn't felt that way with Audrey. Their relationship had been surface, which Audrey had made blatantly clear when she'd walked away. Too late he realized the truth. Frank had being drawn to Audrey by her outward looks, not by an inner beauty.

Colleen was beautiful inside and out, but it wasn't her looks that attracted him to her. It was her focus, her strength and her need to right the wrong that drugs had caused her sister. Frank knew that drive. It's why he had joined the military and eventually transferred to the CID. He wanted to right wrongs and help those in need.

If only he could explain his feelings to Colleen, but she was centered on finding the memory card and bringing Trey to justice. No reason to mix personal relationships with an investigation. He knew better, even if Colleen had pulled him off course.

He drove down the hill faster than he should have and braked to a stop beside the barn.

"Where's my car?" Colleen demanded, the first comment she'd made since climbing into his truck at his sister's house.

"Stay here."

"I will not." She threw open the door and jumped down. "What did you do with my Honda?"

"Nothing."

"Did the local cops impound the car?"

"I'll find out."

Frank pulled his cell from his pocket and called the Freemont PD. He asked to speak with Officer Stoddard.

"I told you about the car buried in debris in the barn," Frank said when Stoddard came on the line.

"Yes, sir."

"Did your crime scene team check it out?"

"Ah, I'm not sure. Give me a minute."

Frank waited, his frustration rising.

"Sir." Stoddard returned. "Our crime scene team scheduled the Honda for late afternoon."

"That would work except the car is gone."

"Gone?"

"Exactly. Someone's taken the car, and I want it found."

"Yes, sir."

Frank disconnected. "The cops don't know what happened," he told Colleen.

"Someone does."

A horse and buggy clip-clopped along the road. Frank flagged down the bearded farmer. He wore a light blue shirt and a straw hat that nearly covered his eyes. A teenage boy, clean-shaven and similarly dressed, sat next to him.

"Mr. Fisher?"

"Whoa, there. Whoa." He pulled his horse to a stop.

Frank pointed to the barn. "There was a car in that barn. Do you know where it's been taken?"

The Amish man shook his head.

Frank turned to the teen. "What about you, Isaac? Did you do anything to the car?"

The bearded man bristled. "Why do you ask this of my son?"

Holding up his hand, Frank said, "Sir, let him answer the question."

"A bulldozer was in the area." The teen pointed across the street to the construction worker clearing debris around the farmhouse. "Ask that man."

Frank nodded his thanks and waited until the buggy had passed before he hurried across the street.

Spotting his approach, the driver shoved the gear in Neutral and allowed the bulldozer to idle in place.

"Paul, isn't it?" The guy who had worked around the barn yesterday.

He nodded. "That's right. Paul Yates."

"What happened to the car that was in the barn?" Frank pointed back to where Colleen stood staring at the ground.

"Someone loaded it on a flatbed." Paul rubbed his chin. "Junkyard Jack? Junkyard Jason? Seems it started with the letter *J.*"

"Junkyard Joe's."

The guy nodded. "That's it."

"Who authorized the pickup?" Probably a long shot to think the Atlanta construction worker would know, but no harm asking.

"No clue about authorization, but the guy in charge of the whole cleanup was talking to the driver of the flatbed. Someone said he was the mayor."

"Allen Quincy. Did you see anyone else?"

"Just the two guys from the junkyard."

Frank nodded his thanks and hustled back to Colleen, who was picking through the hay and debris.

"I'm checking the ground in case the memory card ended up outside the car," she explained as he neared. "When the twister hit, my only thought was staying alive."

"Find anything?"

"Lots of stuff. No memory card. Any luck on your end?"

"Seems the mayor may have gotten carried away with his cleanup campaign and had your car hauled off to the local junkyard."

"That's our next stop?"

He nodded. "But first, let's give this area a thorough search so we don't have to backtrack."

Frank worked back and forth, in a grid-like pattern, just as he had been trained to do with crime scene investigations. Colleen walked beside him, and both of them seemed satisfied when they left in Frank's pickup forty-five minutes later.

"Junkyard Joe's sits on the other side of town," Frank said. "I'll give you a tour of Freemont on the way."

He turned off Amish Road and headed due east, first through a residential area that had escaped damage and then along a country lane.

"Such a beautiful area." She took in the rolling hills and sprawling farms that stretched on each side of the roadway.

A newer home with an expansive back deck was visible in the distance, situated on a road that ran parallel of the one they traveled.

"Dawson Timmons, a former CID agent, lives there." Frank pointed to the house and surrounding farmland.

"He got out of the army, married a local girl, bought land and started farming. They're nice folks who go to Evelyn's church."

"But you don't?"

Frank glanced at her. "Don't go to church?"

She nodded.

"I haven't yet. Maybe one of these days."

Silent for a long moment, Colleen finally spoke. "I didn't think much about religion until my sister died. Since then I've tried to do better, but I haven't joined a church."

"You were busy tracking down Trey."

"Looking back, I realize trying to take him down by myself was probably a mistake."

"It's fairly obvious you don't trust law enforcement."

There, he'd stated the major obstacle that stood between them. She didn't trust anyone with a badge, yet she couldn't achieve her goal without law enforcement's help.

"Not all of us are on the take, Colleen."

"As I recall, you have trust issues, too." Her voice was tight, her focus still on the road.

"Because I question information that can't be substantiated?"

"Because you don't believe me."

He pulled in a ragged breath. He wanted to believe Colleen. When he looked into her eyes, he saw a good woman who was trying to do what was right, but he had this fear of not making the right decision or seeing things the way they really were.

Was that holding him back?

"It's not personal."

She harrumphed. "You've talked yourself into thinking you're doing what's right, yet you can't see the truth."

"The truth about—"

"The truth about me. I'm trying to gather enough evidence to put Trey Howard in jail for life. You and I are actually on the same side of the law. The problem is you're always questioning your own ability and your compromised strength and your weakened condition."

Did he appear weak to her?

"You think your injury and infection affected your investigative skills," she continued, hardly pausing long enough to take a breath. "You're still the man you were before, Frank. You're still a CID agent able to track down evidence and bring the guilty to justice. You just lack confidence. You're looking back at what happened in Afghanistan and during your long hospitalization. It must have been difficult, but you've healed. You're ready to get back to work, to embrace life fully."

She sighed. "You're the same man, only maybe a bit more cautious and more aware of your own mortality. That's not a bad thing. Sometimes when we think we can do it all ourselves, we forget about God. But we can't do anything without Him. Allow Him into your brokenness, and you'll be able to heal."

He hesitated for a long moment. Then pulling in a deep breath, he asked, "What about you, Colleen? Have you healed?"

She shook her head. "I still can't get over losing Briana. Much as I want to believe the tough love was for her own good, I keep wondering if it led to her death. If only I'd opened my heart and brought her back into my life, I could have taken care of her. I could have loved her. I could have helped her battle her addiction."

"She needed rehab."

Colleen shook her head. "She'd been to rehab. It hadn't stopped her from finding drugs."

"Chances are she wouldn't have done anything different the second time. Drug addiction is like quicksand. She couldn't free herself even if she wanted to, and you couldn't have pulled her out. It's not easy to realize drugs have such control over someone we love, but it's the truth. She loved drugs more than she loved herself."

"More than she loved me," Colleen whispered.

Frank didn't know anything else he could say that would ease Colleen's guilt or assuage her grief. If Trey had been guilty of drug trafficking, he needed to be stopped so that no other woman was sucked into the downward spiral of addiction. The addict wasn't the only one affected. The entire family was, as well.

Colleen was proof of that.

She deserved more than heartbreak over a sister's dependence on cocaine. Colleen deserved to be loved and accepted. If only she would lower the wall she had raised around her heart.

Frank didn't know how to change her opinion of law enforcement, but he wanted her future to be bright. He was beginning to think being part of her future might be good for him, as well.

FOURTEEN

A musty smell wafted past Colleen and mixed with the haze of dust and the cloying scent of rusted metal when they drove into the junkyard. Stepping out of the pickup, she tried to hold her breath but quickly ran out of air.

"Are you okay?" Frank asked.

"I'm fine." Which she wasn't. Her head ached, and she was tired of arguing about trust and the lack thereof.

A man left the ramshackle shack that served as an office and headed to a Ford 4x4 parked nearby. The truck looked new.

"Joe?" Frank waved to the guy as he opened the door and started to climb behind the wheel.

Evidently the owner. Joe looked as scruffy as his junkyard, although his truck was pristine. Untrimmed beard, long hair pulled into a ponytail topped with a baseball hat. His name was embroidered on the front chest pocket of his work shirt.

"You need something?" he called back to them.

"A blue Honda injured in the tornado. You or a couple of your workers picked it up this morning." Frank held up his CID badge.

"They unloaded in the west end." Joe pointed them

in the right direction. "Head along the path around the mound of old parts. You'll see the Honda."

Frank reached for Colleen's hand. She hadn't expected his grip to be so strong.

"Let's go."

She hurried after him.

Passing the pile of car parts and twisted metal, she groaned when the expansive west end, as Joe had called it, came into view. The junkyard extended for acres. "This might take some time."

Two paths wove through a graveyard of discarded cars. Doors hung open. The hoods on many of the vehicles were raised, allowing engines to rust from the elements. Trunks were cocked at odd angles. Birds perched on the bottom rims pecked at bugs that lived in the shaded interior.

Colleen glanced at the ground, expecting to see vermin underfoot.

Frank squeezed her hand.

"I'm imagining rats and other creatures," she admitted.

"We'll make noise to scare away anything on four legs."

"What about the two-legged vermin?"

"I'll watch for them, as well."

Trey would do anything to save himself and his profitable drug operation. Colleen stood in his way.

He'd tried to kill her before. He'd try again.

She glanced at Frank's hand that still held hers.

He didn't believe her, yet Frank was helping her find the memory card. Probably because he needed the evidence that would end Trey's hateful abuse of the women he trafficked and the men and women—many young kids who didn't make good decisions—who used the drugs he brought illegally into the United States.

He had to be stopped.

Frank would help her bring Trey to justice. He'd also work to keep her safe, but once he had the digital memory card, he'd no longer need Colleen.

She dropped his hand and started down one of two paths winding through the rows of cars.

Colleen had to rely on her own ability, her own strength. She'd made a mistake letting her guard down around Frank. A mistake she already regretted. At least she hadn't made an even bigger mistake by giving him her heart.

Frank didn't know why he had taken Colleen's hand, especially after the tension that had sparked between them earlier.

He blamed it on his protective nature when he was around her. An inner voice kept warning him to be alert to danger.

Joe was a typical redneck who ran a fairly profitable business despite his scrubby beard and ponytail. The junkyard was a fixture in Freemont, and even Evelyn gave her stamp of approval when Frank had called her and mentioned Joe's name.

Still, something niggled within Frank, a nervous anxiety that had him looking over his shoulder and wanting to keep Colleen close by his side.

She, on the other hand, had charged off in one direction to cover more area, while he followed on the neighboring path.

He cupped his hands around his mouth. "See anything?"

She shook her head. "A lot of junk but no blue Honda."

Frank spotted an old woody station wagon, a Studebaker and other makes and models that had to be classics by now. Some of them could be refurbished into a decent ride, for the right price.

That was the point. No one would spend hard-earned cash for a rusty car that had been exposed to the elements. Joe made money by selling parts, which left the cars picked over like roadkill.

His eyes scanned rows of automobiles, trucks, even a couple of buses and an RV that had all seen better days. Some had been plucked clean. Others sat seemingly untouched in the afternoon sun.

The two paths came together up ahead. In the distance, Frank noted movement on a small hill that formed a natural end to Joe's acreage.

He squinted, trying to determine what he'd seen. A gust of wind stirred trees on the gentle slope. Surely that's what had diverted his attention.

He glanced over his shoulder, ensuring they weren't being followed.

Turning back to the hill, he focused on a narrow dirt path, barely wide enough for a compact car.

"Something wrong?" Colleen asked.

"Just checking the area."

"I see a blue car just beyond the fork where the two paths meet."

Frank followed her gaze. "Looks like your Honda."

He hurried to meet up with her.

The Honda sat behind a wall of vehicles.

"How do we crawl through all that wreckage?" she asked.

"We'll go around some of the cars and over others." He glanced at her feet, glad to see she was wearing shoes with rubber soles.

"Let me check it out. You stay on the path."

She shook her head, just as he'd known she would. "We go together."

"You could twist an ankle or get cut on a piece of metal."

She nodded. "That's a risk I'll take. Plus, I could offer the same warning to you."

"Shall I lead then?"

"Be my guest."

Frank climbed onto the hood of a four-door sedan and offered Colleen his hand. She put her foot on the front bumper, and he helped her up to where he stood. The hood buckled. "Watch your step."

He leaped to the next car and reached for her as she followed. "Two more cars to go."

They crawled across the front seat of a third car and inched their way around a fourth to reach the Honda.

Frank jerked open the driver's door. Colleen looked under the front seat. "The memory card was in my purse."

"Did anything else fall out?"

She nodded. "Everything, including my wallet and lipstick." She patted the floorboard and shook her head when she came up empty-handed. "Maybe it's in the backseat."

"Watch out for broken glass," Frank cautioned.

She searched the rear, but found nothing.

With a sigh, she extracted herself. "It's not there."

"Let me try."

She stepped back to give him room. Bending down, he tugged at the carpet. Two sections were attached by Velcro. Pulling the rug away from the floorboard, he smiled, seeing a small square card.

Grabbing it, he started to stand.

"Look what—"

A shot pinged against the car.

Colleen screamed.

He grasped her shoulders and shoved her down, protecting her body with his own.

Reaching for the Glock on his hip, he glared at the hill and the narrow path where he'd seen movement.

Another ping. Glass exploded as the shot hit the window of the car behind them.

"It's Trey, isn't it?" Colleen cried.

"At this point it doesn't matter who's shooting at us. We need to get out of here."

Frank pulled his cell phone free. He called 911 and relayed the information to the operator. "Tell the police to get here now."

A narrow path led toward a rusted school bus that offered better protection.

"Keep low."

More shots followed them.

"Are you hurt?" Frank asked, once they were behind the bus.

Fear flashed from her eyes, but she shook her head. "I'm okay."

He peered around the corner of the bus and studied the hillside.

Movement. A man aimed a rifle.

Frank raised his Glock and fired three shots.

The guy ducked into the underbrush.

Glancing behind him, Frank searched for another exit. Leaving the protection of the bus would put them in the shooter's sights.

Another volley of fire. A bus window shattered. Frank threw himself over Colleen to shield her from the falling shards.

"Stay down," he warned again.

Frank stared at the hillside. The breeze blew the trees, but a bush moved in the opposite direction. The guy was trying to escape.

Frank took aim and squeezed the trigger.

Sirens sounded in the distance.

He fired again.

The police cars rolled into the junkyard. Four cops jumped from their sedans, weapons drawn, and raced to the bus.

Frank quickly filled them in and pointed to the hill.

Another police car circled around the perimeter of the junkyard and raced up the slope. The cop screeched to a stop and took cover as he climbed from his vehicle. After a quick search, he raised his hand and shook his head.

Behind Frank, an officer spoke into his radio. "The area's clear?"

Static squawked.

"Roger that. Looks like our shooter left before we arrived."

He stepped to where Frank helped Colleen to her feet.

"The shooter took off, sir. We'll set up roadblocks. You were looking for something in the blue Honda?"

"That's correct. He must have followed us."

"We've got a BOLO out on Trey Howard. I'll notify you if we spot the suspect."

Frank took Colleen's hand and helped her back to his truck.

She looked exhausted and scared. He put his arm around her shoulders.

"We'll get him," he kept saying, although he didn't think she believed him.

"He wants to kill me," she whispered, her voice thick.

"You saw him shoot Vivian. He doesn't want you to testify against him. He may plan to escape to that Colombian resort he told you about."

"You can't let him leave the country." She grabbed Frank's hand.

"I'll have CID contact the airlines in Atlanta and the surrounding areas, Birmingham, Jacksonville, Nashville. He won't leave by air. At least not if we can help it."

She rested her head against his shoulder and sighed. "If only we'd found the memory chip, then we'd have proof. All I wanted was enough evidence to see him behind bars."

"I found it, Colleen."

"The memory card?"

He nodded.

She grabbed his hand, pried it open and found it empty. She stared up at him, perplexed and almost angry. "I'm not laughing if you think teasing me is funny."

"Trust me," he said as he dug into his pants pocket and pulled out the memory card.

"Oh, Frank, you found it. Now you can arrest Trey and try him for drug trafficking."

Frank looked at the hill where two additional police cars now searched for any clue that would lead them to the shooter.

To Colleen it all seemed so simple. They had the evidence. The photos along with Vivian's testimony would be enough to try him and hopefully find him guilty in a court of law.

But finding Trey was the challenge.

Even with the mounting police effort, he could elude

the roadblocks. If he left the country, they'd never bring him to justice.

The old Frank wouldn't have felt discouraged, but the injured Frank—the one who was still out of shape—didn't know who would win in the end.

FIFTEEN

"Go on, Frank," Colleen said once they were back at Evelyn's house. "You need to take the memory card to CID Headquarters. Show it to Colby. I'm sure Special Agent in Charge Wilson will be interested, as well."

"We could look at the photos here on my computer, and then email them to Wilson," he suggested.

"Doesn't he need the evidence in hand?"

Frank nodded but still hesitated.

"Your sister and I both insist you get going," Colleen continued. "We'll be fine. Duke will protect us if anyone unsavory comes around."

"Trey's on the loose. He knows you're here."

"And didn't police notify you that the highway patrol apprehended a man who fit his description?" Evelyn interjected.

"His identify hasn't been verified yet."

"Maybe not," Colleen said with a sigh, "but he was stopped on the interstate, heading to Atlanta, soon after the shooting at Junkyard Joe's. The rifle in his car had recently been shot. It all adds up, Frank."

"Except he claims to have been hunting earlier today."

"You two can keep arguing." Evelyn picked up the

telephone. "I'm calling Ron and asking him to stay with us while you're gone."

She raised her brow at her brother. "Will that convince you that we'll be safe?"

"Does Ron know how to use a gun?"

"He served in the military and goes hunting with his uncle. The awards hanging in his office attest to his marksmanship."

Frank nodded. "Tell him I'll leave a weapon in the top drawer of my dresser. It'll be loaded, just in case."

Evelyn passed on the information to Ron after he accepted the invitation to visit.

She hung up with a smile. "He considers it an honor to defend two lovely women."

Colleen ignored the niggling concern she still had about Ron, and instead smiled at the twinkle in Evelyn's eyes. She was lucky to have someone who cared for her.

Feeling a tug at her heart, Colleen glanced at Frank, wishing things could be different between them. He was a good and caring man and a good investigator even after the medical problems he'd undergone.

The way he talked about the military and the CID, he was ready to return to active duty. Maybe Special Agent in Charge Wilson would say he was needed now.

Peering out the kitchen window, Colleen stared at the cleanup and reconstruction going on along Amish Road. The collapsed structures and downed trees had been cleared and either piled at the edge of the road or already transported to the town landfill and dump.

Frank came up behind her and touched her arm. "You're okay with me going?"

"Of course." She wouldn't tell him about the tingle of concern that had her rubbing her arms and asking for the Lord's protection.

Trey was probably already in custody.

Pulling in a cleansing breath, she smiled. Frank had a newfound energy and enthusiasm in his step. Going back to work would be just what the doctor ordered.

"Don't worry," she insisted. "We'll be fine."

"I won't be long."

He looked at Duke, lying in the corner. "Stay. Take care of Colleen and Evelyn."

Duke tilted his head as if he understood.

"Frank," Colleen called after him, "be safe."

But he'd already left the house.

Frank headed toward town and River Road, which would take him to post. Colleen was right. He and Colby needed to go over the photos on the memory card. The authorities in Atlanta would have to be notified. DEA would also be interested in what they uncovered.

His cell rang. "Special Agent Gallagher."

"Sir, this is Officer Stoddard, Freemont PD. I notified you that Georgia Highway Patrol pulled over a white male wearing a red plaid shirt."

"That's right. Trey Howard. Is he in custody?"

"Not yet, sir. They need someone to ID him."

Frank had seen him in the hospital and on the video. "Give me directions."

Five miles north of Freemont on the interstate. The detour wouldn't take long. "I'm headed there now."

Frank disconnected and increased his speed. Knowing Trey would soon be in custody gave Frank a sense of satisfaction. Working on the case felt good. Knowing Trey wouldn't be able to draw others into his drug world was even better.

Frank would like to tell the guy a thing or two, in a professional way, of course. Then he'd drive to post and drop off the memory chip. Colby could do the initial review of the pictures while he hurried back to be with Colleen.

Was he crazy to be attracted to a woman who didn't trust law enforcement? Probably, but he'd never taken the easy route in life, and right now, he wanted to tell her how she made him feel.

After Frank left the house, Colleen tried to convince herself that everything was working out just the way she had wanted. Trey had been apprehended, but she was unsettled by a sense of concern she couldn't shake. She wandered back to the kitchen, where Evelyn was washing dishes.

Reaching for a dish towel, Colleen stepped toward the sink. "Mind if I dry?"

"No need, unless you want something to do."

Evelyn had a knack for knowing what was on Colleen's mind. "Frank's ready to get back to work."

"He's been ready for some time, although his strength needed to improve." Evelyn sighed. "The explosion in Afghanistan was traumatic enough, but he had to face the surgeries in Landstuhl and then more at Walter Reed and in Augusta. He wanted to move on with his life."

She ran more hot water in the sink. "Did he tell you about Audrey?"

Colleen shook her head. "We haven't discussed personal matters. Usually we're talking about Trey." And struggling with trust issues, which she didn't mentioned.

"Frank doesn't talk about the past to me either. It's as if he wants to bury the memories with the rubble that buried him in Afghanistan."

Colleen dried a glass and placed it in the cabinet, waiting for Evelyn to continue.

"He dated Audrey before his unit deployed. Frank thought she'd wait for him."

"They were good together?" Colleen asked.

"Frank thought so."

"But you didn't agree?"

"What do sisters know?" Evelyn shrugged. "I didn't tell Frank, but Audrey seemed more interested in having a handsome guy on her arm than being with Frank."

Colleen nodded, thinking of Briana's attraction for wealth and power and surface attractions.

"When Audrey left him, Frank tried to shrug off the hurt, then the infection set in. At one point, I feared he'd lose the will to live."

"That doesn't sound like Frank."

"He lost so much weight. He was on a ventilator. His kidneys started to shut down. The doctors didn't give me much hope."

"I'm sure you kept praying."

Evelyn nodded. "I prayed. Ron prayed. The whole church community prayed. His recovery was slow and hard, but Frank turned the corner, although he's still testing his own ability as if he's not quite sure of himself."

"He's stronger than he realizes. He'll be fine."

"Maybe, but he needs a good woman to encourage him."

"I doubt Frank thinks he needs anyone's help."

"Maybe not, but he does. I see the way he looks at you."

Colleen's breath hitched. "What do you mean?"

"You touch a spot in him. Someplace he's kept hidden. You've been a good influence."

She shook her head. "The only thing I've done is cause problems."

"That's not true. You've made him interested in life again."

Taken aback by Evelyn's comment, Colleen searched for a way to change the subject. "Ron seems like a great guy."

She nodded. "I'm very thankful he came into my life. He's everything Dan wasn't."

Colleen reached for another glass. "Is there something you want to talk about?"

Evelyn nodded. "How to tell Ron. He needs to know the truth about a guy I dated and thought was Mr. Right. I believed all his sweet talk and was naive to think our relationship would lead to marriage."

"Dan didn't feel the same way?"

"He invited me to meet him at a nearby state park for a late-afternoon picnic lunch. Of course, I expected something special. Storm clouds hovered overhead, but I didn't let that dampen my enthusiasm. Only Dan didn't plan to propose. He wanted to soothe his conscience and tell me about his wife and three children."

"Oh, Evelyn, I'm so sorry."

"I had no idea. He'd been so good at keeping everything secret, and I hadn't seen through his duplicity."

"What happened?"

"I railed at him. Told him he was despicable for what he'd done to his family as well as me. I told him I never wanted to see him again."

Evelyn sighed, and the weight of her upset was still evident. "The storm hit as I left the park. The road was slick. Visibility was bad. I was driving much too fast and didn't make one of the curves."

"The accident that hurt your leg. Frank told me he came home to help you."

"I was too embarrassed to tell him about Dan or the

reason for the accident. Growing up, Frank never struggled with relationships. He had lots of girlfriends over the years. He was tall and strong and handsome. I was always the sister no one noticed."

Colleen knew the feeling. "That's a hard place to be."

"I love Frank. He's got a heart of gold, but he needs to find God and learn what's important in life. As much as I hated to see him suffer through all those operations and the infection, they've opened his eyes. He realizes he can't take care of everything. If only he would start relying on God."

"You're a good influence on him, Evelyn."

"Which is what I said about you." She laughed. "Maybe we both have a positive effect on him."

"And Ron?"

"I want to tell him about Dan, but I'm not sure how he'll react."

"Ron cares deeply for you, Evelyn. He'll understand."

"I hope so." Evelyn checked her watch. "Wonder what's keeping him. He was ready to leave the house when I called. The drive only takes a few minutes."

"He's probably on the way."

"I'm going to phone just to be safe."

Safe. That's what Colleen wanted. She wanted Trey behind bars so she wouldn't have to worry anymore or look over her shoulder to see if she was being followed.

"Ron?" Evelyn held the phone close to her ear. Her voice held more than a note of concern. "You don't sound well. Tell me what happened."

So there had been a problem.

Colleen finished drying the dishes. She didn't want to eavesdrop, but the tremble in Evelyn's voice was worrisome.

"I'm coming over." Evelyn's face was pale and her hand shook as she disconnected.

She grabbed the keys to her car and her purse. "I have to hurry. Ron blacked out earlier. He came to feeling queasy and weak. You'll be okay?"

"Of course. Don't worry about me."

"Pray for Ron," Evelyn said as she left the house.

Lord, help Ron. Don't let anything happen to him.

Colleen locked the door and called Duke.

No reason for her to be worried about her own safety. She wasn't alone. Duke would protect her. At least, she hoped he would.

Frank drove hurriedly through town and headed for I-75, the interstate that stretched from Florida to Atlanta and then farther north into Tennessee.

Two miles outside Freemont, he spied a gathering of highway patrol cars parked on the side of the interstate. Their lights flashed, warning motorists to move to the far lane and give them a wide berth.

Frank braked to a stop and parked behind a Freemont police cruiser. Before exiting his car, he called Colleen.

"You're okay?" he asked when she answered. With a growing concern for her well-being, he feared leaving had been a mistake.

"I'm fine. Where are you?"

"Parked on the side of the interstate with the highway patrol. They want me to ID Trey."

Frank had planned to visit CID Headquarters next, but he felt a sudden need to change his plans. "I'll stop by the house on my way to Fort Rickman."

"You don't have to worry."

"I want to ensure you're safe," he said before he disconnected.

Crawling from his truck, he flashed his badge to the closest officer and introduced himself. "Freemont police called. You've apprehended a possible suspect in a shooting?"

The cop nodded. "His rifle's been fired recently. We received the BOLO. The latest update said he could be wearing a red plaid shirt."

Frank nodded. "Take me to him."

The officer led the way through a swarm of uniforms. Twenty feet from the road, a man sat on the ground, hands cuffed behind his back.

"Who's in charge?" Frank asked.

The officer pointed to a big guy wearing a highway patrol uniform and a Smokey Bear hat. Again Frank showed his badge and provided his name.

"Trey Howard shot a military wife at a roadside park near Freemont. Army CID is working the investigation," he quickly filled in.

"Can you ID the guy?" the patrolman asked. "His driver's license says he's Vince Lawson."

The memory of the man in the white lab coat who threw the fire extinguisher appeared in his mind's eye.

Frank nodded. "I can identify Trey Howard."

"Come with me."

Frank followed the patrolman to the suspect.

The guy turned and glared up at Frank. Brown hair. Dark eyes.

Frank shook his head. "That's not Howard."

"Then who is he?" the cop asked.

"I guess he's who he said he was."

Frustrated by the wild-goose chase, Frank walked back to his car and stared into the distance.

Where was Trey?

SIXTEEN

Duke whined at the door.

"Didn't Frank take you for a walk earlier this morning? He'll be home soon, but I know you want to go out now."

The dog barked.

"You need another romp, right?" She laughed at Duke's attempt to win her heart, which he'd already accomplished.

She unlocked and opened the door. Duke lunged onto the porch and bounded down the steps. He picked up a stick and returned to the open doorway where she stood.

Feeling her mood lighten, she took it from his mouth and threw it into the woods. He scurried off to retrieve the impromptu toy.

Colleen closed her eyes, inhaling the fresh air. The warm breeze brought thoughts of summer vacation when she and Briana were young. Life seemed full of promise then. Now Briana was gone and Colleen was stranded in Freemont.

As a youth, her younger sister had often complained that life wasn't fair. Colleen had known that as soon as Briana had been born. Even at a young age, she'd struggled to accept her curly red hair and had been awed by her sister's beauty right from the start.

Maybe it wasn't fair, but it was also life. Some were given more, some less.

God loves all his children. Words from her Sunday school class played in her mind.

Duke barked.

"Fetch the stick." She opened her eyes.

He barked again.

"Come, Duke."

He refused to obey and stared at something in the woods. A skunk or raccoon? Neither of which she wanted to confront.

"Come on, boy." She slapped her leg as she'd seen Frank do.

Duke growled at the underbrush and held his ground.

The afternoon turned ominously quiet. Birds stopped chirping. Even the cicadas went silent.

Feeling exposed and vulnerable, Colleen stepped back into the house. A sense of relief washed over her as she closed and locked the door. Duke would let her know when he wanted in.

Foolish of her to be so nervous. Trey had been apprehended, and Frank would return soon. She hadn't told him about her being alone when he phoned. He had enough worries.

Once Trey was behind bars, her anxiety would ease, and she'd see everything in a new light.

Then she'd no longer be stranded in Freemont. She would testify when Trey stood trial, but that wouldn't take more than a day or two. He'd trafficked drugs in Atlanta. The trial might be held there. Either way, she would take the stand and tell the truth so that Trey would be stopped forever.

The house phone rang. Maybe it was Frank with news of Trey's arrest.

Evelyn's voice was tight with concern when she greeted Colleen. "Ron's clammy and doesn't remember everything that happened to him. I'm afraid it's his heart. I called an ambulance. Tell Frank when he gets home. Are you sure you're okay?"

"I'm fine. Take care of Ron."

Duke barked.

Colleen returned the phone to the cradle and opened the door to get Duke. She stopped short. A man stood at the foot of the steps, dressed in a red plaid shirt, with a gun in his hand.

Trey.

Taking a step back, Colleen tried to close the door. Trey raced up the steps. His hand reached for her.

She screamed, anticipating his grasp.

Duke snarled, running toward Trey.

"What the—"

He stopped.

Seeing it unfold as if in slow motion, her heart broke.

Trey raised his gun, aimed at Duke and fired.

The dog yelped. His head flew back, his body twisted in air before he fell to the ground.

"No!"

Trey fired again. The shot went wide and hit the side of the porch. Wood splintered.

She pushed on the door that wouldn't close. His foot was wedged across the threshold. She ground her heel into his toes. He growled and lunged.

The door flew open. The force threw her against the table in the foyer. A lamp overturned and crashed to the floor. She ran for the hallway, skidded around the corner.

Frank's room.

His words played through her mind. *Loaded gun... dresser drawer.*

She slammed his bedroom door and turned the lock. Would it hold?

Heart pounding, she pulled open the top drawer on the closest dresser. Socks and underwear neatly arranged. She threw them aside, searching for the gun she couldn't find.

Frantic, she opened a second drawer. T-shirts and running shorts. No weapon.

Crossing the room, she grabbed the phone off the nightstand and yanked on the top drawer of the second dresser.

An army beret. Boxes of military medals. Searching, her hand connected with cold, hard metal.

Relief swept over her. Her fingers wrapped around the grip.

Trey's footsteps sounded in the hallway. He jiggled the knob, pounded on the door.

"I know you're in there, Colleen."

She backed into the bathroom.

He threw himself against the bedroom door. Once, twice.

The wood buckled.

Colleen screamed. Trey crashed into the room.

She slammed the bathroom door. Mouth dry. Heart in her throat. Her hands shook. She could barely turn the lock.

Hitting 9-1-1, she raised the phone and her voice when the operator answered. "This is Colleen Brennan. I'm at Evelyn Gallagher's house just off Amish Road.

An intruder with a gun is after me. Send the police. His name is Trey Howard. I'm armed, and I'll shoot if he comes near me."

"Stay on the line—"

Trey threw his weight. The bathroom door flew open.

He stood in the doorway, hair disheveled, eyes wild with fury.

"I'll kill you. Then I'll go to the hospital and finish off Vivian. You can't get away from me. I have too much power. The cops will never believe you. They didn't believe the others."

Like Briana.

He lunged for her.

No time to think. She squeezed the trigger.

Bam!

A deafening explosion. The gun kicked. She flinched. Her ears roared.

Blood darkened Trey's shirt, but he kept coming.

Bam! A second round.

More blood. He grabbed his thigh.

"Why you—" Foul words spewed from his mouth.

Before she could fire again, he turned and hobbled from the bedroom and into the hallway.

Trembling, she stood in the bathroom, unable to breathe, unable to hear anything except for the ringing in her ears.

She slid to the floor, the gun still raised and aimed in case Trey returned. At her feet, she saw spatters of his blood.

SEVENTEEN

Frank saw the police cars as he pulled off the main road and headed back to Evelyn's house. Heart in his throat, he floored the accelerator and screeched into the driveway, where a group of police officers stood. A body lay at their feet.

Colleen? He jumped from the car, pushed through the uniforms and almost cried out when he saw Trey.

"Where is she?"

"Your sister's at the hospital."

His worst fear. "What's her condition?"

"She's fine. Ron Malone may have suffered a heart attack."

"Was he shot?"

"Negative."

"What about Colleen Brennan?"

"She's inside."

Dead or alive? Frank was afraid to ask.

He pushed past two officers in the kitchen, wild to find her.

"Where is she?"

One of the men pointed to the hallway.

Frank tore around the corner. The door to his bedroom lay in pieces. His dresser drawers hung open.

Stepping over the clothing scattered on the floor, he saw her.

She was alive.

He ran to where she sat on the bed, her eyes dull, her face pale.

"He hurt you?"

She shook her head and pointed to the bathroom, where two patrolmen were photographing the broken door and blood-covered tiles where his gun lay.

"You shot Trey?"

"He came after me. I called 911. I told them I'd shoot."

"Having the gun saved her life," one of the cops said from the bathroom. "She wounded him in his right arm and left thigh. He stumbled outside just as we pulled into the driveway."

"We warned him to drop his gun," a second officer volunteered. "Instead he opened fire."

The police had taken Trey down, but only after Colleen had tried to protect herself.

"I remembered your gun, Frank."

"Oh, honey, you did the right thing." He pulled her into his arms, feeling the rapid beat of her heart.

Frank hadn't been here to protect her. He should have waited until the cops determined if the guy on the highway was Trey. His impetuousness had almost cost Colleen her life.

He pulled her closer and whispered words of comfort, all the while chastising himself for failing her once again.

Colleen didn't need him. She and the police had taken Trey down. She'd return to Atlanta and her life. What would Frank do?

He inhaled the sweet smell of her hair and pulled

her even closer, knowing he had already lost Colleen before he'd even told her how he felt. Her life would go on. Frank would put in his papers to get out of the army and make a new life for himself.

He'd survived without Audrey, but he didn't know if he could survive when Colleen walked out of his life.

"He tried to protect me," Colleen told Frank as he knelt next to Duke.

"Good boy." He rubbed Duke's neck. "You're going to be okay."

Colleen wasn't so sure. The bullet had grazed his hip, leaving him dazed and subdued.

One of the officers had wrapped the wound and placed him on a mat in the kitchen. "It's a makeshift fix, but it'll stop the bleeding until you can get him to the vet."

Footsteps sounded in the hallway. Evelyn rushed into the room. "The police told me."

Her eyes were wide, her face drawn. She reached for Colleen and pulled her close. "Are you okay?"

The embrace, so nurturing, so comforting, brought tears to her eyes. She struggled to blink them back, needing to be strong.

"Duke was hit," she said, her voice heavy with emotion.

"He's a good watchdog." Evelyn squeezed Colleen's arm and stepped toward Frank. She rubbed her hand over his shoulder. "How is he?"

"Probably frustrated that he couldn't take Trey down."

Frank was transferring his own feelings to the dog. Colleen didn't understand his need to be the hero. Trey was dead. Did it matter who had fired the fatal round?

"You'd better get him to the vet," Evelyn suggested. "The police will be here for some time. I'll fix coffee. Colleen can rest."

"Probably a good idea," the cop standing nearby said. "The wound needs to be cleaned. The vet might put him on an antibiotic. You don't want to mess around with a gunshot wound."

Frank glanced at Colleen. "You'll be okay if I leave?"

No, but Duke needed treatment. She didn't want anything to happen to that faithful dog who had tried to protect her. As much as she wanted to go with Frank, she knew there wouldn't be room with Duke stretched out on the passenger seat. Plus, the police would probably have more questions for her to answer.

"Your sister's right. Take Duke to the vet. The danger's passed. Trey can't hurt me now."

Frank loaded Duke in his pickup and drove to the veterinary clinic on post.

"It looks worse than it is," the doc said once he completed his examination. "I'll keep Duke overnight for observation. He should be able to go home tomorrow with a slight limp that will improve with time."

Frank knew about limps and walkers and reprogramming his mind to guard the weakened portion of his body. When Frank had finally walked without relying on a cane, he thought he was ready to go back to work. Then the raging fever and infection had landed him back in the hospital.

"One overnight seems doable." He scratched the scruff on Duke's neck. "You need to stay with the doc tonight."

He licked Frank's hand and laid his head on his paws as if to show he understood.

"See you in the morning, boy." Frank had full confidence in the vet and was grateful Duke was in good hands.

Frank drove across post and parked in front of the CID Headquarters building.

Colby glanced up when Frank entered his cubicle. He looked tired and irritable.

"I take it your wife isn't home yet."

"Becca's temporary duty was extended a few more days."

"Tough break."

Colby nodded. "I wander around the house not knowing what to do when she's not there."

Frank thought of how empty Evelyn's house would seem today without Duke and, even more so, when Colleen returned to Atlanta. It was time for him to find his own place. A small condo that wouldn't bring Colleen to mind.

"I wanted to talk to Wilson. Someone's in his office. I told Sergeant Otis to let me know when he's available."

"Can I help?"

Frank shrugged. "I need to iron out my options."

"You mean when you should come back to work?"

"More or less."

Colby stared at him for a long moment. "I heard what happened. Are you okay?"

"Because Duke was hurt?"

"That and because Trey came after Colleen. I heard she found one of your guns and wounded him."

"All true. He stumbled out of the house and into the sights of the Freemont cops, only he made a fatal mistake and opened fire."

Frank tossed the memory card on Colby's desk.

"This is what she took from Trey's office. I thought we needed to take a look."

"She never mentioned a memory card the night we questioned her."

"Colleen wasn't sure she could trust me."

Colby raised his brow and shrugged. "If that's the way you see it."

"You don't?"

"Let's check the photos on the card. We might learn more about why she withheld information."

"A lot had happened. I'm sure she wasn't thinking clearly."

Colby pursed his lips. He didn't appear to accept Frank's explanation.

Sergeant Otis peered into the cubicle. "Sir, the chief can see you now."

"Thanks, Ray."

"While you're talking to Wilson," Colby said, "I'll go over the memory card."

Frank hurried to the chief's office. Wilson was at his desk and glanced up when Frank knocked.

He entered and saluted. "Sir, we need to talk."

Wilson pointed to a chair. "Colby updated me about Colleen Brennan. Sounds like the Freemont police got our man."

Without Frank's help. "Yes, sir. Trey Howard appears to have trafficked drugs into the US. Vivian Davis acted as his mule."

"We haven't been able to question her. The doctor said her condition has improved, but she's still intubated and unable to talk."

"Has her husband provided evidence?"

"Negative. He was completely in the dark. Tough place to be. Redeployed back to Fort Rickman and eager to move to his next duty station at Fort Hood, then his wife is shot and he learns she's been involved in criminal activity." Wilson sniffed. "That's a hard homecoming."

Frank thought of his own medical evacuation back to the States and his eagerness to see Audrey. "Life isn't always fair."

"Roger that." The chief leaned back in his chair. "Thanks for all your help on the relief effort. Says a lot about you, Frank, that you rolled up your sleeves even though you were still on convalescent leave."

"That's what I want to discuss, sir."

"What's on your mind?"

"Whether I should continue on active duty."

Too much had happened too fast, and Colleen had a hard time trying to come to terms with Trey's death.

She hadn't wanted that for him. She'd wanted him stopped and put behind bars. Now he wouldn't stand trial, and the truth wouldn't come out about his drug-trafficking operation.

The police would consider the case closed and not pursue the other people involved. The whole operation had to be far-reaching, stretching to Colombia and the resort where Trey had invited her to stay.

The memory of Briana played and replayed in her mind. Trey had introduced her to drugs and enticed her to do his bidding, but other folks had worked with him.

Colleen crossed her arms and looked out the French doors beyond the screen porch. Police cars were still parked in the drive, and the crime scene team was finishing up its work.

Evelyn had called a local carpenter who was replacing the doors Trey had broken.

Thinking back to when he'd crashed into the bathroom made her shiver. It all seemed surreal, almost like a dream.

Then she'd been in Frank's arms, feeling his strength and support, which she'd needed. She hadn't wanted to leave his embrace, but he had to take care of Duke. That sweet, faithful dog had done his best to save her from Trey. If Duke took a turn for the worse, she'd never forgive herself.

Tears burned her eyes. Frank had mumbled something about not being there for her. Then he'd left with Duke.

Evelyn had hovered nearby, no doubt sensing Colleen's unease. Although she appreciated Evie's support, Colleen longed to have Frank standing at her side.

Not wanting to answer any more questions, she had retreated to the guest room, claiming she needed rest.

She couldn't relax. All she could do was think back to what had happened and glance at her watch.

What was taking Frank so long?

EIGHTEEN

Frank left the chief's office still unsure of his future. Wilson had listened to the concerns Frank had about his compromised condition. An extended PT program would build him up physically, but a bigger problem was whether he was still an effective investigator. Although Frank hated to admit his limitations, after everything that had happened with Colleen, he was convinced he'd lost his edge.

The chief wasn't known for empathy, but he'd offered advice. "Give yourself more time. Return to active duty, but not to full-blown investigative work at first." Wilson suggested a desk job that wouldn't be as taxing, either physically or mentally.

The thought of pushing papers left a bad taste in Frank's mouth.

He exited the chief's office still unsure of what he should do. The decision didn't get any easier when he faced Colby again.

The other agent was at his desk and pointed to his computer screen. "I've been going over the photos on the memory card."

"What'd you find?"

"It's more like whom." Colby hesitated. "I found Colleen."

Frank nodded. "With a couple guys who work for Trey. She told me all about it. Trey insisted on taking the snapshot. Her refusal would have raised suspicion."

"Not one photo, Frank. Many photos with known drug dealers."

Colby scrolled through the digital pictures and stopped at one that showed Colleen on a couch flanked by two men, neither of whom looked like salt-of-the-earth types.

"Do you recognize those guys?" Colby asked.

"Negative."

Colby provided names. "Atlanta's Narcotics Enforcement Unit said they're bad dudes."

"You called them?"

"And emailed a copy of the photo."

Frank sighed with exasperation. "I told you, Colleen needed to be careful and not raise Trey's suspicion."

Colby shook his head. "I not only question Colleen's judgment but also the other dealers'. Why would they expose themselves to the camera and allow Trey to take their pictures? It doesn't make sense unless they didn't know they were being photographed. Maybe Trey wanted to have the goods on them in case they turned on him. He keeps the photos on the memory card. If the dealers give him a hard time, he's got a way to blackmail them. He could control Colleen that way, too." Colby sniffed. "Isn't that what you thought Vivian and Colleen might be doing with that phone video?"

"Blackmailing Trey?"

"Exactly."

"Vivian could have been, but Colleen just wanted more evidence to prove Trey's guilt."

"If that were the case, she took the wrong memory card. Trey's not in any of these photos."

"What are you trying to say, Colby?"

"I'm saying be careful. Colleen isn't who you think she is."

Frank clamped down on his jaw. The two men had known each other since their early days in the military, but Colby was walking close to the edge of their friendship.

"I'm heading back to Evelyn's."

"I may have it wrong, Frank. Colleen may be innocent, but—" Colby turned back to the monitor and tapped the screen. "In this photo everyone's having fun. Laughing, eating, drinking. Some of them are smoking what looks like weed. The bowls of white powder on the table could be cocaine."

Frank stared at the screen, unable to make sense of what he saw. "Colleen doesn't do drugs. Her sister died of an overdose."

"Which doesn't mean she's not involved. When Briana died, the Atlanta PD thought Colleen might have been her supplier."

"How'd you find that out?"

"Ulster called again. He talked to Anderson."

"Anderson's got it wrong." Frank mumbled a terse goodbye and headed back to his truck, frustrated with Colby.

He thought of the picture he'd seen of Colleen surrounded by a roomful of known criminals.

She was innocent of any involvement with drugs.

Frank was sure of it. Or would Colleen prove him wrong?

Colleen checked the time and then berated herself for being so concerned about Frank. The investigation was winding down, and Frank's attention was back on his job. Trey was dead, and the CID had the memory chip. She was no longer needed.

Grabbing a tissue from the box near the bed, she wiped her eyes and pulled in a cleansing breath before she opened the door.

Evelyn was in the kitchen, making sandwiches that she offered to the police officers who stood nearby.

"May I help?" Colleen wanted to feel useful.

"I thought you were resting."

She looked down at her hands. "I cleaned up a bit, but I couldn't rest. I kept reliving what happened. It's better if I have something to do."

"There's a pitcher of iced tea in the refrigerator. Fill some glasses and see who wants to take a break. The police have been working nonstop."

Pounding came from the hallway.

"That's Zack Barber. He's a retired carpenter from my church. He was nearby, helping to restore one of the Amish farmhouses. He had some spare doors in the back of his truck that hadn't fit the house he was helping to refurbish. He assured me the repairs wouldn't take long."

Colleen poured the tea and kept glancing down, expecting to see Duke. Not having him close by was unsettling. Remembering the reason troubled her even more.

She grabbed a tray from a cabinet and loaded it with the filled glasses.

"I'll be outside."

The officers thanked her profusely as they reached for the refreshing tea. A few followed her back into the kitchen. Evelyn was talking to Ron on the phone and smiled as they helped themselves to the sandwiches she had prepared.

"We'll be finished shortly, ma'am," one of them told Colleen, his voice low so he wouldn't interfere with Evelyn's phone call.

Colleen had struggled with law enforcement in Atlanta, but these men had come to her rescue when the 911 operator had notified them about the break-in. Their rapid response had stopped Trey and potentially saved her life.

Yesterday, Officer Stoddard, the blond marathon runner, had been considerate when he questioned her. His voice had been filled with compassion, and he made note of everything she told him without raising his brow or shaking his head in disapproval.

Frank had been right. Not all cops were on the take.

As soon as he returned, she'd tell him she'd been wrong. She'd also thank him for inviting her to stay at his sister's house and for helping her track down the memory card. He had protected her at the hospital and again the night Trey had broken into the screen porch as well as at the junkyard.

All Frank focused on was his bad timing, but he'd left Duke to guard the house and had counted on Ron and the loaded gun to ensure her safety. His foresight had allowed her to survive.

She steeled her spine. She could take care of herself. She'd done so in the past and she could again, but when Frank walked into the kitchen, she realized her mistake. She didn't want to go back to Atlanta and be alone again. She wanted what Evelyn and Ron had.

Colleen wanted to smile and laugh and flirt whenever she saw Frank. She wanted to let her eyes twinkle with merriment and joy, which was the same look she'd seen in Evelyn's eyes when Ron was nearby.

Stepping closer to Frank, she asked, "Is Duke okay?"

"The vet said he'll be fine, but he needs to stay overnight for observation."

"I know it was hard for you to leave him." She pointed to the sandwiches. "Evelyn prepared food for the workers. I could pour you a glass of iced tea."

He shook his head. "Don't trouble yourself."

The sharpness in his tone cut her to the core. Why was Frank acting so aloof?

The carpenter lumbered into the kitchen and nodded to Frank. "Tell Evelyn I finished working on those doors. I'll come back in a few days in case she has any other repairs."

When Evelyn got off the phone, she had a lightness to her step, which was a good sign.

After greeting Frank, she shared the news. "The doctor thinks Ron's problem was a lack of potassium. He's been working out recently and probably overdid it being in the sun so long with the relief effort. The doctor ordered more tests for tomorrow, but he's optimistic and so is Ron."

The good news lifted Colleen's spirits. "Are you going back to the hospital?"

"Ron assured me he'll be fine. I'll visit him in the morning."

She stepped closer to her brother. "He wanted to apologize for not coming over while you were gone. I told him he was silly to even give it a thought."

Frank steeled his jaw. "I'm glad Ron's doing better. He doesn't need to worry. Colleen was able to handle the situation."

She stared at him, unable to determine what he meant or what was bothering him.

"I need to talk to the police before they leave." Frank left the kitchen.

Evelyn patted Colleen's hand. "He's struggling because he wasn't here to rescue you."

She shook her head. "There's more to it. It's not about Frank. It's about me."

"Give him a little time. He's still trying to find himself."

Colleen was running out of time. She needed to leave Freemont. Evidently she needed to leave Frank, as well.

NINETEEN

Frank had gotten a full summary of the crime scene investigation from Stoddard before he and the other officers left the area. They had bagged Frank's weapon and had taken blood specimens from the bathroom floor. They'd lifted prints that were probably Trey's and had photographed the entire house.

Once satisfied they'd gotten everything they needed, the police caravan pulled out of the driveway, and Frank headed back inside. Colleen was still in the kitchen, rinsing dishes and placing them in the dishwasher.

"Evelyn's in her room. She looked tired. I told her to get some rest."

"You should, as well."

"As soon as I finish here." She placed a glass in the upper rack. "I… I'm sorry about Duke."

"He'll be fine, I told you."

"Still. I know how close you are."

Frank nodded. "He's a good dog, and he's been a faithful companion. I can trust him."

From the expression on her face, Frank knew his words had hit hard. He wasn't talking about Duke, and she knew it.

More than anything, Frank wanted to believe Colleen. Colby was convinced of her involvement with the drug operation. The pictures proved it. At least that's what Colby thought.

Frank wanted to defend her, which he had tried to do at CID Headquarters. Unfortunately, Colby had already made up his mind. Frank needed information that would prove her innocence without a shadow of a doubt. Information he could shove in Colby's face and take to Special Agent in Charge Wilson.

"Are we back to trust issues again?" she asked.

"Colby found photos of you with a number of known drug dealers." Frank wouldn't mince words. He wanted everything out in the open.

She bristled, immediately on guard. "Haven't we been over this before? I told you about the photo and why I agreed to have my picture taken."

"There were more photos, Colleen. Lots of them showing you fraternizing with drug dealers."

"I wasn't fraternizing."

"What were you doing?"

"Gathering evidence. Just as you do with your investigations."

"I'm trained. You're not. Why didn't you let law enforcement handle it?"

"Because I don't trust cops."

He let out a lungful of hot air. "What about the joints everyone was smoking? The cocaine on the table?"

She shook her head. "I don't know what you're talking about."

"I'm surprised the dealers would let Trey take their photo."

"They might not have known."

"What?"

"One night, I saw him hide a camera behind books

on a shelf by his fireplace and program the shots to snap at a certain time."

"You knew about the secret photos?"

Coleen was digging a bigger hole. One Frank didn't want her to step into because the water in the hole wasn't clear. It had turned a murky brown.

"He didn't see me spying on him. I feigned a headache and went home early that night. I thought that was the only time he'd taken photos on the sly. Evidently I was wrong."

"Did he plan to blackmail the others?"

"I'm not sure. He didn't like people questioning his authority."

"Did he suspect you?"

"Not until I took the memory card."

"Vivian admitted to working for Trey."

Colleen nodded.

"Was she blackmailing him? Is that why you arranged to meet at the roadside park?"

He waited for her to prove him wrong, but she just stared at him. Her cheeks were flushed and her eyes filled with sorrow because she couldn't deny what she knew to be the truth.

Had Colby been right all along?

Frank wanted to hit his hand into his other palm and feel pain for what he'd done to Colleen. He had wanted to prove her innocence. Instead her reticence was telling. His gut twisted. How had he been so wrong?

Colleen turned and hurried down the hall to the guest bedroom. The door slammed, slamming the door to his heart, as well.

Frank was back to when he'd first stumbled upon Colleen in the barn.

He didn't know what to believe.

* * *

Tears burned Colleen's eyes. She couldn't stand there and listen to his accusations any longer. Nothing had changed. Frank didn't see things clearly anymore. Maybe he'd suffered some traumatic brain injury when he'd been caught in the rubble. He couldn't get past thinking she was guilty.

What a fool she'd been to trust him with the memory card and with her heart.

She wouldn't make that mistake again.

Throwing herself on the bed, she cried for all she'd lost. Her sister and now Frank's trust that she'd never had. Tomorrow she'd leave Freemont and head back to Atlanta.

She didn't want to see Frank again. The pain of his betrayal was too deep and too raw. Just as planned, she'd catch a flight to California and never return to Georgia again.

Frank picked up one of the sandwiches on the counter. His stomach was empty, and he needed food, but when he took a bite, it lodged in his throat. How could he have been so mistaken about Colleen?

He checked the doors to ensure they were secure out of habit. Trey would never hurt her again.

Turning off the overhead light, Frank headed to his room, but the thought of what had happened there kept playing in his head.

If he hadn't left a loaded gun—just in case—the night would have had a completely different ending.

At least Colleen hadn't been hurt.

He sat on the edge of his bed and dropped his head in his hands. If Duke were here, the trusty dog would have licked Frank's hand and offered support. His near-

ness and the understanding in his brown eyes would
have brought comfort.

But Duke wasn't here, and Frank had nowhere to
turn.

Come back to me.

Words from scripture he'd heard after the storm repeated again in his mind.

He rubbed his forehead. The reconstruction was
going well, and the Amish were getting their lives back
together while his was falling apart. They were a faithful people who put their hope in God.

He'd stopped relying on the Lord years ago. In those
days, the old Frank could take care of himself. He made
good decisions and was quickly earning a name for himself in investigation channels. Then he'd made a fateful
mistake that nearly cost him his life.

*Lord, forgive me for being too haughty, too proud
to realize I needed you. The injury and illness opened
my eyes to what's important in life, and it isn't good
looks or brains and brawn. It's you, Lord. I need you.*

His heavy heart weighed him down. He needed Colleen, but not if she was mixed up with drug dealers and
trafficking.

Help me see clearly, Lord.

All through the night, Frank sat on his bed and
prayed for strength. He'd give himself more time to
heal, but he needed clear vision about Colleen.

Was she holding on to things in the past with her sister? Frank realized he was doing the same thing. Audrey was then. Colleen was now.

Opening the drawer on his nightstand, he pulled out
a photograph and looked down at the woman with blond
hair and blue eyes he had once thought he loved.

He'd been wrong.

True love wasn't about good looks and good times, and it wasn't easy. It could hurt and get twisted and tied up with other events and other people.

Love was painful. It was now.

He dropped Audrey's photo on his dresser and left the house before Colleen got up. He wanted Duke back at his side, and he wanted to stop by CID Headquarters and review the photos again.

He wouldn't lose Colleen without a fight. Colby had his opinion, but Frank didn't buy it. He believed in Colleen, even if she didn't think he did.

TWENTY

Colleen woke with a pounding headache probably brought on by all the tears she'd shed. After getting dressed, she tidied the room and packed her carry-on bag.

She met Evelyn in the kitchen. "I'm heading to the hospital early. Ron thinks he might be released by noon. I want to talk to the doctors when they make their rounds."

Colleen poured a mug of coffee. "Thanks for all you've done for me. I can't tell you how much I appreciate your kindness."

Evelyn tilted her head. "If I didn't know better, I'd think you were saying goodbye."

"I need to get back to Atlanta. I'd taken a leave of absence from my job. I have to tell them to put me back on the schedule."

"I'm sure Frank will drive you to Atlanta." She smiled. "Something tells me he'll be making quite a few trips into the city in the days ahead."

For all her thoughtfulness, Evelyn didn't realize what had happened last night. Colleen wouldn't tell her.

"I doubt he'll have any spare time once he returns to work. You mentioned a bus station in Freemont."

"The number's in the phone book." She pointed.

"First drawer next to the fridge, but I'm sure Frank will find a way to take you himself. You're welcome to stay as long as you like, Colleen. You know Frank and I both enjoy having you here with us."

Evelyn's sincerity touched Colleen. Tears welled up in her eyes. To hide her emotions that seemed so raw this morning, she peered from the window and looked down into the valley.

"The Amish have rebuilt so much, so quickly."

"I'm glad to see it. They help one another and come together as a community."

"The whole town did. It's been encouraging to see."

"I guess you weren't raised in a small town."

Colleen shook her head. "We lived in Savannah and moved to Atlanta soon after my sister was born."

"Small towns take care of their own. From what Frank says, the military is the same way. Maybe even more so since they're often far from family and home."

Family. The word brought another lump to Colleen's throat.

"You've made me feel part of your family, Evelyn. Thank you."

"Why wouldn't we?" She wrapped her arms around Colleen and gave her a hug. "All this talk has me upset, thinking about you leaving."

She pulled back and laughed as she reached for her purse. "I'll expect to see you this evening. I'll bake chicken and have some fresh vegetables. Ron might join us if he feels up to it."

Colleen stood at the door and waved when Evelyn backed out of the drive. Once the car disappeared from sight, Colleen returned to the kitchen and pulled the phone book from the drawer. After finding the number for the bus station, she called and got an automated recording that listed the arrivals and departures. A bus left for Atlanta at ten this morning.

Unsure how long it would take to get to the station, Colleen called for a cab. Returning to her room, she grabbed her carry-on and placed it by the door so she'd be ready when the ride arrived.

Turning, she glanced over the house. So much had happened here. She needed to accept the good along with the bad.

She wanted to retrace the steps she'd taken yesterday so broken doors and blood spatters wouldn't be her last memories of the home. Entering Frank's room, she inhaled the lingering scent of his aftershave and had to close her eyes to keep the tears at bay when she thought of being in his arms.

Peering into the bathroom, she appreciated Zack's workmanship and all that had been done to remove any trace of the tragedy that had unfolded here.

Now Colleen could move on and remember the room as it should be remembered. Leaving the bathroom, she noticed a photo on the dresser.

The picture was of a beautiful blonde with big eyes and an engaging smile that was sure to melt the hardest heart. Curious, Colleen turned the photo over.

To my wonderful Frank. I'll always love you, Audrey.

Colleen dropped the photo and hurried from the room. Frank still loved Audrey. Colleen had been so wrong about everything. He had never wanted anything from her except information.

She hoped he and Audrey could get together again. That would make Frank happy, which is what Colleen wanted for him.

A knock sounded at the front door.

She glanced at her watch. The cab was twenty minutes early. At least she'd get to the bus station ahead of schedule.

She hurried to the foyer and opened the door.

A man. T-shirt. Baseball cap. Not the cabbie.

"Excuse me, ma'am. I'm Steve Nelson."

Frank had mentioned his name. "You're with the construction company here to help with the relief effort."

"That's right." He smiled. "I'm having problems with my cell phone and need to call the mayor's office downtown. We're scheduled to do some demolition today. I was driving by your house when I realized my problem and thought you might be able to help."

"Of course, come in. But it's not my house. I'm just visiting."

He wiped his feet on the doormat and pointed to her carry-on bag as he followed her to the kitchen. "Looks like you're going someplace."

She nodded. "The bus station."

"I'm headed downtown. Let me give you a lift."

"I've already called a cab."

"Easy enough to cancel."

He motioned her to the phone.

She waved him off. "No, you go ahead. Call the mayor."

Grabbing her cell, she checked the coverage. "I'm not having any trouble with my cell reception." Which didn't make sense.

"Really?" He stepped closer. Too close.

Colleen tried to move aside.

He grabbed her arm. "Where's the memory card? Trey said you have it."

"Let me go." She struggled to free herself.

"Trey said you sent a picture to the cops, only it

wasn't his operation. It was mine. I need to destroy the memory card."

"You'll never find it."

His grip tightened on her arm. She clawed at his cheek and screamed for help.

The guy pulled a gun. She tried to back away.

"Tell me or you'll die."

"You'll go to jail." Colleen had never seen the photos on the memory card, but she needed something to hold over his head. "Trey took pictures of you that prove your guilt."

Rage twisted his face. "I don't want to hear anything about Trey."

"He outsmarted you," she pressed.

"Shut up." He raised the gun and slammed it against her head.

She gasped with pain.

Darkness settled over her.

Colleen's last thought was of Frank.

TWENTY-ONE

"He had a good night," the vet said when Frank arrived at the clinic.

Duke licked his hand. "I missed you, boy. How's the leg?"

"The wound's healing." The vet handed Frank ointment. "Change the dressing daily and apply more ointment. If it starts to bleed or looks infected, bring him back. Otherwise Duke should be feeling like his old self in seven to ten days."

Frank still didn't feel like his old self, but he appreciated the vet's help, and having Duke by his side made the overcast day seem less gray.

Opening the passenger door, he smiled as the dog hopped into the truck seemingly without effort. "You're going to be chasing squirrels again before long. I'll have to hold you back."

Duke barked. Frank laughed and rounded the car.

"If you don't mind, I want to stop at CID Headquarters and look at some pictures."

The drive across post took fewer than ten minutes. Colby's car was in the parking lot.

"I need to see those photos," Frank said as he entered Colby's cubicle.

"Hey there, Duke." Colby scratched the dog's scruff. Then he stood and motioned Frank to take his place at the computer.

"Have at it. I'm getting a refill of coffee. Can I get a cup for you?"

"Sounds good. Black."

Frank started scrolling through the photos and stopped when he saw the one Colleen had sent to the police. He enhanced the picture until he could read the name tag on the camera case sitting next to the shrink-wrapped bricks. *Howard.*

Colby came back, carrying two cups. He handed one to Frank.

"Colleen was right about the camera case." He pointed to the monitor. "Looks like it may have belonged to Trey."

"Lots of people are named Howard."

Colby's outlook hadn't improved.

"Has anyone questioned Vivian?" Frank took a slug of the coffee.

"Not yet. The doctor wants to wait another day or two before he weans her off the ventilator."

"And her husband?"

"Faithfully sitting at her bedside."

Frank continued to scroll through the photos, searching for anything that would incriminate the dealers and shed more light on Colleen's innocence.

Colby leaned over his shoulder and sipped his coffee. The process was slow and monotonous.

Many of the shots showed the Colombian resort after its completion. Trey had taken pictures for the travel brochures and advertisements that drew tourists from all over the world. The property was top of the line.

An army wife like Vivian with a deployed husband

could easily be swayed by Trey's talk of a modeling career, especially when he included an all-expenses-paid vacation to such a plush resort.

A number of photos showed parties in full swing. Groups of people mixed and mingled, many sipping cocktails. The men were a diverse group. Some wore sport coats; others were in polo shirts and slacks. Attractive women mingled with them, serving drinks and hanging on their arms. Colleen stood to the side, looking very much alone.

Frank's heart went out to her. She hadn't been part of the drug operation. Colleen was an outsider trying to fit in—and failing, in Frank's opinion. It was a wonder Trey hadn't seen through her charade. Determined to bring down the man who had hooked her sister on drugs, Colleen had put herself in danger. Just as she'd told Frank from the beginning, she needed evidence and she found it by infiltrating a large and corrupt drug-trafficking operation.

Frank had to apologize to her for the way he'd acted. She deserved a medal instead of chastisement.

Colby looked at his watch and patted Frank's shoulder. "You keep searching. I've got to be at Post Headquarters in fifteen minutes for a meeting with the chief of staff about the reconstruction. The Freemont mayor will be there to talk about their efforts. The last project is the warehouse demolition by the river."

Frank waved his hand in farewell and glanced down at Duke once Colby had left the room. "Time for us to get going, boy. I need to talk to Colleen and apologize for my actions."

Even with Trey dead, Colleen still needed to be careful, especially if the photos ever got out. Just as she had said, the pictures had served as protection for Trey in case anyone tried to do him harm, but Colleen was front and center. Not a safe place to be.

Frank needed to warn her.

Duke lay his head on Frank's knee, blocking the chair. "What is it, boy? Not ready to leave yet? You like being back at work?"

He chuckled and reached for the mouse. "A few more minutes here won't hurt."

The next section of photos showed the beginning construction effort for the resort. A large sign announced the groundbreaking for La Porta Verde.

Three men stood in front of the sign. A short man with dark skin appeared to be the local contact. Another man, dressed in a flowery Hawaiian shirt, held a stack of papers and must have been part of the initial building project.

A third man shook the Colombian's hand. He was standing to the side, his face in profile. In the distance, a backhoe was poised, ready to break ground.

Frank zoomed in. His gut tightened.

The man in profile was Steve Nelson, the head of the company helping with Freemont's reconstruction.

Frank grabbed his cell and called Evelyn's house.

His sister answered.

"I thought you'd be at the hospital."

"I just got home. Ron's tests came back. The doctor said it was an electrolyte imbalance and released him. I dropped him off at his place and came home to check on Colleen."

"Let me speak to her."

"That's the strange thing, Frank."

He jammed the phone closer to his ear.

"A cab was waiting out front when I pulled up. He said someone needed a ride to the bus station in town."

Colleen was leaving?

"I have to talk to her."

"She's not here."

Frank pushed back from the desk, raced from the cubicle and out the rear door that led to the parking lot. Duke ran beside him.

"I'm on my way to the bus station. If Colleen calls, convince her not to leave town, and tell her she's still in danger."

"You're scaring me, Frank. What's going on?"

"I'll tell you once I find Colleen. What time does the bus leave for Atlanta?"

"Give me a minute to check."

Frank didn't have a minute. He was at his truck. Duke hopped in through the driver's side.

"The bus departs in twenty minutes, but there's something else you need to know."

Climbing behind the wheel, Frank started the ignition. "What is it, Evelyn?"

"Colleen left her carry-on bag by the front door. Her things are strewn all over the floor."

Pain!

Colleen thrashed, trying to escape the burning fire that seared through her head. She moaned, then blinked her eyes open and stared into the damp dimness.

A small room. Table.

She struggled to sit up, realizing too late her hands and feet were bound. A wave of nausea washed over her and sent her crashing back to the musty mattress and pile of rags.

The faint light filtering through the open doorway caused another jolt of pain. She shut her eyes and groaned.

"Coming around?"

A deep voice.

Frank?

She blinked again. Not Frank.

The construction boss. What was his name? Steve. Steve Nelson. Bile rose in her throat as she remembered his attack. "Where...where am I?"

"Someplace safe. At least for now. Where's the memory card?"

"Gone...in the storm."

He bent down, his face inches from hers. His sour sweat and stale breath made her want to gag.

"You only have a few minutes to tell me the truth."

"What...what happens then?"

"Poof!" He threw his hands in the air. "An explosion brings down the building. Tell me about the memory card or you'll die in the blast."

"You're worried. Trey took incriminating photos of you, along with the other dealers." At least she presumed he had.

Steve's eyes widened with fury. "I brought Trey into the operation, but he got greedy and started running his own girls. If the cops hadn't killed him, I would have. They saved me the trouble."

"You're despicable. Trey hooked my sister, Briana, on drugs that caused her to overdose. You're responsible, too."

His lips twisted into a maniacal smile. "Briana wanted out. She went to the cops and told them about Trey. Only one of the cops needed money and passed the information on to me."

Colleen gasped. "You killed my sister."

"She forced my hand. I had to kill her. Just like I have to kill you because you know too much."

"The police have the memory card from Trey's camera. They'll find you and everyone else in your operation. You're finished, Steve."

He shook his head. "I can move to Colombia."

"They'll extradite you back to the States, where you'll spend the rest of your life in jail."

He stepped to the table, leaned over a small gym bag and fiddled with the contents. Nodding to himself as if satisfied with what he'd done, he wiped his hands on his pants and then turned back to her.

"You've got ten minutes. Tell me now or tell me never."

"I'll never tell you anything. The cops will find you and bring you to justice."

"Cops?" He raised his brow. "Or your boyfriend, Frank?"

Her heart lodged in her throat. "He doesn't know anything."

"Of course he does. You gave him the digital card. After I leave the building, I'll go back to his sister's house and wait for him there."

"No." She struggled to free herself.

He turned for the door. All she heard were his footfalls on the old oak floor and his laughter.

Lord, save me. Save Frank.

TWENTY-TWO

Frank left Fort Rickman and increased his speed. River Road wove along the water and led to the older section of downtown Freemont, where the bus station was located. Hopefully Evelyn had phoned Colleen to warn her.

He tried again. All he got was her voice mail.

"Call me, Colleen. Don't leave Freemont. You're in danger."

Which she had been all along. Frank hadn't been able to protect her. He hadn't been there when she'd confronted Trey. Now someone else was after her.

"Steve Nelson is part of the operation in Atlanta," he relayed to her voice mail. "Watch out. I'll be at the bus station in less than five minutes. Stay safe."

After disconnecting, he called Freemont police.

"Head to the old part of Freemont around the bus station. Apprehend anyone wearing an American Construction Company T-shirt or driving one of their vehicles."

He threw the phone on the dashboard and gripped the steering wheel. Pushing down on the accelerator, he willed his truck to go faster. The stretch of road had never seemed so long and so winding.

Frank had been wrong about Colleen. How could he ever prove himself to her?

Lord, forgive me. Lead me to Colleen.

The outskirts of Freemont appeared in the distance.

Although traffic was light, Frank didn't want to stop at intersections in the downtown area. Instead, he remained on River Road. A side street, farther north, would lead to the bus station.

He passed the first of a row of warehouses on his left. The tornado had damaged a portion of the old brick facades on the formidable structures with historic charm.

In days past, boats would unload their wares, and the goods would be stored in the warehouses until wagons transported them to local markets. He didn't have time to bemoan the destruction of a treasure from the past. He needed to find Colleen.

Passing the second building, something caught his eye. He glanced left.

A utility truck sat parked next to a side door.

He stared for half a heartbeat at the company name painted on the van's side panel.

American Construction.

Frank turned the wheel and screeched into the narrow alleyway. He braked to a stop and hit the pavement running.

The big burly guy sat at the wheel. Frank threw open the door. He grabbed Steve's arm and yanked him to the pavement.

The guy reached for the gun tucked in his waistband. Frank kicked it out of his hand.

"Where is she?"

"You'll never get to her in time." The big guy lunged. His fist jammed into Frank's side, close to his incision.

Air whooshed from his lungs. He doubled over.

Steve stumbled back and grabbed his own gun.

He took aim. "Your girlfriend dies in five minutes, but you die now."

Duke leaped, and his teeth sank into Steve's arm. He screamed with pain. The gun fell from his hand and slid under the van.

The dog didn't let go. Steve toppled backward. His head crashed against the pavement. Gasping in pain, he backpedaled. "Get…the dog…off me."

Sirens sounded nearby.

"Duke, guard." The dog bared his teeth and hovered over Steve. Once big and strong, the construction worker looked like a blubbering baby as he covered his face with his hands and cried.

Frank ran into the warehouse. Shadows played over the expansive area inside. Cobwebs tangled around central support beams and wove their way to the ceiling rafters.

"Colleen!" Her name echoed across the scarred oak floors and bounced off windows fogged with decades of dirt.

Where was she?

Please, God.

He checked his watch. How much time did he have?

Five minutes max.

"Colleen?"

He raced forward. An enclosed office sat in the middle of the giant empty space.

He shoved the door open. A library table, overturned chairs. Two bookcases.

A sound.

Another door.

He turned the knob. The door creaked as it opened. An antique safe stood against the far wall. The room was so dark and so confined that he almost missed the pile of bedding in the corner.

A rustle of movement. Another moan.

He pulled back the blanket and gasped in relief.
Colleen.

Blood matted her beautiful hair and stained the mattress on which she lay. She'd suffered another blow in the same spot. Three strikes.

"I'm here, honey. I'll get you free."

"Explosives…detonate…"

"I know. We don't have much time." Using his pocketknife, he cut through the plastic ties that secured her hands and feet.

He wrapped his arm around her shoulders and helped her to her feet. She faltered.

Half supporting her, half carrying her, he ushered her through the office.

"We have to hurry," he warned.

Sirens sounded outside. Pulsating lights flashed through the filthy windows.

The side door opened. A cop started inside.

"Stay back," Frank shouted. "It's ready to blow."

His side screamed with pain, but he had to save Colleen. She staggered beside him.

Glancing at his watch, his heart lurched. No more time.

"Run." He pushed her toward the open door. She had to get to safety.

The cop grabbed her hand and tugged her through the doorway.

"Take cover," Frank screamed.

He followed her to the threshold of the door. The police had backed off. The cop was ushering Colleen away from the building. She turned, searching for Frank.

Her scream was lost in the blast.

Duke ran toward him.

Frank put up his hand to stop his faithful dog just as an avalanche of bricks started to fall.

Afghanistan. The IED.

Duke wouldn't be able to rescue him this time.

But Frank had saved Colleen.

She was alive.

Nothing else mattered.

"Frank," Colleen screamed.

She fought her way free from the cop who had pulled her from the building. He'd held her back and kept her from Frank.

Duke bounded onto the fallen bricks, the dust thick.

He barked, then sniffed the pile of debris that covered the doorway where Frank had stood seconds earlier.

Now he lay buried beneath the rubble.

She raced forward and clawed at the bricks. Duke dug with his paws, neither of them making progress.

Frank had to be alive. She wouldn't give up hope.

Please God, save him.

Policemen swarmed around them. They shoved aside pieces of brick and piles of dirt that came down with the building.

"Frank, hold on. We'll get you out."

Only she didn't know if he could hear her.

Duke barked. If anything, Frank would hear his trusty dog.

A large beam stretched across the fallen rubble, forming a protective pocket.

If only—

Colleen peered into the opening and glimpsed a hand. She reached to touch him. Cold. Lifeless.

"Don't leave me, Frank."

His fingers moved.

"He's alive," she shouted. "Hurry."

In a matter of seconds, the cops removed the remaining bricks covering the opening.

Frank's face. Swollen, battered, scraped and bleeding. His eyes shut.

"Watch his neck."

A backboard. They hoisted him carefully onto the wooden brace.

The cops hustled him toward the ambulance.

An EMT approached Colleen and pointed to her forehead. "Ma'am, you need to be examined."

He helped her into the ambulance where two EMTS worked on Frank. She sat opposite them and took his hand. She wouldn't let go.

Duke climbed in beside her.

The doors closed, and the ambulance took off, siren screaming.

Colleen couldn't stop watching the rise and fall of Frank's chest. He was breathing. He was alive, but just barely.

TWENTY-THREE

Although his prognosis wasn't good, Colleen was so grateful Frank was still alive. His condition was critical when he was raced into the Fort Rickman Hospital emergency room yesterday.

An entire medical team had worked on him in the trauma room until a bed opened in the ICU. Since then, he'd been hooked to wires that monitored his pulse, oxygen level, heart rate and blood pressure.

The occasional beep and the thrust and pull of the medical machinery made Colleen even more anxious about his condition.

She'd sat by his side throughout the night. Evelyn said she would stay, but fatigue had increased her limp and her eyes lacked their usual sparkle. She had been worried about Ron. Now her concern was for her brother.

"Go home, Evelyn. Sleep. You can spell me in the morning," Colleen had told her.

Civilians weren't usually treated at military hospitals, but one of the emergency room docs had checked Colleen over. Another slight concussion. Her third. The doc laughed as he said that she'd struck out. At least he didn't seem overly concerned, especially since she planned to stay the night at Frank's bedside.

The RN on duty had provided blankets and showed her how the vinyl chair extended into a semiflat position. Colleen had tried to sleep, but with the constant flow of medical caregivers who checked on Frank, she'd dozed off only a few times and then not for long.

The morning-shift nurse had provided a sealed plastic container of toiletries that included a toothbrush and comb. Colleen had given up trying to bring order to her matted hair and had used a rubber band to pull her unruly locks into a makeshift bun that at least got the curly strands out of her face.

Since first light, she'd hovered close to Frank's bedside, watching in case his eyes opened. She'd prayed throughout the night that God, who heard all, would answer her request and restore Frank to health.

"If he does respond," the doctors cautioned, "a full recovery will take time."

She sighed as the weight of that one comment sank in. If he recovered? A full recovery will take time? How long?

It didn't matter. She'd wait forever, if Frank wanted her to stay. That was the problem. She didn't know what he wanted.

She glanced at the floor, wishing Duke were with her. The military doctors hadn't been as welcoming as the EMTs in the ambulance had been. As soon as Ron and Evelyn arrived at the hospital, they'd been instructed to take the dog home.

A knock sounded. The door to Frank's room opened, and a man in uniform entered. He was tall with a full face and gentle smile.

"I'm Major Hughes, one of the chaplains on post."

"Thank you for coming."

He glanced at Frank. "Mind if I say a prayer?"

She rose from the chair. "Of course not. Yours might bring better results than mine."

"You've had a long night. The nurse told me you've been at his bedside."

"Praying." She tried to smile, but tears filled her eyes. She didn't want to cry in front of the chaplain.

He reached for her hand. "God knows our hearts. He responds. Although sometimes he's not as timely as we'd want."

"That's what worries me."

"We need to trust."

She nodded. Her weak suit, especially when it came to Frank. "He's a good man. Compassionate, caring, but he's been through so much."

"I was told a war injury and multiple surgeries followed by a life-threatening infection."

Colleen nodded. How much could someone endure? "He ignored his own condition to help me. I... I made a mistake and wasn't completely forthright."

She turned her head and bit her lip.

The chaplain patted her shoulder. "Our limitations are always easier to see in hindsight. When we're in the middle of a stressful situation, our vision is often cloudy. The Lord is a God of forgiveness. You can trust him." He glanced at Frank. "I have a feeling you can trust Special Agent Gallagher, as well."

Buoyed by the chaplain's words, she folded her hands and bowed her head as he prayed, knowing God was in charge. He was the Divine Physician who would return Frank to health.

That was her hope.

That was her prayer.

Someone patted Frank's arm. He heard voices and tried to comprehend what they were saying.

"I think he's coming around."

Evelyn?

He sensed someone else bending over his bedside. "Agent Gallagher? Frank? Can you hear me?"

He fought his way from the darkness.

"Open your eyes?"

He tried. They remained shut.

"My name's Molly. I'm the nurse who's taking care of you today. You're in the hospital at Fort Rickman. Do you remember what happened?"

He turned his head.

"Open your eyes, Frank." Evelyn's voice. She patted his hand.

Still so tired, but he wanted to see—

Light. Too bright.

"That was great. Try opening your eyes again."

He blinked. Twice.

"Even better. Keep working. I bet your eyes are blue."

Brown. He licked his lips, but the word wouldn't form.

"Eyes opened wide. That's what I want to see."

Again, he blinked against the light. The nurse smiled down at him.

He turned his head ever so slightly. Evelyn came into view.

"Oh, Frank," she gushed. A tear ran down her cheek. "I've been so worried."

She squeezed his hand. He squeezed back.

"Wh...where—"

Slowly, his gaze swept the room. A knife stabbed his heart. He had expected to see Colleen.

Audrey had left him. Now Colleen.

He didn't want to keep struggling any longer. He was worn-out and unwilling to fight back from the brink of despair again.

He had almost died last time. He wasn't willing to bear the hurt again.

"Keep your eyes open, Frank."

He ignored the nurse and slipped back into the darkness, where he couldn't feel pain. Why should he open his eyes? He didn't want to see anything if he couldn't see Colleen.

"You need to go back to my place and get some sleep," Evelyn suggested.

Colleen shook her head. "The last time I stepped out for coffee, Frank opened his eyes. I want to be here next time."

"If there is a next time," Evelyn said. Her voice contained all the fear Colleen felt.

She shook her head. "Don't say that."

"The doctors warned us. We need to realize what could happen."

"God won't take him from me. I've lost Briana. I can't lose Frank."

Evelyn rubbed her shoulder. "Life isn't always fair."

Colleen nodded. How well she knew that to be true.

She thought of Evelyn's first love and the pain she'd experienced when he revealed the truth about his marriage.

"You've had your share of suffering."

"But now I have Ron."

"Did you tell him about Dan?"

Evelyn nodded. "Just as you mentioned, he was loving and caring. Although like a typical male, Ron wanted to punch Dan. Even if he hadn't been married, what he and I had wasn't true love. It was something that fell far short. Looking back, I know God saved me for Ron."

Colleen squeezed Evelyn's hand. "I wasn't sure about Ron because of seeing him with Trey the night of the tornado, but I was wrong, too. He's got a big heart and a lot of love to shower on you, Evelyn."

She glanced at her brother. "Frank does, too. He just needs to wake up and accept your love."

The phone rang. Evelyn reached for the receiver. "Yes?"

She smiled. "You're downstairs? I'll be right there." She hung up and patted Colleen's hand.

"Ron's in the lobby. I'm going to meet him for coffee in the cafeteria. Can I bring you anything?"

"Bring your brother back, and I'll be happy."

"Ron and I are praying. The whole church community is, as well."

Would it be enough? Colleen wasn't sure.

Colleen heard Frank's voice in her dream. She smiled and squeezed his hand.

"Ouch."

Her eyes popped open. Sitting in the chair at Frank's bedside, she had rested her head on the edge of his mattress and dozed off.

His eyes were still closed. Her dream had been so real. Had she imagined his voice?

Maybe the three strikes were finally catching up to her.

She rubbed her hand over his. His fingers moved.

Her heart skittered in her chest.

"Frank?"

One eye blinked open.

The IV solution was providing fluids, but that didn't keep his lips from being cracked and chapped.

"C…ol…leen?"

Surely he didn't think she was Audrey.

His smile widened. His fingers wrapped through hers. "You…you…didn't leave me."

"Oh, Frank, I'll never leave you."

Tears filled her eyes and spilled down her cheeks.

She moved closer to him. His other eye opened. "Now… I…see you."

"I haven't even combed my hair."

"You…you're beautiful."

"Do you remember what happened?"

He nodded ever so slightly. "I…saved…you."

She smiled. "That's exactly right. You saved my life."

His brow wrinkled. "D… Duke?"

"He's fine. Evelyn claims his sense of smell returned, since he was able to find you in the rubble. I'm sure you heard him barking."

Frank wrinkled his forehead. "I… I heard…your voice. You…gave…me…will to live."

"Oh, Frank, I was so wrong about you and about law enforcement. You were trying to find the truth, and I kept holding back information."

The words gushed out. Colleen couldn't stop them. "Briana's death had taken me to the depths of despair. I'd turned my grief into a need to bring all those involved with drug trafficking to justice."

She shook her head, frustrated at her own actions. "Only I was headstrong and foolish to take on Trey and his operation. You kept trying to protect me, but I wasn't sure of where I stood with you. I'd been so determined to bring Trey down that I almost got myself killed and you killed, as well."

Frank rubbed her hand. "Before…thought I was invincible…didn't need God…didn't need anyone. Dated a girl. She…must have known. Only person… I… I… loved was my…self."

"You're not that man any longer. You're not self-serving or self-centered. You're a wonderful man who has a bright future ahead in law enforcement. You check every detail and make sure hearsay isn't taken as fact. I thought Trey had caused Briana's death, but Steve Nelson was to blame. I went after the wrong man."

"Trey…led you to Steve."

"You're right. Colby stopped by after work last night. He said the photos on the memory card revealed even more drug dealers involved in Steve Nelson's far-reaching operations. The resort is being cleaned out in Colombia, and the DEA is going after traffickers throughout the Southeast. Colby called it a good day for law enforcement."

"Be…cause of you."

"Because you helped me find the memory card."

Frank smiled.

"Colby said Anderson, the cop I contacted in Atlanta, was tied in with Trey. He's been arrested."

"Vi…vian?"

"She confessed to smuggling drugs into the US and provided information about others involved. Colby said the judge will take that into consideration."

"I'm…sorry… I…"

She smiled. "Didn't believe me?"

He nodded.

"You were being that wonderful investigator who I'm beginning to think I love."

His eyes opened a bit wider, and the smile that filled his face made her heart soar with joy.

"I…love…you, Colleen."

Her grip tightened on his hand, and she bent over

his bedside. His condition was still fragile, and he had a long recuperation ahead, but Colleen wanted him to know the way she felt. She had waited too long to tell him the truth.

"I love you, Frank."

She gently lowered her lips to his, and for one long moment the earth stood still.

Pulling back ever so slightly, she added, "And I'll never leave you." She smiled. "Cross my heart."

His eyes closed, and he fell back to sleep. Resting her cheek against his hand, she gave thanks to God for bringing this wonderful, strong man into her life.

TWENTY-FOUR

Frank sat on Evelyn's front porch and listened for the sound of tires on the driveway. Seeing Colleen's new red Mustang convertible, he hurried down the steps and opened her door as she pulled to a stop.

Before either of them spoke, he reached for her and pulled her into his arms. Their lips met, and the lingering kiss did more for him than all the physical therapy he'd been having over the past five weeks.

Evelyn stood in the open doorway and waved. Duke bounded around her and barked with glee, causing Colleen to push away from Frank and laugh.

"Are you jealous of Frank?" she asked as the dog danced at her feet. She patted his sleek coat and scratched behind his ears.

"How was your flight?" Evelyn asked from the porch.

"Easy. I'm enjoying working short domestic flights again."

"And we like having you spend time between trips with us."

Frank grabbed her carry-on from the backseat. "The Mustang suits you."

"Oh? Is it the color?"

"You mean because it matches your hair?"

She laughed. "I didn't think you noticed."

"I notice everything about you."

"Be still my heart. I like having a man who's observant."

"And I like your hair loose around your face. It suits you just like the car."

He ran his hand through the curls that fell free around her shoulders. Leaning close, he inhaled the flowery scent of her shampoo, which made him want to kiss her again.

She giggled. "Looks like you're feeling better. Did you talk to Wilson?"

"He's wants me back doing CID investigations as soon as I'm ready."

Colleen narrowed her gaze. "What'd you tell him?"

"Next Monday. I'm ready."

She nodded. "I know you are."

"What smells so good?" Colleen asked as they followed Evelyn into the kitchen.

"I've got a rib roast in the oven, and Isaac selected fresh corn from the Amish Craft Shoppe for us, along with homegrown lettuce and an apple pie for dessert."

"You always spoil me, Evelyn."

"Ron's joining us for dinner."

"How's he feeling?"

"Strong as an ox."

Colleen laughed. "Is he still working out?"

Evelyn nodded. "He has to keep in shape to keep up with me." She winked at Colleen, who laughed again.

Her joy was infectious, and Frank's heart soared. "Let's go for a drive."

She looked confused. "I… I just got here."

"I know, but there's something I want to show you."

She glanced at Evelyn, who smiled knowingly but didn't say anything.

He took her hand and hurried her to his truck. He held the passenger door for her, and lowered the back for Duke. They were soon heading along the country road they'd traveled weeks before.

They passed Dawson Timmons's house. Frank turned at the next intersection and headed north for a little over three miles.

"This area is so beautiful." Colleen's smile said as much as her comment.

He stopped at the top of a small rise and helped her out. Duke jumped from the rear and immediately chased after a gray squirrel that scurried up a sturdy oak.

Frank pointed to a small pond and the gentle rise where more hardwoods grew.

"I thought a house overlooking the pond might be nice. The trees would provide shade in summer."

Her eyes widened with surprise. "You're buying the land?"

"I went to the bank, but I haven't signed the papers yet."

"Does that mean you're getting out of the army?"

"Not now. I've got ten years on active duty already. I'll stay in for at least ten more before I retire from military service. I thought farming the land, raising a few head of cattle, might be something for the future. I'll live here for the next three years while I complete my assignment at Fort Rickman. When I'm transferred, I'll still need a place to come back to for vacations and to visit Evelyn."

Colleen turned to look at the expanse of land. "It's lovely. A good place to call home."

"How would you feel about living here?"

She took a step back. "I'm not sure what you're saying."

He laughed, realizing his mistake. "Looks like I got ahead of myself."

Digging into his pocket, his fingers touched a small box. He pulled it out. "I'm not overly romantic, and I may not have the right words, but I love you, Colleen. You're my everything, and I never want to spend a day without you. Will you—"

He opened the box. "Will you marry me?"

Colleen's heart stopped for a long moment as Frank removed the solitaire diamond and held it out ready to put on her finger.

"Will you marry me?" he asked again when she failed to respond.

Tears filled her eyes. She brushed them away, knowing her cheeks would blotch and her mascara would run, but she didn't care. All she cared about was Frank.

"Yes," she almost screamed, holding out her hand. He slipped the ring over her finger, then he pulled her into his arms.

"I love you."

"Oh, Frank, I love you, too."

They kissed under the shade of the oak tree. Duke fetched a twig and raced back to where they stood, wrapped in each other's arms. He danced at their feet, trying to get their attention until another squirrel caught his eye. Then he bounded off in pursuit, while Frank pulled Colleen even closer, and she nestled in his arms.

His kisses were as sweet as the wildflowers blooming on the hillside and as warm as the sunshine overhead.

This land, their home, would be the perfect place to seal their love and raise a family.

Colleen glanced at the ring and then raised her lips again to the wonderful man, the strong and determined man with whom she planned to spend the rest of her life.

God had answered her prayers. Every one of them.

* * * * *

SPECIAL EXCERPT FROM

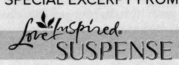

*When a guide dog trainer becomes a target
of a dangerous crime ring, a K-9 cop and his loyal
partner will work together to keep her safe.*

Read on for a sneak preview of Trail of Danger
*by Valerie Hansen, the next exciting installment
to the True Blue K-9 Unit miniseries,
available September 2019 from Love Inspired Suspense.*

Abigail Jones stared at the blackening eastern sky and
shivered. She was more afraid of the strangers lingering
in the shadows along the Coney Island boardwalk than
she was of the summer storm brewing over the Atlantic.

Early September humidity made the salty oceanic
atmosphere feel sticky while the wind whipped loose
tendrils of Abigail's long red hair. If sixteen-year-old
Kiera Underhill hadn't insisted where and when their
secret meeting must take place, Abigail would have
stopped to speak with some of the other teens she was
passing. Instead, she made a beeline for the spot where
their favorite little hot dog wagon spent its days.

Besides the groups of partying youth, she skirted
dog walkers, couples strolling hand in hand and an old
woman leaning on a cane. Then there was a tall man and

enormous dog ambling toward her. As they passed beneath an overhead vapor light, she recognized his police uniform and breathed a sigh of relief. Most K-9 patrols in her nearby neighborhood used German shepherds, so seeing the long floppy ears and droopy jowls of a bloodhound brought a smile despite her uneasiness.

Pausing, Abigail rested her back against the fence surrounding a currently closed amusement park, faced into the wind and waited for the K-9 cop to go by. His unexpected presence could be what was delaying Kiera.

"Come on, Kiera. I came alone, just like you wanted," Abigail muttered.

Kiera had sounded panicky when she'd phoned.

"Here. Over here" drifted on the wind. Abigail strained to listen.

The summons seemed to be coming from inside the Luna Park perimeter fence. That was not good since the amusement facility was currently closed. Nevertheless, she cupped her hands around her eyes and peered through the chain-link fence. It was several seconds before she realized the gate was ajar. *Uh-oh. Bad sign.* "Kiera? Is that you?"

A disembodied voice answered faintly. "Help me! Hurry."

Don't miss
Trail of Danger *by Valerie Hansen,*
available September 2019 wherever
Love Inspired® Suspense books and ebooks are sold.

www.LoveInspired.com

WE HOPE YOU
ENJOYED THIS BOOK!

Love Inspired®
SUSPENSE

Uncover the truth in these thrilling
stories of faith in the face of crime
from Love Inspired Suspense.
Discover six new books available
every month, wherever books
are sold!

LoveInspired.com

LISHALO2019

SPECIAL EXCERPT FROM

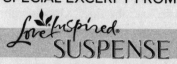

Love Inspired.
SUSPENSE

*When a rookie K-9 cop becomes the target of a
dangerous stalker, can she stay one step ahead of this
killer with the help of her boss and his K-9 partner?*

Read on for a sneak preview of
Courage Under Fire *by Sharon Dunn,
the next exciting installment to the*
True Blue K-9 Unit *miniseries, available in
October 2019 from Love Inspired Suspense.*

Rookie K-9 officer Lani Branson took in a deep breath as
she pedaled her bike along the trail in the Jamaica Bay
Wildlife Refuge. Water rushed and receded from the shore
just over the dunes. The high-rises of New York City,
made hazy from the dusky twilight, were visible across
the expanse of water.

She sped up even more.

Tonight was important. This training exercise was an
opportunity to prove herself to the other K-9 officers who
waited back at the visitors' center with the tracking dogs
for her to give the go-ahead. Playing the part of a child lost
in the refuge so the dogs could practice tracking her was
probably a less-than-desirable duty for the senior officers.

Reaching up to her shoulder, Lani got off her bike and
pressed the button on the radio. "I'm in place."

The smooth tenor voice of her supervisor, Chief Noah Jameson, came over the line. "Good—you made it out there in record time."

Up ahead she spotted an object shining in the setting sun. She jogged toward it. A bicycle, not hers, was propped against a tree.

A knot of tension formed at the back of her neck as she turned in a half circle, taking in the area around her. It was possible someone had left the bike behind. Vagrants could have wandered into the area.

She studied the bike a little closer. State-of-the-art and in good condition. Not the kind of bike someone just dumped.

A branch cracked. Her breath caught in her throat. Fear caused her heartbeat to drum in her ears.

"NYPD." She hadn't worn her gun for this exercise. Her eyes scanned all around her, searching for movement and color. "You need to show yourself."

Seconds ticked by. Her heart pounded.

Someone else was out here.

Don't miss
Courage Under Fire *by Sharon Dunn,*
available October 2019 wherever
Love Inspired® Suspense books and ebooks are sold.

www.LoveInspired.com

LISEXP0919